The Frost Fair

The Frost Fair

EDWARD MARSTON

First published in Great Britain in 2002 by
Allison & Busby Limited
Bon Marche Centre
241-251 Ferndale Road
Brixton, London SW9 8BJ
http://www.allisonandbusby.com

Copyright © 2002 by EDWARD MARSTON

The right of Edward Marston to be identified as
author of this work has been asserted by him in
accordance with the Copyright, Designs and
Patents Act, 1988

A catalogue record for this book is available from the British Library

ISBN 0 7490 0600 5

Printed and bound in Ebbw Vale,
by Creative Print & Design

EDWARD MARSTON was born and brought up in South Wales. A full-time writer for over thirty years, he has worked in radio, film, television and the theatre. Prolific and highly successful, he is equally at home writing children's books or literary criticism, plays or biographies and settings for his crime novels range from the world of professional golf to the compilation of the Domesday Survey. *The Frost Fair* is the fourth book in the series featuring architect Christopher Redmayne and Puritan constable Jonathan Bale, set in Restoration London after the Great Fire of 1666.

Also by Edward Marston:

The Redmayne Mysteries
The King's Evil
The Amorous Nightingale
The Repentant Rake

The Domesday Books
The Wolves of Savernake
The Ravens of Blackwater
The Dragons of Archenfield
The Lions of the North
The Serpents of Harbledown
The Stallions of Woodstock
The Hawks of Delamere
The Wildcats of Exeter
The Foxes of Warwick
The Owls of Gloucester
The Elephants of Norwich

The Nicholas Bracewell series
The Queen's Head
The Merry Devils
The Trip to Jerusalem
The Nine Giants
The Mad Courtesan
The Silent Woman
The Roaring Boy
The Laughing Hangman
The Fair Maid of Bohemia
The Wanton Angel
The Devil's Apprentice
The Bawdy Basket
The Vagabond Clown

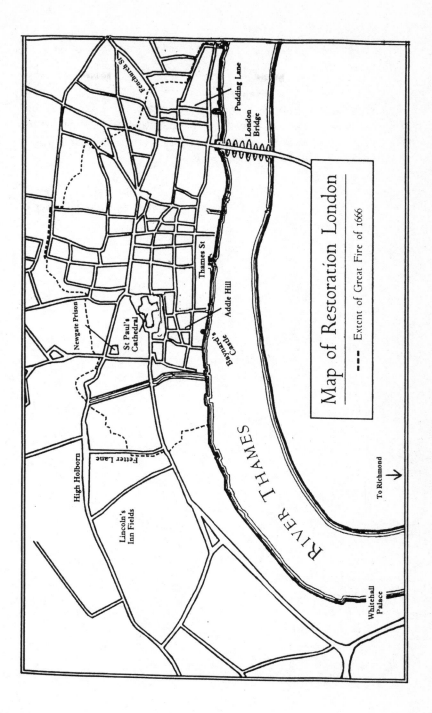

Map of Restoration London

- - - - Extent of Great Fire of 1666

RIVER THAMES

Fenchurch St

Pudding Lane

London Bridge

Thames St

Addle Hill

Baynard's Castle

Newgate Prison

St Paul's Cathedral

High Holborn

Fetter Lane

Lincoln's Inn Fields

To Richmond →

Whitehall Palace

The frost still continuing more & more severe, the Thames before London was planted with bothes in formal streetes, as in a Citty, or Continual faire, all sorts of trades and shops furnished and full of Commodities, even to a printing presse...

John Evelyn: *Diary*
January 24, 1684

Chapter One

Snow came like a thief in the night. Quickly and silently, it fell over the whole of London, searching every last corner and robbing the city of its distinctive appearance. When they awoke next day, Londoners found that they were in the grip of a raging blizzard. Not only did it smother the streets and coat the buildings in white, the snow was blown hither and thither by a mischievous wind that was determined to cause the greatest possible inconvenience. Heavy drifts leaned against doors, sealed up windows and blocked off lanes and alleyways. Wherever there was a gap in a threshold, a hole in a roof or even a tiny opening in some shutters, the snow blew in unbidden. Those who had slept in warm beds were fortunate. Beggars, urchins and stray animals that had spent the night in the open were destined to slumber forever. Unable to escape from the blizzard, they had curled up in doorways or hidden beneath benches, only to be frozen to the marrow by the chill wind and covered by an ever-thickening shroud of snow.

Fires were lit in grates all over the capital but they only added to the general discomfort. They might bring relief to those who huddled around them but the smoke they produced could not disperse in the cold air. A sulphurous stench invaded the streets. Even when the snow finally abated, the smoke continued to belch from the chimneys, darkening the sky and swirling down to attack the throats and eyes of any citizens unwise enough to be abroad. London was brought to a standstill. Markets were cancelled, trades abandoned, shops left shut. Few visitors entered the city by means of its gates or its famous bridge and none tried to leave. For most people, it was a time to wrap up and stay indoors. Hardier souls took on the task of clearing the streets as best they could so that some movement could take place. It was slow and laborious work.

The snow had a deadly accomplice in its wake. Frost set in with a vengeance. Icy fingers took London by the throat and sought to throttle it. The old, the sick and the very young were its first victims, weakened, tormented, then finally killed off by the freezing temperatures. Even the most robust citizens found themselves prey to the infections that winter always brings. Thoroughfares that had been matted with snow were now glistening with ice, waiting to catch the unwary traveller and send him flying. Broken legs, arms, wrists and ankles were inflicted indiscriminately. But it was the Thames that underwent the most dramatic change. Ice formed first along the banks then, gradually and imperceptibly, extended its reach across the whole river. The water that was the life-blood of the city disappeared from sight. Above the bridge, and partially below it, the Thames was one long sheet of cold, solid, continuous, unrelenting ice.

No ships could sail, no boats could ferry passengers from one bank to another. London was starved of everything that came in by water. The huge trade in coal from Newcastle came to a complete halt. Fuel prices soon soared. The city shivered on. Yet there was no sense of doom. Having endured virulent plague and a devastating fire in recent years, the capital met the latest crisis with a mixture of bravery and resignation. At a time of suffering, it also found a new source of pleasure. They held a frost fair.

'It's wonderful!' exclaimed Susan Cheever, clapping her gloved hands together. 'I've never been to a frost fair before.'

'No more have I,' said Christopher Redmayne, gazing around in amazement. 'A hundred architects could not effect such a transformation. Mother Nature has redesigned the whole city. In place of a river, we have the widest street in Europe.'

'Our pond freezes every year, and so does the stream at the bottom of our garden. But I never thought that a river as broad and eager as the Thames would turn to ice. Still less, that a fair could be set on its back.'

'That is to blame,' he explained, pointing to the huge bridge that spanned the river. 'The piers that support it are set into starlings that restrict the flow of water. Above the bridge, as you see, it freezes more thoroughly.' He smiled at her. 'Shall we test it?'

Susan laughed. 'Everyone else has done so.'

'Then we must not be left out.'

They were standing on the northern bank of the river, midway between London Bridge and the Tower. To keep out the sharp pinch of winter, Susan was wearing a long coat that all but brushed her ankles and a bonnet that protected her head and ears. A woollen scarf at the neck added both warmth and decoration. Enough of her face could be seen to remind her companion how beautiful she was. The sparkle in her eyes and the softness in her voice were a constant delight to him. He escorted her to the stone steps.

'Take my arm,' he offered. 'The stairs are slippery.'

'Thank you.'

'Descend with care.'

'I shall,' she promised.

Arm in arm, they went slowly down the steps and Christopher enjoyed every moment of their proximity. They had known each other long enough to dispense with some of the formalities but too short a time for him to take any real liberties. An aspiring young architect, Christopher was helping to rebuild the city after the ravages of the Great Fire and one of the most appealing commissions that had come his way was a contract to design a town house for Sir Julius Cheever, elected to Parliament to represent the county of Northamptonshire. Sir Julius was a truculent man by nature and not always easy company, but his daughter knew exactly how to handle him. During the building of the house, her friendship with its architect had steadily developed and he was thrilled that she took every excuse to quit her home in the Midlands so that she could visit the capital. The affection between them was unspoken but no less real for that.

'Well,' he said, as they stepped on to the ice, 'here we are.'

She tapped a foot. 'It feels so solid.'

'There's talk of a thaw but I've not seen a sign of it.' He released her arm. 'When you return home, you'll be able to boast that you achieved a true miracle.'

'A miracle?'

'You walked on water.'

'Some people are doing much more than that.'

'Let's take a closer look at them.'

Wanting her to take his arm again, Christopher contented himself with the merest touch of her back as his palm eased her forward. Like her, he wore his winter attire, a long blue coat and a wide-brimmed hat keeping the wind at bay. He was tall, slim and well-favoured with an open face that glowed with intelligence. Peeping out from beneath his hat was curly brown hair with a reddish tinge. As they strolled towards the fair, they made a handsome couple, their reflections walking ahead of them in the ice. Christopher looked down to study her moving portrait but Susan only had eyes for the fair itself.

'Half of the city must be here,' she observed.

'Can you think of a better place to be?'

She pointed a finger. 'What's that they are roasting?'

'An ox, I think,' he said, staring across at the spit, 'and I fancy we'll see a pig or two being turned over a brazier as well. Warm meat sells well on cold days.'

'Will the fire not melt the ice?'

'It appears not.'

'Another miracle.'

'You'll have much to tell them in Northamptonshire.'

'I plan to linger here for a while first,' she said, turning to him with a smile.

He met her gaze. 'Call on me for anything you should require.'

They walked on into the heart of the fair. Lines of booths had been set up to form an avenue that was known as Temple Street since it ran from the bottom of Temple stairs. Every conceivable item of merchandise was on sale and there was loud haggling over each purchase. Large crowds and horse-drawn coaches went up and down the street with complete confidence. In some of the tents, freaks of nature were on display. Lurid banners advertised a cow with five legs, a sheep with two heads and a dog that could sing like a bird. Feats of strength were displayed by a giant of a blacksmith, bare-armed to show off his rippling muscles and seemingly impervious to the cold. Two dwarves in yellow costumes had a mock fight to entertain the children. Puppet plays and interludes were also drawing their audiences. Horse races were being held at regular intervals and sizeable bets were being made. Those who preferred more brutish pleasures flocked to the bull ring that had been erected below the Tower to cheer on the vicious hounds that baited the animals.

Watching it through startled eyes, Susan took it all in, anxious to miss nothing of the phenomenon. She paused beside a booth that housed a printing press.

'Look at that,' she said. 'Someone is actually *printing* upon the ice.'

'It's a wise tradesman who knows how to create a demand.'

'For what?'

'Do you not see what he is about?' asked Christopher, as the printer handed a piece of paper to a grinning customer. 'He prints but one line to certify that the bearer attended the frost fair and he charges sixpence for the privilege. Here's a shrewd businessman. I dare swear that he'll make five pounds a day at the enterprise.' He put a hand to his pocket. 'I'd be happy to buy a certificate for you.'

'A kind offer,' she said gratefully, 'but one I decline.'

'If anyone refuses to believe that you came here, turn to me for an affidavit.'

'Thank you.'

She gave him another warm smile and they moved on. They passed a woman selling pies and another with a basket of trinkets and dolls under her arm. Strong drink was in good supply and sounds of revelry came from a large tent. Even in the wintry conditions, prostitutes found ways to ply their trade. Hearing the rustle of taffeta to his left, Christopher took care to block Susan's line of vision so that she did not see the woman was smiling provocatively through a gap in a booth at the men who passed by. An old man selling brooms competed aloud with other pedlars who were trumpeting the merits of their wares. A scarecrow of a ballad singer then claimed their attention, singing of the frost fair and thrusting his copies of his ballad at anyone who came within reach. The man's daughter, a tiny creature swathed in rags, followed him with a wooden bowl in which she kept the day's takings.

Christopher guided his friend between two booths and out into a wide expanse of ice. Sleds were darting to and fro. Skaters were everywhere, some with more sense of balance than others. Deprived of their livelihood, the notoriously foul-mouthed watermen who usually rowed people from one bank to the other, had just cause to turn the air blue with their oaths. Some of them, out of desperation, had harnessed their craft to horses so that the Thames could still yield some income for them. Christopher was glad that Susan never got close enough to any of them to hear their bad language. They came to a halt to survey the scene. It was, in the main, one of joy and merriment. London was defying the elements with a show of celebration. Christopher noticed something else.

'*Civitas in civitate*,' he remarked. 'Here is truly a city within a city, and one without the constraints we find on shore. Do you not *feel* the difference?' he went on. 'We are all one on the ice. Degree vanishes and an earl has no more status than an eel-catcher. The King himself was here yesterday to rub shoulders with his subjects and to carve his name in the ice as readily as any child. The frost fair abolishes rank and makes us all the same age. That is the *real* miracle.'

'I believe it is,' she agreed.

'Thank you for letting me bring you here.'

'I would not have missed it for the world.'

'It pleases me so much to have you here in London.'

'The pleasure is mutual, I assure you.'

Their eyes locked for a moment and Christopher suddenly realized just how fond he had become of Susan Cheever. While they had met as a result of the commission to design a house, it was the murder of her brother, Gabriel, which really drew them together. A bond had developed between them and Christopher was now aware just how strong that bond was. He felt an upsurge of affection for her. He was on the point of putting it into words when, out of the corner of his eye, he saw someone approaching them. Christopher turned to see two familiar faces. They belonged to Jonathan Bale and his wife, Sarah, who were strolling arm in arm across the ice. Delighted to meet his friends again, Christopher nevertheless wished that they had delayed their arrival by a few minutes. They had interrupted a special moment.

After a flurry of greetings, Jonathan smiled politely at Susan.

'I'll wager you've seen nothing like this in Northamptonshire,' he said.

'No, Mr Bale,' she replied. 'It's a source of great wonder to me.'

'And to us,' admitted Sarah. 'We've had bad frosts before and blocks of ice in the river but I can't remember it freezing over completely like this. It's such an adventure for the boys. We simply had to bring them.'

'Where are they?' asked Christopher.

'Skating over there,' she said, waving an arm in the direction of the bridge.

'*Trying* to skate,' corrected Jonathan with paternal fondness. 'Richard has taken well to the sport but Oliver is too clumsy on his feet as yet. There they are,' he added, jabbing a finger. 'Close by that boy on the sled. Do you see them?'

Christopher picked them out at once. Oliver Bale was moving gingerly across the ice while his younger brother, Richard, was skating with a degree of skill on the skates that their father had fashioned out of wooden blocks and straps of leather. Like so many other children on the river, they were enjoying themselves hugely. The parents watched their sons with indulgent smiles. Christopher liked the whole family but he had a particular fondness for Jonathan Bale.

In character and in background, the two men had little in common. Jonathan was a big, sturdy, diligent constable whose Puritan sympathies made him a stern critic of what he saw as the excesses of the restored monarchy. Dour by inclination, he had the kind of misshapen face, disfigured by two large warts and a livid scar, that even his doting wife could never describe as handsome. For her part, Sarah was a stout, bustling, warm-hearted, gregarious woman who had kept her good looks, if not her figure, well into her thirties. Since Jonathan had played a crucial part in pursuit of the men who had killed her brother, Susan, too, had a great respect for the constable.

'This weather must make your job somewhat easier,' she remarked.

'Easier?' he echoed.

'Yes, Mr Bale. Burglars will have too much sense to prowl the streets on chilly nights. We may put up with more disruption but we have less crime.'

Jonathan became solemn. 'If only it were so. Evil men pay no heed to the cold and they work by day as well as night. The frost fair is a boon to them for they know that so many houses will be empty. And here on the Thames, the pickpockets are still with us, alas. Wherever there's a crowd of people, there are criminals mingling with them.' A great roar was heard from the bull ring. Jonathan's face hardened. 'Baiting a poor animal is a sinful pleasure,' he said. 'Left to me, there'd be none of it.'

'Left to you,' teased his wife, 'there'd be no frost fair.'

'That's not true, Sarah.'

'You hate to see too much merriment.'

'Not if it's kept within the bounds of decency,' he said. 'We are entitled to get some enjoyment out of this terrible frost. What I hate to see are the thieves, rogues, liars, gamblers, charlatans, drunkards and lewd women that a fair will always attract.'

'That's no reason to shun such an event as this,' argued Christopher.

'Nor have we done so, Mr Redmayne. I was only too ready to call on my skills as a carpenter to make some skates for my sons.'

17

'Yes,' said his wife proudly. 'Jonathan has kept all the tools he used during his days as a shipwright and he can still use them like a master.'

'I wanted Oliver and Richard to have their fun while they could. This weather will not last and they may never see such a frost fair again.'

'I'll certainly not forget this one,' said Susan.

'Nor shall I,' added Christopher with an affectionate glance at her.

'I'm sorry that Father could not be persuaded to join us on the river.'

'How is Sir Julius?' asked Jonathan.

'Fretful.'

'Because of the weather?'

'It has made the roads impassable,' said Susan, 'and that irritates him. We can neither return home to Northamptonshire nor even visit my sister and her husband in Richmond. Snow and frost have kept us in London, though I make no complaint. I'm the happiest of prisoners. I could spend every afternoon here on the ice.'

Christopher grinned. 'We'll have to get Jonathan to make you a pair of skates.'

'Shame on you, Mr Redmayne!' scolded Sarah playfully. 'It's a pastime for small boys, not for refined young ladies.'

'And yet,' confessed Susan, 'I do envy your sons.'

They all turned to watch the progress of the two skaters. Oliver and Richard Bale had now moved much further away to find a patch of ice they could have entirely to themselves. They were engaged in a race that could only have one conclusion. Though they set off together, Oliver was too preoccupied with staying on his feet to move at any speed. Richard was soon several yards in front of him. Putting more effort into his skating, he lengthened each stride and pulled right away. The younger boy was thrilled. Accustomed to being in Oliver's shadow, he had finally found something he could do better than his brother. It bred a fatal arrogance. When he was thirty yards clear of Oliver, and still skating with verve, he could not resist looking over his shoulder and emitting a mocking laugh. Richard soon discovered that he still had much to learn. Losing his balance, he fell forward and skidded crazily over the ice on his chest. He let out such a cry of horror that both Jonathan and Christopher hurried off simultaneously to his aid.

'Dear God!' exclaimed Sarah. 'The poor lad must have broken something.'

'I hope not,' said Susan.

And the two women walked swiftly in the direction of the fallen boy.

Jonathan was also afraid that an arm or a leg had been fractured in the accident and he cursed himself for letting the boys get too far away from him. As they ran past Oliver, he was still having difficulties staying upright. Richard, meanwhile, was backing away on all fours from the spot where he had finished up. Christopher and Jonathan soon realized why. When his father grabbed him, the boy was gibbering with fear and pointing in front of him. A jagged line, first sign of a thaw, was etched in the ice but that was not what had frightened the boy. Through the crack, the two men could see the hazy outline of a body. Two large, dark, sightless eyes stared up at them out of a deathly white face.

Chapter Two

When he alighted from his coach, Sir Julius Cheever used a stick to support himself. A thaw had set in but the streets were still treacherous. On the journey from his house in Westminster, the coach had slid from side to side and the horses had occasionally lost their footing. Sir Julius was a big, strapping man of sixty with the physique of a farmer dressed incongruously in the apparel of a gentleman. If he slipped and fell, his weight would tell against him. The walking stick was therefore a sensible accessory. It was also useful for rapping hard on the door of the house in Fetter Lane that he was visiting. His imperious summons was soon answered. The servant who opened the door gave him a deferential smile of recognition.

'Good morning, Sir Julius,' he said.

'Is your master in?'

'Mr Redmayne is working in the parlour.'

'Then don't keep me shivering out here, man,' said Sir Julius, using the end of the stick to move the servant aside. 'Let me in.'

'Yes, Sir Julius.'

Opening the door to its full extent, Jacob Vout, the old servant who was butler, cook, chambermaid, ostler and everything else in the household, stepped back to admit the visitor. He did not need to announce the man's arrival. The booming voice of Sir Julius Cheever had already brought Christopher Redmayne out of his parlour. Pleased to see his former client, the architect was disappointed that he had not brought his daughter with him. After an exchange of greetings, he conducted Sir Julius into the room where the drawing on which he had been working all morning was spread out on the table. His visitor gave it a cursory glance before choosing the most comfortable chair into which to lower his bulk. He held his hat in his lap.

'You are designing a new house, I see.'

'Yes, Sir Julius. I have a commission from Lady Whitcombe.'

'Whitcombe? That name sounds familiar.'

'She is the widow of the late Sir Peregrine Whitcombe,' explained Christopher. 'In his time, he was a distinguished Member of Parliament.'

20

Sir Julius was scornful. 'There's no such thing as a distinguished Member of Parliament. They are all such dolts, rogues or charlatans that I can scarce forbear knocking their heads together. Whitcombe, eh?' he went on, scratching a bulbous nose. 'I remember the fellow now. A damnable Cavalier. He fought at Naseby and at Worcester, as did I. On both occasions, I thank God, we gave his army a bloody nose. I'm sorry to hear that you are working for the family of such a despicable creature.'

'The war is long over,' said Christopher tactfully.

'Not to me. It continues in other ways.'

Christopher did not argue with him. Sir Julius was an unrepentant Roundhead who still talked of Cromwell with affection. Knighted by the Lord Protector, he ignored the taunts that came from those whose honours had been bestowed by royal patronage and who therefore felt them to be superior. In addition to the battles he had mentioned, he had also fought at Bristol, Preston and Dunbar, liberally donating his blood to the soil in all three places. Sir Julius carried the scars of battle with pride. In his own mind, he was still a colonel in a victorious army.

'May I offer you some refreshment?' asked Christopher.

'No, no. This is only a brief visit.'

'At least, remove your coat.'

'There is no point,' said Sir Julius. 'The first thing that I must do, Mr Redmayne, is to thank you. Susan has told me what transpired at the frost fair. In keeping her away from the horror that you uncovered, you acted like a true gentleman.'

'There was no need for her to view such a hideous sight.'

'Susan has always been far too curious.'

'Yes,' said Christopher with a fond smile. 'Your daughter was determined to see the body for herself. I had some difficulty persuading her that it would be unwise for her to do so. Most young women would be too squeamish even to make the request. That was not the case with her.'

'She has a headstrong streak, I fear,' said her father, 'though I cannot imagine from whom she got it. Her mother was a docile woman and I am known for my gift of restraint.' He gave a chuckle. 'Except on a battlefield, that is.'

Christopher had never met anyone less restrained than Sir Julius but he made no comment. As he looked into the face of his visitor with its surging brow, its rubicund cheeks, its wild eyes and its square chin, he could see that Susan's beauty had certainly not come from her father. His features were arresting but hardly prepossessing. What she had inherited from him was an iron determination and a sense of independence.

'My real concern was for Richard,' he said. 'Jonathan Bale's younger son. He actually chanced upon the body. It will give him nightmares for a long time to come.'

'Mr Bale is a good man. He fought with us at Worcester.'

'That will not advantage his son.'

'It will,' insisted Sir Julius. 'The boy has his father's blood in his veins. He'll be able to look on death without turning a hair.'

'The poor lad was crying like a baby. It was a dreadful shock for him.'

'He'll soon get over it.'

'I beg leave to doubt that.'

'Be that as it may,' said the other irritably. 'I did not come here to talk about a small boy who stumbled upon a corpse. I simply wanted to thank you for the way you behaved towards Susan and to acquaint you with the fact that, as soon as the roads are passable, I will be quitting London.'

Christopher was upset. 'For how long, Sir Julius?'

'Until the King sees fit to recall Parliament.'

'But that may be months away.'

'I do have an estate in Northamptonshire to run.'

'Naturally,' said Christopher, trying to conceal his fear that he and Susan might be parted for a considerable time. 'But I hope that you'll not neglect the many friends you have here in the capital.'

'I entered Parliament to clean up this city, not to sink into its corruption myself.'

'Do not judge the whole of London society by its more wayward members.'

'Prejudice has not made me that blind, sir.'

'I trust that you'll be able to dine here before you depart,' said Christopher, anxious to arrange at least one more meeting with Susan. 'It may be a week or so before the ice has completely thawed.'

Sir Julius rose to his feet. 'It's a tempting invitation,' he said, 'but I'll have no time to take advantage of it. There's too much work to do before I leave. I've letters to write, reports to deliver and committee meetings to attend. Because I consider you one of the few decent men in this cesspool of a city, I felt that I owed you the courtesy of telling in person about my decision.'

'I appreciate that, Sir Julius.'

'One day, perhaps, we can lure you back to Northamptonshire.'

'This commission will keep me in London for the time being.' said Christopher, indicating his drawing, 'but the situation may ease in the springtime. I'd be happy to come then.'

'Our door is always open to you.'

'I'm flattered.'

'A word of advice, Mr Redmayne,' said Sir Julius, tossing a disapproving glance at the table. 'Reject this approach from Lady Whitcombe. You are far too talented an architect to be short of work. Choose clients whom you can respect, not those who bear the names of confounded Royalists.'

'I make no distinctions.'

'You should, man.'

'I disagree.'

'What scoundrel introduced you to this particular lady?'

'You did, Sir Julius.'

'Me?' protested the other. 'But I've never even met the woman.'

'It makes no difference,' said Christopher, amused at his reaction. 'Indirectly, you were responsible for my coming to Lady Whitcombe's attention. When she was driven through Westminster, she was so impressed with the town house I built for you that she demanded the name of the architect. I was promptly engaged to design something similar, though on a larger scale, for her.'

'Do you mean that she's copying my house?' demanded Sir Julius. 'I'll not allow it, do you hear? Is the lady incapable of having ideas of her own?'

Christopher smiled ruefully. 'Far from it. Lady Whitcombe invents new refinements every time we meet. Her house will be no slavish copy of yours. The façade has a superficial resemblance to your own,' he continued, looking down at the drawing, 'but there are features that set the two properties far apart. Between the two interiors, there will be little comparison.'

'I still feel that you should refuse her tainted money.'

'Architects do not make moral judgements about their clients.'

'They ought to.'

'Then our commissions would be few and far between.'

'But you'd have the reward of a clear conscience.'

'My creditors prefer to be paid in coin.'

'I took you for a man of principle.'

'Then you were right to do so, Sir Julius,' said Christopher. 'Nobody adheres so closely to the principles of architecture as I do. The first principle is that an architect must have food, drink and a roof over his head in order to pursue his profession. I'm grateful to anyone who makes that possible.'

'So be it,' said the visitor, putting his hat on. 'I'll waste no more breath on you.'

'I wish you a safe journey.'

'And I wish you a better class of client.'

Turning on his heel, Sir Julius made his way to the front door. Christopher did not want them to part on such a sour note. When his guest tried to open the door, he put a restraining hand on it.

'How shall I know when you leave London?' he asked.

Sir Julius snorted. 'The city will sink back into a morass of depravity.'

'I'd like to be there to see you off, Sir Julius.'

'There's no need for that.'

'I could wish you both God-speed.'

'I abhor the sight of well-wishers,' said Sir Julius, opening the door, 'however well-meaning they may be. Besides, I'll simply go when the moment is right. There'll be no time to advertise my departure.'

'I see.'

'Good day to you, sir.'

'Thank you again for taking the trouble to call.'

'I had to,' said Sir Julius, walking to his coach. He paused at the door held open by his coachman. 'Dear me!' he added with a wry grin. 'I all but forgot the main reason that brought me here. While I will be shaking the dust of London from my feet, Susan will not. She's decided to stay with her sister at Richmond.'

Christopher's spirits were lifted. 'This is excellent news!'

'I thought it might be.'

'I'm doubly grateful that you came, Sir Julius.'

'Then repay me in the best possible way,' said the old man with a twinkle in his eye. 'While I'm away, look after Susan for me. It will bring me some comfort to know that she has such a reliable friend in London. Do I ask too much of you?'

'Not at all. No request could be more welcome.'

'Then let me burden you with a second one.'

'As many as you wish, Sir Julius.'

'Since that body was discovered in the ice, Susan has taken a personal interest in the crime. I'd like that interest to be firmly discouraged. It's not right for a young lady to concern herself with such things.'

'I understand.'

'Has the body been identified yet?'

'Not to my knowledge.'

'When it is,' said the other, 'confide no details in my daughter. Susan is showing an unhealthy curiosity in the whole business. I trust that I can depend on you to keep her ignorant of any developments.'

'I'll do my best, Sir Julius,' Christopher promised.

But he doubted if he would be able to keep his promise.

But he doubted if he would be able to keep his promise.

Jonathan Bale got back from his patrol that evening to find that his children were already in bed. Sarah was in the kitchen, preparing a meal for her husband. Like all the other properties in Baynard's Castle Ward, their little house in Addle Hill had been burned to the ground in the Great Fire but it was among the first to be rebuilt. Grateful to have their home back again, they treated it with exaggerated care, keeping it spotlessly clean and making sure that their sons showed it due respect. Every night, they prayed that their house would never again be destroyed by flames.

Jonathan went into the kitchen and gave his wife a token kiss on the cheek.

'Are the boys asleep?' he asked.

'No,' she replied. 'They are waiting for you to read to them.'

'I'll go up in a moment. How is Richard?'

'He's still very upset. I spent most of the afternoon cuddling him.'

'Poor lad! He was all but frightened out of his skin.'

'I know,' she said, putting the food on the table for him. 'Richard has hardly slept a wink since. Thank heaven that Oliver did not have to see that gruesome sight!'

'I made sure of that, Sarah.'

'If only you'd been able to keep everyone away.'

'Yes,' he sighed, 'but that was impossible. As soon as word spread, the ghouls came in their hundreds to peer at the corpse as if it was part of the frost fair laid on for their pleasure. In truth, it made me ashamed of my fellow men.'

'There were a few women in that crowd as well.'

'They were among the worst offenders.'

'So I saw.' She folded her arms. 'Did you call on the coroner today?'

'I spent an hour with him this afternoon.'

'Does he know how the body got into the water?'

'Not by accident,' said Jonathan sadly. 'That much is certain. There were stab wounds in the man's back, it seems. He was dead before he was thrown into the Thames. What the killer did not anticipate was that the river would freeze over. The ice preserved the body in a better state than might have been the case. Most corpses that are hauled out of the water are bloated beyond all recognition.'

Sarah gave an involuntary shiver. 'So this man was murdered?'

'I fear so.'

'Do they have any idea who he might be?'

'Yes,' he said. 'The coroner has no doubt on that score. The man had been reported missing and, even in their sorry condition, his brother was able to identify the remains. My ears pricked up when I heard that the murder victim had lived in this ward.'

'Who was the man?'

'His name was Jeronimo Maldini.'

'An Italian?'

'Yes, Sarah. A fencing master by profession and one with a fine reputation, I gather. In short, a man who was well able to defend himself. It would have taken a cunning swordsman to get the better of him.'

'Is that what happened?'

'Who knows?' said Jonathan. 'I mean to look closely into the matter.'

'Why?'

'Because I feel involved. It was my son who first saw the body.'

'I doubt if he'll ever forget that.'

'The man lodged no more than a few hundred yards from here. I've probably passed him in the street a number of times without

26

realising who he was. Baynard's Castle Ward is very precious to me,' he went on with a proprietary glint in his eye. 'It's my territory, Sarah. If someone is murdered here, I want to do everything possible to catch the culprit.'

'Be careful,' she said, putting an affectionate hand on his arm.

He kissed her gently. 'I always am.'

'Sit down and eat your supper, Jonathan.'

'Let me read to the boys first. Where's the Bible?'

'In their bedroom.'

'Good,' he said, moving to the door. 'I must find a passage that will help to still Richard's fears. He needs a lot of love and attention.'

'That was Mr Redmayne's view.'

'Mr *Christopher* Redmayne?'

'Yes, Jonathan.'

'How do you know?'

'He called in this afternoon to see how the boys were,' she said, her face beaming at the memory. 'Mr Redmayne is such a kind man. He brought presents for both of them to cheer them up. They've grown very fond of him. And so have you,' she continued with a smile, 'if only you had the grace to admit it.'

Jonathan was impassive. 'Mr Redmayne has many good qualities,' he said. 'I respect him for that. But he and I live in different worlds. You may choose to forget that but I'm unable to do so. There is a gulf between us as wide as the Thames.'

'Even when the river is frozen?'

'Even then, Sarah.'

An evening out with friends imposed a whole set of decisions on Henry Redmayne. He had to make up his mind where to go, how best to get there and what to wear in order to achieve the maximum effect. An hour at least was devoted to the selection of his apparel. Henry had a large wardrobe and, in spite of his tendency to leave his tailors' bills unpaid, he was always adding to it, desperate to keep abreast of the latest fashion. No less than four mirrors adorned the walls of his bedchamber and he examined himself meticulously in each one before settling on a particular garment. Thomas, his long-suffering valet, was a martyr to Henry Redmayne's vanity.

'How does this look, Thomas?' asked his master, parading in a lime green coat.

'It becomes you, sir.'

'You said that about the red one.'

'They suit you equally, sir.'

'How can they,' complained Henry, 'when they are so different in colour, cut and finish? Damnation, man! Green and red are opposing hues. One must surely flatter my complexion more than the other.'

'Then it must be the green, sir,' said Thomas, ready to agree with him on any choice. 'It makes you look handsome and elegant.'

'Everything I wear does that.'

'It goes without saying, sir.'

'I'm reminded of it every time I court a looking glass.'

Henry preened himself in front of the largest mirror, twisting around so that he could see himself from various angles and adjusting his coat as he did so. Thomas waited patiently. A short, neat, alert man in his fifties, the valet knew the ritual all too well. The secret was to watch his master get to the verge of a decision before applying the gentle pressure needed to help him actually make it. Having got him as far as the coat, Thomas felt that he was doing well.

'No,' said Henry, clicking his tongue. 'I think that I prefer the blue one, after all.' He held out both arms. 'Take this one off, Thomas.'

'Is that wise, sir?'

'I can hardly put on a blue coat until a green coat has been removed. Would you have me wear two at the same time and be the laughing stock of London?'

'No, sir,' said Thomas. 'I merely question the wisdom of dispensing with the green coat. The colour is ideal for you. Change to the blue and we have to replace both the shirt and the waistcoat for neither will match it.'

'Could we not try the combination?'

'We've already done so three times, sir.'

'Ah,' said Henry. 'In that case, perhaps it's time to settle for the green.'

'It was my choice from the start.'

'Then why lead me astray by letting me try of every other coat in my wardrobe?'

Henry appraised himself once more in the mirror. Now in his thirties, he was tall, slim and striking with a long face that was pitted with the signs of dissipation and hair that was vanishing so rapidly that its remaining wisps were hidden beneath an expensive periwig. Henry Redmayne shared little with his younger brother, Christopher, beyond a surname and one surviving parent. While the architect would spend the evening working on his drawings by the light of candles, Henry intended to sit at a gaming table with his friends and, in all probability, run up even more debts that he could not afford to pay. One brother lived for his profession but his older sibling dedicated himself exclusively and unashamedly to pleasure.

'The green coat, it will be,' announced Henry, fiddling with his wig. 'All that remains is to choose a hat and cloak.'

'I believe that they will choose themselves, sir,' said Thomas.

'Every last detail must enhance the whole.'

'Shall we descend?'

Relieved to have come through another ordeal of indecision in the bedchamber, the valet led the way downstairs to the hall. The house in Bedford Street was large and its ornate furniture and rich hangings reflected the taste of its owner. Some of the paintings that covered the walls were by maritime artists but the majority featured buxom young women in a state of undress. Among ships and nude females, Henry felt supremely at home. In the spacious hall was a cupboard that contained a wide selection of hats, cloaks and canes as well as variety of swords and daggers. Thomas opened the doors so that his master could survey the possibilities. From the street outside came the sound of approaching horses.

'I believe that the coach is here to pick you up, sir,' said Thomas.

'Then it can wait.'

'You were asked to be ready at eight o'clock, sir.'

'I'll not be rushed into a wrong decision, Thomas,' said Henry, taking out the warmest cloak he could find and handing it to his valet. 'Put that around my shoulders so that I can judge its relation to the rest of my attire.'

Thomas did as he was bidden. There was a loud knock at the door. A nod from Henry sent him off to open it. Expecting to see a friend on his doorstep, Henry swung round with a smile of welcome, only to find himself confronted by four officers of the law. Their grim expressions suggested that it was not a social visit. One of the men stepped past Thomas and waved a scroll at the master of the house.

'Mr Henry Redmayne?' he enquired.

'Away with you, man! How dare you enter my home like that?'

'I have a warrant here for your arrest, sir.'

'Is it a crime to choose a cloak that does not match this green coat?' asked Henry, removing the cloak with a flourish and hanging it back in the cupboard. 'For that is the only misdemeanour of which I've been guilty today.'

'This is no occasion for levity, Mr Redmayne.'

'Then take yourself off at once.'

'You have to come with us, sir,' said the man with calm authority. 'I must warn you that we'll brook no delay.'

'Is this some kind of jest?'

'No, sir. I arrest you, Henry Redmayne, on a charge of murder.'

'But that's utterly ludicrous!'

'Reserve your protestations for the judge.'

'Murder?' said Henry with disdain. 'You accuse a decent, honest, respectable, peace-loving, law-abiding man like me of *murder*? It's quite absurd. Who on earth am I supposed to have killed?'

'The victim's name is Jeronimo Maldini.'

Henry was struck dumb. His righteous indignation was quickly replaced by a mingled surprise and apprehension. His eyes filled with horror, his mouth was agape. Thomas had never seen his master tremble so violently before. When he saw him begin to sway, the valet rushed forward. He was just in time to catch Henry as the latter collapsed in a dead faint.

Chapter Three

Over the years, Christopher Redmayne had seen his brother in many embarrassing situations. He had watched Henry being pursued by creditors, harassed by discarded lovers, thrown out of gaming houses, afflicted by shameful diseases, mocked by his colleagues at the Navy Office and, on more than one occasion, so hopelessly drunk that he could barely recall his own name. There was also a time when Henry was subjected to a violent assault that put him in bed for a week and gave him the perfect excuse to whinge, whimper and feel thoroughly sorry for himself. He had been battered and bruised enough to arouse anyone's sympathy. Nothing he had seen before, however, prepared Christopher for the image that he beheld in Newgate prison that morning. Henry Redmayne was in despair.

Locked in a tiny, dark, dank cell, he was sitting on the ground beneath a barred window with his knees pulled up to his chest and his arms wrapped tightly around his shins. His face was drawn, his eyes rimmed with fatigue. In spite of the cold, he wore nothing but a shirt, breeches and stockings, all of them sullied with filth. Without his wig, he looked a decade older than his true age. Henry was so caught up in his tragedy that he did not seem to notice the stink that pervaded his cell nor the rat that was rustling the straw. When the turnkey showed the visitor in, the prisoner did not even raise his eyes. It was only when the heavy door clanged shut that he came out of his reverie.

'I want no food,' he declared. 'I'd sooner starve than eat that offal.'

'Henry,' said his brother, putting a hand on his shoulder. 'It's me, Christopher.'

'Thank God!'

'How came you to this sorry state?'

'You may well ask!'

'Your valet rushed to my house yesterday evening with news of your arrest, but they would not let me see you until this morning. I had to bribe the turnkey to be left alone with you for ten minutes.'

'This whole place is run on bribes and favours.'

'Tell me what happened,' said Christopher, shocked at his

brother's condition. 'Your valet said that officers came to your house.'

Henry put a hand to his brow. 'It's been like a descent into Hell.'

'Have you been badly treated?'

'I've been *everything*, Christopher. Manacled, fettered, browbeaten, bullied, interrogated, humiliated and even threatened with torture. Had I not had sufficient money to buy a room of my own, they'd have tossed me in with the sweepings of London. Can you imagine that?' he asked with a flash of his old spirit. 'Me, Henry Redmayne, a man of delicate sensibilities, locked up with a seething mass of thieves, cutthroats and naughty ladies, all of them infected with maladies of some kind or another. They'd have torn me to shreds as soon as look at me.' He stared down at his stockinged feet. 'I had to give my best shoes to the prison sergeant – the ones with the silver buckles – so that he'd spare me from being chained to the wall.'

'I'll protest strongly on your behalf.'

'There's no point.'

'Even a prisoner has certain rights.'

'Not in Newgate.'

'It's not as if you're a convicted felon,' argued Christopher. 'You're simply on remand. When this whole business is cleared up, you'll be found innocent, released and able to resume your normal life.'

'Normal life!' echoed Henry gloomily. 'Those days are gone.'

'Take heart, brother.'

'How can I?'

'We'll help you through this nightmare.'

'It's too late, Christopher. The worst has already occurred. The very fact of my arrest has blackened my name and, I daresay, cost me my sinecure at the Navy Office.'

'Not if you are completely exonerated.'

'Nothing can exonerate me from the torment I've suffered so far,' moaned Henry, running his fingers through the vestigial remains of his hair. 'I was arrested in front of my valet, taken by force from my house, questioned for hours by rogues who had patterned themselves on the Spanish Inquisition, deprived of my wig and most of my apparel, then flung into this sewer. By way of a jest, the turnkeys pretended to lock me next door.'

'Next door?'

'Can you not smell that noisome reek?'

Christopher nodded. 'It's the stench of decay.'

'They made me see where it came from,' said Henry, glancing at the wall directly opposite. 'In the next cell are the quartered remains of three poor wretches who were executed earlier this week. They are being kept there until their relatives can get permission to bury what's left of them. The turnkeys took a delight in pointing out that there were no heads in the cell. They'd been parboiled by the hangman with bay-salt and cummin seed so that they would not rot. Those heads have now been set up on spikes for all London to mock.' He grabbed his brother. 'Do not let that happen to *me*, Christopher. Save me from that disgrace.'

'Only those found guilty of treason suffer that indignity.'

'They'll do their best to pin that crime on me as well.'

'Nonsense!'

'There's nothing they like more than to see a gentleman brought down,' wailed Henry. 'I'm like one of those bulls they had at the frost fair, a noble animal forced to its knees by a pack of sharp-toothed mongrels. I can feel the blood trickling down my back already.'

'Enough of this!' said Christopher, determined not to let his brother wallow in self-pity. 'Our main task is to get you out of here today.'

'There's no chance of that.'

'Yes, there is. I'll speak to the magistrate who committed you.'

'I'm more worried about the judge who'll condemn me.'

'The case will not even come to trial, Henry.'

'It must. The law will take its course.'

'Only if there's enough evidence against you,' argued Christopher, 'and, clearly, there is not. A gross miscarriage of justice has taken place here. You'll be able to sue for wrongful arrest.'

'Will I?'

'Yes, Henry. The charge against you is preposterous.'

'They do not seem to think so.'

'Only because they do not know you as well as I do. What better spokesman is there than a brother? You have your faults, I grant you – and I've taken you to task about them often enough – but you are no murderer, Henry. I've never seen you swat a fly, still less raise your hand against another man.'

'I do not always reign in my temper,' confessed Henry.

'All of us have lapses.'

'Not of the kind that lead to arrest.'

'I'd be surprised if you even knew the murder victim.'

'But I did, that's the rub. I knew and loathed Jeronimo Maldini.'

'Maldini? Who was he?'

'The man they found in the river.'

Christopher was startled. 'The fellow they had to cut out of the ice?'

'According to report.'

'But I was there at the frost fair when the body was discovered. Good Lord! What a bizarre coincidence we have here! Is *that* what has brought you to this pass? I did not even realise that the man had been identified yet. It was one of Jonathan Bale's sons who actually stumbled on the corpse. The lad was frightened to death.'

'So was I when four constables came knocking at my door.'

'What was name again?'

'Maldini. Jeronimo Maldini.'

'And you disliked him?'

'I detested the greasy Italian,' said Henry petulantly. 'At one time, I made the mistake of going to him for fencing lessons but we soon fell out. Our enmity began there and grew out of all proportion.'

'You said nothing of this to me.'

'If I told you about every acquaintance of mine with whom I have a disagreement then it would take up an entire week. Life is a process of constant change, Christopher. We learn to see through people. Friendships fall off, antagonism takes over.'

'How antagonistic were you towards Signor Maldini?'

'*Very* antagonistic.'

'Could you give me more detail?'

There was a pause. 'I'd prefer not to.'

'But this is important,' said his brother. 'If I'm to help you, I need to be in possession of all the facts. I had no idea that there was any connection between you and the man they hauled out of the Thames. When I heard that you'd been arrested, I assumed that some grotesque error had been made.'

'It has!' Henry looked up at him in dismay. 'At least, I hope that it has.'

'Why did they issue a warrant against you?'

'Judicial spite.'

'They must have had some grounds for suspicion.'

'Witnesses had come forward.'

'Witnesses?' repeated Christopher, feeling anxious. 'What sort of witnesses?'

'Ones who were there at the time.'

'At what time? There's something you're not telling me, Henry.'

'I despised Maldini. I admit that freely.'

'Did you quarrel with him?'

'Several times.'

'And did you do so in public? In front of witnesses?'

Henry bit his lip. 'Yes,' he murmured.

'What was the nature of the argument?'

'It was a heated one, Christopher.'

'Did you come to blows?'

'Almost. His insults were too much to bear.'

'And how did you respond?' Henry put his head in his hands. *'Please,'* said his brother, leaning over him. 'I must know. I came to Newgate in the confident belief that some appalling mistake had been made and that, when I'd spoken up for you, I'd be in a position to take you home or, at the very least, to set your release in train. Yet now, it seems, there *were* grounds for suspecting you. Is that true, Henry?'

'I suppose so.'

'Heavens, man! Your life may be at stake here. We need more than supposition.'

'It's all I can offer,' bleated Henry, looking up at him once more. 'For a number of reasons, there was bad blood between Jeronimo Maldini and me. It came to a head one evening when we had a chance encounter. His language was so vile that he provoked me beyond all endurance.'

'So what did you do?'

'I expressed my anger.'

'How?'

'I said something that, on reflection, I should not perhaps have said.'

'And what was that, Henry?'

'Does it matter?'

35

'It matters a great deal,' insisted Christopher. 'I've known you make incautious remarks before but never ones that might land you in a prison cell. Now let's have no more prevarication, Henry. What did you say?'

'I threatened to kill him.'

Christopher was staggered. It had never occurred to him for a moment that his brother was guilty of a crime serious enough to justify arrest and imprisonment. He knew his brother's defects of character better than anyone and a homicidal impulse was certainly not among them. Or so he had always believed. Now he was forced to look at Henry through very different eyes. Strong drink could corrupt any man and few indulged as frequently as his brother. Whole weeks sometimes passed without his managing more than a few hours of sobriety. Such a life was bound to takes its toll on Henry. The thought made Christopher put a straight question him.

'Did you murder Jeronimo Maldini?' he asked.

'I don't know,' replied Henry with a forlorn shrug. 'I *may* have done.'

Word of the arrest spread throughout London with remarkable speed. Within a couple of days, it was the talk of every tavern and coffee house in the city. Since she had been there when the murder victim was found, Susan Cheever took a keen interest in the case and seized on every scrap of information related to it. She was astonished to hear that Henry Redmayne was the chief suspect. Her father, an unforgiving man, was plainly disgusted.

'He should be hanged by his scrawny neck at Tyburn,' he announced.

'But he's not been convicted yet, Father,' she reminded him.

'The fellow is guilty. Why else would they arrest him?'

'There are all kinds of reasons. Mistaken identity is but one of them.'

'*We* have been the victims of that, Susan.'

'What do you mean?'

'We took the Redmayne family for honourable men,' he said, gesticulating with both arms, 'and we were most cruelly deceived.'

'Not so, Father,' she rejoined with vehemence. 'Christopher Redmayne is the most honourable man I've ever met and his brother, Henry, can be quite charming when you get to know him.'

'I've no wish to know him, Susan.'

'At least, give him the benefit of the doubt.'

'What doubt?' he asked. 'Henry Redmayne consorts with some of the most notorious rakehells in the capital. That says everything. It pains me to admit that my son, Gabriel, was once embroiled in that same twilight world of decadence and debauchery. He paid for it with his life.'

'And who helped to *solve* his murder? Christopher Redmayne.'

'I've not forgotten that.'

'But for him, the villains would never have been caught.'

'That was one crime, this is quite another.'

'It's unfair to reproach him because of what's happened to his elder brother.'

'Certain traits run in families.'

Susan exploded. 'That's a dreadful thing to say!'

'Nevertheless, it happens to be true.'

'But their father is the Dean of Gloucester.'

'You know my opinion of Anglicans,' he said with a sneer. 'That may be the reason the sons were led astray. Brought up on debased values, they had a false start in life. It's ended at the gallows.'

'It's done nothing of the kind, Father,' she said, 'and I'll thank you to stop talking about the two brothers as if they are the selfsame person. They most assuredly are not. It's Henry who has been charged with this terrible crime and I, for one, will presume him innocent until he's proved guilty in a court of law.'

'I *know* the man did it. I feel it in my bones.'

'That's no more than old age creeping up on you.'

'Old heads are the wisest.'

'Not when they make unjust accusations.'

'The fellow has been arrested, Susan,' he said, slapping the table with the flat of his hand for emphasis. 'Evidence has been gathered and a warrant issued for his arrest. That's proof positive to me.'

Susan bit back a reply. In his present mood, Sir Julius would not even listen to her properly. His mind was already made up while her own was still very confused. The tidings about Henry Redmayne had alarmed her. In her heart, she could not accept that any member of the Redmayne family could be capable of murder. Vain and feckless, he might be, but Henry was not, in her opinion, a potential killer. Yet he had been indicted and such a step would not be taken lightly. Her real concern was for Christopher. Though he was the younger brother, he always seemed older and more responsible than Henry. The latter's peccadilloes were an unceasing source of discomfort to him and he had rescued his brother from countless embarrassments. This time, Susan feared, even Christopher would be uncertain what to do. She felt an urge to go to him.

Sir Julius Cheever seemed to read his daughter's mind.

'Stay away from him, Susan,' he warned.

'Who?'

'Mr Redmayne.'

'But he must be in great distress.'

'That's a problem he must cope with alone. It does not affect us.'

'It does. At a time like this, he wants friends around him.'

'Well, he'll not number us among them.'

'He will and he ought to,' she said hotly. 'Do you condemn one brother for the alleged sin of another? What a miserable species of friendship that is! It's callous to desert Mr Redmayne when he needs us most.'

'We do it for our own protection.'

'From what?'

'The taint of evil.'

'That's a monstrous suggestion!'

'I'll not have you associating with any member of that family.'

Susan was defiant. 'Would you forbid me?'

'No,' he said, taking a deep breath to calm himself. 'I'd not go that far. I'd simply appeal to your love and loyalty. For my sake, keep away from Mr Redmayne. I know that you are fond of him, Susan, and I know that he has many virtues. Why,' he went on, looking around the room, 'he designed this very house in which we stand and I'm very grateful to him for that.'

'He did much more than that to earn our gratitude, Father.'

'Do not harp on about Gabriel.'

'He was my brother,' she said with tears in her eyes. 'You shut him out of your life in the same way that you now want to exclude Mr Redmayne and his brother. Did you never stop to think that, if Gabriel had been kept *within* our family, he would not have met such an untimely end?'

'No!' yelled Sir Julius, rounding on her. 'That's not true!'

'Be honest with yourself, Father.'

'Silence!'

He was so furious that he did not trust himself to say anything else until he had regained his composure. Crossing to a large oaken court cupboard, he opened the door to take out a bottle of brandy and a glass. He poured himself a measure and drank it down in one gulp, waiting until it had coursed through him. When he turned back to his daughter, there was sadness as well as anger in his voice.

'Never dare to say that to me again,' he cautioned.

'I did not mean to hurt you so.'

'Gabriel's death lies heavy enough on my heart, as it is. I need no additional burden of anguish. Let him rest in peace, Susan. Please do not tax me on his account.'

'No, Father.'

He opened his arms to give her a hug of reconciliation and she kissed him on his cheek. Since he was due to leave London the following day, Susan did not want any disagreement between them. It might be months before they were reunited. On a subject as important as her friendship with Christopher Redmayne, however, she could not stay silent. Sir Julius held her by the shoulders to look at her.

'It's so ironic,' he reflected.

'What is?'

'Here am I, telling you to spurn Mr Redmayne when, only a few days ago, I called at his house for the express purpose of asking him to keep an eye on you while I was away from London.'

She took a step back. 'You talked to Mr Redmayne about me?'

'Yes.'

'Why did you not say?'

'It was a private matter between the two of us.'

'Not if it concerns me,' she said, hands on hips. 'I'm not sure that I like the idea of anyone keeping an eye on me. Am I a child that needs to be assigned to a new parent whenever my own goes away on his travels?'

'No, Susan. You misunderstand the situation.'

'I understand it all too well. You do not trust me to fend for myself.'

'That's not the case at all.'

'I'm wounded by this news. It's galling enough to be packed off to Richmond to stay with Brilliana when I could just as easily remain here.'

'Not on your own.'

'There are servants in the house.'

'They are hardly adequate companions.'

'I've friends in London on whom I can call.'

'That's my fear. Mr Christopher Redmayne is one of them.'

'A few days ago, you were urging him to look after me.'

'That was before I learned the ugly truth about his family,' said Sir Julius. 'It changes everything. Tomorrow, I depart for home but not before I've delivered you into Lancelot's hands. His coach will arrive by mid-morning at the latest.'

'You do not have to stand over me like that, Father.'

'I do it by choice. That imbecile of a brother-in-law will hardly be entertaining company but Lancelot will at least get you safely back to Richmond. I've written to Brilliana to tell her what's afoot here.'

'There was no need to do that.'

'Brilliana is your sister. She has a right to know what's going on.'

'She's too critical of Mr Redmayne.'

'With just cause, it seems.'

'This will only feed her misconception.'

'Brilliana will take a dispassionate view of it all.'

'She'll only interfere.'

'Precisely,' he said with a cold smile that signalled the end of the conversation. 'Brilliana will agree with me and her husband will, as usual, do what she tells him. That contents me. Between the two of them, they'll keep you well away from Mr Redmayne and that murderous brother of his.'

Susan felt helpless. She could do nothing but smoulder in silence.

The first thing that Christopher Redmayne did when he left the prison was to fill his lungs with fresh air. It helped to clear his head and rid his nostrils of the abiding stench of Newgate. His visit had been deeply disturbing. It was bad enough to find his brother in such an appalling state. To learn that there were genuine grounds for suspecting Henry Redmayne of murder was truly shocking. What made it even worse was that Henry himself could neither deny nor confirm his guilt, making it almost impossible for Christopher speak up in his defence. On previous occasions when he had been arrested, Henry had been fined for being drunk and disorderly before being discharged. He had never spent a night in a prison cell before, especially one as cramped and fetid as the bare room that he now occupied. Unused to squalor, he was having it rubbed in his face and his ordeal seemed likely to continue until he went to trial for murder.

Christopher walked away from Newgate then turned back to study it. Razed to the ground in the Great Fire, the prison had been rebuilt and work was still continuing on it. As an architect, Christopher had to admire the magnificent façade, decorated, as it was, by emblematic figures and statues. Among other civic worthies of the past, Richard Whittington and his cat looked down on the hordes of people going in and out of the city. Behind the sumptuous exterior of Newgate, however, was a grim prison that retained all the faults of its hated predecessor. Bad ventilation, an inadequate water supply and serious overcrowding made it a breeding-ground for disease. Those who survived the brutal regime imposed upon them often fell victim to gaol fever. In one way or another, Newgate left an indelible mark on anyone incarcerated there.

Fearing for his brother, Christopher heaved a sigh and turned his steps homeward. The stroll back to Fetter Lane gave him an opportunity to reflect on the situation. Henry Redmayne had mourned the loss of his job and of his reputation but there was another potential loss, so great and so frightening that Henry had not even been able to address his mind to it. Out of consideration to his brother, Christopher had said nothing but the dilemma now had to be faced. What of their father, the eminent Dean of Gloucester? Should he be informed of the disgrace brought upon the family by his elder son or should he be kept in the dark in the hope that Henry would be found innocent and set free? It was a thorny problem.

Christopher's first instinct was to keep his father ignorant of the events in London but he soon came to accept how unfair and unwise that would be. If, by any chance, Henry were convicted of the murder, the Reverend Algernon Redmayne would never forgive his younger son for holding back information about the arrest. He would see it as the ultimate betrayal. There was another consideration. Even if Christopher remained silent, others would not. The Dean of Gloucester had enemies in the Church hierarchy and they would revel in the situation, taking an unholy delight in telling him that one of his sons faced execution. Given the name of the murder suspect, Archbishop Sheldon himself

41

might be moved to write to their father. The truth could not be hidden indefinitely.

Christopher accepted that it was his duty to pass on the sad tidings. He knew that the Dean would travel immediately to London. It would be an additional blow for the prisoner. Henry would view a visit from his father as worse punishment than being stretched on the rack but it could not be helped. In a time of crisis, the Redmayne family needed to come together. When he got home, Christopher went straight to the parlour and sat down at the table.

He began to compose the most difficult letter that he had ever written.

Chapter Four

Jonathan Bale was in a quandary. The news that Henry Redmayne was being held as a chief suspect in the murder investigation was profoundly troubling to him. Having met Henry a number of times, he had no affection at all for the man and even less respect. In his estimation, the elder of the two Redmayne brothers was a symbol of all that was wrong with the country since a venal King had returned to rule over it. Henry Redmayne was conceited, egotistical and corrupt. He was a confirmed sybarite whose circle included some of the most blatant voluptuaries in London. Since Henry was guilty of so many deplorable sins, Jonathan had no difficulty in believing him capable of a heinous crime. That was how the quandary arose. It was a murder that the constable was helping to investigate. What exercised his mind was whether or not he should get in touch with Christopher Redmayne. He agonised over the decision for hours. It was his wife who finally helped him to make it.

'Go to him, Jonathan,' she advised. 'Mr Redmayne needs you.'

'He may not want me near the house, Sarah.'

'How will you know unless you offer your sympathy?'

'I'm not sure that I feel any,' he admitted. 'Henry Redmayne never struck me as a violent man but there's evidence enough to arrest him. That speaks volumes. You can hardly expect me to feel sorry for a man I think might well be a killer.'

'Put yourself in his brother's place. How do you think *he* feels?'

'Low and dispirited.'

'Is that all?'

'No, I daresay that he's been badly shaken by this business. Mr Redmayne is a decent man who deserves better than to have something like this happen within the family. It will cause him great pain. He'll be mortified.'

'That's why you must call on him.'

'It's not my place to do so, Sarah.'

'You're his *friend*.'

They were in the kitchen of their little house in Addle Hill. Sarah was seated at the table, sewing a pretty blue dress with deft fingers. In warmer weather, she took in washing to help the family finances but winter found her leaning much more on her skills as a needlewoman. It was something she fitted in around running the house, looking after two children and caring for a husband whom she loved dearly even when she disapproved of his actions. Her opinion on the matter in hand was dictated by her fondness for Christopher Redmayne. She simply could not accept that any brother of his would commit such a terrible crime as murder. Notwithstanding the arrest, she clung to the belief that he must somehow be innocent.

Still sewing away, she raised questioning eyes to Jonathan.

'Did you hear what I said?'

'Yes, Sarah.'

'I know what Mr Redmayne would do in *your* place.'

'Do you?'

'He'd be knocking on our door to offer you his help.'

'What possible help can I give?'

'You're an officer of the law. You can advise him.'

'I doubt if he'd even agree to see me.'

'How do you know if you refuse to call on him?'

'It's not as simple as that,' he said, running a ruminative hand across his chin. 'There's more to this than you understand, Sarah. If it was merely a question of going to a friend in need, I'd be there now. But his brother is accused of murder.'

'Does that make Mr Redmayne a criminal as well?'

'No, but it does oblige me to think carefully.'

'What do you mean?'

'I'm deeply involved in this investigation. It was our son who found that body in the first place. Richard keeps asking me when I'm going to arrest the killer.'

'That should not stop you going to Fetter Lane.'

'But it does, Sarah,' he argued. 'Don't you see? I'm gathering evidence that may lead to the conviction of Henry Redmayne. What will people think if I'm seen helping the brother of the accused man?'

'Since when did *you* worry about what people thought?'

'I have to keep an open mind.'

'Mr Redmayne would expect no less of you, Jonathan.'

'Then it would be safer if I kept well away from him.'

'Why?'

'Because there'd be no complications then.'

Sarah put her sewing aside. 'You disappoint me, I must say.'

'What do you mean?'

'I never thought that you could be so selfish.'

'It's not selfishness, Sarah. It's commonsense.'

'Oh, is that what it is?' she said with light mockery in her voice. 'It sounds more like putting your own needs first, Jonathan Bale, and I'm ashamed of you for doing so.'

'I have to do my duty.'

'And don't you have a duty towards a friend as well?'

'It's not the same thing.'

'So it seems.'

'I'm in an awkward position,' he explained. 'I'm searching for evidence that will lead to the prosecution of Henry Redmayne and you want me to go running off to the one person in London who is trying to defend him.'

'You see it your way, I see it mine.'

'If I arrived on his doorstep, Mr Redmayne would feel embarrassed.'

'No, Jonathan. *You* would. And that's what really holds you back.'

'It would be wrong and it would be foolish.'

'My parents once told me it was wrong and foolish of me to marry a shipwright named Jonathan Bale,' she recalled with a wistful smile. 'But I listened to my heart instead.'

His tone softened. 'Do you have any regrets?'

'None at all – until now.'

'Sarah!'

'Yes, I know. I'm a woman. I couldn't possibly understand.'

'That's not what I was going to say.'

'What's the point in talking about it?' she asked, taking up her sewing again. 'You tell me that you must keep an open mind but it's shut tight against sympathy or reason. You pay no attention at all to me.'

'I do, I promise you.'

'I see precious little sign of it.'

'There are some decisions I can only make on my own.' He gave a smile. 'Did your parents really say that it was wrong and foolish of you to become my wife?'

'They thought it would never last.'

'We proved them wrong.'

'In some ways,' she conceded. 'Prove *me* wrong, Jonathan.'

'You?'

'Show me that you're not the fair-weather friend that you seem.'

'Now, that's unjust!' he protested.

'Is it?'

'Yes.'

'Mr Redmayne is waiting for you.'

'Then he must wait in vain.'

'Why is that?' she challenged. 'Are you going to let him down?'

When she plied her needle again, Jonathan felt as if it were piercing his brain.

Susan Cheever had always liked her brother-in-law. Lancelot Serle was a willing, affable, tolerant man who was passably handsome and never less than impeccably dressed. He had none of the arrogance that wealth often brings and he was endlessly obliging. Ordinarily, Susan would have been pleased to see him again but circumstances militated against her. Serle had come to take her away from the city and put distance between her and Christopher Redmayne. It made her fretful. She gave her brother-in-law only a muted welcome. Sir Julius Cheever did not even bother with a greeting.

'Where, in God's name, have you *been*?' he demanded.

'We were delayed, Sir Julius,' replied Serle with a shrug of apology.

'I can see that, man. I wanted you here by mid-morning and it is well past noon. Are there no clocks in Richmond? Or have you lost the ability to tell the time?'

'We reached London hours ago but we were held up on the bridge. Every cart, carriage and coach in England seem to have congregated there. It took an age to battle our way through. That's the beauty of living in the country,' he said, turning to Susan. 'We have the freedom to move at will.'

'I was hoping to enjoy that freedom myself,' said Sir Julius testily, 'but you've kept me cooling my heels in Westminster.'

'Not deliberately, Sir Julius.'

'You should have set out earlier.'

'Nobody could have foretold that amount of traffic.'

'London Bridge is always an ordeal to cross.'

'Except when the river freezes over,' observed Serle with an almost childlike smile. 'The ice is breaking up now or we could have ridden across the Thames itself. What an adventure that would have been! I'm so sorry that we missed the frost fair but Brilliana refused to stir from the house during the cold spell.' His smile broadened into a polite grin. 'Brilliana sends her love, by the way.'

'I'd have been more grateful if she could have sent a punctual husband.'

'I did not mean to hold you up, Sir Julius.'

'You never mean *any* of the idiocies that you commit.'

'Do not be so choleric, Father,' said Susan, trying to save their visitor from further abuse. 'Lancelot has made the effort to get here and you have not even had the grace to offer him refreshment.'

Sir Julius was dismissive. 'He does not deserve any.'

'Forgive him, Lancelot,' she said. 'Father is so eager to be on the road that he has forgotten his manners. I'm sure that you'd like refreshment after your journey and the horses will appreciate a rest.' She turned to Sir Julius. 'Carry on, if you must. There's nothing to detain you now.'

Sir Julius hovered. The three of them were standing in the hall of the house in Westminster. Milder weather had banished the icicles under the windowsills and the hoar frost on the garden. Winter sunshine was chasing away the last few deposits of snow. It was only Sir Julius who seemed impervious to the thaw. He regarded his son-in-law with glacial contempt. What upset him most was that he was forced to part with his younger, and favourite, daughter. It would be a long and lonely journey to Northamptonshire and, when he got there, his manor house would feel desperately empty without her. But Susan was determined to remain near the capital so a compromise was reached. Sir Julius grudgingly allowed her to stay behind on condition that she moved in with her sister in Richmond. He felt a flicker of paternal interest.

'How is Brilliana?' he asked gruffly.

'Extremely well, Sir Julius,' said the doting husband. 'She's full of plans for Susan's visit and regrets that you are unable to join us yourself.'

'I've business elsewhere.'

'We understand that. When can we expect your return?'

'When I choose to make it.'

'Ignore him, Lancelot,' advised Susan. 'Father is in a peevish mood today.'

Sir Julius was always in a peevish mood when he was close to his son-in-law, a man whose personality and politics he found it impossible to admire. Lancelot Serle had none of the intelligence, thrust or ambition that would have impressed the older man. Instead, he was kind, considerate and inoffensive. He did not seem to mind that he was firmly under the thumb of his wife, indeed, he accepted his servitude with alacrity. Serle was proud to be linked to the Cheever family.

'Brilliana was grateful for your letter, Sir Julius,' he said.

'I felt that she needed to be made aware of the facts.'

'As it happened, word of the crime had already reached us. We are not so cut off in Richmond that we do not hear the latest scandal. Brilliana was as shocked as I was,' he went on, looking at Susan. 'Who would have thought that Mr Redmayne's brother would be guilty of such a foul murder?'

'He is only *suspected* of the crime,' corrected Susan.

'They would not arrest him without firm evidence.'

Sir Julius was blunt. 'The fellow deserves to hang and there's an end to it!'

Susan was dismayed that the subject had even been raised. Her aim had been to send her father on his way so that she could work on her amenable brother-in-law while they dined together. Before they left London, she believed, she could persuade Serle to let her call at a certain house in Fetter Lane. Her urge to see Christopher had hardened into a firm resolve. If nothing else, she wanted him to know that he was in her thoughts. Sir Julius was dressed for departure. His luggage had been loaded on to the coach that stood ready at his door. He reached for his hat and cane.

'One last request, Lancelot,' he said.

'Yes, Sir Julius?' asked Serle.

'When you leave here, drive straight to Richmond.'

'That was my intention.'

'Do not be shifted from it,' said the old man with a reproving glance at his daughter. 'Especially if you are asked to direct your coachman to an address in Fetter Lane. I want no contact to be made between Mr Christopher Redmayne and my daughter. Do you understand?'

'I understand and endorse your wishes, Sir Julius.'

'It would be a relief to know that you got something right at last.'

'Brilliana takes the same view,' said Serle.

'So I should hope.'

'She thinks it would be unwise and improper for Susan to maintain a friendship with anyone in the Redmayne family, however personable he may be. It's a name that now bears the most hideous stigma.'

'Do you hear that, Susan?' asked her father. 'Forget all about Mr Christopher Redmayne. Your friendship with him is at an end.'

Susan saw the futility of protest. Her hopes had been completely dashed.

As soon as he stepped into the house, Jonathan Bale knew that he had made the right decision. Christopher Redmayne was not only pleased to see him, he was deeply touched. There was none of the awkwardness that the constable had feared. He was invited in, given a drink by Jacob and taken immediately into his friend's confidence.

'I hoped that you'd come,' said Christopher.

'Did you?'

'I need your assistance.'

'What can I do, Mr Redmayne?'

'Two things,' explained the architect. 'Firstly, you can help me to drive out some of the demons that have been inside my skull since my brother was arrested. Secondly, you can trust my judgement.'

'Your judgement?'

'I firmly believe that Henry is innocent.'

'Any brother would feel like that,' said Jonathan cautiously. 'But you have to accept that there must be substantial evidence against him for an arrest to be made.'

'I know what that evidence is.'

'Do you?'

'I visited Henry this morning in Newgate.'

'How was he?'

'Still overwhelmed by the turn of events.'

'Prison comes as a terrible shock for a gentleman.'

'It comes as a shock for anyone, Jonathan,' said the other. 'I saw some of the filthy cells in which the prisoners are kept. I'd not house animals in conditions like that.'

'Newgate is better than some of the other gaols.'

'Then they should be pulled down and rebuilt. Even criminals have the right to be treated as human beings. If I'd designed Newgate, I wouldn't spend all that money on a beautiful exterior that none of the prisoners can see. I'd make sure they had clean water, proper drains and larger windows to let in more light and air. Yes,' said Christopher, 'and there'd be far more single cells to allow a degree of privacy.'

'Privacy costs a lot of money in prison,' said Jonathan.

'That's what Henry has found. He's already spent everything in his purse. Luckily, I was able to replenish his funds.'

'Were you able to speak to him alone?'

'Yes, I was. Thanks to a bribe.'

'Did he plead his innocence?'

'No,' said Christopher, shaking his head, 'that was the strange thing.'

Jonathan was astonished. 'He *confessed* to the murder?'

'Not exactly. What Henry admitted was the possibility that he *might* have been guilty of killing Jeronimo Maldini. He was not entirely certain.'

'He must have been. Either he stabbed the victim or he did not.'

'There was more than just stabbing involved,' Christopher reminded him. 'The body was dropped into the freezing water of the Thames and that's one charge that could never be laid at Henry's door.'

'Why not?'

'Because he was too drunk to walk properly, let alone carry a dead body.'

'I thought that drink might be involved,' said Jonathan ruefully.

'Henry's eternal weakness, I fear. One of them, anyway,' added Christopher sadly, 'for my brother is liberal in his choice of vices.'

'They appear to have caught up with him at last, Mr Redmayne.'

'Newgate has certainly been a sobering experience for him.'

Christopher was standing behind the table on which his latest architectural drawing was set out. Lying on top of it was a piece of paper that he used to make some jottings. He picked it up to glance at what he had written.

'What's convinced you that your brother is innocent?' asked Jonathan.

'His account of what happened.'

'It sounds as if he's very confused.'

'Henry is completely bewildered.'

'Rumour has it that he and the murder victim were arch enemies.'

'They were certainly not the best of friends. Thus it stands,' said Christopher, keen to rehearse the facts for his own benefit as much as for that of his visitor. 'Henry was enjoying the pleasures of the town one evening when he happened to cross the path of Signor Maldini. There was a violent argument – in front of witnesses – during which my brother became so incensed that he threatened to kill the man.'

'Is he in the habit of issuing such threats?'

'No, Jonathan, that's what makes this so worrying.'

'What was it about the Italian gentleman that enraged him so much?'

'Henry believed that he cheated at cards.'

'Is that reason enough to murder him?'

'To *threaten* him with murder,' said Christopher. 'And the answer is yes. Cheating is a cardinal sin to those who wager large amounts on the turn of a card. But there were other reasons why my brother disliked the fellow so intensely. I've yet to drag all of them out of him.'

'Go on,' encouraged Jonathan. 'I'm sorry to interrupt.'

'Signor Maldini was a hot-blooded man. When Henry threatened him, he drew his sword and would have attacked my brother there and then if the others had not pulled him away. It was, apparently, an ugly scene.'

'What happened then?'

'Henry and his friends rolled on to a tavern for supper. If they were not drunk when they went in there, they certainly were by the time they came out. They split up and went their separate ways. My brother had forgotten all about the quarrel with Jeronimo Maldini. The gentleman himself, however, had not.'

'He was lying in wait for your brother,' guessed the constable.

'Yes,' said Christopher, 'and he, too, was emboldened by drink.'

'It's the root of so much crime and evil in this city.'

'Henry went in search of a calash to take him home. Out of the shadows came Signor Maldini, still shaking with fury and demanding satisfaction. He was waving his rapier in the air.'

'Duelling is against the law.'

'That will not prevent it, Jonathan.'

'Did your brother draw?'

'He wore no sword,' said Christopher, 'and even if he had done so, he would have thought twice about taking on a fencing master in a duel. The only way he could defend himself was with his dagger and he remembers taking that out. In fact, it's one of the last things that he does remember.'

'Why?'

'He passed out. Whether from drink or fear or a combination of both, he does not know. Henry has a vague memory of a pain at the back of his head before falling to the ground so he might have been struck from behind.'

'By an accomplice of Signor Maldini?'

'Possibly.'

Jonathan pondered. 'It's not a convincing story,' he said at length. 'A man as skilful with a sword as a fencing master would not need a confederate. It would be a matter of pride to him to dispatch an enemy on his own.'

'Yet he left Henry untouched.'

'When did your brother recover his senses?'

'A watchman found him and helped him to his feet,' said Christopher, resuming the tale. 'There was no sign of the Italian. Henry's only concern was to get home safely so the watchman summoned a calash for him. When he got back to Bedford Street, the servants put him to bed.' He pursed his lips. 'They've had plenty of practice at that, I fear.' He tossed the piece of paper on to the table. 'I think I know what you are going to ask me, Jonathan.'

'Where was your brother's dagger?'

'It disappeared along with Signor Maldini.'

'According to the coroner, he was stabbed to death before he went into the river.'

'The dagger was still embedded in his back,' said Christopher. 'It bore my brother's initials and Henry was forced to identify it as his own. Yes,' he continued when he saw the doubt in his friend's eyes, 'I know that it's telling evidence against him but you have to remember the condition that my brother was in at the time.'

'Too sodden with drink to know whether or not he stabbed a man in the back.'

'He'd never do that, Jonathan.'

'Not even in self-defence?'

'What chance would a dagger have against a rapier?'

'Very little if the two men faced each other,' said Jonathan. 'However, if your brother chanced upon his adversary from behind, it would be a different matter.'

'I can see that you're not persuaded of his innocence.'

'I'd need far more evidence to do so.'

'Let me speak to Henry again. Newgate will have jogged his memory.'

'With respect, Mr Redmayne, it would be foolish to rely only on what your brother tells you. Drink befuddled his mind. That much is beyond question. You'll never get the truth out of a man who does not know it himself.'

'So what do you suggest that I do?'

'Speak to the witnesses who were present when the argument flared up. They may be able to shed more light on why your brother and Signor Maldini hated each other so much. Do you have their names?'

'They are here before me,' said Christopher, indicating the piece of paper. 'When I got back from the prison, I made a note of everything that Henry told me, incoherent as it may be. But he did remember who his companions were that night.'

'How many of them were there?'

'Three.'

'Begin there,' counselled Jonathan. 'And when you have finished with his friends, track down this watchman who discovered your brother lying on the ground. He might yield some valuable information.'

Christopher was resolute. 'I'll do all that I can to save Henry,' he affirmed.

'If he is innocent.'

'If he is guilty, he deserves to suffer the full rigour of the law. If my brother killed a man in a drunken brawl, I would hesitate to lift a finger in his defence. But that's not the case, Jonathan,' he argued. 'Henry could not have committed this crime and I'll not rest until I've proved that.' He looked deep into his friend's eyes. 'Will you help me?'

'I am already making enquiries that relate to this investigation.'

'I know,' said Christopher. 'Signor Maldini lodged not far from you. But I would ask you to go further afield. This watchman, for instance. You'll find him much quicker than I would and win his confidence more easily.'

Jonathan was cynical. 'The right coins will do that.'

'I need a partner in this enterprise. I'm too guided by filial love to see everything as clearly as I should. That's why your help would make such a difference, Jonathan. You are cool, detached and objective.'

'There are others with those same qualities.'

'I'm asking *you*.'

'Then you've come to the wrong man, Mr Redmayne.'

Christopher was hurt. 'Why? We've worked so well together in the past.'

'That was different. We were both of one mind in the past.'

'What are you telling me?'

'What honesty compels me to say,' replied Jonathan uneasily. 'You assume your brother's innocence but I cannot bring myself to do that. On the face of it, the evidence against him is too strong. He threatened Signor Maldini in the hearing of others, and he had the motive, means and opportunity to carry out that threat. His only defence is that he was too drunk to recall what he did. If you'd heard that excuse offered in court as many times as I have, you'd know how unwise it is to believe it.'

'I thought that I could count on you above all others.' Jonathan's face was impassive. 'If you are not ready to help me, why did you bother to come?' His visitor averted his gaze. 'Will you proceed on this basis, then?' asked Christopher, anxious to have an ally. 'Work to establish Henry's guilt while I struggle to prove his innocence. We can still carry on side by side. Sooner or later, one of us will have to change his mind.' He knelt before his friend. 'I'd not ask this of anyone else, Jonathan. Help me. Please.'

'Help you to send your brother to the gallows?'

'No,' said Christopher. 'Help me to find the man who *did* kill Signor Maldini?'

Chapter Five

Devoted to a life of outward show, Henry Redmayne had never felt the need to look beyond his reflection in a mirror at the inner man. He was now forced to do so and found it a thoroughly disagreeable experience. It soon dawned on him that he had neither the character nor the strength to cope with the predicament in which he found himself. Gregarious by nature, he was lost when cut off from human company of the kind that he favoured. Yet he shuddered at the thought that any of his acquaintances should see him in such distress, locked away in a grimy cell, deprived of even the most basic comforts, drooping with fatigue and trembling with fear. In his fevered mind, the prospect of execution was a very real one. Henry knew that it would be preceded by a series of other humiliations. His name would be besmirched, his friends would fall away, his enemies would rejoice and his family would suffer horrendously. It was that same family which now preoccupied the prisoner.

While his brother, Christopher, was standing by him with unquestioning loyalty, his father would definitely take a more trenchant view of his plight. Henry was as terrified of the Dean of Gloucester as he was of the hangman. At least he would not have to endure a blistering sermon from the latter. Overcome with guilt, he could not bear the notion of being confronted by an outraged parent in homiletic vein, yet the truth could not be hidden from his father. One thing he had learned about the Church was its remarkable capacity for disseminating bad tidings. A messenger might already be on his way to Gloucester and he would not return to London alone. The Reverend Algernon Redmayne, stirred into action, would surely accompany him, armed with stinging rebukes and dire predictions about his elder son's reception at the Last Judgement. It would be worse than being flayed alive. Henry was unequal to it. Falling to his knees in the straw, he prayed, with a fervour he usually reserved for amorous encounters, that his father was kept away from him by whatever means.

The grating of a key in the lock made him jump to his feet and flatten himself against the wall, frightened that the Almighty had spurned his request and delivered the Dean of Gloucester to scourge him for his sins. When someone stepped into his cell, Henry did not dare to look. The door was locked behind the visitor.

'My dear fellow!' said a kindly voice. 'Look at the state of you!'

Henry peered at him. 'Is that you, Martin?' he asked, torn between gratitude and embarrassment. 'What are you doing here?'

'I came to see you and to bring you some sustenance.'

Martin Crenlowe was a fleshy man in his thirties with a reddish tinge to his nose and cheeks. A goldsmith by trade, Crenlowe had expensive tastes in clothing. His periwig framed a podgy face that was creased with sympathy. He was a fastidious man who had taken the precaution of carrying a pomander to ward off the stink of Newgate and the risk of infection. He had also brought a flagon of wine and some food. Unhappy at being seen in such a miserable condition, Henry was revived by the sight of the turkey pie, cheese and fruit. He accepted them with profuse thanks.

'It's good to know that one of my friends has not disowned me,' he said.

'Why should I disown you?'

'Because I'm held here on a charge of murder.'

'I know,' said Crenlowe, shifting his feet uneasily. 'I came to apologise for my part in that. I do not believe for one moment that you were the killer, Henry, but they put me under oath and I was compelled to speak the truth. I was there when it happened. I heard you threaten Signor Maldini.'

'I've never denied it.'

'The three of us had to bear witness against you. Sir Humphrey Godden, Captain Harvest and myself. We had no choice.'

'I do not blame you for that, Martin.'

'But our evidence helped to land you in Newgate. Can you ever forgive us?'

'You spoke honestly. I did threaten to kill him.'

'Only because you were sorely provoked,' said Crenlowe. 'And there's all the difference in the world between a wild threat uttered in the heat of the moment and the determination to carry it out. Let them say what they will. I'll never accept that Henry Redmayne is a ruthless killer, nor will Sir Humphrey.'

'What of Captain Harvest?'

Crenlowe sighed. 'James has let you down badly, alas.'

'In what way?'

'He's convinced of your guilt and is telling everyone who'll listen to him that you are a dangerous man with a temper you could not control. Sir Humphrey and I are so appalled by his behaviour that we've cut him dead.'

'The villain!'

'Forget him, Henry. Lean on your friends.'

'I did not know that I still had any.'

'One stands before you,' said Crenlowe loyally, 'and there are others who do not doubt your innocence. If there's any way that we can help, you've only to ask.'

'Your visit has been a medicine in itself, Martin. It's cured my one malady – the fear that the whole of London had turned against me. As for help,' said Henry, 'the person you must turn to is my brother, Christopher. He's trying to marshal my defence and would welcome aid from any source. He lives in Fetter Lane.'

'You once pointed out the house to me.' He heard the key in the lock again. 'My time is up. I was only permitted a brief moment with you.'

'You've brought me more comfort than I can say.'

'Enjoy the wine,' said Crenlowe as the door creaked open. 'And do not despair, Henry. We'll get you out of this somehow.'

'God bless you!'

The house was in Covent Garden and Christopher Redmayne spent several minutes admiring its exterior before he knocked on the door. It was typical of the properties that were being built in increasing numbers in the area, tall, imposing and elegant with a narrow frontage. Marble pillars supported the portico. Evidently, a considerable amount of money had been spent on the house by someone with firm views about architecture. A manservant opened the door and, after listening to the visitor's name and request, invited him into the hall while he went off to speak to his master. There was a long delay during which Christopher inspected the paintings on the wall. Like his brother, Sir Humphrey Godden had an insatiable curiosity in the naked female form. Nudes of varying shapes and sizes abounded. In the one portrait where a young lady was fully dressed, she was raising an expressive eyebrow while exposing a rounded breast to the artist. Christopher was still studying a picture of a Bacchanalian orgy when footsteps clacked across the marble floor. He turned to see a tall, striking man in his forties with a black moustache that matched exactly the colour of his wig. Dressed to go out in a scarlet cloak, he was carrying a hat and cane. He eyed his visitor with frank displeasure.

'Sir Humphrey?' asked Christopher.

'You come at an inopportune moment, Mr Redmayne,' replied the other, putting on his hat. 'I was about to leave.'

'I'll not detain you long. I'm sure that you can guess why I'm here.'

'If it is to ask me to change my evidence, you are wasting your time. I spoke as my conscience dictated. Your brother threatened to kill Jeronimo Maldini and I heard him loud and clear. That's what I reported.'

'Henry admits it himself.'

'Then this conversation is superfluous.'

'Not so, Sir Humphrey,' said Christopher, wondering why the man was so unwilling to talk to him. 'I came here on my brother's behalf because I understood that Henry counted you among his friends.'

'We've shared many pleasurable times together.'

'In view of that, is it too much to ask that you might try to help him?'

'I have an appointment, Mr Redmayne.'

'So does Henry, unless he is cleared of the charge. I venture to suggest that his appointment is of more significance than yours since it would be with the hangman.'

'Very well,' said Sir Humphrey with undisguised irritation. 'Ask what you will.'

'Thank you.'

Christopher could see at a glance why his brother had befriended Sir Humphrey Godden. They were birds of a feather, confirmed hedonists with a passion for all the vices of the city. Like Henry, his friend wore ostentatious apparel and cultivated an air of suppressed boredom. The handsome features were marred by the clear signs of late nights and loose company. The difference between the two men was that Sir Humphrey had unlimited money to support his indulgences while Henry Redmayne did not, though that fact did not deter him in the least.

'What manner of man was Jeronimo Maldini?' asked Christopher.

'He was a confounded foreigner and we already have too many of those here.'

'Yet an accomplished swordsman, obviously.'

'Yes,' said Sir Humphrey. 'Give the fellow his due. He could handle any kind of blade with masterful skill. None of us could touch him.'

'You were a pupil of his, then?'

'We all were at some time or another, Mr Redmayne. Captain Harvest was first. Then I took lessons from him, followed by Martin Crenlowe. Henry was the last to seek instruction and the quickest to abandon it.'

'Why did he do that?'

'Because he found Signor Maldini too infuriating.'

'Infuriating?'

'He liked to humble us, to expose our weaknesses in front of others. Henry could not bear that. He felt that the man was there to improve our skills, not to demonstrate that his own were far superior. I left the fencing school for the same reason and so did Martin Crenlowe. The only person who could tolerate him was James.'

'James?'

'Captain Harvest.'

'My brother said he was a fine swordsman in his own right.'

'He was. Try as he might, even that mocking Italian could not make James look like a novice. Soldiers are trained to fight for their lives, not merely for pleasure. James had picked up too many tricks to be humiliated by a fencing master.'

'Why did he need the lessons in the first place?'

'You'll have to ask him that.'

'So you left the school because of Signor Maldini's habit of goading you?'

'That was only part of the reason,' replied Sir Humphrey, adjusting his cloak. 'I disliked the man intensely. He was vain, insolent, disrespectful and lacking in all the virtues of an English gentleman. In short,' he said with disgust, 'he was an *Italian*.'

'I have great respect for Italians,' said Christopher, responding to the other's manifest prejudice. 'No nation on earth has produced so many wonderful artists and architects. This house bears many traces of Classical influence.'

'I need no lecture on architecture, Mr Redmayne.'

'Nor would I presume to give you one.'

'Then do not try to excuse the faults of Jeronimo Maldini by citing the artistic achievements of his countryman. I knew the man for what he was – a low, cunning, deceitful rogue with a rare skill as a fencing master. I'll not mourn him,' he asserted, wagging a finger. 'I think he deserved to die.' He moved across to the front door. 'And now, I fear, you must excuse me. I've given you all the time I can.'

'One last question, Sir Humphrey.'

'Well?'

'Do you believe that my brother killed Signor Maldini?'

'Of course not,' said the other, opening the door. 'Henry Redmayne would not stab anyone in the back. He's like me. He would have run the man through with a sword so that he could have enjoyed the look of horror in the eyes of that odious Italian. What's the point of revenge if you cannot savour it to the full?'

Captain James Harvest proved to be an elusive quarry. Jonathan Bale did not track him down until well into the following day. When the man was not at his lodgings, Jonathan pursued him through his various haunts, guided by the advice of Harvest's landlord and a succession of tavern keepers, all of whom seemed to be on close terms with the ubiquitous soldier. It was almost as if the man knew that the constable was on his tail and kept one step ahead of him. Jonathan was not to be shaken off. A combination of patience and dogged determination eventually brought a result. Captain Harvest was run to ground at the Peacock Inn. Located in Whitefriars, it was at the heart of a lively district, inhabited by people of contrasting fortunes. While the area attracted lawyers, doctors and members of other professions, some of its streets were warrens of poverty and neglect.

Jonathan paused to study a row of houses that had been rebuilt the previous year. During the Great Fire, he had helped to pull down the properties that stood there before in order to create a firebreak but the inferno scorned his efforts by vaulting over the empty space with ease. Whitefriars had a cosmopolitan feel to it. In its noisy streets, English was not the only language that drifted into his ear. Jonathan lost count of the number of taverns and ordinaries that he passed. The area seemed to have its fair share of bookshops as well. The Peacock Inn was a popular establishment, occupying a corner site. When he heard the clash of steel and the sound of raised voices, Jonathan went around to the courtyard at the rear of the premises and saw two men engaged in a sword fight, encouraged by a handful of spectators with tankards of beer in their hand. The constable did not stop to notice that the younger of the two combatants was having difficulty in fending the other one off.

'Stop!' he ordered, rushing forward. 'The law forbids duels.'

'This is no duel,' explained the older man, lowering his rapier. 'I was merely giving this young fellow a lesson in how to defend himself.'

'You've taught me enough for one day,' said his opponent, glad of the interruption and sheathing his weapon. 'Come inside and I'll honour my promise.'

'I'll hold you to that, my friend.'

The young man went into the inn with the onlookers and Jonathan was left alone with a sturdy individual in his forties whose face was half-hidden by a red beard and further obscured by an pair of enormous eyebrows that all but met on the bridge of his nose. The stranger had the ready grin and easy manner of a born adventurer. He wore a bright red coat that was frayed slightly at the edges and a wide-brimmed hat that he doffed with a flourish.

'Captain James Harvest, at your service, sir,' he announced.

'Good,' said Jonathan, relieved that he had finally caught up with him. 'My name is Jonathan Bale and I've been searching for you all morning.'

'A not unusual situation, alas. Constables are forever barking at my heels.'

'I only came to ask a few questions, sir.'

'Then I shall endeavour to provide you with a few answers, Mr Bale.' Replacing his hat, Harvest scrutinized him for a moment. 'You were a military man, I think.'

'I've borne arms, Captain Harvest, it's true.'

'For whom did you fight? King and country?'

'I fought for a just cause.'

'Then I applaud you, sir,' said Harvest. 'A soldier who is driven by belief in a cause is worth ten whose swords can be hired for money. So, you were one of Noll's men, were you? He was a doughty commander. I fought against him three times and was thrice hounded from the battlefield.' He nodded towards the inn. 'Shall we step inside?' he suggested, sheathing his sword. 'That little bout has made me thirsty and my pupil owes me a drink.'

'I'd rather speak to you out here where we have some privacy.'

'As you wish, Mr Bale.'

'I believe that you were a friend of Mr Henry Redmayne.'

'I knew him,' conceded Harvest with a frown, 'but I'd hardly describe myself as a friend. I always found him too smug and self-satisfied to merit my friendship. Henry was a silly man at bottom. I did not care for him at all.'

'Yet you spent time with him.'

'Only when it was necessary.'

'How did you meet Mr Redmayne?'

'By chance. We were taught by the same fencing master, not far from here, as it happens. When it comes to swordsmanship, Whitefriars has some of the finest tutors in London. We were fortunate to study with the best of them.'

'Signor Jeronimo Maldini.'

'The very same.'

'I would not have thought that you needed lessons, Captain Harvest. With your experience, you should have been a fencing master yourself.'

'Why, so I am when occasion serves,' said the other, tapping the hilt of his rapier. 'But I like to keep my art in repair and Jeronimo did that for me. He also employed me to practice with novices in return for a modest fee. I taught as I learned.'

'Did you ever teach Mr Redmayne?'

'He thought himself above that,' said Harvest, 'and spurned my offer. Jeronimo soon cut him down to size and made him look the arrant fool that he was.'

'The two men fell out, I believe.'

'They were never kindred spirits, Mr Bale.'

'Why not?'

'Because Henry was too irredeemably *English*. In other words, he was haughty, selfish and quite unable to turn his gaze beyond our narrow shores.'

'A common complaint, sir.'

'Henry seemed to think that he had a divine right to look down on other nations, especially Italy. His condescension knew no bounds. If he'd seen as much of the world as I have, he'd know that every country has valuable lessons to teach us.' Harvest took a step closer. 'Have you ever met Henry Redmayne?'

'Yes, Captain. A number of times.'

'What was your opinion of the man?'

'It's immaterial.'

'Nevertheless, I'd like to hear it.'

'He's not a person I could readily admire,' admitted Jonathan. 'But, then, nor am I the sort of companion that he would ever seek.'

'What was your trade before you became a constable?'

'I was a shipwright.'

'A good, honest, worthwhile occupation.' He gave a ripe chuckle. 'I could see from the size of your shoulders and the roughness of your hands that you were not a ladies' hairdresser. There's the difference between the two of you, Mr Bale. You served the Navy with the strength of your arm and sweat of your brow. Henry pretends to work at the Navy Office but spends most of his time at play.'

'I'm aware of his habits, Captain Harvest.'

'So why did you come to me?'

'For confirmation of certain facts. Mr Redmayne, as you know, is in prison.'

'And rightly so. He stabbed Jeronimo Maldini to death.'

'That remains to be proved in a court of law.'

'I need no lawyers to tell me who the killer was.'

'You supped with him that night.'

'So?'

'What state was he in when he left you?'

'Quivering with anger.'

'At Signor Maldini?'

'Who else?' asked Harvest. 'Henry loathed the man and made no secret of it. He claimed that Jeronimo once cheated at cards but his hatred went deeper. When two men are at each other's throats like that, there's usually only one reason for it.'

'A pretty woman?' said Jonathan.

'A *beautiful* woman, Mr Bale. A truly gorgeous and enchanting young lady who had every red-blooded man in London lusting after her. Henry Redmayne was among them, convinced that she'd bestow her favours on him. Then Jeronimo Maldini joined in the hunt and that was that.'

'Was it?'

'Well, you've seen Henry. His good looks deserted him years ago. He could never forgive Jeronimo for being so young, dashing and handsome. Fencing is not the only skill in which the Italians are superior to us. They are also proficient in the arts of seduction.' He chuckled again. 'It was a terrible blow to Henry's self-esteem. He not only lost the lady in question. He surrendered her to a despised rival, who, in his opinion, came from a lower order of creation.'

'How can you be sure that he murdered Signor Maldini?'

'Because it was on his mind when he left the tavern that night.'

'Mr Redmayne claims that the man was lying in wait for him.'

Harvest gave a contemptuous snort. 'He would! It was the other way round, Mr Bale, mark my words. It was Henry who laid the ambush. He caught Jeronimo off guard. That was the only way he could have secured an advantage over him,' he said, thrusting his beard close to Jonathan's face. 'Henry could never hope to beat him in a fair fight so he stabbed him in the back then threw the body in the river.'

'What evidence do you have to support that belief?'

'The evidence of my own eyes,' affirmed Harvest, widening them for effect. 'Henry Redmayne is a killer. I'd stake my reputation on it.'

Christopher Redmayne spent the whole afternoon with the lawyer whom he engaged to take charge of his brother's defence but the man was unable to give him any grounds for optimism. By the time he left, Christopher was more worried than ever. It was early evening as he began the walk home and the light was fading. Frost and ice had been expelled from the city but the thaw had left the streets wet and slippery. Christopher moved along with due care.

He was so taken up with his brother's plight that he had neglected his own work. Drawings lay untouched on his table and he had forgotten about his demanding client. All of his energy was directed towards securing Henry's release from prison. He was suddenly struck by the thought that the murder of Jeronimo Maldini might have serious consequences for his career. Nobody would be eager to employ the brother of a man who had been convicted of such an atrocious crime and his existing client, Lady Whitcombe, might wish to disown him in the light of recent developments. A contract had been signed but Christopher did not feel that it would be sufficiently binding to hold such a forceful woman. The dagger that ended the life of a fencing master might also have severed in two a valuable commission.

Lady Whitcombe was not the only person who had been ousted from his thoughts for the past couple of days. Susan Cheever, too, had faded to the back of his mind even though she had been at the frost fair with him when the body was discovered in the ice. He was too busy to contact her and too uncertain about the reception he would have got at the house in Westminster. Christopher hoped that he might count on sympathy from Susan but he sensed that her father would be much more censorious. Sir Julius Cheever had no respect whatsoever for Henry Redmayne and could hardly be expected to offer support to a man whom he considered to be a worthless rake. He would not scruple to prevent his daughter from getting in touch with Henry's brother.

The change in the weather meant that the truculent knight had probably left for Northamptonshire, which meant that Susan, in turn, would have withdrawn to Richmond. At the very moment when Christopher was starting to get closer to her, she had moved out of his reach. It was galling. In getting arrested and imprisoned, Henry had not simply endangered his brother's career as an architect, he might well have poisoned the dearest relationship in his life. There would no doubt be other appalling losses to come.

It all served to strengthen his resolve to establish his brother's innocence but he recognised that that would not be easy. The one person who was assisting him did so with grave misgivings. Jonathan Bale was too honest to pretend that he shared his friend's belief in a wrongful arrest. The constable had personal reasons for taking an interest in the case and was not impelled by any affection for the suspect. All that mattered to him was the weight of the evidence. He was far more accustomed to the processes of law than Christopher and that disturbed the latter. Hoping for uncritical assistance from his friend, he was settling for something far less. On the other hand, he told himself, Jonathan would certainly unearth some important new facts and he could only hope that they would be instrumental in helping to clear his brother's name.

He left the city through Ludgate and strode along Fleet Street.

Candlelight burned in windows or showed through the chinks in shutters. People were going home on foot or on horseback. London was beginning to close down for another day. Within the hour, watchmen would begin their nocturnal perambulations. When he turned into Fetter Lane, he did so with a sense of guilt. While he would sleep beneath warm sheets that night, Henry would shiver in the cold of Newgate. In place of a devoted servant like Jacob, his brother would have a coarse and uncaring turnkey. Most important of all, Christopher could enjoy a freedom that was denied to the prisoner.

Jacob had an uncanny gift for anticipating the return of his master. When the latter was within ten yards of the front door, it opened wide. Rubbing his hands together, Jacob put out his head to look down the street. Christopher's approach made him smile with quiet satisfaction.

'Good evening, sir.'

'How did you know that I was coming?'

'It was simply a guess.'

'I wish that my guesses were as accurate,' said Christopher, going into the house. 'When I chose a lawyer this afternoon, I guessed that he might send me home feeling more sanguine. That was not the case, Jacob.'

'Oh dear!'

The old man closed and bolted the door before following him into the parlour.

'It's been such a disappointing day.'

'Would a glass of wine lift your spirits, sir?'

'Not unless I could share it with Henry and toast his release.'

'That moment will come in due course,' said Jacob confidently.

'Is this another of your guesses?'

'I merely offer it as my opinion.'

'Then I accept it with gratitude,' said Christopher, taking off his coat and hat before handing them to Jacob. 'It's comforting to be with someone who believes in my brother's innocence. Jonathan Bale does not and, more to the point, neither does Henry himself.' He lowered himself into a chair. 'Has anything happened while I was away?'

'A gentleman called, sir. Mr Martin Crenlowe.'

'One of Henry's friends.'

'He visited your brother in Newgate and urged you to call on him for any help.'

'Then I'll certainly take up that offer. Any other news?'

'A letter arrived for you, sir.'

'A letter?' said Christopher, hoping that it was from Susan Cheever.

'Here it is,' said Jacob, taking it from the table to hand to him. 'It was delivered by one of Lady Whitcombe's servants.'

'Oh, I see.'

Christopher lost all enthusiasm for opening the missive. A single line from Susan would have rallied him but he could expect no such inspiration from his client. As he studied the neat calligraphy on the front of the letter, he feared that he knew exactly what it would contain. News of his brother's arrest must have found its way to the home of Lady Whitcombe. She was writing to dismiss her architect summarily. Seeing the distress in his master's face, Jacob made the same assumption.

'There'll be many other houses to build, sir.'

'And many other architects to design them.'

'Your reputation will stand you in good stead.'

'I begin to doubt that, Jacob.'

Breaking the seal, he opened the letter and braced himself for the loss of a lucrative commission. Miraculously, it did not come. Instead, he was simply reminded of his promise to deliver his final drawings to Lady Whitcombe that week. His client had either not heard of Henry's disgrace or chosen to ignore it. Whichever it might be, Christopher was placed in an awkward situation. Time that should have been spent at his work had been mortgaged elsewhere. Long hours were still required for the drawings to be in a presentable state. Christopher leapt to his feet.

'Jacob!'

'Yes, sir.'

'Light more candles. I must work.'

'Will that glass of wine be needed now?'

'Only brandy will suffice,' said Christopher. 'I'll have to ride to Sheen tomorrow morning and I need to take the drawings with me. They'll keep me up all night.'

'You're going to Sheen, sir?'

'Yes, Jacob.'

'Then you'll not be far from Richmond.'

'How true!' said Christopher with a slow grin, realising that he might be able to meet Susan Cheever after all. 'Thank you for pointing that out, Jacob. I may have two calls to make tomorrow.'

'I thought you might, sir.'

'Fetch that brandy.'

Christopher was soon poring over the table with renewed enthusiasm.

Chapter Six

Now almost two centuries old, Serle Court was a fortified manor house, complete with towers, turrets and crenellation. It was set on the brow of a hill and surrounded by rolling parkland. A delightful prospect met the eye from every window of the property and the rear gardens, in particular, were a work of art. Since there was no other building in sight, the occupants had a wonderful sense of isolation, of being untroubled by the presence of neighbours and free to explore the extensive acres that comprised the estate without any danger of meeting strangers. For all its size, Susan Cheever always found the house uncomfortably small but that was less to do with its design than with the necessity of being under the same roof as her sister. However large a house, Brilliana would somehow contrive to shrink it in size. Though she loved her sister dutifully, Susan often had difficulty in actually liking her, especially when she felt, as now, that she was being watched over by Brilliana. She was seated in the parlour that morning when her sister sailed into the room.

'What are you doing?' asked Brilliana.

'Reading a book,' replied Susan, looking up from the volume in her hands.

'I never read anything these days. It's such a pointless exercise, I always think. When we were first married, Lancelot used to read poetry to me but his voice started to irritate me after a time.'

'You are too easily irritated, Brilliana.'

'I hate being bored.'

'Then find something that excites your mind.'

'I'll not find it on a *bookshelf!*' said the other with disdain.

Brilliana Serle was older, taller and more ambitious than her sister. She had the kind of porcelain beauty that defied the passage of time and dressed with such exquisite style that she always stood out in a crowd. When she was younger, Susan had resented her sister's ability to monopolise male attention but she came, in time, to appreciate its advantages. It rescued her from the wooing of a whole gallery of unappealing suitors, who made a fool of themselves over her sister instead. Marriage to Lancelot Serle had shaken off the chasing pack but it had not dulled Brilliana's fondness for dominating a dinner table or for being the cynosure at any gathering. She crossed the room to look over Susan's shoulder.

'What are you reading?' she demanded.

'It's a book about Italy, full of the most charming drawings.'

'Why on earth should you wish to read about Italy?'

'Because my interest was aroused by Mr Redmayne,' replied Susan. 'He's visited the country to study its architecture. He made me want to know more about Italy.'

'I think that you should know less about Mr Redmayne.'

'Brilliana!'

'It's high time that you removed him from your list of acquaintances.'

'Christopher is a friend of mine.'

'He's also the brother of a killer.'

'That's not true.'

'Father's letter was very exact on that point. Henry Redmayne is a dangerous criminal who has brought shame and ignominy on his entire family. You are to have nothing to do with them forthwith.'

'I prefer to make my own decision in that regard.'

'Not as long as you're in this house.'

Susan winced. Serle Court was turning out to be a luxurious version of Newgate to her, a place where she was confined against her will and kept deliberately apart from the company of the person she most wanted to see. Every decision that affected her was made by someone else. It was demeaning but Susan knew that she had to endure it. Apart from the fact that she would inevitably lose any argument with her sister, she did not wish to upset Brilliana. In due course, she hoped, she would persuade her sister to take her to London, ostensibly to visit the shops but really to be back in the city where her dearest friend lived, so that she could somehow contrive a meeting with him. If she so much as challenged Brilliana on the subject of Christopher Redmayne, she would not get within a mile of him. Putting the book in her lap, Susan looked up with a patient smile.

'What plans have you for today, Brilliana?'

'My dressmaker is due to call this afternoon.'

'Good,' said Susan, thinking that she would have at least three hours of escape from sisterly vigilance. 'Has she finished that new dress you told me about?'

'She's not coming for my benefit, but for yours.'

'Mine?'

'Yes,' said Brilliana airily. 'Your wardrobe has grown so stale and dowdy. If you want to catch a rich husband, as I did, you must look the part. That's why I intend to take your appearance in hand.'

'I've no wish to have it changed.'

'Wait until you've spoken to my dressmaker. She'll transform you.'

'Brilliana, I have dresses enough of my own.'

'But none of any real *quality*.'

'There's no need to insult me.'

'It was meant in the kindest possible way, Susan. You choose your apparel for comfort rather than effect. It's a habit that no young woman in your position can afford.'

'My position?' echoed Susan, trying to maintain her composure.

'A spinster in search of a husband.'

'But that's not my position at all.'

'Of course, it is,' said her sister with a brittle laugh. 'What do you think we were put on this earth for, Susan? It was not to read books about ridiculous countries like Italy, that much is certain. It was to make a good marriage. Yours is already long overdue.'

'That's a very unkind remark.'

'Strike now while you still have your beauty. It will not last forever.'

'Some men prize other qualities above beauty.'

'Not the ones that you need to attract.'

'And who might they be?'

'Men like Lancelot. Wealthy, cultivated and infinitely obliging.'

'Nothing could be further from my mind at the moment than marriage.'

'Then you are betraying your womanhood,' said Brilliana, 'and will live to regret it before very long. Since Mother died, I've tried to take her place and offer you the love and advice that I know she would have given you.'

Susan did not trust herself to reply. There was not even the faintest resemblance between the roles of her mother and that of her sister. Brilliana had shown her precious little love and showered her with the sort of cynical advice that a kind and caring woman like their mother would never dream of foisting on any of her daughters.

Susan found her sister's comments offensive. She was grateful when Lancelot Serle came into the library to interrupt their conversation. His face was reddened by an hour in the saddle and his eyes glistening. He stood in the doorway and beamed.

'So, here you are!' he declared, noting the book in Susan's lap. 'Have you found my library to your taste?'

'Yes, thank you,' said Susan.

'I think that I may call it a library now that I have over seventy volumes on my shelves. Many were inherited from my father, of course, for he was a learned man but I have bought several on my own account. Brilliana will vouch for that.'

'Books are so tedious,' said his wife.

'You did not always think so, my love.' He turned to Susan. 'There was a time when Brilliana liked me to read poetry to her. John Donne was her favourite.'

'Those days have gone, Lancelot.'

'You were fond of Shakespeare's sonnets as well.'

'I slept through most of them.'

Serle laughed. 'Brilliana will tease,' he said.

'Did you enjoy your ride?' asked Susan.

'It was not so much of a ride as an errand. Has your sister not told you?'

'Told me what?'

'Brilliana wanted me to invite some friends over to meet you. We could have dispatched a servant, naturally, but I felt that a personal touch was needed.'

'That's why I sent you,' said his wife crisply. 'Is everything in hand?'

'It is, my love. All is arranged and the cook is standing by for your instructions. It promises to be an interesting evening, Susan,' he went on, still beaming happily. 'You'll have the pleasure of meeting a very special gentleman.'

It sounded ominous. Susan felt a warning tremor.

After a long but profitable night at work, Christopher Redmayne set out with his drawings finished and packed away safely in his satchel. An accomplished horseman, he looked forward to the ride and found the keen morning air very bracing. Once clear of London, he discovered that the ground was firm and dry but not frozen. It enabled his horse to maintain a steady canter. Fear of ambush would have made most riders seek company before they set out but Christopher felt confident that he could repel or outrun any highwaymen who might be lurking along the way. In the event, he encountered no hazards on the road to Sheen apart from a stray dog that pursued them for a while and tried to bite the horse's fetlocks. A warning swish from Christopher's sword had got rid of the animal.

The village itself looked rather insignificant now that it had lost its royal and monastic associations. Sheen Palace, in various forms, had served generations of kings and queens before and well after its name was changed to Richmond Palace. Largely destroyed by the Parliamentarians, it had, after the Restoration, been partially repaired by the King for his mother but she found it far too bleak to live in. Christopher was saddened to see that it looked more ruin than royal place. He was even more dismayed when he rode past the dilapidated remains of the priory, a fine building that had been allowed to crumble over the years. As an architect, Christopher felt a profound sense of loss when noble edifices were reduced to shadows of their former glory.

Whitcombe Manor was less than a mile from Sheen and, in a sense, it was an attempt to preserve a royal connection because it was so obviously and unashamedly inspired by the Queen's House in Greenwich. Those who had never seen the beautiful house that Inigo Jones had designed for one queen, and finished for another, were struck by the symmetrical perfection of Whitcombe Manor, with its long, low, clean outlines, its arresting Palladian features and its proportions so subtly altered that it no longer resembled the Italian villa on which it was based. Visitors who were familiar with the Queen's House, however, recognised a smaller version of the building, more compact, less chaste in its aspect and with enough minor variations to absolve the architect of simply copying his predecessor. As he rode up the long drive and through the formal gardens at the front, Christopher wondered why Lady Whitcombe had opted for plagiarism rather than originality, for it was she who had been the moving spirit behind the construction of the house. The new town house she had commissioned was also, in essence, a copy of an existing structure. Her notions of architectural excellence were always second-hand.

It was only when he dismounted from his horse than Christopher realised how tired he was. The sleepless night and the long ride had taxed his strength. It was an effort to keep his eyes open. Handing the reins to an ostler, he tried to shake off his fatigue and strode towards the front door of the house. He was soon conducted to the parlour and given plenty of time to examine its contents. It was his third visit to the house but it still had a strange novelty for him. Lady Whitcombe was an acquisitive woman. If she saw something that she liked, she was determined to have it, no matter what its cost. Christopher looked around at the array of gilt-framed paintings, rich tapestries, abundant statuary and all the other ornamentation that had been assembled. A vast, red, patterned, circular Turkish carpet occupied the centre of the room with furniture arranged carefully around its circumference. There was an abiding sense of order and balance.

When Lady Whitcombe finally swept into the room, her daughter was trotting obediently at her heels. Both women smiled when they saw their visitor.

'It is so reassuring to see you, Mr Redmayne,' said Lady Whitcombe, extending a hand for him to kiss. 'I began to fear that you'd forgotten us.'

'How could I possibly do that?' he said gallantly.

He kissed her hand politely then gave a token bow of acknowledgment to Letitia Whitcombe. She suppressed a giggle. Though almost twenty, Letitia had the manner of someone far younger. She was a desperately plain young lady with bulbous eyes, a snub nose and a pronounced jaw. Unsure whether a modest smile or a sly grin best suited her features, she kept shifting nervously between the two, however inappropriate they might be. Her mother, by contrast, had a natural dignity that gave her an almost regal air. Now approaching fifty, Lady Cecily Whitcombe had preserved some of the beauty that had made her such a catch in her younger days. What in other women might be considered an unbecoming plumpness looked, in her case, an attractive aspect of a Junoesque figure. Pink was Letitia's chosen colour but her mother wore a dress of pale blue with a row of darker blue bows adorning the front of the bodice. Both women had looped skirts that revealed petticoats with delicate embroidery. Anticipating his visit, they had taken great care with their appearance. Christopher felt untidy by comparison.

'Do sit down, Mr Redmayne,' said Lady Whitcombe, perching on a chair and adjusting her dress accordingly. 'The long ride must have wearied you.'

'I am fine, my lady,' replied Christopher, grateful to be able to take a seat himself. 'The sight of Whitcombe Manor revived me at once.'

Letitia gave an involuntary giggle before lowering herself on to a chair.

'We are so grateful for this milder weather,' said her mother. 'You'd have found it impossible to travel when there was snow on the ground.'

'It was the frost that caused the real problems,' he said. 'Until this week, the Thames was one long sheet of ice.'

'We heard about the frost fair, Mr Redmayne,' said Letitia, venturing into the conversation. 'I wish that I could have seen it.'

Her mother gave a disapproving smile. 'It was far too vulgar an event for you to attend, Letitia. I'm sure that Mr Redmayne agrees.'

'The King did not feel it beneath him, Lady Whitcombe,' said Christopher. 'His Majesty joined the rest of London on the ice. The frost fair was a splendid sight.'

'We preferred our own sights, here at Sheen.'

'I do not blame you.'

'The last thing I wanted to do was to rub shoulders with the common people on the Thames. One has to set standards. Fairs are a licence for crime and bad behaviour.'

'And for enjoyment as well,' said Letitia wistfully. 'It must have been a wondrous experience to be there. Was it, Mr Redmayne?'

'Oh, yes,' he confirmed.

'There you are, Mother.'

'We had sufficient amusements of our own, Letitia,' said the older woman.

'Yet it would have been nice to visit the frost fair.'

'It was quite out of the question.'

Letitia gave a resigned nod. 'Yes, Mother.'

'London is at its least alluring in the winter,' declared Lady Whitcombe. 'My late husband often remarked upon it. Cold weather seems to bring out the worst in people. It makes them angry, unsettled and disrespectful. You must have noticed the changes that the season brings, Mr Redmayne. Winter somehow strips people of their finer feelings. They become tetchy and more inclined to violence. The streets of London are simply not safe to walk down.'

'They are if you take sensible precautions,' said Christopher.

'The most sensible precaution is to stay away. Everyone who has been there recently comes back with tales of woe. They complain of fraud, theft, assault and affray. And, as everyone knows,' she went on, turning a pair of large, blue, searching eyes on him, 'the most gruesome murders are always committed in London.'

Christopher shifted uneasily in his seat. Lady Whitcombe's face was so impassive that it was difficult to tell if she was referring to the crime that involved his brother or not. He hoped that she might still be unaware of the murder but that set up the possibility of a revoked contract at a later stage when the news did trickle into her ears. He was certainly not going to volunteer any information on the subject. She stared at him for some time as if trying to communicate something. Relaxing slightly, she glanced at the satchel he had brought with him.

'Is the design for my new house finished?'

'It is, my lady.'

'Let me see it,' she said, rising to her feet. 'I've been looking forward to this moment for weeks. So has Letitia.'

'Yes,' agreed her daughter, getting up. 'It's very exciting.'

Christopher opened his satchel. 'I hope that the drawings meet with your approval,' he said, taking them out and unfolding them. 'Shall I put them on the table?'

'Please do, Mr Redmayne,' said Letitia.

'Did you include the modifications?' asked Lady Whitcombe.

'Every suggestion you made has been followed to the letter,' he said.

Christopher went over to the table under the window. When some ornaments had been moved off it, he set out his drawings. The women were either side of him, bending over to study the designs and brushing his legs with their skirts as they did so. He caught a whiff of the most enchanting perfume. Letitia giggled with pleasure at what she saw but her mother inspected every detail in silence. Eventually, she gave a murmur of assent. Letitia pointed to an upstairs window in one drawing.

'Is this my bedchamber, Mr Redmayne?' she asked.

'It is, indeed,' he said, 'and it overlooks the river, as you see.'

'Which is Egerton's room?'

'Here at the front of the house,' said her mother, tapping the spot with her finger. 'You've not met my son yet, have you, Mr Redmayne?'

'That's a pleasure still to come.'

'He's due back from France very soon. It was Egerton who kept agitating for a house in London. Life in Sheen is idyllic in some respects but our opportunities for entertaining are rather limited. In London, our table will be more readily supplied with guests.' She straightened up to look at him. 'I trust that you'll be one of them.'

'How could I refuse such an invitation?'

'We look upon you as rather more than our architect, Mr Redmayne.'

'I'm very flattered, Lady Whitcombe.'

'Your company is so congenial.'

'I hope that my work brings satisfaction as well.'

'Oh, it does. I cannot fault it.'

'Nor can I, Mr Redmayne,' said Letitia, still surveying the drawings. 'How on earth did you conjure such a beautiful house out of your imagination? It is magical.'

'Thank you,' he said.

'I have always wanted to live in the city.'

'It is only an occasional residence for us, Letitia,' her mother reminded her. 'This will always remain our principal home. Egerton will spend most of his time in London because he needs the society of young men. Country pleasures are no longer enough for him. You and I, however, will be more selective in our visits.'

'Yes, Mother.'

'We'll certainly not spend winter months in the capital.'

'You'll be warm enough, if you do so, my lady,' promised Christopher. 'I took especial care to give you large fireplaces in every room. Italian marble.'

'That was exactly what I required. Well,' she said, taking a final look at the drawings, 'I think that you deserve our congratulations, Mr Redmayne.'

'It was a labour of love, Lady Whitcombe.'

'We, too, have found it a most pleasurable experience.'

'Yes,' said Letitia with a grin.

'All that remains,' added her mother, 'is to get the house built. Who was the fellow you recommended?'

'Mr Popejoy,' replied Christopher. 'I've worked with him before. He built the house in Westminster that you admired so much. I'd recommend Sidney Popejoy without the slightest reservation. There are few more conscientious builders in London.'

'Would he be available?'

'I took the liberty of speaking to him about the project at the very start.'

'Then engage him forthwith.'

'Will your son need to approve the designs first?'

'Egerton?' she asked. 'No, he has no interest in architecture. His only demand was for a large house in London where we could entertain a much wider circle of friends than is possible here in Sheen. My son will be very grateful for what you've done, Mr Redmayne. His needs are simple and you've met every one of them.'

Christopher would never have described the house in terms of simple needs. It was a large property that would occupy a site overlooking the river and contain features that bordered on extravagance. Cost had been incidental. Lady Whitcombe had not merely inherited her husband's substantial wealth, she had independent means of her own. She was ready to lavish a huge amount of money on a house that she would only occupy at certain times of the year. It was her son, Egerton, who would derive most benefit from the place. As a wave of fatigue hit him, Christopher's legs buckled slightly.

'Are you hungry, Mr Redmayne?' asked his hostess.

'I am, Lady Whitcombe.'

'We shall dine very shortly.'

'Thank you.'

'It will give you time to get used to sharing our table.'

'I regard that as a privilege.'

'And we regard you as a friend, Mr Redmayne,' she said, bestowing her sweetest smile on him. 'Letitia made the same observation only this morning. We have not seen all that much of you and yet it feels as if you are one of the family.'

Letitia gave a nervous giggle. Christopher's legs wobbled again.

Jonathan Bale walked along the riverbank that afternoon until he was roughly opposite the point where the body had been found.

His sons would not be able to skate on the ice now. Cracks had been turned into deep crevices and thinner patches had broken up altogether. Blocks of ice floated in open water, melting gently in the sun. As the Thames slowly reasserted itself, the frost fair had been abandoned. Jonathan was glad. The city might be deprived of its winter merriment but the constable's younger son would be spared the visible reminder of the discovery he had made in the ice. There was a secondary reason why Jonathan was pleased at the thaw. Many of his friends earned their living from the river. In places like Shadwell, Ratcliffe, Poplar and Wapping, something like six out of ten men worked either as sailors, watermen or lightermen, occupations that had been frozen out of the Thames. Fishermen, too, had suffered. Sole, cod, herring, sprat and whitebait had continued to be caught in the estuary but those whose income depended on the smelt, eels, salmon and other fish they netted in the shadow of London had been badly hit.

As he gazed out of the river, Jonathan tried to work out where the body had been thrown in and how it had reached the spot where the ice had formed around it. He knew that the current could do strange things with any object tossed into the water. Human and animal bodies had been carried several miles downstream from the point where they had been hurled into the Thames. In this case, however, he sensed that the corpse had not drifted very far. Indeed, it might well have entered the water no more than a few hundred yards from where he stood. Jonathan looked up and down the riverbank, estimating the nearest point to the tavern that Henry Redmayne and his friends had visited on the night when the murder had probably taken place.

After pondering for some time, he moved away and walked alomg Thames Street in the direction of his home. His thoughts turned to his meeting with the jovial Captain Harvest. Before he met the soldier, Jonathan had been convinced that the killer had already been arrested and imprisoned in Newgate. Yet when his judgement had been buttressed by the confident assertions of Captain Harvest, he began to have doubts. There was something about the man that provoked distrust. He was too glib, too plausible and far too hasty to condemn Henry Redmayne. Harvest claimed to have been a friend of the murder victim. Jonathan asked himself why, if Henry had had left the tavern that night in such a vengeful mood, Harvest had not tried to restrain him or at least have gone off to warn Jeronimo Maldini of the imminent danger. The constable still believed in Henry's guilt but with far less certainty than before.

When he got back to Addle Street, he found his wife cleaning the house with a broom. After collecting a kiss from him, Sarah passed on her news.

'Jacob called here earlier on,' she said.

'Jacob?'

'Mr Redmayne's servant.'

'Oh,' said Jonathan. '*That* Jacob. What did he want?'

'To give you a message. Mr Redmayne had to go out of London today. He'll not be back until tomorrow but is anxious to speak to you then.'

'I'm just as eager to talk to him, Sarah, and hoped to do so this evening.'

'Jacob saved you a wasted journey to Fetter Lane.'

'So it seems.' He looked around. 'Where are the boys?'

'Oliver is in the kitchen and Richard is upstairs. I had to separate them.'

'Why?'

'For the usual reason,' she said, leaning on her broom. 'They were arguing over who first saw that body in the ice. Oliver insists that it was him even though he knows perfectly well that it was Richard.'

'They must try to forget the whole thing, not argue about it.'

'That's what I told them, Jonathan.'

'I'll speak to Oliver later,' he decided, crossing to the staircase. 'Richard is the one who needs most attention. I'll not be long.'

As he ascended the steps, they creaked under his weight. Jonathan went into the little room at the rear of the house where his sons slept. Richard was huddled in a corner with his collar turned up against the cold.

'It's warmer downstairs by the fire,' said his father, kneeling beside him.

'I was sent up here.'

'Only because you and Oliver were bickering again. I warned you about that.'

'I'm sorry.'

'We both know that you were the first person to see that poor wretch in the ice,' said Jonathan, slipping an arm around the boy. 'Nobody can dispute it. I'll make sure that Oliver understands that. But it's time to put it behind you, Richard.'

'I've tried, Father. I've tried so hard.'

'Does it still prey on your mind?'

'Day and night.'

Jonathan gave him an affectionate squeeze. 'The memory will fade away in time.'

'Not until it's all over.'

'Over?'

'That man was murdered. Someone has to pay for that.'

'He will, Richard.'

'When he does, I may stop thinking about it.'

'I hope so, son.'

The boy looked up at him. 'Do you know the man?'

'The victim?'

'No, the one who killed him. Mother says he's in prison.'

'Yes,' said Jonathan. 'He's locked away in Newgate so you need have no fears about him. And I do know the man slightly, though he's no friend of mine.'

'What's his name?'

'Never mind about that.'

'I want to know, Father.'

'You know too much already.'

It was not the only reason that he held back the name of Henry Redmayne from his son. Both boys were very fond of Henry's brother. Christopher had been very kind to them and, on one occasion, even read to them from the Bible when they were in bed. To tell them that the murder suspect was his elder brother would be to destroy their faith in the architect and Jonathan did not want to do that. If and when Henry was convicted, it might be impossible to keep the name from them. Until that time, however, Jonathan wanted the suspect to remain anonymous.

'Did you help to catch him, Father?' asked the boy.

'No, Richard.'

'But you're helping in some way?'

'That's part of my job.'

'When are they going to hang him?'

'There has to be a trial first.'

'But they know that he did it.'

'They *believe* that they do,' corrected Jonathan. 'There's evidence against him and it will be presented in court in due course.'

'Will they hang him then?'

'If he's found guilty.'

'Oliver wants to be there,' said the boy. 'So do I. Will you take us, Father?'

'No!'

'But we'd like to see him hang for what he's done.'

'You'll do nothing of the kind,' said Jonathan sternly, 'and you're not to talk about it with Oliver ever again. Do you understand? As far as you're concerned, the matter is over and done with. Forget all about it, Richard. Pretend that it never happened.'

It was late afternoon before Christopher Redmayne finally rode away from Whitcombe Manor and it required an effort of will to do so. Lady Whitcombe had pressed him to stay, offering him a bed for the night and doing all she could by way of persuasion. It was a tempting offer. Under other circumstances, he might have accepted since he felt far too weary to travel back to London but something prompted him to leave. During the long discussion they had over dinner about the new house, Christopher became aware of Letitia's growing fondness for him. It became so obvious that it was embarrassing. Letitia praised his drawings, hung on his every word and never took her eyes off him. Every time she giggled aloud at one of his remarks, he cringed. What convinced him that he should depart was the fact that Lady Whitcombe quit the table at one point and left him alone with the daughter. Letitia was too gauche and unsophisticated to initiate an intelligent conversation herself so she merely agreed enthusiastically with everything that he said. Christopher's discomfort increased markedly. It was one thing to be promoted from architect to friend of the family but Letitia, abetted by her mother, seemed to have an even closer relationship in mind for him. Escape was imperative.

Back in the saddle, he rode swiftly in the direction of Richmond. When he came to a wayside inn, he stayed long enough to reserve a room for the night before continuing his journey. Silhouetted against the darkening sky, Serle Court eventually came into sight on its high eminence. Christopher was not impressed with it as a piece of architecture. It looked striking from afar but had too many contradictory elements in it to appeal to his taste. Its jagged outline was a denial of symmetry. He felt such a great need to see Susan Cheever once more that he did not even think of postponing his visit until the following morning when he would be in a better physical condition. At such a difficult time, Christopher sought the warmth of her friendship and the reassurance of her support.

Reaching the house, he dismounted, tethered his horse and rang the bell. The prospect of meeting her again helped him to shrug off his exhaustion. When the door was opened, Christopher introduced himself to the manservant and asked if he might see Susan. He was invited into the hall while the man went off to pass on his request. It produced an immediate response. The door of the parlour opened and a woman came bustling out but it was not Susan Cheever. It was her sister, Brilliana, and her mood was anything but hospitable.

'What on earth are you doing here, Mr Redmayne?' she asked indignantly.

'I was hoping to see your sister.'

'You came all the way from London for *that* purpose?'

'No, Mrs Serle,' he explained. 'I was visiting a client in Sheen. As I was so close, I thought I would take the liberty of calling here.'

'I suggest that you think twice before you do so again.'

'All that I wanted was a chance to speak to Susan.'

'That's impossible,' she said with a dismissive wave of her hand. 'She's not here.'

'But your servant gave me the impression that she was.'

'He was mistaken.'

'Sir Julius talked of leaving London as soon as the weather improved.'

Her eyes flashed. 'Pray, sir, do not concern yourself with the travel arrangements of our family. I should have thought that it was your own family that required your attention. As it happens, my father has indeed quit the city.'

'Then Susan must have come to Richmond.'

'I've told you she is not here and that is all I'm prepared to say.'

Christopher could see that she was lying but he did not dare to challenge her. Brilliana's hostility was so blatant that she had obviously heard about the arrest of Henry Redmayne. Her response was no surprise to him and he sensed that it would identical to that of her father. Polite withdrawal was the only option for him.

'As you wish,' he said, backing away. 'If, by any chance, your sister arrives this evening, be so good as to tell her that I'll be staying overnight at the Falcon Inn, a few miles from here.'

'I'll do no such thing,' said Brilliana with vehemence. 'You are not welcome here, Mr Redmayne, for reasons that I need hardly explain. The next time you come knocking on our door, you'll not be admitted. My husband and I have no wish to see you and neither, I am sure, does my sister. I bid you farewell, sir.'

When Christopher backed out, she closed the door firmly in his face.

Chapter Seven

Balthazar Pegge was a retired brick maker with such a strong sense of civic duty that he took on the thankless task of being one of London's watchmen. While the majority of people were at home with their families, visiting friends or revelling in a tavern, Pegge and his companion spent the night trudging the streets of the capital in their distinctive garb. Each had a lantern and they took it in turns to carry the large bell that they used to warn citizens of their approach. Pegge also took a staff on his patrols but it was less a weapon than a means of steadying him on his spindly legs. Allan Kiffin, his fellow-watchman, always bore a halberd even though he had never been called upon to use it. Old, tired, slow and with failing eyesight, the two men were out in all weathers, admired by few, ridiculed by many and ignored by most, yet confident that their very presence helped to ensure a degree of safety in the city of their birth.

When they turned into Fenchurch Street that evening, they were accosted by a burly figure that came out of the gloom ahead of them. Pegge rang the bell but the man stood his ground. Fearing confrontation, the watchmen slowed their pace but there was no danger. The stranger's voice was very friendly and their lanterns soon revealed him to be a parish constable.

'A word with you, good sirs,' he said.

'We've plenty to spare,' replied Pegge, weighing up the newcomer.

'My name is Jonathan Bale and I need your help in the pursuit of a murderer.'

'It's yours for the asking, Mr Bale.'

'To whom do I speak?'

'I'm Balthazar Pegge,' replied the other, turning to his colleague, 'and this is Allan Kiffin, as fine as fellow as you could hope to meet.'

'Thank you, Balthazar,' said Kiffin.

'How can we help, Mr Bale?'

'Do you walk down this street every night?' asked Jonathan.

'Without fail,' said Pegge proudly. 'Around this time, you'll always find us here or hereabouts. We know every inch of Fenchurch Street even though it's changed a lot since the Great Fire.'

'Then you must be familiar with the Elephant.'

The watchman gave a dry cackle. 'Everyone knows the Elephant, sir. Those who built it were schooled in their trade. The stone they used was so thick and solid that the Elephant did not fall to the fire. The Mitre did, more's the pity. I remember seeing Daniel Rawlinson, who owned it, crying as he stood in the ruins. Other taverns were turned to cinders as well.'

'My only interest is the Elephant.'

'Why is that, Mr Bale?'

'Because a certain person supped there some weeks ago,' said Jonathan. 'When he left the tavern, he went looking for a calash to take him home and claims that he was ambushed by a man who brandished a sword. All that he can remember after that is that he was picked up from the ground by a watchman.'

'Drunk, sir?'

'Very drunk, Mr Pegge.'

'Then he could be any one of a dozen fellows we've helped to their feet.'

'Cold weather drives people to drink,' observed Kiffin darkly.

'This gentleman was in a bad state,' said Jonathan.

'They always are after a night at the Elephant.'

'The landlord serves good wine and strong ale,' added Pegge. 'Some people, alas, never know when they've had too much. We see them stumbling out of there as if their legs did not belong to them.'

'I think you'll remember this particular gentleman,' said Jonathan.

'Oh?'

'The watchman who got him to his feet also found a carriage to take him home to Bedford Street. He'd never have got there otherwise.'

'Bedford Street?' repeated Pegge, scratching his straggly grey beard. 'Now, that does sound familiar. Where have I heard that address before, Allan?'

'Why ask me, Balthazar?' said Kiffin. 'It's new to my ears.'

'I told a driver to go to Bedford Street. When was that?'

'Who knows? We've put many a man into a carriage.'

'This one would have been tall, slim and extravagantly dressed,' said Jonathan. 'He was probably wearing an expensive periwig. An arrogant fellow in every way. Even when drunk, he'd have had airs and graces.'

'They often do,' said Kiffin before spitting philosophically on to the ground.

'His name was Henry Redmayne.'

'Bless you, sir,' said Pegge, leaning on his staff. 'Most of the gentlemen that we help to their feet can barely remember what day it is. As like as not, they've forgotten their names and everything else about them.'

'Mr Redmayne did manage to give his address.'

'Yes, it's Bedford Street that sticks in my mind somehow. I wonder why that is.' He snapped his fingers. 'You are right, Mr Bale. I *did* ask a driver to take a gentleman back there one night.'

'When?'

'Weeks ago, I fancy.'

'Where did you find him?'

'Not here, sir,' said Pegge.

'But if he came out of the Elephant,' argued Jonathan, looking towards the tavern, 'this is where he would have searched for a lift back home. He was in no condition to walk far from Fenchurch Street.'

'You are mistaken there, sir.'

'What do you mean?'

'If it's the man I believe it was, we found him much nearer the river.'

Jonathan blinked in surprise. 'Are you sure, Mr Pegge?'

'Dead certain. Allan will bear me out.'

'Will I?' asked Kiffin, mystified.

'We found him in that alley off Thames Street,' recalled Pegge, nudging him. 'He was lying face down and we thought at first he'd been attacked by thieves. His hat had been knocked off and his wig was all askew, but he still had his purse about him.'

Kiffin's face lit up. 'I think that I remember him now, Balthazar.'

'Drunk as a lord, he was.'

'I held your lantern while you got him off the ground.'

'I soon began to wish I'd not bothered.'

'Why?' asked Jonathan.

'Because he tried to punch me,' said Pegge ruefully. 'When I got him upright, he lashed out at me with both fists. Drunk he might be, but he was still strong. I had a job to hold him and I'm no weakling, Mr Bale. Forty years of making bricks for a living has left some muscle in these old arms.'

'So you overpowered him?'

'I had to. He'd else have knocked me down.'

'I never took him for a violent man,' said Jonathan.

'You'd not have called him peaceable that night. And the worst of it was, he kept calling me by this strange name. It was an odd, curious, foreign sort of name.'

'Maldini, by any chance?'

'Yes,' said Pegge. 'Or something very much like it. He swore he'd kill me.'

'You or this fellow, Maldini?'

'He took us for one and the same.'

'What happened then?'

'Well, sir, when I'd got the better of him, I stood him against a wall and asked him where he lived. He mumbled what sounded like Bedford Street so that's where I sent him. To be honest, I was glad to see the back of him.'

'So was I,' agreed Kiffin. 'Watchmen deserve more respect.'

'You'll get it from me,' promised Jonathan. 'You do a valuable job, my friends. As for this fight, it all took place some distance away from here, you say?'

'Close by Thames Street.'

'Could you show me the place?'

'We'll take you there now, Mr Bale,' volunteered Pegge, pleased that he might be able to furnish useful evidence in a murder enquiry. 'This way, sir.' Jonathan fell in beside them as they headed towards the river. 'What did you call the gentleman?'

'Mr Redmayne,' said the constable. 'Mr Henry Redmayne.'

Night was an unrelieved torment. Noises that were unsettling during the day became unbearable during the hours of darkness. Cries of pain and howls of anguish echoed throughout Newgate. Sounds of a violent argument would erupt when least expected and rise in volume until those involved in the brawl were beaten into submission by brutal turnkeys. Eerie silences then followed before a fresh clamor would arise. Female screams could last for an hour. Though he kept his hands over his ears, Henry Redmayne could not shut out the prison cacophony. He began to think that he was locked in a madhouse. Money had bought him a flickering candle that he set in his lap, grateful for its tiny warmth as much as for its light. It was his only source of consolation.

Martin Crenlowe's visit seemed an eternity away now. Henry had eaten all the food that his friend had brought and drunk all the wine, hoping that the latter would dull his senses enough to allow him to sleep. It did not happen. Part of his punishment, he now understood, was being forced to stay awake, listening to the deafening protests of other prisoners and reflecting on his fate. He also came to realise how dependent he was on other people for his welfare. When Henry was in his own house, a servant woke him and brought him breakfast, a barber arrived to shave him and a valet helped to dress him. There were no servants, barbers or valets in Newgate. Henry was hungry, unshaven and wearing soiled clothes. A more immediate problem troubled him. Since he had no access to a privy, he had to relieve himself in a corner of the cell and share his space with his own excrement. Unaware how privileged he had been, he had taken for granted the perfumed elegance of his normal life. To be reduced to the level of a caged animal was a horrifying experience for him.

The longer he stayed in Newgate, the more certain he became that he would end his life on the gallows. His brother had sworn to work for his release but there had been no sign of Christopher for days. Martin Crenlowe might profess to believe in his friend's innocence yet his evidence had been partially responsible for Henry's incarceration. The same could be said of Sir Humphrey Godden, another member of his circle. Crenlowe had at least come to offer his sympathy and bring some welcome gifts. Sir Humphrey had done neither, nor had Captain Harvest, a man who was reportedly informing the world aloud of Henry's guilt. The last time he had seen the three of them, they had been sitting at a table with him at a tavern in Fenchurch Street, enjoying a delicious meal, albeit spiced with an argument. Now he was entombed in a cold, filthy, noisome prison with a rat as his only companion. Henry wondered what he had done to deserve such a reversal in his fortunes.

His trial was yet to come but the judge he feared most was his father. No leniency would be shown by the Dean of Gloucester, no appeals for mercy would be heeded. The Reverend Algernon Redmayne would surely have heard the grim tidings about his elder son by now. He would be on his way to London to administer his punishment. Henry could almost hear his voice and see his raised finger. The only way that he had remained on speaking terms with his father was to conceal from him the true nature of his life in London, giving him instead the impression that he was a model of Christian sobriety and industriousness. That illusion could no longer be sustained. His father would see him as the feckless and decadent spendthrift that he really was. Unable to defend or excuse himself, Henry would be exposed as a complete rake whose habit of drinking to excess had led him down the path to damnation. He shuddered so violently that the flame he nursed was blown out, plunging him into complete darkness. Shrieks and bellows from other cells reached a new pitch of intensity. Henry added his own impassioned yell to the general tumult.

'Christopher!' he shouted. 'Where *are* you?'

Having retired to bed early at the Falcon Inn, he fell asleep almost immediately. So deep was his slumber that the lusty crowing of the cock failed to rouse him at dawn, as did the sound of a cart rumbling out of the courtyard. It was only when the landlord's strong fist thundered on his door that he was brought awake.

'Mr Redmayne!' called a voice.

'Yes?' said Christopher, opening a bleary eye.

'You asked to be woken, sir.'

'Thank you.'

Annoyed that he had overslept, Christopher hauled himself out of bed and reached for his clothes. He had planned to be on the road at daybreak and had lost valuable time. His body might have needed the rest but his mind was full of self-reproach. Spurning breakfast, he gathered up his things, paid for his room then made for the stables. He was just leaving the inn when he heard the drumming of hooves behind him. Christopher turned to see a rider emerging from a copse nearby. When he recognised who it was, he could not believe his eyes. Riding sidesaddle and cantering towards him, Susan Cheever waved a hand in greeting. When she brought her horse to a halt beside him, her face was flushed with pleasure.

'Thank heaven I got here in time!' she said.

'Yes,' he agreed. 'I'd intended to be miles away by now.'

'I'll not hold you up. I just wanted to speak to you.'

'Detain me for as long as you wish, Susan.'

Christopher dismounted and helped her down from her own saddle. After tethering the horses to a fence that ran alongside the inn, they stepped into the shadow of one of the outbuildings. He feasted his eyes on her.

'Brilliana misled you,' she began.

'I knew that you were at the house.'

'I was in the parlour when you came and overheard you speaking to my sister. I could have joined you both there and then but that would have led to a fierce argument with Brilliana, and you would have been shown the door.'

Christopher smiled wryly. 'Your sister was a harsh porter,'

'When I heard you mention the Falcon Inn, I saw my opportunity.'

'I'm so pleased that you took it.'

'Nothing would stop me. I *had* to see you, Christopher.'

'Supposing that I'd already left?'

'Then I'd have tried to overhaul you,' she said. 'I'm no stranger to a saddle. If at all possible, I ride every day.' Susan lowered her eyes. 'I must apologise for Brilliana.'

'There's no need.'

'She was rude and inconsiderate.'

'Your sister was only responding as many others have done. The name of Redmayne is not as welcome as it was on some doorsteps.'

'Well, it's still a welcome sound in my ears,' she affirmed, looking up at him again. 'That's what I needed to tell you, Christopher. I can only imagine the pain you've suffered these past few days.'

'My problems are nothing compared with those endured by Henry.'

'I refuse to believe that he's guilty of the crime.'

'Thank you,' he said, touching her arm in gratitude. 'I, too, am persuaded of his innocence and not merely because he's my brother. I'll do all in my power to secure his release and to vindicate the reputation of the family name.'

'Even if he *did* commit a murder – and I'm convinced he did not – it would make no difference to my opinion of you, Christopher. I wanted you to know that.'

Christopher was moved. 'Such sentiments are the breath of life to me.'

'Unfortunately, Brilliana does not share them.'

'Nor, I suspect, does Sir Julius.'

'Father tried to forbid me to see you,' she confessed. 'He would not leave the house in Westminster until he'd handed me over to my brother-in-law, for fear that I might try to reach you.'

'Would you have done so?'

'Most assuredly.'

'That gladdens my heart.'

'I'd hoped to inveigle Lancelot into stopping his coach in Fetter Lane but Father was wise to that possibility. He warned my brother-in-law accordingly.'

'I do not blame Sir Julius,' said Christopher resignedly. 'In his view, he's only trying to protect you. So are your sister and brother-in-law.'

'I need no protection from any of them.'

'They see me as a corrupting influence.'

'Only because they do not know you as well as I do.'

'Their opinions may change when Henry's innocence is established.'

'How soon will that be, Christopher?'

He grimaced slightly. 'I wish that I knew. At the moment, the evidence points to my brother as the culprit. The surest way to exonerate him is to find the real killer.'

'Have you made any progress in that direction?'

'Very little,' he admitted. 'Being called out of London was an interruption that I could not afford, though it's had a happy conclusion. This brief meeting with you has made the whole journey worthwhile.'

'But you need to get back to the city.'

'As fast as I can, Susan.'

'Then you must be on your way,' she said, 'and so must I. If I ride hard, I can be back at Serle Court before Brilliana and Lancelot have even risen.'

'I'd hate the thought that coming to see me would get you into trouble'

'They'll not even know that I've left the house.'

'I know,' he said fondly, 'and I'll not forget this kindness.'

He untied her horse then helped her to mount the animal, enjoying the momentary contact with her body. Susan looked down at him with a wan smile.

'Remember that I'll be thinking of you, Christopher.'

He grinned. 'You'll be in my thoughts as well, have no fear.'

After a frugal breakfast of bread and whey, Jonathan Bale set out early from his house in order to have another meeting with Captain James Harvest. His intention was to get to the man's lodging before he went off on his morning peregrinations. Jonathan felt that there was much more still to be learned from, and about, the genial soldier. Harvest worried him. He had a surface charm that hid his true character and a fondness for drink that did not impress a Puritan constable. There was also something faintly shabby about him and Jonathan was bound to ask how a man who earned a little money by giving impromptu fencing lessons in a tavern courtyard could afford to consort with people like Henry Redmayne and his friends. It was only one of many questions he wished to put to Captain Harvest. In the event, he was baulked.

'Not here?' he said with disappointment. 'Then where is he?'

'That's what I'd like to know.'

'What do you mean?'

'He's flown the coop, Mr Bale. During the night.'

'Are you sure?'

'Why else should he take all his belongings with him?'

The owner of the house was a short, stubby man in his fifties with a world-weary expression on his whiskered face. Captain Harvest had been his lodger for over six months and given him no indication that he wanted to leave. Jonathan guessed the reason for the sudden departure.

'Was there any rent outstanding?' he asked.

'A month in total.'

'And before that?'

'Captain Harvest always paid eventually,' said the other. 'I liked him, sir, that's the sad part of it. I made allowances for the captain I'd not make for all my lodgers. He was such pleasant company. Well, if you've met him, you know how engaging a fellow he was. It was worth having him here just to listen to some of his tales.'

'Tales or excuses?'

'Yes,' sighed the landlord, 'we had our share of those as well.'

'Yet he always gave you the rent in the end?'

'Either him or his friend.'

'Friend?'

'An Italian gentlemen, Mr Bale. A handsome fellow with a fine tailor, judging by his apparel. I believe that Captain Harvest worked for him from time to time.'

'Then it must have been Jeronimo Maldini.'

'That was the name,' confirmed the other. 'Maldini. He called here once or twice and the captain got him to settle his debts. They seemed quite close.'

'How well did you know Captain Harvest?'

'Not well enough, it seems.'

'Did he ever borrow any money from you?'

'Occasionally.'

'Has it all been paid back?'

'No, Mr Bale. I was a fool to trust him, I see that now.'

'Was he a creature of habit?'

'Oh, yes. He always left the house early and came back late. If he came back at all, that is, for sometimes he was out all night.'

'I can well imagine it.'

'The captain was very popular with ladies.'

'Did he ever invite any of them here?'

'No,' said the landlord, glancing over his shoulder. 'It's a decent house, as you see, but he only rented two rooms from me and they were rather small. He'd not wish to entertain female company in there.'

'Yet he brought friends like Signor Maldini here.'

'That's true.'

'Can you remember any others?'

'Only the gentleman with the coach.'

'Coach?'

'He came more than once to drop him off. It's not often you see a coach as fine as that in this street. Captain Harvest had some wealthy friends. No mistake about that.'

'Can you recall the name of this particular friend?'

'Oh, yes.'

'Well?'

'It was Godden,' said the other. 'Sir Humphrey Godden.'

After calling at his house to let Jacob know that he was back, Christopher Redmayne rode on to the address that had been left by Martin Crenlowe. It was not far from Foster Lane, where the Goldsmiths' Hall had once stood, and Christopher was interested to see that it was in the process of being restored after the ravages of the Great Fire. The premises occupied by Crenlowe were in a lane nearby and the first thing that Christopher noticed was the solidity of the doors and shutters. Constructed of stout timber, they had iron strap hinges and thick bolts. When he knocked, a grill was opened in the door so that he could be questioned by an apprentice whose face peered through the bars. It was only when he gave his name and stated his business that Christopher was admitted. He was conducted past the workshop at the rear of the building and into the room that served as Crenlowe's office. Attention had been given to security here as well. There were iron bars at the window and the heavy chest that stood in the corner had no less than six large locks along its edge. Christopher was in the presence of gold.

'I'm so pleased to see you, Mr Redmayne,' said Crenlowe, shaking his hand. 'Pray, take a seat. I'm sure that we have much to discuss.'

'Thank you, Mr Crenlowe,' said Christopher, sitting in the chair in front of the long table that served the goldsmith as a desk. 'I'm sorry not to come earlier but business called me out of the city for a day.'

'You are a celebrated architect, I hear.'

'I aspire to be one but it may take several years yet.'

'London has need of your skills now that so much of it is being rebuilt.'

'I hope to make a small contribution to that work. But I did not come here to talk about my career, Mr Crenlowe. That's in abeyance from now on until I've managed to rescue my brother from the appalling situation in which he finds himself.'

'Naturally.'

'You visited him in Newgate, I believe?'

'I did,' said Crenlowe with a look of distaste, 'and took some food and wine with me. Henry was in a dreadful state. I hardly recognised him as the man I knew.'

'The shock of imprisonment has been too much for him.'

'He was so obviously ashamed to be seen like that.'

'Most of us would be, Mr Crenlowe.'

'I was not allowed to stay long,' said the goldsmith, 'but I think I was able to give him fresh heart. The wine, especially, would have been a treat for him.'

'It was thoughtful of you to take it.'

'I just wanted him to know that we had not abandoned him.'

'We?'

'His friends, Mr Redmayne. We're standing by him. Neither of us will accept that Henry is capable of a foul murder. He's a man of hot words rather than rash deeds. Sir Humphrey and I in agreement on that.'

'How long have you known Henry?'

'Some years.'

'Long enough to understand his failings, then.'

'And to appreciate his virtues, for he has those as well.'

Christopher appraised him. In appearance and inclination, Sir Humphrey Godden had seemed a natural companion for his brother but the goldsmith somehow did not. He seemed too quiet, intelligent and responsible. Unlike many of Henry's friends, Crenlowe worked for a living and clearly made a good profit by doing so. Looking at him now, Christopher had to remind himself that the man had been a pupil of the Italian fencing master and spent the evening with Henry on the night of the murder.

'I've spoken with Sir Humphrey Godden,' said Christopher.

'What did he tell you?'

'Almost nothing of value, Mr Crenlowe. Indeed, he was loath to talk to me at all as he was late for an appointment. You've shown Henry true friendship, and I'm grateful to you for that, but I saw little of it when I visited Covent Garden.'

'Sir Humphrey can be brusque at times.'

'This was one of them.'

'Do not be deceived by his manner. He's very fond of your brother.'

'I saw no desire in him to work for Henry's release.'

'That will surely come when the facts emerge.'

'It was those same facts that landed him in prison in the first place.'

'Henry is the victim of circumstance,' said Crenlowe, stroking his double chin. 'It was his misfortune to be in the wrong place at the wrong time.'

'And why was that?'

'Because we all went our separate ways in Fenchurch Street.'

'Yes,' said Christopher, 'but Sir Humphrey travels by coach. Bedford Street is not far from his own home. He could easily have given my brother a lift, could he not?'

'He offered to do so, Mr Redmayne.'

'Then why did Henry not accept?'

'Because he was in a contentious mood,' explained the goldsmith. 'The meeting with Jeronimo Maldini had stirred up his ire. Throughout the meal, Henry could talk of nothing else but settling a score with the fencing master. Sir Humphrey had no love for the fellow but even he tired of hearing the endless rant. He wanted to leave. When he suggested that Henry should go with him, he was waved away so off he went.'

'What of you and Captain Harvest?'

'We, too, had places to go. My wife was waiting up for me and James – Captain Harvest, that is – had promised to call on friends. We urged Henry to find a carriage to take him home.'

'Then walked off and left him.'

'Unhappily, yes. I've been writhing with guilt ever since.'

'My brother was not your responsibility.'

'I should have done *something*, Mr Redmayne. Henry had drunk far too much. He was in a dangerous mood. The least I could have done was to make sure that he was driven home.'

'What of Captain Harvest?'

'He went off in the other direction.'

'Did he not think of taking care of my brother?'

'I fear not.'

'Why was that?'

'Because he was a good friend of Jeronimo Maldini. The rest of us had fallen out with him but James still went to the fencing school and even taught there. That was part of the trouble,' said Crenlowe with a sigh. 'He came to his friend's defence when Henry started to attack Signor Maldini. That only enraged your brother the more. He accused James of being in league with the Italian against him. Henry's language became very intemperate.'

'How did Captain Harvest respond?'

'He tried to laugh it off, as he always does. But he was angry, I could see that.'

'What did he do?'

'Stalked off as soon as we left the tavern.'

'Henry can look for no support from him, then?'

'On the contrary,' said Crenlowe, shaking his head, 'he'll get nothing but abuse. James is voicing it abroad that your brother was

97

the killer. Jeronimo Maldini was more than a friend of his, you see. He was source of income for James. He borrowed a little money from me and even more from Sir Humphrey, but it was the fencing school that allowed him an income of sorts. Signor Maldini was generous to his friends. I know that he loaned James money on several occasions.'

'Was it ever paid back?'

'Oh, yes. James often had a run of luck at the card table.'

'Henry says that he cheated.'

'That was his opinion.'

'There's no truth in the charge?'

'Not as far as I know,' said the goldsmith. 'James had a knack for card games, there's no doubt about that. I've seen him win five hundred guineas in a night.'

'What did he do with his money?'

Crenlowe laughed. 'Lose it just as quickly the following day.'

'That was very careless of him.'

'James is a soldier of fortune,' said the goldsmith with grudging admiration. 'He takes life as it comes and makes the most of it. Rich or poor, he's happy with his lot. It's not an existence that I envy, Mr Redmayne.'

'I can see that.'

Christopher was glad that he had decided to call on Martin Crenlowe. There was a quiet complacency about the goldsmith that made it impossible to like him but he was much more forthcoming than Sir Humphrey Godden. He also evinced far less hostility towards the murder victim. Christopher wondered why.

'What did you make of Signor Maldini?' he asked.

'I respected him greatly as a fencing master.'

'And as a man?'

'I had less time for him. He was not the most appealing individual.'

'Did he ever try to humiliate you at the school?'

'Yes,' said Crenlowe with a frown. 'He goaded me unmercifully. You can see from my shape that I'm no swordsman of note. Jeronimo Maldini was and he made me look ridiculous in front of my friends.'

'Is that why you left the school?'

'It was, Mr Redmayne. I like to be treated with respect.'

'Henry, too, suffered at his hands.'

'Even more than I did. He was livid. He talked of shooting Signor Maldini.'

'But not of stabbing him in the back.'

'He could *never* do that,' asserted Crenlowe, rising to his feet. 'Henry Redmayne is first and foremost a gentleman. You, above all people, should know that.'

'I do,' said Christopher loyally. 'I can see that you're a busy man, Mr Crenlowe, so I'll not impose on you for much longer. But I would like to ask about that evening when the four of you had a meal together.'

'Ask anything you wish.'

'Henry told me that you had a chance meeting with Signor Maldini?'

'And so we did. It was not far from Fenchurch Street.'

'So the four of you were walking along together when you were accosted by the fencing master. Is that what happened?'

'No, Mr Redmayne.'

'Then perhaps you could explain what did.'

'Certainly,' said the other. 'There were only *three* of us strolling along that evening – Sir Humphrey Godden, Henry and myself.'

'Where was Captain Harvest?'

'He arrived with Jeronimo Maldini.'

Christopher was astonished. 'Even though he knew how much you all disliked his friend? Some people might say that that was an act of provocation.'

'James said that he had met Signor Maldini by accident. He'd arranged to meet us at the tavern and did not expect to encounter the three of us in the street. In fairness to him, when the argument started, James was the one who tried to quell it.'

'Do you believe that the meeting with his friend was accidental?'

'I did at the time.'

'And now?'

'I think that James was lying,' said Crenlowe seriously. 'He merely pretended to intervene in a quarrel that he had deliberately set up. Henry Redmayne and Jeronimo Maldini were like two fighting cocks. Captain James Harvest was the man who sharpened their spurs.'

Chapter Eight

Jonathan Bale always felt uncomfortable when he visited the house in Fetter Lane. It was spacious, well-furnished and filled with the individual touches that only a man of artistic talent could devise. It made his own home seem small, bare and lacking in any real character. The presence of a servant was another factor that set the two abodes apart. Employing someone to cook, clean and run the house was a concept that Jonathan would never have considered, even if he could have afforded the expense. There was streak of self-reliance in him that rebelled against the very notion. While he liked Jacob Vout as a person, therefore, the man's role as a servant made their relationship uneasy for him. The constable was soon shuffling his feet.

'I'd best be on my way,' he decided.

'Mr Redmayne will be back very soon,' said Jacob.

'I'll call again later.'

'Why bother when you can see him now? He's eager to speak to you, Mr Bale.'

'And I wish to speak to him, Jacob.'

'Then try to be patient. You'll not have long to wait.

Jonathan sat back in the chair but he could not relax. Anxious to pass on what he had learned, he had called at Christopher's house that afternoon and been disappointed that his friend was not there. Twenty minutes had elapsed so far and he was increasingly restless. Since he had no interest in the architectural beauties of Europe, the paintings that covered the walls held little charm for him. Holding his hat between his knees, he played nervously with the brim. It was left to Jacob to strike up a conversation.

'How is your son, Mr Bale?' he asked.

'Which one?' replied Jonathan. 'I have two.'

'His name is Richard, I think. He found the body in the ice.'

'Oh, yes. He did, alas, and the memory still haunts him.'

'Have you told him that a man has been arrested for the crime?'

'Yes,' said Jonathan, 'but Richard does not know his name. I see no reason why he should, unless the prisoner is convicted of the murder. The boy has been shocked enough already. He'd be even more upset if he realised that it was Mr Redmayne's own brother who is held in Newgate. That's why I kept it for him. Richard has great respect for your master.'

'Mr Redmayne speaks fondly of both your children.'

'There may come a time when the truth can no longer be suppressed.'

'In other words, you believe in his brother's guilt.'

'I've yet to be persuaded of his innocence, Jacob. What about you?'

'I've no opinion to offer, Mr Bale.'

'But you must incline one way or the other.'

Jacob was discreet. 'I'm just grateful that I serve one brother and not the other.'

'They are hardly like two peas in a pod,' said Jonathan. 'I've never known two brothers have so little in common. My sons look, talk and think alike. It's only natural that they should do so. But your master is so different from Henry Redmayne that the two of them might be complete strangers.'

'Adversity brings out family feeling.'

'True. And I admire Mr Redmayne for standing by his brother.'

'Even though you believe that he is wasting his time?'

'I can only follow my instinct, Jacob.'

'Then I'll do the same,' said the old man, moving to the front door as he heard the sound of hoof beats in the street. 'Unless I'm very much mistaken, Mr Redmayne has come home at last.'

Jacob opened the door in time to see his master dismounting from his horse. Hearing that he had a visitor, Christopher handed the reins to his servant and went straight into the house. After an exchange of greetings, he sat opposite Jonathan.

'I'm sorry to keep you waiting,' he said with a gesture of apology, 'but it's been a busy day. As soon as I got back from Richmond, I had to call on Martin Crenlowe and, after that, I spent an hour or so with the lawyer I've engaged to represent my brother.'

'Did you learn anything of value from Mr Crenlowe?'

'A great deal, Jonathan. He was much more helpful than Sir Humphrey Godden. It was good to meet someone who's wholeheartedly on my brother's side.' He saw his friend wince slightly. 'Crenlowe even took the trouble to visit Henry in Newgate. I'll go there myself this afternoon.' Christopher leaned forward. 'But what of you?'

'I've not been idle, Mr Redmayne.'

'You wouldn't know *how* to be. Did you speak to Captain Harvest?'

'Yes,' said Jonathan, 'and I also tracked down the watchman who helped your brother to his feet that night. I was glad that I did so. Many new facts came to light.'

Christopher was hopeful. 'Did they help to change your mind?'

'I fear not.'

'Then they confirmed your opinion that Henry is guilty?'

'In some ways.'

'Oh. I see.' He was crestfallen. 'Well,' he said, rallying quickly, 'perhaps the evidence that *I* gathered will persuade you.'

'I long to hear it, Mr Redmayne.'

Christopher sat back in his chair and gave him a succinct account of his respective visits to Sir Humphrey Godden and Martin Crenlowe. He did not pretend to like either man though he had found the latter far more pleasant. Jonathan listened intently and waited until his friend had finished before he offered any comment.

'Sir Humphrey Godden was adamant that your brother is innocent?'

'Yes, Jonathan.'

'It did not appear so from your description of what was said.'

'He was in something of a hurry when I questioned him.'

'That should not prevent him from coming to the defence of a friend.'

'Martin Crenlowe assures me that he and Sir Humphrey are of the same mind.'

'But that's not quite the same thing as hearing it from the man himself,' said Jonathan. 'According to you, Sir Humphrey accepts that your brother had reason enough to kill Signor Maldini and even thinks him capable of murder. It's only the nature of the fatal wound that makes him believe the crime was the work of someone else.'

'Sir Humphrey was with Henry that night. He knew my brother's frame of mind.'

'Drink can have strange effects on a man.'

'It left my brother tottering down the street.'

'That's not the picture that I was given, Mr Redmayne.'

'Oh?'

'When the watchmen found him on the ground, your brother was nowhere near the place that he claimed to be. He was able to walk better than you imagine.'

'Are you certain?'

'I can only tell you what Balthazar Pegge told me.'

It was Jonathan's turn to present his findings. He talked about his conversation with Captain Harvest, the subsequent disappearance of the soldier from his lodging and the time spent in the company of the two old watchmen. His recital was more laboured and methodical than Christopher's but the salient facts were all there. They caused a shift of perspective in his friend's thinking.

'Henry lied to me,' he complained. 'He swore that he was set upon by Signor Maldini, somewhere in Fenchurch Street. How did he get so close to the river?'

'How did he lose his dagger?'

'What do you mean?'

'Could it be that he lied to you about that as well?'

'No,' said Christopher, groping for an explanation. 'He was probably too drunk to remember the details with any clarity. The main part of his story is true. Let's give him credit for that. Henry was found by a watchman and sent home in a carriage. His servants confirm it.'

'It's what happened earlier that matters, Mr Redmayne.'

'I agree.'

'Did you brother mention that he mistook the watchman for Jeronimo Maldini?'

'No,' admitted Christopher.

'Or that he wrestled with Mr Pegge and threatened to kill him? That, too, seems to have slipped his mind. Unless, as you say, drink blinded him so completely that he did not know what he was doing. It clearly left him with enough strength to attack an old man, I know that. If he can brawl with one person and forget all about it, could he not have done the same with Signor Maldini himself?'

'I suppose so.'

'Mr Pegge told me that your brother had obviously been in a fight of some sort. His hat was off, his wig askew, his clothes dishevelled. He seemed tired rather than dazed. As soon as he was lifted to his feet, he became violent.'

'That does not sound like Henry.'

'How well do you know your brother?'

'Not as well as I thought, it seems,' conceded Christopher. 'But it's this Captain Harvest who interests me. Did he flee from his lodging in order to avoid paying his rent or has he quit the city before the trial is held?'

'Why should he vanish from London?'

'Because he's afraid to be cross-examined in court by a barrister.'

'He's already given sworn evidence that he heard your brother threaten the life of Signor Maldini. He was not too frightened to do that. I've met Captain Harvest. He's the sort of man who's not afraid of anything.'

'Except paying his landlord.'

Jonathan smiled. 'I fancy that he makes a habit of changing his lodgings.'

Christopher was lost in thought for a moment. 'I still feel that he's more involved in this whole business than we realize,' he said at length. 'Everything you've told me agrees with Mr Crenlowe's view of the man and he knew him better than any of us. Could it really be the case that Captain Harvest *arranged* the encounter between Henry and the fencing master?'

'To what end?'

'Provoking them into a duel.'

'But your brother would stand no chance against Signor Maldini.'

'Unless the Italian were also drunk or disabled in some other way. Or perhaps,' Christopher went on, offering another possibility, 'this mischievous soldier brought the two enemies to the verge of a duel then took a hand in the proceedings himself.'

Jonathan was startled. 'Captain Harvest may have been the killer?'

'It would not be the first time he had blood on his hands.'

'But he stood to lose most from Signor Maldini's death,' argued Jonathan. 'The two men were friends. Captain Harvest worked at the fencing school. He earned his keep there. Why murder a man who employed him and who often loaned him money?'

'There has to be a reason, Jonathan.'

'I fail to see it.'

'Perhaps he wanted to take over the fencing school himself. Perhaps he had a disagreement with Signor Maldini. Perhaps he owed the man far more than he could ever repay. All kinds of motives may have impelled him,' said Christopher. 'What we do know is that he has no affection for my brother.'

'He spoke very slightingly of him, Mr Redmayne.'

'And is now openly proclaiming Henry's guilt. What better way to throw suspicion off himself than by accusing another man? That must be the answer.'

'I have my doubts.'

'Don't you see?' asked Christopher, excited by the idea. 'He instigated a duel between Signor Maldini and my brother to act as a shield for his own designs. Henry was *used*. Captain Harvest must have followed him that night, knowing that the Italian was lying in wait for him.' He was dismayed by Jonathan's obvious lack of enthusiasm for the theory. 'You must confess that it's *possible*.'

'Anything is possible.'

'You met the fellow. You said that he was untrustworthy.'

'That's a far cry from accusing him of murder.'

'Why is he the only one of the three who is not supporting my brother?'

'I prefer to ask another question, Mr Redmayne,' said Jonathan calmly. 'Why has neither Sir Humphrey nor Mr Crenlowe suggested that Captain Harvest is involved in some way? I only met him once. They've shared his company many times. So has your brother, for that matter. Did he tell you that he was the victim of a plot that was hatched by the captain?'

Christopher heaved a sigh. 'No, Jonathan,' he confessed, 'he did not. And I apologise for letting my imagination run away with me. I'm so desperate to help my brother that I'm confusing possibility with proof. However,' he continued, 'I do think that Captain Harvest will bear more examination.'

'That's why I went in search of him again.'

'I'd like to speak with the gentleman myself.'

'He's an affable character, Mr Redmayne.'

'Yet rather slippery.'

'Captain Harvest is a man who lives on his wits.'

'So I gathered,' said Christopher. 'But I'd like your opinion of the other witnesses as well. Mr Crenlowe is an approachable man. I'm sure that he'd be prepared to talk to you about the case.'

'What of Sir Humphrey Godden?'

'Choose the time you call on him with care.'

'You'll need to furnish me with their addresses.'

'And I'll require some guidance to find Captain Harvest. Where might he be?'

'In one of his favourite taverns, I daresay.'

'Give me a list of them before you go.'

'I will, Mr Redmayne. Did you say that you'd visit your brother today?'

'I must,' replied Christopher. 'Henry is suffering badly in Newgate. There are no friendly faces to comfort him in prison. I'll take food and drink, and do my best to instil some hope into him.'

'Will you tax him about his hatred of Signor Maldini?'

'In what way?'

'Well,' said Jonathan, getting to his feet, 'your brother told you that it was because the Italian cheated at cards.'

'Sir Humphrey Godden supplied another reason. He said that Henry was ridiculed at the fencing school by Signor Maldini. That would inflict a terrible wound on his pride.'

'Captain Harvest took a different view.'

'So you said.'

'He insisted that a third party was involved. According to him, a certain lady was the real cause of dissension between the two men.' There was a note of profound disapproval in Jonathan's voice. 'I wonder why your brother never even mentioned her.'

Christopher swallowed hard. 'It's something that I intend to ask him.'

The first time they carried a litter past his cell, the corpse was not even covered. As he looked through the grill, Henry Redmayne saw the body of a woman, dressed in rags, misshapen by age and skeletal from hunger, being borne away by two of the turnkeys. Her face was so disfigured by disease that Henry turned away in disgust. Gaol fever had claimed another victim. On the second occasion, the body was hidden beneath a shroud that was sodden with blood around the neck and chest. Henry was at the grill again. Seeing his face, the bearers of the litter stopped briefly outside his cell so that he could look more closely at the cadaver.

'What happened?' asked Henry.

'He took the easy way out of Newgate,' replied one of the turnkeys.

'How did he do that?'

'With a razor. He cut his throat.'

Henry recoiled. 'Why?'

'He wanted to cheat the hangman.'

'And he took his own life?'

The turnkey grinned. 'You'll warm to the notion yourself before too long.'

They went on their way and left Henry to meditate on horror of what the other prisoner had done. He was sufficient of a Christian to know that suicide was an unforgivable sin. The dead man would be denied the privilege of being buried in hallowed ground and would never go to meet his Maker. What had forced the man to take such a wild and irrevocable step? What was his crime? How had he come by the means to kill himself? Did he have any family and friends to grieve for him? Henry was so preoccupied with the misery of another prisoner's lot that he all but forgot his own. Then a rat ran across his foot and made him yelp. He looked round the four bare walls that hemmed him in. The straw in his cell was clogged with filth and the prison stench was now so strong that it made him retch. His clothing was in an appalling state. The shirt on which he had spent so much money was caked with grime and his breeches were badly torn. He looked worse than the meanest beggar.

Henry curled up in a corner to reflect on the malignity of fate. An hour crawled slowly past. He was still cursing his misfortune when something was dropped through the grill on to the straw. He groped about in search of it then drew his hand away sharply as it made contact with the blade. Someone had tossed a razor into his cell but it was not to help him shave. It had already drawn blood from his finger and he licked it hard. On impulse, he picked the razor up and went to push it back through the bars then something stopped him. The razor was a weapon of last resort. He did not feel the need of it now but it would be foolish to spurn it altogether. Suicide would be less painful than execution. He understood that very clearly. One swift slice with the razor across his throat and he would bleed to death quietly in the privacy of his cell. If he slit his wrists first, he would die even more quickly. Set against the ignominy of a trial and the agony of a public hanging, suicide began to have a growing appeal.

Propped against the wall, he considered his future. It was grim.

He had been locked up for days like a common criminal with nothing to soften the wretchedness of his day. Those who were working for his release had obviously had no success and he had come to accept that perhaps he was, after all, the man who ended the life of Jeronimo Maldini. He had certainly been involved in a fight of some sort on the night in question and he did remember reaching for his dagger. How it had got into the Italian's back, he did not know. His fear was that he would go to his grave without ever learning the truth. His brother and two of his friends might believe in his innocence but they were not judge and jury in the case. Men had been hanged on less evidence than that presented against him. Henry was so dejected that he could not even entertain the vague possibility of release. What obsessed him was the image of a noose being put around his neck to strangle the life slowly and painfully out of him in front of a jeering crowd.

The razor was his only means of escape. He held it tentatively against his throat. Knowing in his heart that it was wrong, he nevertheless felt that it was necessary. His hand shook and the blade brushed gently against his skin. Henry steeled himself. Before he could discover if he had the courage to take his own life, however, he heard the sound of the key in the lock and dropped the razor into the straw. The door opened to admit his brother. Henry leapt to his feet to embrace him.

'Christopher!' he shouted. 'I thought you'd forsaken me.'

'I'd never do that, Henry,' said his visitor, lifting up the bag that he was carrying. 'I've brought you decent food and good wine. And I've bribed the prison sergeant to let you have fresh water to wash and shave.'

Henry ran a hand across his face. 'I'll not touch a razor while I'm in here,' he said, ashamed of his earlier impulse to commit suicide.

'Take a pride in your appearance. You always did in the past.'

'It's another world in here, Christopher.' He looked at the provisions. 'I thank you for these. When I tried the prison gruel, I thought they were trying to poison me.'

'I'll bring food every day from now on.'

'That means there's no chance of my release.'

'Not in the immediate future,' admitted Christopher, 'but I promise you that we are all working hard to that end.'

'We?'

'Myself, your lawyer and your friends.'

'Have you spoken with Martin Crenlowe?'

'Yes, he told me about his visit here. I called on Sir Humphrey Godden as well.'

'What about Captain Harvest?'

'I left him to Jonathan Bale.'

'What!' exclaimed Henry, pulsing with anger. 'You let that sour-faced Puritan know about my disgrace? How could you? Keep him away, Christopher. I want none of the fellow. His solemnity oppresses me.'

'Jonathan is a good friend.'

'Not to me.'

'He's also a constable with a keen eye and a good brain.'

'Yes,' said Henry bitterly, 'but he employs them both in the prevention of harmless pleasures. If he had his way, we'd all be in a state of never-ending penitence, wearing sackcloth and ashes as we shuffle our way to church. Jonathan Bale is helping *me*?' he cried in disbelief. 'He's more likely to turn public executioner for the privilege of putting a rope around my neck.'

'You do not know the man.'

'I know what he thinks of me. I see it in that ugly face of his. Nothing will convince me that that gloomy constable has my best interests at heart. He despises all that I stand for. Be honest, Christopher,' he urged. 'Does the fellow really believe in my innocence?'

'Not entirely,' said his brother.

'So what have you done? Hired him to prove my guilt?'

'No, Henry.'

'Then what?'

'I need to lean on his experience.'

'Even though loathes me?'

'Henry –'

'Why must you torment me like this?'

He burst into tears and flung himself into his brother's arms. Henry was more despondent than ever now. Hoping that some progress had been made towards securing his release, he had learned of major setbacks. Christopher waited until the sobbing had stopped before he spoke. He eased his brother gently away from him.

'The person who can help you most is yourself,' he said.

'Me?'

'Any new detail you can remember about that night may be crucial.'

'I've tried and tried,' said Henry, wiping tears away with the back of his hand. 'But my mind is a very blur. This is no place for contemplation, Christopher. It's worse than Bedlam.'

'Is there *nothing* that you can recall?'

'Nothing at all. But I must tell you this,' said Henry, grabbing him by both arms. 'It may help in my defence. Granted, I *could* have killed that posturing Italian. But I'm sure that I did not because I feel no remorse. Do you see what that means? If I'd done the deed, I'd have felt sorry afterwards, when my anger had subsided. But I feel nothing. I neither rejoice in his death nor regret it. Explain that, if you will,' he demanded, releasing Christopher. 'How can a person of high emotion like me feel nothing whatsoever?'

'No twinges of conscience?'

'None.'

'No satisfaction that a despised enemy was killed?'

'That would only come if I'd been the one lucky enough to kill him.'

Christopher was alarmed. He hoped that his brother would never have to go to trial but it was a contingency that had to be taken into account. Henry's comments might persuade him of his own innocence but they would hardly sway a jury in his favour. His last remark had made his brother blench. Uttered in the courtroom, it would suggest a heartless man with a burning hatred of the murder victim. Christopher knew that he had to mix strictness with his sympathy.

'You did not tell me the whole truth, Henry,' he chided.

'I did. I told you all.'

'Not according to Sir Humphrey Godden.'

'Does he call me a liar?'

'No,' said Christopher, 'he merely doubted that his alleged cheating at cards was enough to make you turn against Signor Maldini. Apparently, you were exposed to scorn at the fencing school.'

'I prefer to forget that shameful episode.'

'It's important, Henry.'

'Is it?'

'It provides you with a motive. Tell me what happened.'

'Must I?'

'Yes,' insisted his brother. 'If I'm to help you, I must know *every-thing*.'

'Very well,' said Henry with a sigh of reluctance. 'I was the victim of the most dreadful act of spite at that fencing school one day. It was utterly humiliating. I'm no mean swordsman, as you know. I've worked hard to master all the accomplishments of a gentleman – fencing, dancing, drinking and gambling.'

Christopher was sardonic. 'Not to mention the arts of the bedchamber.'

'I had a natural excellence in that direction.'

'What did Signor Maldini do?'

'He set me up so that he could cut me down, Christopher. He waited until the school was full then chose me for a demonstration. I was flattered at first. That illusion did not last,' he said with rancour. 'While I had a rapier, Jeronimo Maldini seemed to have a magic wand in his hand. It did whatever he wished. He slashed my sleeves open, hacked off my buttons and made me look such a blundering clown that everyone jeered at me. It was quite insupportable.'

'Why do you think he did that?'

'To prove that he was the superior swordsman.'

'That was evident before you started. Why pick on you, Henry?'

'To vent his dislike of me.'

'Was there not another reason as well?'

'Not that I know of.'

'Think again.'

'He simply wanted to shame me.'

'And we both know why,' suggested his brother. 'You talked of cheating at cards and Sir Humphrey Godden mentioned this bout at the fencing school, but there was another cause of strife between you.' He lowered his voice. 'What was her name?'

Henry was shaken. 'I've not the slightest idea of what you are talking about,' he said, trying to muster some indignation. 'This conversation has taken an unsavoury turn.'

'Who was the lady, Henry?'

'What lady?'

'The one who came between you and your fencing master.'

'There's no such person.'

'Who *was* she?'

Henry faltered. 'That's a personal matter and has no relevance here.'

'So you confess that there *was* someone?'

'Place what construction you will on my statement.'

'Then I can only believe that you actually welcome trial and conviction,' said Christopher levelly, 'for you shun what might be significant evidence in your favour. Does it not occur to you that this lady may be in a position to save your life?'

'She'd be more inclined to break my heart.'

'Is that what she did when she went off with Signor Maldini?'

'He tricked her,' yelled Henry, turning on him. 'He used every foul device he knew to woo her away from me. When he'd done that, when he'd lured her with false promises, when he'd sneaked his way into her bed and taken his evil pleasures, he cast her aside like a broken doll.' His face went blank. 'I loved her, Christopher,' he said in a hollow voice. 'I loved her as I've never loved anyone else. Yes,' he went on before his brother could interrupt, 'I know you've heard me say that before but this time it was different. It was not mere lust disguised as love. It was true passion of a kind I'd not felt before.' He bit his lip and shook his head. 'I loved her, I swear it.'

'What was her name?'

'Forget her. Please. It's all in my past.'

'But she may be able to have some influence on your future as well,' reasoned Christopher. 'She'll have intelligence about your rival that nobody else has. It may help you. And, I daresay, the lady will be overcome with regret at the way she treated you. Let me speak to her, Henry.'

'It would serve no purpose.'

'Are you afraid of what she might tell me?'

Henry sagged. 'I still care, Christopher. I want to spare her any more pain.'

'That's a laudable objective but not a very practical one. It was Captain Harvest who revealed the existence of the lady. He would not divulge her name but he'll have no choice if he's put under oath in the witness box.' Christopher put a hand on his arm. 'Who is she, Henry, and where do I find her?'

'I dare not tell you.'

'Why not?'

'Because you've always taken such a critical view of my *amours*.'

'Only when they have deserved my reproach. More often than not, you pay for your pleasures then profess to love the lady, even though her favours are for hire. I'm bound to look askance at that, Henry.'

'This time it was different.'

'Then I'm pleased for you,' said Christopher with a kind smile. 'I'm delighted that you found someone who rescued you from that dark and licentious world that you inhabit and taught you the value of true love. Who was she?'

'I'll not betray her name.'

'Captain Harvest will have no compunction in doing so.'

'Damn the fellow!'

'Let me speak to her.' His brother turned away. 'I'll be discretion itself.' Henry shook his head. 'What is holding you back?'

'Fear of your censure.'

'But I've already told you how thrilled I am that you found someone who could inspire such feelings in you. The lady must be special indeed if she could make you think of romance instead of mere conquest. Why should I be censorious?'

'Because she is married.'

'Oh,' said Christopher.

'Unhappily married to a brute of a husband,' continued Henry, anxious to justify his behaviour. 'It would have been cruel to have let her suffer his ill-treatment of her without offering some relief. I felt honour bound to go to her aid.'

'You intended to rescue her from her marriage?'

'No, from her unhappiness.'

'It sounds to me as if you might well have increased it, Henry. Think of the danger you would have put her in if her husband had discovered the truth.'

'The old fool suspected nothing.'

'How can you be so sure?'

'He was always too caught up in his own affairs.'

'I need to speak to her,' said Christopher. 'I need to speak to everyone who may be in a position to help you in some way. The lady must have cared for you.'

'She did – until that snake of an Italian took her from me.'

'Tell me her name.'

'Only if you promise not to rebuke me.'

'You have my word, Henry.'

'Then know the worst.' He hesitated for a moment as he wrestled with some inner demon. Then he braced himself. 'Her name is Patience Holcroft.'

Christopher was astounded. '*Lady* Patience Holcroft?'

'I knew that you would chide me,' protested Henry.

'It's surprise more than reproof,' said his brother. 'Her husband is a man of consequence. Sir Ralph Holcroft is a power in the land.'

'That does not entitle him to abuse his spouse. Patience only married him out of sympathy when his first wife died. He offered her all manner of inducements and swore that what he sought was companionship. Sir Ralph is thirty years her senior.'

'That gave you no right to intrude on their marriage.'

'Patience appealed for my help.'

'You were playing with fire, Henry.'

'That was part of the excitement,' said his brother wistfully. 'Surely, you understand that. Have you never cared for someone who was put beyond your reach?'

'Yes,' said Christopher, thinking of Susan Cheever, 'I confess that I have.'

'Then you'll know the wonderful thrill that danger brings, the joy of meeting in secret. Forbidden love is the highest form of pleasure.'

'I'll speak to the lady.'

'Be careful with her, Christopher. Ask her not to think badly of me.'

'From what you say, her regrets concern Signor Maldini. But do not worry. I'll impress upon her that you are completely innocent. It will be the way to win her confidence.'

Henry was agitated. 'Nobody else must know about this.'

'I'll be as close as the grave.'

'Find some way to muzzle Captain Harvest. We must not let him blurt out her name. And most of all,' he pleaded, 'do not let Father get wind of this. He has enough reasons already to disown his elder son.'

'Father would never disown you, Henry.'

'Does he know of my arrest?'

'I felt obliged to write to him.' His brother's face was contorted with pain. 'It could not be kept from him, Henry, and I wanted him to hear it from me rather than from someone else. I, at least, was able to assure him of your innocence.'

'He'll be on his way to London even now.'

'I expect that he will.'

'Help me!' implored Henry, grabbing him. 'Please keep Father away from me.'

Christopher shook his head. 'Only God could do that.'

It was some years since the Reverend Algernon Redmayne had been in the saddle. Since his elevation to the Deanery, he felt that riding a horse was beneath his dignity and only travelled by coach or, at the very least, by pony cart. None were available at short notice and the situation called for an immediate response. As soon as he read Christopher's letter, the old man confided in his bishop, was given permission to leave and, in the interests of safety, joined a party of merchants who were on their way to London. It was the fastest way to reach the capital but, as he soon discovered, it was also the most uncomfortable. Muscles that had grown slack with age now ached and burned. Buttocks that invariably had a cushion beneath them when he sat in the cathedral were bounced and bruised until he was in agony. The Dean rode on without complaint.

During their second day on the road, they paused near a stream to water the horses and stretch their legs. One of the merchants watched the old man dismount in obvious pain. He took pity on him.

'We are riding too hard for you,' he said solicitously.

'No, no,' replied the Dean. 'I can keep up.'

'Perhaps you should move at a more sedate pace. When we reach the next town, wait for travellers who are in less of a hurry to reach London.'

'I prefer your company, sir.'

'But we are men of business with a need to get there soon.'

'I, too, have my needs,' said the old man. 'And I'll not be deflected by any aches and pains. In some ways, I welcome them.'

The merchant was amazed. 'You *welcome* them?'

'Indeed, I do.'

'But you've been in distress since we left Gloucester. You can barely walk.'

'It's a judgment on me,' said the Dean, 'and I accept God's punishment gladly.'

'Why should He punish a man like you?'

'That is what I am going to London to find out. And I mean to get there, sir,' he added with fierce determination. 'Even if I have to be tied across the saddle.'

Chapter Nine

Christopher Redmayne left the prison in a daze. The visit had been a revelation. His faith in Henry's innocence had not wavered but he wished that his brother had been more honest from the start. It was disturbing to hear it confirmed that the real cause of enmity with the fencing master had been rivalry for the hand of a woman, and it was even more alarming to discover her name. Lady Patience Holcroft was a noted beauty, a young lady of good family, who had dismayed her many admirers by accepting a proposal from a most unlikely suitor. In choosing Sir Ralph Holcroft, she had married wealth and political influence, making light of the substantial difference in their years and, it had seemed, enjoying her new status in society. Christopher did not mix in the same circles as the couple but even he had heard the gossip about the crusty old politician with the radiant young wife. Envy and curiosity kept that gossip bubbling away.

That his brother was involved with the lady was deeply worrying to Christopher. He could imagine how they met, for Henry mixed with the elite of society, and he could easily understand why he conceived a passion for her. What baffled him was that Patience Holcroft took the slightest interest in him, let alone reached the stage of requiting his love. Henry had had many dalliances in the past and his brother took care to know as little about them as possible. As a rule, they followed a familiar course from infatuation to conquest, and on to bitter recrimination. It pained Christopher to admit that, in matters of the heart, his brother had the ruthlessness of a true rake, luxuriating in the chase for its own sake before casting the object of his affection carelessly aside. This had patently not been the case with Patience Holcroft. Genuine love was actually involved for once. Henry was truly committed to the lady. To have her stolen away from him must have been a harrowing experience. It was no wonder that he harboured a grudge against Jeronimo Maldini.

As he walked home, Christopher wished that the lady could have been anyone else but Lady Holcroft. Her marital situation made it impossible for him to approach her directly. The irony was that she lived in a magnificent house in Fleet Street that he would pass on his way to Fetter Lane but he could hardly present himself at her front door. If her husband were there, Christopher could find himself in an embarrassing position and, even if he were not, the servants would be so loyal to their master that they would report the visit of a man with a name that had acquired a sudden notoriety. Henry Redmayne's arrest made his brother an outcast in the eyes of those who assumed the prisoner's guilt before it was proved in court. If Henry's relationship with the wife of Sir Ralph Holcroft were to come to light, there would be a huge scandal. Christopher knew that immense tact was required.

What Henry had flatly refused to tell his brother was how he had developed the acquaintance with Lady Holcroft into something far deeper. An intermediary must have been used and secret assignations made. Where had they taken place and who had carried messages between the two lovers? It was puzzling. Christopher was reminded that Henry's courtship had been ruined by the intervention of a rival. That raised the question of how Jeronimo Maldini contrived to meet and ensnare the lady. He had none of Henry's connections yet he managed somehow to supplant him in Lady Holcroft's affections. How were their secret meetings arranged and why did the Italian tire of her? Evidently, there was a way to communicate with her somehow. Christopher had to find it.

Inevitably, his thoughts turned to Susan Cheever. The few snatched moments he had shared with her in Richmond had given him the most intense pleasure. Whatever happened to his brother, she had emphasized, would make no difference to her feelings about Christopher. It was the most heartening news he had received since the arrest. Sir Julius Cheever had turned his back on the architect, as had Brilliana Serle and her husband, but Susan's fidelity was unshaken. In order to see him, she had risen at dawn and sneaked out of the house to the stables. A grave risk had been taken on his behalf and that added a decided spice to their encounter. Henry had talked about the thrill of the forbidden. Given the fact that he had savoured that thrill himself, his brother could hardly blame him for following the dictates of his heart. Susan Cheever might not be married to a politician of high standing but she was being deliberately kept away from Christopher. There was a deep satisfaction in being able to circumvent the efforts of her family.

What he had learned at Newgate made it even more imperative to find Captain Harvest. The man was in possession of information that could spark a scandal and cause greater hardship for Henry. If he had been such a close friend of Signor Maldini, the captain would be able to tell Christopher much more about the Italian than he had so far managed to establish. The three people who had talked to him about the fencing master had painted a picture of a vain, unfeeling, duplicitous man whom they had each left in turn, yet many other people had remained as pupils at the school and its reputation was high. When he put his mind to it, Jeronimo Maldini was clearly able to retain the custom of those he instructed. Christopher hoped that Captain Harvest would be able to tell him how he did it and, in the process, add a few kinder brush strokes to the communal portrait of the dead man.

A stiff breeze made him turn up his collar and lengthen his stride. Temperatures were milder but nobody could doubt that it was winter. Though the frost had abated and the ice was cracking up on the Thames, the citizens still had enough cause to grumble about the cold. Afternoon had shaded into evening by the time that Christopher turned into Fetter Lane and a gloom had descended. It was only when a pedestrian or a rider passed close by him that he could see them properly. He cheered himself with the thought of the warm fire that Jacob would have lit. It made him quicken his pace even more. So eager was he to get back to his house that he did not see the man who was lurking in the shadows nearby. When Christopher let himself in and closed the front door behind him, the man came out of his hiding place. He stared at the house with a smouldering hatred.

Brilliana Serle's headache was a boon to Susan. After exacting as much sympathy as she could, she retired to bed and left her sister alone in the parlour with her husband. Lancelot Serle was full of concern.

'Brilliana is rather prone to headaches,' he said.

'Has she discussed it with her doctor?' asked Susan.

'Endlessly. He's prescribed a medicine that she finds too unappetising to take.'

'Medicines are not supposed to be appetising, Lancelot.'

'My wife believes that they should be. At all events,' he went on with a reassuring smile, 'Brilliana will not be indisposed for long. The headaches rarely persist.'

'That's good to hear.'

Having spent the whole day under her eye, Susan Cheever was relieved by her sister's departure. It not only gave her a sense of freedom, it enabled her to have a private conversation with her brother-in-law. Lancelot Serle was a much more intelligent man than her father ever cared to appreciate. His breeding and his politics would never commend themselves to a gruff Parliamentarian like Sir Julius, who felt that his elder daughter was throwing herself away on a worthless fool. In fact, Serle was cultured, well-informed and effortlessly polite in a way that only served to enrage his father-in-law. Though he would never be her choice for a husband, Susan was very aware of his finer qualities and he, by the same token, recognised her virtues. It enabled them to be friends.

'Father will be back in Northamptonshire by now,' she noted.

Serle pulled a face. 'I can still hear his strictures of me.'

'Take no notice, Lancelot. He's critical of everybody.'

'But he saves his real venom for me. I pretend that it does not hurt, of course, but the wounds do smart. After all this time, I'd hoped that Sir Julius would have accepted me into the family.'

'Well, I do,' said Susan. 'Without complaint.'

'Thank you.'

'I did not believe that anyone could make Brilliana happy. Yet you've done so.'

'It does require hard work,' he confided, 'and considerable patience.'

'You have that in abundance.'

'And so do you, Susan,' he complimented. 'I marvel at the way you handle Sir Julius. It's astonishing. I could never do it. I must confess that he frightens me.'

'Father still has too much of the soldier in him.'

'I agree. His tongue is a deadly weapon.'

'He's fighting battles that were over long ago.'

'Nobody seems to have told him that we are ruled by a King once again.'

'Oh, he's been told many times, Lancelot, but he refuses to believe it.' They shared a laugh. Susan began to probe. 'We are having visitors tomorrow, then?'

'Yes,' he replied. 'Eight in all.'

'Anyone I might know?'

'I doubt it, Susan. Though your sister is anxious that you should meet one of them and I'm equally keen that he should meet you.'

'Why?'

'Because I think that you'll get on splendidly.'

'Who is the gentleman?'

'Jack Cardinal. He's as decent a fellow as you could imagine. His father died a few years ago and he's devoted himself to looking after his ailing mother. Their estate is four or five miles away. Jack is so modest by nature. You'd never guess that he's the best shot in the county or that he can handle a sword as if he were born with it in his hand.'

'What age is Mr Cardinal?'

'A little above my own. Brilliana thinks him more handsome than me.'

'How can she be so disloyal?'

'It was only said to taunt me,' he explained with an uxorious smile. 'But she does admire Jack. What mystifies her – and me, for that matter – is why the fellow has never married. It's noble of him to put his mother first but he deserves rather more out of life.'

Susan frowned. 'I can see why Brilliana wants to dangle me in front of him.'

'Oh, you'll take to Jack Cardinal and he'll certainly adore you.'

'I do not think that I want to be adored, Lancelot.'

'Every woman wants that.'

'Only if the adoration comes from the right source,' she replied with a slight edge in her voice. 'The truth is – and I made this plain to Brilliana – that I'm not in the market for a husband.'

Serle grinned proudly. 'Neither was your sister until she met me.'

Susan did not wish to disillusion him. Unbeknown to Serle, his wife had two broken engagements in her past and there had been a bevy of proposals that she had turned down. From an early age, Brilliana had dedicated herself to finding the right husband and her sister had watched the various suitors come and go with depressing regularity. One of the reasons why Susan had been so unwilling to encourage the attentions of any young men in the area was the likelihood that they already been tested, found wanting, then rejected, by her sister. Out of kindness to her brother-in-

121

law, Susan resolved to conceal the details of Brilliana's previous entanglements.

'We thought that you and Jack would have so much in common,' said Serle.

'In common?'

'You look after a difficult father while he takes care of a sick mother.'

'You are surely not suggesting that we marry the two of them off?' she said waspishly. 'Much as I love Father, I'd not undertake the role of matchmaker for him. I don't think the wife exists who could endure his bad temper and his idiosyncrasies. Mr Cardinal's ailing mother would be the last person to tempt him.'

'Stop these jests,' he chided with a laugh. 'What I meant – as you well know, Susan – was that you and Jack Cardinal have similar interests.'

'I doubt that. I've never fired a gun and have no skill at fencing.'

'But you like books, do you not?'

'So?'

'Jack is also prodigious reader.'

'What does he read?' she asked. 'Books about firearms or manuals on the finer points of swordsmanship?' She fixed him with a stare. 'Answer me this, Lancelot. Does this friend of yours know why he's been invited here?'

'No, Susan. I merely requested the pleasure of his company.'

'Mr Cardinal is not coming to look me over like a prize heifer, then?'

'Heaven forbid!' he exclaimed. 'That's a monstrous notion! If Jack thought that he was being asked to do such a thing, he'd refuse to come anywhere near Serle Court.

'That's a relief.'

'Apart from anything else, he's a rather shy man.'

'It's difficult to be shy with a gun in your hand.'

'That's how he expresses himself, don't you see? By means of his sporting prowess, for he's a wonderful horseman as well. But it's with a rapier in his hand that he's really at his best. Egerton discovered that.'

'Egerton?'

'Egerton Whitcombe. The son of Lady Whitcombe.'

Susan sat up with interest. 'Lady Whitcombe, who lives in Sheen?'

'The same. Have you met her?'

'No, but I've heard of her,' she said, remembering that Christopher Redmayne had been engaged to design a house for the lady. 'What sort of person is she?'

'Very grand. Her late husband was a member of the Privy Council.'

'And is Lady Whitcombe among the guests you've invited?'

'Dear me, no!' he said. 'We are not on visiting terms.'

'You mentioned a son named Egerton.'

'Yes, Susan. He's a surly young man, with little respect for others. There's the essential difference between them. Jack Cardinal is a sterling fellow, who puts his mother first at all times. Egerton Whitcombe is a wastrel, who deserts his family whenever he can. I gather that he's in France at the moment. The pity of it is,' he sighed, 'that Lady Whitcombe indulges him ridiculously. She seems quite blind to his faults.'

'What's the connection between her son and Mr Cardinal?'

'Why, the duel, of course.'

'Duel?' she said. 'They *fought* each other?'

'Only in the spirit of competition,' he told her. 'There was no animus involved. At least, there was none on Jack's side. He only consented to a bout because Egerton pestered him so much. Jack Cardinal has a reputation in the locality, you see.'

'What happened?'

'Egerton Whitcombe thought that he could damage that reputation. In fairness, he's a fine swordsman in his own right and he'd been taking lessons from a fencing master in London to sharpen his skills. He felt that he was ready to topple Jack.'

'And was he?'

'Not from what I heard, Susan. They were well-matched at first, it seems, and Egerton did not disgrace himself but Jack was too quick and guileful for him. He vanquished yet another challenger, leaving his reputation untarnished.'

'I see.'

'Egerton took the defeat badly but that was only to be expected. No,' he went on, 'Lady Whitcombe and her family are not in our circle. Quite candidly, we are relieved.'

'Relieved?'

Egerton Whitcombe is no gentleman. He's brash, boastful and

ungracious. He's certainly not fit company for you, Susan. Put him out of your mind,' he advised. 'He's one suitor that Brilliana would never inflict on her sister.'

A choppy sea and a biting wind had made the crossing from Calais particularly unpleasant. When he disembarked at Dover, the young man was in a foul mood. He adjourned to the nearest inn, hired a room and sent for a flagon of wine. When the satchel containing writing materials was brought in, he dashed off a letter to his mother to inform her that he would be in London the next day. His servant came up the steps, struggling with the last of the baggage. Egerton Whitcombe thrust the letter at him.

'This must reach my mother as soon as possible,' he ordered.

Jonathan Bale was not looking forward to talking to either of the other witnesses but he had given his word. Accordingly, he called on Martin Crenlowe that evening as the goldsmith was about to close up his shop. When he heard why Jonathan had come, he invited him reluctantly into the building and took him to his private office. Crenlowe was civil rather than welcoming.

'I'll not be able to give you much time, Mr Bale,' he said. 'I'm expected at home.'

'Then I'll be brief, sir. You are a friend of Henry Redmayne.'

'And proud to be so.'

'Do you believe him to be innocent of this crime?'

'Yes, I do.'

'On what evidence?'

'My knowledge of the man.'

'You heard him threaten the murder victim. His dagger was in the man's back.'

'I refuse to believe that Henry put it there,' said Crenlowe. 'It's no secret that he and Signor Maldini fell out – I had no time for the fellow myself – but that does mean he was driven to murder. You see, Henry Redmayne is temperamental.'

'I've met the gentleman, sir.'

'Then you know that he's a creature of moods. Older friends like myself and Sir Humphrey Godden are accustomed to his ways. Others are not. That's why Henry tends to lose as many acquaintances as he makes. He is *always* parting with someone or other.

124

Goodness!' he said with a throaty chuckle, 'If Henry killed every man with whom he had a quarrel then you'd need to build a new cemetery to hold them all.'

'One death alone concerns me, Mr Crenlowe.'

'I understand that.'

'Then perhaps you'll tell me what happened on the night in question.'

'I've already given a sworn statement,' said Crenlowe with impatience, 'and spoken to Henry's brother on the subject. Do I really need to go through it all again?'

'There might be some tiny details that you missed earlier.'

'I doubt that. I have an excellent memory.'

'Yet you had been drinking that night, sir.'

'I can hold my wine, have no qualms on that score.'

Jonathan waited. The goldsmith was not as friendly as he had been led to suppose. He could understand why. Martin Crenlowe could be open with Christopher Redmayne because he part of his brother's circle and because he felt that he and the architect were on the same social footing. A lowly constable was a different matter, especially when he exuded such obvious disapproval. Crenlowe ran a searching eye over him.

'You've come to the wrong place, Mr Bale,' he said quietly. 'If you look for evidence that will help to hang a dear friend of mine, you are wasting your time here.'

'All that I seek is the truth, sir.'

'I sense that you've already made up your mind.'

'Change it for me,' invited Jonathan, folding his arms.

'Very well,' said Crenlowe after a long pause. 'I'll try.'

His narrative was short but lucid. He described the quarrel that had flared up between Henry Redmayne and the fencing master, then talked about the meal that four of them had shared at the Elephant. He explained how they had each gone off in a different direction. Jonathan was motionless throughout.

'When did you next see Henry Redmayne?' he asked.

'Not for some days.'

'Did he make any mention of that evening you all spent together?'

'None, Mr Bale.'

'So the name of Signor Maldini never came into the conversation?'

'Why should it?'

'The gentleman must have been missed by then.'

'Only by his friends and we did not count ourselves in that number.'

'Captain Harvest did.'

'James is a law unto himself.'

'Did he not tell either of you that Signor Maldini had disappeared?'

'No, we never saw him. James is not part of our inner circle. Besides, he comes and goes to suit himself. Sometimes, we do not catch sight of him for weeks on end.'

'I spoke to Captain Harvest.'

'Then you'll have some idea of his character.'

'Robust and forthright.'

'A little too hearty for my taste but he can be amusing company.'

'He insists that Mr Redmayne was the killer.'

'He would. He never liked Henry.'

'Captain Harvest is the only person I've met who mourns his friend.'

'Do not expect us to shed tears for him,' said Crenlowe sharply. 'Jeronimo Maldini was a snake in human guise. He got close to people in order to strike at their weak points. He upset me, he insulted Sir Humphrey and he outraged poor Henry.'

'Why did the three of you go to him in the first place?'

'Because of his reputation. He was a brilliant swordsman.'

'With a rapier?'

'With any weapon that man could devise. I've seen him use broadsword, rapier, Toledo, spontoon and backsword with equal proficiency.'

'What of Mr Redmayne? How proficient was he?'

'Henry was the best of the three of us, no question of that. We live in a dangerous city, Mr Bale, as you well know. Wise men learn how defend themselves. Henry was more than capable with sword and dagger.'

'Dagger?' said Jonathan pointedly.

'I was speaking about practice bouts at the fencing school.'

'But he knew how to use the weapon?'

'We all do, Mr Bale.'

'Not as well as Henry Redmayne, it seems.'

Crenlowe angered. 'I can see that you've not been listening to me,' he said with asperity. 'You claim to seek the truth but your mind remains obstinately closed to it. No more of it, sir. I resent the time you've taken up and I must ask you to leave.'

'There's one more question I have to put.'

'Good day to you, Mr Bale.'

'If Mr Redmayne is innocent, then someone else must be guilty of the crime.'

'So?'

'Is it conceivable that the killer could be Captain Harvest?'

Crenlowe was taken aback. He was obviously surprised by the suggestion and needed some time to assess its value. Jonathan could see his brain working away. The goldsmith was uncertain at first but the expression on his face slowly changed.

'Yes,' he concluded. 'I suppose that it is.'

Captain Harvest had a gift for being at ease in any surroundings. Whether mixing with aristocracy or consorting with the lower orders, he felt completely at home. He was also quick to make new friends, mastering their names with disarming speed and finding a way to be on familiar terms without causing the slightest offence. The three men with whom he was playing cards had been total strangers to him an hour earlier but Harvest chatted to them as if had known them for years. They sat around a table in the corner of the tavern, drinking beer and using a large candle to illumine their game. The Hope and Anchor was not the most salubrious inn along the riverbank. In the main, it catered for sailors, watermen, lighter-men and others who earned their living from the Thames. The atmosphere was rowdy, the air charged with pipe tobacco. Wagers were only small but they mounted up as the evening progressed. Hitting a rich vein of luck, Harvest scooped the winnings time and again but he was generous with his gains. The beer that he bought for his companions kept them at the table to lose even more to him. Eventually, their purses could withstand no more assaults by the soldier and so they peeled away. Their place at the table was imme-diately taken by someone else.

'Captain Harvest, I believe,' said Christopher Redmayne.

'At your service, sir,' replied the other. 'How did you know my name?'

'You are not difficult to recognise.'

Harvest peered at him. 'Nor are you, my friend, unless I'm deceived. I see a distinct family likeness to a certain gentleman who is at present domiciled in Newgate prison. Am I right, Mr Redmayne?'

'You are, indeed. I'm Henry's brother, Christopher.'

'Then you've obviously not come to play cards with me.'

'I've been warned against that.'

'Rightly so,' said Harvest with a chuckle. 'Well, sir, I can guess why you are looking for me. I'm also mightily impressed that you found me. For a whole host of reasons, I like to cover my tracks.'

'Jonathan Bale discovered that.'

'Ah, yes. The earnest constable.'

'He gave me a list of your haunts. One led on to another.'

'You've been a veritable bloodhound, Mr Redmayne.'

'Mr Bale told me that I would have to be,' said Christopher, realising how exact his friend's description of the captain had been. 'He spoke with your landlord today. It seems that you quit your lodgings and forgot to pay your rent.'

'That oversight will soon be repaired,' promised Harvest, tapping his purse. 'One good day with pack of cards can make all the difference.' He moved the candle nearer to Christopher so that it lit up his face. 'Yes, there's a definite likeness but it's not strong. You look so much healthier than your brother. Henry boasted about you from time to time. An architect, I hear.'

'True.'

'An honourable profession. Unlike the one that your brother follows.'

'He does valuable work at the Navy Office.'

'On the rare occasions when he actually goes there. It's no wonder that the Dutch surprised us in the Medway if the fate of our navy is in the hands of people like Henry Redmayne.' He gave a snort of disgust. 'Thank Heaven that we have an army!'

'You fought against the Dutch?'

'That's how I earned my commission.'

'Then I'm surprised you do not choose a tavern frequented by soldiers,' said Christopher, glancing round. 'If you have such a low opinion of the navy, why do you come to the Hope and Anchor?'

'I told you, Mr Redmayne. I like to cover my tracks.'

'Are you hiding from someone?'

'Only my creditors.'

'Mr Bale tells me that you are denouncing my brother at every opportunity.'

'It's my bounden duty to expose him for the brutal killer that he is.'

'Did you witness the murder, Captain Harvest?'

'Not with my own eyes.'

'Then how can you be so certain that my brother is the culprit?'

'Call it a soldier's instinct.'

'I'd prefer to call it an unfair and over-hasty judgement.'

'Henry left that tavern with one thing on his mind, Mr Redmayne. I know when a man is about to kill. He'd spent the whole evening working himself up to it.'

'Yet you did nothing to stop him?'

Harvest spread his arms. 'What could I do?'

'Prevail upon him to see sense,' said Christopher. 'Made sure that he went home afterwards or, at the very least, stayed with him to calm him down.'

'Calm him down? He was well beyond that. Besides, I had somewhere else to go.'

'Signor Maldini was your friend. Did you not try to warn him?'

'Of what?'

'My brother's intentions.'

'It was Henry that I warned. Even when he was sober, he was no match for Jeronimo. What chance did he stand against him when he was drunk?'

'In other words, you let my brother go in the belief that he would be the one to suffer in any duel. You've a strange idea of friendship,' said Christopher with sudden passion. 'You sup with my brother yet you do nothing to prevent him from engaging in a brawl that could well lead to his death.'

'Henry was never a real friend.'

'So you deliberately sent him off after Signor Maldini?'

'It was no concern of mine. I had somewhere else to go.'

Christopher was scornful. 'Yes, Captain Harvest. I'm sure that you did. No doubt you had to cover your tracks.'

'You are beginning to annoy me, sir,' said the other, bristling.

'Then I have something in common with my brother, after all.'

'Rather too much, for my liking.'

'Why did you despise him so much?'

'Henry?' said the other, playing with his beard. 'Chiefly, because of the way that he treated other people. He was cold and patronising. I've learned to love my fellow men. Henry loathed them, unless they could carouse with him through the night. Look at those closest to him,' he sneered. 'Martin Crenlowe and Sir Humphrey Godden, each as supercilious as the other. What right had they to look down on Jeronimo Maldini? Yet they treated him like dirt. Sir Humphrey was the worst. He hates foreigners. He was happy enough to take lessons from Jeronimo because he thought he might learn something, even though he believed that, as an Italian, the man was beneath contempt.'

Christopher nodded. 'I've heard Sir Humphrey's views on foreigners.'

'Martin Crenlowe shares them.'

'I found him the more amenable of the two.'

'Neither of them would earn my admiration.'

'Yet you were ready to spend time with them and with my brother.'

Harvest gave an elaborate shrug. 'One has to eat.'

'Who paid for your meal that evening, Captain Harvest?'

'What does it matter,' said the other with a wolfish grin, 'as long as I did not have the inconvenience of doing it myself?'

The man was shameless. Christopher could see how he had ingratiated himself with Henry and the others. Captain Harvest had a devil-may-care charm that would have had a surface appeal to men bent on pleasure. The soldier was urbane and quick-witted. Most of those whose friendship he courted would not even realise that he was an amiable parasite. Yet he was loyal to the people he really cared about. Christopher felt obliged to approve of that.

'Tell me about Signor Maldini,' he said.

'Why?'

'Because nobody else had a good word to say for him.'

'Then you've been talking to the wrong people,' said Harvest. 'Most of his pupils at the fencing school worshipped him. Jeronimo was supreme at his trade.'

'Is that why you liked him?'

'No, Mr Redmayne. It was because I sensed that we were two of a kind, men who had not been blessed at birth and who therefore had to make their own way in the world. I know what it is to live in a foreign country where most people turn instinctively away from you. That's what it was like for Jeronimo at first,' he said. 'But he worked hard to master the language and soon began to win people over.'

'Some people.'

'Your brother and his friends were always beyond his reach.'

'He loaned you money, I understand.'

'He did more than that,' replied Harvest. 'He gave it to me out of love.'

'Could he afford to be so generous?'

'He ran the most popular fencing school in the city, Mr Redmayne. That's why he employed me as his assistant. There were too many pupils. Jeronimo was never short of funds, in spite of his weakness.'

'Weakness?'

'He was an Italian. He adored women.'

'I gathered that.'

'Romance costs money,' said Harvest, 'and he had many romances.'

'There's only one that interests me. According to my brother, a certain lady was the real cause of the rift between him and his fencing master.'

'You do not need to tell me that.'

'What did Signor Maldini do?'

'He took pity on her, Mr Redmayne. He rescued her from Henry's clutches.'

'That's not how my brother describes the situation.'

Harvest laughed aloud. 'You surprise me!'

'Did your friend confide in you?'

'Only up to a point. He was very discreet where ladies were concerned. But this case was slightly different.'

'Why?'

'There was an element of revenge,' explained the soldier. 'Jeronimo felt that your brother had slighted him. What better way to get his own back? He could sport with the lady and enrage Henry at the same time.'

'It was no true romance, then?'

'Only for her.'

'And who might she be?'

'Your brother will tell you that, Mr Redmayne.'

'He prefers to protect the lady's reputation.'

'He'd have done that best by leaving her well alone for she was married.'

'That did not seem to hinder Signor Maldini.'

'Jeronimo is like me,' said Harvest, reaching for his tankard. 'He takes his pleasures where he finds them. That's what I meant when I said we were kindred spirits,' he went on, downing his beer in one gulp. 'We are both soldiers of fortune.'

'You did not give me the lady's name,' pressed Christopher.

'Why are you so eager to learn it?'

'So that I can tax my brother with it.'

'I would have thought he has enough troubles, as it is. Why remind him of a lady who was snatched away from beneath him? It would only torment him.'

'You are doing that by spreading lies about him, Captain Harvest.'

'Take care, sir,' warned the other, sitting up. 'I'll brook no insults.'

'You are quick enough to hand them out.'

'I speak as I find.'

'Was Signor Maldini as hot-blooded as you? Is that why you liked him?'

'We understood each other, Mr Redmayne.'

'You both preyed on innocent women, you mean?'

Harvest beamed. 'Jeronimo's conquests were not innocent,' he said. 'Far from it. He had a preference for married women and they for him. Take the lady whom your brother was sniffing after. She deliberately cuckolded her husband.'

'Why?'

'Because Jeronimo wooed and won her. He was a very handsome man.'

'And a vengeful one, too. He made sure that my brother knew about it.'

'I applauded that.'

'What happened to the lady afterwards?'

'Who knows?' asked Harvest with a shrug. 'Who cares? Such dalliances come to a natural end. Jeronimo simply walked away and never looked back.'

'But she must surely have loved him to take such a risk.'

'She was obsessed with him.'

'Then it would be a kindness to let her know of his fate,' said Christopher. 'If she was truly enamoured of him, it's only fair to let her mourn him.'

'That thought never struck me,' he admitted, 'but you are right.'

'Tell me the lady's name and I'll apprise her discreetly of the facts.'

'I'd do that myself, if I could.'

'What prevents you?'

'Jeronimo never told me who she was, Mr Redmayne. Only *what* she was.'

Christopher was relieved. After only a minute in the company of Captain Harvest, he knew that he could never gag the man. If he were asked in court what was the source of discord between the prisoner and the fencing master, Harvest would not lie. He would disclose a possible motive for murder. But he would not be in a position to create additional scandal by naming the lady in question. It was compensation for the effort that Christopher had put into finding the man that evening.

Captain Harvest got to his feet. When Christopher rose, he saw for the first time how brawny the man was. The soldier glared at him with a mixture of hostility and amusement.

'Go your way, sir. I'll not help your brother to escape the gallows.'

'You still think him guilty?'

'Yes, Mr Redmayne. Guilty of murdering a good friend of mine.'

'Yet when he left you in Fenchurch Street, my brother could barely stand.'

'He was not too drunk to stab a man in the back.'

'Perhaps not,' said Christopher, 'but I very much doubt if he could then carry a dead body to the river and have the presence of mind to throw it in.'

'I agree with you.'

'Then why do you still name him as the killer?'

'Have you not worked it out yet?' taunted Harvest. 'Henry had an accomplice.'

Chapter Ten

Jonathan Bale rarely discussed his work as a constable with his wife. Most of it was too tedious even to talk about and he sought to protect her from the more gory aspects of his occupation. His children always pressed him for details of terrible crimes but he refused to satisfy their ghoulish interest. It was his belief that a home should be a place for quiet, pleasant, restorative family life, safe from the horrors that stalked the streets of London. This time, however, it was different. His younger son had actually been the person to discover a murder victim so it was impossible to say nothing about the investigation when he stepped into the house. Both boys were eager to know when the killer would be tried and hanged. Richard, in particular, was agog for any news.

Their day began with family prayers. It was followed by a breakfast of bread, whey and the remains of a meat pie that Sarah Bale had baked the previous afternoon. When the meal was over, she took her sons off to their petty school nearby. On her return, she found Jonathan still in his seat. He was brooding darkly.

'I wonder if they should have gone this morning,' she observed.

'They must learn to read and write, Sarah.'

'I know that but I worry about Richard. He has no chance to forget what he saw at the frost fair. No sooner does he get to the school than the other children ask him to tell his tale once more. It keeps it fresh in his mind.'

'We must hope that the whole business is soon over.'

She saw his furrowed brow. 'This case is troubling you badly.'

'No more than any other,' he said, trying to make light of it. 'I've been a constable for too many years to let the work distress me.'

'You do not fool me, Jonathan Bale. You hardly slept a wink last night.'

'How do you know?'

'How do you *think* I know?' she said, kissing the top of his head. 'Something is keeping you awake and it's not difficult to guess what it is. You are worried.'

'I'm confused, Sarah.'

'Why?'

'I find it hard to explain.'

'Did it make you feel better when you went to see Mr Redmayne?'

'In one way.'

'And what was that?'

'I let him see that I was concerned for him,' he explained. 'I know what a shock it can be to someone when a member of the family is arrested for a serious crime. They are dazed by it. Mr Redmayne was grateful. I was pleased about that.' He glanced up at her. 'But the truth is that he thinks that his brother is innocent and I do not. It makes me feel so uneasy, Sarah. He asks me for my help yet I'm trying to find evidence to convict Henry Redmayne.'

'And is he guilty?'

'I think so.'

'Think? You were almost certain at first.'

'The case is not as straightforward as I imagined.'

'Then they could have arrested the wrong person?'

'No,' he said firmly. 'He's all but confessed to his brother.'

'Then why does Mr Redmayne fight to clear his name?'

'It's what anyone would do in his position, Sarah. I do not blame him for that.'

'Was he hurt because you did not support him?'

'Deeply,' said Jonathan with a sigh. 'I think that he was counting on me.'

'Are you still friends?'

'I hope so.'

'What if his brother *is* convicted?'

'That's what troubles me most, Sarah. I'd hate to lose Mr Redmayne's friendship but there may be no way to stop that happening. He turned to me and I let him down. I feel that it's a kind of betrayal.'

'You could never betray anyone.'

'Then why does my conscience keep me awake at night?'

'Only you know that, Jonathan.'

She put an affectionate arm around his shoulders. Sarah was very concerned. Ordinarily, her husband was a strong, reliable, phlegmatic man who remained cool in any crisis. She knew that his work as a constable must have confronted him with serious dangers and hideous sights, yet he took them all in his stride without the slightest murmur of complaint. For once, however, he was unable to hide his suffering. Sarah cast around for a way to ease his pain

'How often have you met Mr Redmayne's brother?' she asked.

'Often enough.'

'You do not like the man, do you?'

'I do not approve of any person who lives that kind of life.'

'What do you mean?'

'He's proud, selfish and given to the pursuit of pleasure.'

'Then he's not like his brother at all.'

'No, Sarah,' he replied. 'He's an embarrassment to Mr Redmayne, even more so now. I think that he's sainted the way that he's standing by him. It must be galling for him to see his brother locked away in prison.'

'It must be even more galling for his brother.'

'A man has to pay for his crime.'

'But he's not been convicted yet,' she argued. 'Have you spoken to him?'

'Why should I do that?'

'Well, it might give you a better idea if he's guilty or not.'

'Henry Redmayne has no wish to talk to me, Sarah.'

'How can he prevent you? As an officer of the law, you have a right to see him.'

'He's already been questioned.'

'But not by you,' she pointed out. 'You have to act on the opinion of others. It's unlike you not to question him, Jonathan. You prefer to dig around for yourself.'

'That's unnecessary in this case.'

'When a man's life is at stake? I'd have thought it very necessary.'

'Sarah —'

'Think how grateful Mr Redmayne would be.'

He was checked. 'What?'

'It would show that you were trying to hear both sides.'

Jonathan became pensive. He was irritated that his wife was arguing with him but honest enough to admit that she was making an important point. In accepting the probability of Henry Redmayne's guilt, he had denied the man the right to defend himself and left contact with the prisoner to his brother. He recalled that Martin Crenlowe had also visited Newgate to offer succour to his friend.

Yet Jonathan had deliberately kept away from the prison. He sought to justify his decision.

'It would be a waste of time, Sarah.'

'Why?'

'Henry Redmayne dislikes me. He'd never let me near him.'

'Things may have changed since he's been in there. You've often told me how glad prisoners are to have any visitors. It means that someone is thinking about them.'

'I'd not be there as a visitor. He'd see me as an enemy.'

'Even though he knows you are a friend of his brother?'

'Mr Redmayne might not wish me to go.'

'Have you asked him?'

'No, Sarah.'

'Then why not do so? He might even want the two of you to go together.'

'That would be different,' he conceded.

'He'll not refuse the offer. Besides,' she went on, 'you are much more used to visiting a prison than he is. You've been to Newgate dozens of times. You know some of the turnkeys there. Talk to them about Mr Redmayne's brother.'

Jonathan hesitated. His wife's advice was sound yet he found it difficult to accept. He was afraid that he would be spurned by Henry Redmayne and that his visit would simply widen the rift between him and the prisoner's brother. On the other hand, he knew the value of studying a man who was behind bars. The way that a suspect bore himself in custody could give a strong indication of his guilt or innocence. A word with the turnkeys who looked after Henry Redmayne might be profitable. It was worth trying. After making his decision, Jonathan stood up and wrapped his arms gratefully around his wife.

'Where would I be with you to counsel me, Sarah?'

'I do not do it for your benefit,' she said with a smile, 'but for my own. If you stay awake at night, then so do I. And we both need our sleep.'

Exhaustion had finally got the better of Henry Redmayne. His body had been drained of all its powers of resistance. Even the pervading stench and nocturnal pandemonium of Newgate could not keep him awake. He lay on the straw and went off into oblivion. It was only when the turnkey shook him hard next morning that he opened his eyes.

'Wake up, sir!' grunted the man. 'You've a visitor.'

Henry was bewildered. 'Where am I?' he asked, looking around.

'Where you belong – in Newgate.'

'I'm in *prison*?'

The realisation brought him fully awake and he sat up to wipe the sleep from his eyes. When the turnkey left the cell, Christopher stepped into it and the door was locked behind him. He was carrying a pile of clothing over his arm.

'Good morning, Henry,' he said.

'Is it morning? I've no sense of time in here.'

'Do you not hear the bells chiming the hour?'

'All I can here is the pounding of my own heart, Christopher.' He stared at the suit that his brother had brought. 'What do you have there?'

'A change of apparel.'

'I need none.'

'Those things are filthy,' said Christopher. 'You must take them off.'

'There's no call for fashion in here.'

'But there is a call for self-respect. That's one of my favourite tenets. Come, now. You'll feel much better when you look something like your old self.'

'I never expect to do that again,' moaned Henry.

'We'll see. The turnkey will be back soon with warm water and a razor. Since you did not shave yesterday, I'll be your barber today. I've also turned valet. That's why I called at your house on the way here to pick up this fresh attire.'

'I'll not wear it.'

'Would you let Father see you in that state?'

Henry quailed. The thought of meeting his father at all was unnerving. To receive him in a prison cell when he was soiled and unkempt would be to give the old man additional reasons for outrage and condemnation. A shaven chin and a smart suit would at least offer Henry a slight degree of protection. It would also remind him of whom he was. He thanked Christopher for his thoughtfulness then bent down to retrieve something from the straw.

'You'll not need a razor,' he said. 'I have one here.'

'Where did that come from?'

'A friendly hand dropped it through the bars to help me escape.'

'Escape?' said Christopher with alarm. 'You surely did not think that you could kill the turnkey and get out of here. That's madness, Henry.'

'There's a simpler means of escape.'

He pretended to slit his throat with the razor. Christopher was so appalled that he dropped the clothing on the straw and snatched the razor from him. Slipping it into his pocket, he grabbed his brother by the shoulders.

'I do not believe that you even contemplated such a thing,' he said.

'It seemed the only way out.'

'Of what?'

'This unbearable misery, Christopher.'

'But that will not last forever.'

'No,' said Henry mournfully. 'It will end on the gallows when I dance on fresh air to amuse the crowd. I did not think that I could face that.'

'You'll not have to, Henry. Your case may not even come to trial.'

'I feel that it already has. That's why the razor had a gruesome appeal for me.'

'Then I'll make sure it's not left in the cell,' affirmed Christopher, 'and I'll speak to the prison sergeant. He needs to know that someone is encouraging one of his charges to commit suicide. Has it really come to *this*?' he asked, shaking his brother vigorously. 'Taking your own life is an unpardonable sin, Henry. It's a crime against God and an act of cruelty against those who love you. How could you even think about it?'

'I was desperate.'

'Then pray for deliverance.'

'There's no hope of that, Christopher.'

'Yes, there is,' rejoined the other. 'You are innocent of the charge against you.'

Henry was bemused. 'Am I?'

'When the real killer is apprehended, they'll have to release you.'

'When will that be?'

'Soon, I trust. Very soon.'

'But not before Father reaches London.'

'Perhaps not.'

'Do not tell him about the razor,' begged Henry. 'Spare me that.'

'I'd not dare tell him,' said Christopher, 'for I know how hurt he'd be. Father is on his way here in order to comfort you, Henry. How do you think he would feel if he learned that you had committed suicide? He'd be utterly destroyed. He'd see it, as everyone else would see it, as an admission of guilt.'

'But I *may* be guilty. That's what torments me.'

'You were guilty of drinking too much and losing your temper. Nothing more than that. Bad behaviour is not a crime. You were foolish but you are no killer.'

'Yet I wanted that villain dead. I own that freely.'

The door was unlocked and the turnkey handed Christopher a razor and a bowl of warm water. Christopher thanked him then the door was shut again. He looked at Henry with a sympathy that was tempered with disgust. At least, he told himself, his brother had confessed to the thoughts of suicide. That was a positive sign. But it did not take away his sense of shock. The razor suddenly felt hot in his hand.

'I'd never have done it,' Henry assured him. 'I was not brave enough.'

'A brave man would never even have considered it.'

'I'm sorry, Christopher.'

'Sit down under the window so that I can see to shave you.'

Henry was contrite. He put the stool where it would catch the best of the light then lowered himself on to it. Christopher had never shaved anyone else before, and these were hardly the ideal conditions in which to try it, but he did his best. After using the water to wash the grime from his brother's face, he plied the razor with great care.

'I've brought more food as well,' he said. 'I left it with the prison sergeant.'

'You are very kind to me, Christopher.'

'Kinder than you are to yourself, it seems.'

'I had a moment of weakness.'

'Your life is a succession of them,' said Christopher harshly. 'This is by far the worst. I thank God that you stayed your hand. Now, hold still,' he ordered as Henry moved his head. 'You may wish to cut your throat but I do not.'

When his beard had been slowly scraped away, Henry felt considerably better. He stripped off his dirty clothing and put on the clean apparel. Christopher had been right. His brother looked something like his old self and that instilled a new confidence in him. Henry told himself that was no longer a condemned man in grubby attire. He was the victim of a dreadful error.

'Thank you, Christopher,' he said, embracing him warmly.

'You thank me best by *believing* in yourself.'

'I will, I will.'

'Then let's have no more moments of weakness.'

'I give you my word.' Henry became afraid. 'When shall I expect Father?'

'That depends on how fast he travels from Gloucester,' said Christopher, folding up his brother's discarded clothing. 'The most he could manage in a day is thirty miles and only that if the roads are clear.'

'I thought he'd come down from heaven like a bolt of lightning.'

'You've already been struck by that.'

'Too true, brother!'

'Father will bring you more solace than stricture.'

'They are one and the same thing to him,' said Henry with a shiver. 'Father always travels with a pulpit.' He thought of his tattered reputation. 'What do they say about me, Christopher? How am I proclaimed in the city?'

'I do not listen to any hostile comment.'

'My enemies must be dancing with delight at my predicament.'

'Think only of your friends,' advised Christopher. 'They do not doubt you. I've spoken with Martin Crenlowe and with Sir Humphrey Godden. Both of them swear that you could never have committed this crime.'

'Martin was good enough to visit me.'

'Do not rely on the same consideration from Sir Humphrey. Though he supports you to the hilt, he is too full of his own affairs to come and see you. I had the impression that he was a fastidious man who'd never dare to let the stink of prison enter his nostrils.'

'Sir Humphrey has a fondness for perfumes and powders.'

'And an even greater fondness for himself.'

'He's good company when you get to know him properly, Christopher. Sir Humphrey Godden is cheerful, amusing and generous to a fault. I've lost count of the number of times his purse has bailed me out.'

'He loaned money to Captain Harvest as well, I believe.'

'Most people in London have done that,' said Henry with a cynical smile. 'A few of them have even had it repaid. James is a worthless hanger-on. This business has shown him in a true light.'

'He's the only one of the three who's turned against you.'

'Good riddance to him!'

'Sir Humphrey seemed to think him a likeable rogue,' said Christopher. 'Having met the captain myself, I saw a more sinister streak in him. Of the four of you who shared a meal that night, Captain Harvest was the most likely back-stabber.'

Henry was astonished. 'Do you believe that *he* killed Jeronimo Maldini?'

'Someone did, Henry, and it was not you.'

'But James and the Italian were on friendly terms.'

'How reliable is Captain Harvest's friendship? You've seen how quickly he's turned against you. Martin Crenlowe and Sir Humphrey were both disgusted by that.'

'No,' said Henry. 'I refuse to accept that James was involved. He had somewhere else to go that night. I watched him stride off down Fenchurch Street. Martin, too. He was eager to go home to his wife.'

'What of Sir Humphrey? Does he have a wife?'

'Oh, yes. And a comely creature she is.'

'Why did you not travel in his coach when he went back to Covent Garden that night?' wondered Christopher. 'His house is not far from Bedford Street and I understand that he offered you a lift. Why turn him down?'

'Because he was not going back home,' said Henry. 'Sir Humphrey wanted us to go elsewhere in order to carouse until dawn. I was in no mood for that. I preferred to make my own way back to Bedford Street.'

'But you were intercepted by Signor Maldini.'

'Yes, Christopher. Not far from the tavern.'

'That was in Fenchurch Street. How do you explain the fact that you were found by two watchmen much closer to the river?'

Henry blinked. 'Was I?' he asked in surprise. 'How did I get there?'

'I was hoping that you could tell me that.'

'It's all so vague. The truth is that I'm not sure what I remember about that night beyond the fact that I was seething with rage at that glib Italian.'

Christopher did not press him. Whether from drink or as a result of a blow he might have received to the head, his brother was genuinely confused about events. It made the task of defending him that much more difficult. The door was unlocked as a signal that it was time for the visitor to leave. Christopher gathered up the discarded clothing and made sure that the two razors were not left in the cell.

'Thank you for everything,' said Henry, embracing him again. 'I'm sorry that you've been dragged into this mess. It must perforce have dulled your own lustre.'

'Do not worry about me.'

'But I do. One act of folly from me will inflict damage on your career as well. Instead of being a successful architect, you'll be pointed at as the brother of a killer.'

'Not by people whose opinion I value,' said Christopher. 'I'll admit that I had fears in that direction but they've proved groundless. My latest commission is quite unthreatened by what's happened to you.'

'Then your client must not yet know about my disgrace.'

'I believe that she does, Henry. She hinted as much to me.'

'Oh?'

'Lady Whitcombe is given to impulses. When she sets her heart on something, she means to get it whatever the obstructions. I feel secure in her employ. She is so eager for me to design her new house in London that I fancy she'd not dismiss me even if my brother had assassinated the entire royal family.'

'But how can you attend to her needs when you are entangled with mine?'

'Forget her,' soothed Christopher. 'Lady Whitcombe is in Sheen and unlikely to stir from there until building gets under way. That will not happen until the Thames unfreezes completely, for the stone we require for the house will have to come by water. No,' he said confidently, 'I do not expect to see Lady Whitcombe for weeks.'

The coach moved slowly along the rutted track so that the occupants were not bounced about too much. Supported by cushions,

Lady Cecily Whitcombe sat in the coach with a blanket over her knees. Her daughter, Letitia, also wrapped up in warm clothing, was seated beside her. In spite of their discomfort, the two women were excited.

'I'm so pleased that Egerton has come back at last,' said Lady Whitcombe. 'He's been away too long. I've missed him terribly.'

'So have I, Mother. Life is so dull without Egerton to brighten our day. But I'm even more pleased that he wishes to stay in London,' said Letitia with a giggle. 'It gives us an excuse to visit him there.'

'Egerton is not the only person we'll visit, Letitia.'

'I know. I have every hope that we'll see your architect again.'

'Be assured of that.'

'Will I be able to meet him?'

'I'll insist on it.'

'Thank you, Mother.'

'Do you like Mr Redmayne?'

'Very much.'

'I could see that he's taken to you,' said the older woman complacently. 'Though you must strive for more composure in his presence. You giggle far too much. That's irritating. It shows a lack of maturity. Mr Redmayne is a serious young man. Try to impress him.'

'It's he who impresses me. What an imagination he must have!'

'That's why I chose him, Letitia.'

'He's so clever and yet so modest. I love being close to him.'

'Good,' said Lady Whitcombe, patting her hand with maternal approval. 'That's as it should be. I'm sure that Egerton will get on with him as well.'

'Nobody could take a dislike to Mr Redmayne.'

'Precisely. He is truly exceptional. There are lots of people we shall call on while we are in London and Christopher Redmayne will certainly be among the first.'

The coffee house was in a street behind Charing Cross. Jonathan Bale had walked past it many times without daring to venture in but he had no choice on this occasion. One of the customers was just arriving in a sedan chair. He was an elderly man with a walking stick and a servant had to help him up the stairs. The constable followed them. Before he even stepped into the room itself, he could hear the babble of voice and smell the aroma of coffee mingling with that of tobacco smoke. Jonathan was relieved to see that the place was half-empty at that time of the morning. It lessened the degree of discomfort he felt and made it easier to pick out the man he sought. The room was long and narrow with tables set out in parallel lines along both walls. It was an exclusively male preserve for fashionable Londoners. He could see why coffee was sometimes called politicians' porridge for the snippets of conversation he heard from nearby all concerned the affairs of the day. Christopher Redmayne had given him an accurate description of the customer he was looking for so Jonathan soon identified Sir Humphrey Godden. Seated alone at a table in the corner, the man was taking snuff from a silver box.

Jonathan approached him, introduced himself and explained the purpose of his visit. Sir Humphrey was not pleased to be accosted by a parish constable.

'How did you know that I'd be here?' he said with indignation.

'I called at your house,' explained Jonathan. 'I was told that you always visited this coffee house at a certain time of the morning.'

'I come here to see friends, not to be interrogated.'

'I thought that Henry Redmayne was one of those friends.'

'Well, yes,' said the other,' he is. More often that not, he'd be sitting in that chair opposite me. Henry is a fine fellow. But, like me, he loathes any interruptions.'

'He needs your help, Sir Humphrey.'

'He has it, man. He knows that I'll speak up for him in court.'

'There are a few questions I wish to put to you first.'

'This is not a convenient moment,' said Sir Humphrey testily. 'I've arranged to meet someone and he'll be here at any moment.'

Jonathan folded his arms. 'Then I'll wait.'

'I can't have you standing over me like that.'

'Would you prefer that I sat down?'

'No!'

'The questions are important, Sir Humphrey.'

'So is drinking my coffee in peace.'

'I won't disturb you.'

Jonathan stood there obstinately with his feet wide apart. Other customers were glancing across at him and speculating audibly on why he was there. Though he felt incongruous among the moneyed and over-dressed habitués of the coffee house, he was determined not to budge. Sir Humphrey eventually capitulated.

'Very well,' he snarled. 'Ask your questions then get out of here.'

'My first question is this. Why are you so unwilling to assist your friend?'

'I'll assist Henry in any way that I can.'

'That was not his brother's opinion, Sir Humphrey, nor is it mine. Both of us have seen how you put your own interests before those of a man in a desperate situation.'

'What more can I do?'

'You might visit him in prison to offer your sympathy.'

'Go to Newgate?' said Sir Humphrey, offended by the suggestion. 'The place is rife with disease, man. You'll not find me going into a fetid swamp like that.'

'Mr Crenlowe had enough compassion to call on a friend.'

'Then Martin will have spoken for both of us.'

'Are you trying to disown Mr Redmayne?'

'That's a scandalous suggestion, Mr Bale, and I resent it.' He made a visible effort to sound more reasonable. 'Look, man,' he said. 'Nothing can be achieved by my visiting Henry in prison. I know him. He'd be mortified to be seen in such dire straits. It's a kindness not to trouble him. But that does not mean I've forgotten the poor fellow. Only yesterday, I spent half an hour with the lawyer whom his brother has engaged to defend Henry. I spoke up strongly for him.'

'Could you offer any firm evidence to prove his innocence?'

'It does not need to be proved. Henry would never do such a thing. It's as simple as that. You do not spend so much time in the company of a friend without understanding his essential character.'

'He's prone to lose his temper.'

'Most of us are, Mr Bale,' said the other, glaring at him. 'When provoked.'

'Were you sorry to hear that Signor Maldini had been murdered?'

'Not at all. I was delighted.'

'Did you dislike him so much?'

'I dislike all foreigners, sir. They should be sent back where they belong.'

'The Queen is a foreigner,' noted Jonathan, arching an eyebrow. 'Would you have Her Majesty sent back to her own country?'

'Of course not, you idiot! Royalty is above reproach.'

'That's a matter of opinion, Sir Humphrey.'

'Jeronimo Maldini was a scheming Italian without a decent bone in his body. He was a fine swordsman, I grant him that. I've never seen a better one. But he did not respect his betters, Mr Bale.' His eyes ignited. 'He did not know his place.'

'Who stabbed him in the back?'

'It was not Henry Redmayne.'

'Who else could it have been?'

'I wish I knew, sir. I'd like to congratulate him.'

'Do you condone an act of murder, then?'

'I abhor the taking of life but applaud the result in this case.'

'That's as much as to say you think the killing was justified.'

'It rid us of a foul pestilence.'

'Captain Harvest does not think so.'

'Do not listen to James,' said Sir Humphrey, flushing with anger. 'He actually liked that execrable foreigner. That was his besetting sin. He could not discriminate. James liked almost everybody.'

'He does not seem to like Henry Redmayne.'

'James had a blind spot where Henry was concerned.'

'Is that all it was?' asked Jonathan. There was no reply. 'Someone must pay the penalty for this crime, Sir Humphrey,' he resumed. 'Most people believe that the culprit has already been caught.'

'Only because they do not know him as we do.'

'If he's innocent, someone else must have wielded that dagger. I realise that Captain Harvest was a friend of the dead man but could *he* have been the killer?'

'That's a ludicrous notion!'

'Mr Crenlowe did not think so.'

'James had no motive,' said Sir Humphrey. 'We all gain by the murder. He is the only one who stands to lose. Why search for a killer among the four of us who shared a meal that night? Nobody knows better than a constable how many hazards there are at night in the streets of London. There are hundreds of villains at large who'd stab a man in the back for the sheer pleasure of it.'

'But they'd have their own weapons,' observed Jonathan. 'They'd not use a dagger that was owned by Mr Redmayne. How do you account for that?' There was another silence. 'And I have to disagree with your earlier comment, Sir Humphrey,' he continued. 'You do not all gain from this murder. As a result of it, Mr Redmayne may well lose his life.'

Before he could respond, Sir Henry saw someone walking down the room and rose to welcome him. Martin Crenlowe was surprised to see the constable there. After an exchange of greetings, the two friends took their seats at the table.

Sir Humphrey was abrupt. 'Will that be all, Mr Bale?'

'For the moment,' said Jonathan. 'I may need to speak to you again.'

'Do not dare to do so in here again. You have created a scene.'

'That was not my intention, Sir Humphrey.'

'What about me, Mr Bale?' asked Crenlowe, adopting a more helpful tone. 'Shall you require some more information from me? I'll be happy to furnish it.'

'Thank you, sir.'

'I'm sorry if I was a trifle brusque with you at our last meeting.'

'You were in a hurry, Mr Crenlowe. I understood that.'

'Henry's welfare comes before my family obligations.'

'I agree,' added Sir Humphrey. 'Now perhaps you'll leave us alone so that we can enjoy a cup of coffee. We have much to discuss.'

Jonathan looked from one to the other. 'I'm sure that you have, Sir Humphrey.' He touched the brim of his hat. 'Good day to you, gentlemen.'

Another day had been swallowed up with frightening speed by the crisis. Christopher Redmayne suddenly found that evening was already starting to chase the last rays of light out of the sky yet again. Much had been done but little had so far been achieved. After his visit to the prison, he had returned to the house in Bedford Street to hand over the discarded clothing to Henry's valet and to assure him, and the other servants who gathered anxiously around him, that their master would eventually be released without a stain on his character. They tried hard to believe him but Christopher could see that they feared the worst. Their own futures looked bleak. It would not be easy for the servants of a convicted murderer to find a new master.

After dining early at home, Christopher went off for another meeting with the lawyer who would fight to save Henry's life in court. Indifferent to the legal costs that he was running up, he spent the whole afternoon with him but the man was able to hold out much hope of success. All that Christopher could offer him were hearsay evidence and intelligent speculation. The prosecution, by contrast, had a murder weapon with his brother's initials on it. He was irritated by the excessive caution of his legal advisor but he could do nothing to dispel it. A mood of pessimism hung over the whole discussion. By the time that he left, Christopher was forced to accept that, unless he and Jonathan Bale found an alternative killer, then Henry Redmayne's initials might already be on the hangman's rope as well.

It was ironic. As prospects were brightening for one brother, they were rapidly deteriorating for the other. Christopher felt guilty about it because he was eternally grateful to Henry for helping him to launch his career as an architect. It was his brother who had secured the first vital commissions for him and whose connections at Court and elsewhere had brought Christopher so many valuable contacts. Now that he was more established, he did not need Henry's assistance but that did not weaken his profound feeling of gratitude. While the architect was about to earn a substantial sum of money from Lady Whitcombe, his brother was languishing in a prison with a possible death sentence hanging over him. The disparity in their fortunes could not have been greater.

Christopher had arranged to call on Jonathan Bale that evening so that they could compare any new intelligence that had come to light. Before he did that, however, he felt the urge to visit Fenchurch Street to view the tavern where his brother had gone with friends on the fateful night. Setting a brisk pace, he walked along Cheapside and took note of the architecture on the way. It was encouraging to see just how much rebuilding had already been completed. Within three years of the Great Fire, almost three thousand new houses had been constructed in the ashes of the old ones. It was an astonishing feat. Christopher was proud to have designed a few of those properties. Taverns, ordinaries, guild halls, warehouses and civic buildings had also risen again and work was continuing on some of the many churches that had been destroyed in the blaze. Precautions had been enforced from the start. Streets were widened, thatch was replaced by tile and brick was the most common building material. Half-timbered houses had gone up like tinder in the blaze. London had learned its lesson.

When he reached the tavern in Fenchurch Street, Christopher was reminded of that lesson once again. The Elephant was well-named. It was big, solid and indomitable. While neighbouring buildings crashed to the ground, its thick stone walls had withstood the fiery siege like an invincible fortress. Christopher was not there to admire the finer points of its construction and the growing darkness would have made it impossible to do so. He gazed around, feeling that conditions were very similar to those on the night when his brother had come out of the tavern. It was cold, murky and inhospitable. People who passed on the other side of the street were conjured out of the gloom for seconds before disappearing into it again. If Henry was too drunk to walk properly, it would have been simple to ambush him.

After looking up and down the street, Christopher made his way towards the river. Jonathan Bale had told him the exact location where the two watchmen had chanced upon the fallen man. It was in an alleyway off Thames Street, too dark to explore without a lantern and too dangerous for any sensible person to enter late at night. Henry must have got himself there somehow but had no memory of the journey. As he stood there and tried to work out how his brother had ended up at that spot, Christopher could hear a strange noise. He soon discovered what it was. When he walked down to the river bank itself, he realised that the ice was still cracking up. Having thawed in the middle, it was now melting towards the banks, splitting into huge blocks that bobbed and jostled in the water. Directly below him, Christopher noticed, a small pond had opened up, still filled with jagged pieces of ice but clear evidence that the Thames was determined to obliterate all signs of the frost fair that had been held upon its back.

There were lots of people passing by and he felt in no danger. He leaned over and peered into the darkness. It was a grave mistake. A hand was suddenly placed in the middle of his back to give him a hard shove. Christopher lost his balance. Unable to stop himself, he tumbled helplessly through space until he hit the cold, swirling, merciless water with a loud splash.

Chapter Eleven

Susan Cheever was not looking forward to receiving the guests at Serle Court. Since her sister's avowed objective had been to find her a husband, she shuddered at the notion that she would be on display. Her first thought was to plead illness and avoid meeting any of the visitors but Brilliana would not be tricked that way. Nor could Susan wear her oldest and least appealing dress as a form of armour to ward off any romantic interest in her. Brilliana insisted on going through her sister's wardrobe to choose the attire that would accentuate her best features. By the time that the first coach rolled up to Serle Court that evening, Susan was dressed in her finery and gritting her teeth.

'Smile,' urged her sister. 'Men like to see you smile.'

'Then they'll need to give me something to smile about, Brilliana.'

'You are being perverse.'

'I'm being serious. I do not intend to smile for the sake of it.'

'It's what men expect of us.'

'Then their expectations will not be met.'

'Susan!'

'This was your idea, Brilliana, and not mine.'

'Need you be so obstructive?'

'And why invite them this evening?' asked Susan with exasperation. 'Had they come to dinner, they would be on their way home by now and I'd feel safe.'

'Safe from what? Meeting someone worthy of you at last?'

'That will not happen today, I promise you.'

'We may surprise you. As for my choice of time, the reason I wanted them here this evening was that Mrs Cardinal will be too weary to return home in her coach and will therefore have to spend the night here.' Brilliana gave a knowing grin. 'And so, of course, will her son.'

Susan groaned. 'I'm to endure their company for breakfast as well?'

'It will give you the opportunity to get to know them better.'

'I may sleep until late tomorrow.'

Brilliana was resolute. 'No, you will not!'

Her face blossomed into a regal smile as the first guests came through the front door. They were four in number and swiftly followed by an elderly married couple from a neighbouring estate. They all received a cordial welcome from Brilliana and her husband. Susan, too, was uniformly polite. Looking around the visitors, she saw that they were exactly what she had anticipated. They were, in their various ways, alternative versions of her sister and her brother-in-law. The latecomers most certainly were not. When Jack Cardinal and his mother finally arrived in a flurry of apologies, Susan was taken aback. The woman caught her eye first. She was an obese lady with a surging bosom, bulging cheeks and tiny pig-like eyes. Hanging on her son's arm for support, she explained that they had been delayed because she had had one of her attacks. Susan was amazed. Mrs Cardinal looked uncommonly healthy to her.

Jack Cardinal was the real surprise. He was a neat, compact man of medium height with a shock of black hair that rose up from a high-domed forehead. Only his mother could have deemed him handsome. His face was craggy in repose and slightly comic when he was animated. Susan was completely disarmed. Cardinal was no threat to her. If anything, she felt sorry for him. Even at a glance, the man was so burdened by a demanding mother that he looked years older than his true age. When he was introduced to Susan, he was too shy to do more than give her a token bow. She began to relax. The evening might not be as onerous as she had feared.

It was an hour before she had a conversation alone with Cardinal. Before the meal was served, Brilliana contrived to divert the majority of the guests by inviting them to see the recent portrait of her that hung at the top of the staircase. Serle had been primed to assist Mrs Cardinal up the steps and to listen to the endless litany of her symptoms. Susan found herself in the parlour with Jack Cardinal. He examined the bookshelves.

'Lancelot has tastes not unlike my own,' he remarked.

'In what way?'

'I, too, am fond of poems. I read them to Mother sometimes.'

'Can she not read them to herself, Mr Cardinal?'

'Not when her eyes trouble her,' he replied. 'Poor sight is one of her many problems. What about you, Miss Cheever?' he asked, turning to look at her. 'Are you interested in poetry?'

'I am, sir.'

'May I know whom you admire?'

'Many of those you'll find on those same shelves,' said Susan. 'But the poet I revere most is not in my brother-in-law's collection.'

'And who might that be?'

'Mr Milton.'

He was astounded. '*John* Milton?'

'I know of no other.'

'I'd not have thought he'd appeal to a young lady such as you.'

'He certainly does not appeal to my sister,' confessed Susan, 'and Lancelot has strong political objections against him. Mr Milton, as you know, was Latin Secretary to the Lord High Protector.'

'That's what makes him so intriguing, Miss Cheever.'

'Intriguing?'

'Poetry transcends political affiliation,' he said solemnly. 'Because I do not agree with a man's politics, I am not unaware of his poetic skills. I take John Milton to be a man of infinite genius. I'm proud to call myself a Royalist but that does not stop me from telling you that *Paradise Lost* is the finest poem I've ever read.'

'You are a religious man, I see.'

'Far from it.'

'Then wherein lies its appeal?'

'In its scope, its ambition and its sheer intelligence.'

'You have surely not read it to your mother.'

'No,' he replied with a rare smile. 'Mother has no time for John Milton or anyone of his persuasion. She believes that he should have been beheaded as a traitor. That attitude does not put her in the ideal frame of mind for appreciating his work.'

Susan warmed to him. 'Lancelot tells me that you are a prodigious reader.'

'I know of no greater pleasure.'

'What about shooting and fencing? You excel at both, I hear.'

'They are manly accomplishments and nothing more.'

'You are too modest, Mr Cardinal. I understand that you are an expert.'

'Hardly! What has Lancelot been saying about me?'

'He talked of a duel that you had with Egerton Whitcombe.'

'Oh, that,' said Cardinal, his face clouding. 'It was a big mistake.'

'But you were the victor.'

'The bout should never have taken place.'

153

'According to Lancelot, the other man goaded you into it.'

'He did, Miss Cheever, and I was foolish to go along with it.'

'Why?'

'Because I did not realise how seriously my opponent was taking the whole thing. Egerton Whitcombe was so confident that he would get the better of me that he'd made a number of wagers with friends.' He gave an apologetic shrug. 'Losing the bout cost him a sizeable amount of money.'

'No wonder he was so embittered.'

'He keeps asking for a return meeting to recoup his losses but I'll not measure swords with him again. Too much rides on it for Egerton – and for his mother, of course.'

'Lady Whitcombe?'

'She was there to cheer her son on the last time,' he said. 'Lady Whitcombe was so outraged that I proved the finer swordsman that she's not spoken to me since.'

'My brother-in-law tells me that she's very grand.'

'Very grand and very determined.'

'In what way, Mr Cardinal?'

'She has the highest ambitions for her family,' he said. 'She drives them on. Lady Whitcombe expects that her son – and her daughter – win at everything.'

Egerton Whitcombe paced angrily up and down the room like a caged animal. He was not accustomed to having his demands rejected. Tall, slim and striking in appearance, he was immaculately dressed in a blue doublet and petticoat breeches. His gleaming leather jackboots clacked noisily on the oak floorboards. When he finally came to a halt, he turned to his mother with an accusatory stare.

'Has work begun on the house yet?' he barked.

'No, Egerton,' she replied. 'The ground is still too hard for them to dig the foundations and the stone they need will not be brought in by boat until the ice has vanished from the Thames.'

'Then we still have time to cancel the contract.'

'I've no intention of doing that.'

'Do you know who the architect is, Mother?'

'Of course. I've met Mr Redmayne a number of times.'

'His brother is in prison on a charge of murder,' he said with disgust. 'I only heard about it today and I was shocked. We cannot let ourselves get involved with a family such as that.'

'We are not getting involved with a family, only an individual.'

'His brother is a killer. That means his name is tainted.'

'His father is the Dean of Gloucester,' she retorted, 'and that says far more about him. It's unfortunate that this other business has cropped up, I agree, but it will not affect my judgement of Christopher Redmayne. He's not merely a brilliant architect, he's a delightful young man.'

'With a criminal for a brother.'

'Egerton!'

'People talk, Mother. What will our friends say?'

The quarrel took place in a room that he had rented at a tavern in Holborn. Lady Whitcombe and her daughter were staying with friends in London but they were spending the evening with the man in their family. Hoping for a joyful reunion with her son, Lady Whitcombe was disappointed to find him in a combative mood. Letitia was too distressed by his truculent behaviour even to speak. Instead of listening to an account of her brother's adventures abroad, she was witnessing a fierce argument. She made sure that she kept out of it.

Lady Whitcombe was imperious. 'My decisions are not subject to the dictates of my friends,' she declared. 'I saw what I wanted and engaged the architect who could give it to me. There's an end to it.'

'No,' retorted her son. 'I'm the person who'll spend most time in the house.'

'So?'

'I should have more of a say in who designs it and it will not be anyone who bears the sullied name of Redmayne. Dismiss the fellow at once.'

'It's too late. His drawings have already been delivered.'

'But no work has yet been done on the site. There's still time to think again.'

'Why should I do that?'

'Because I'm telling you, Mother,' he said, trying to assert himself by standing in front of her with his hands on his hips. 'Let me speak more bluntly. I simply refuse to occupy a building that's been designed by Christopher Redmayne.'

'Then Letitia and I will have to stay there in your stead.'

'What about me?'

'You'll continue to rent a room in a tavern.'

His face was puce with rage. 'But you promised me a house.'

'I've provided one, Egerton. It will be the envy of our circle when it's built.'

'Not if it's been designed by the brother of a murderer.'

'Stop saying that.'

'It's what everyone else will harp on.'

'I care not.'

'Well, I do, Mother,' he announced, stamping his foot for emphasis. 'I'll not let you do this. London is full of architects. Engage another one.'

'I already have the one that I prefer.'

'I'll find someone better.'

'There *is* nobody better,' said Letitia, forced to offer her opinion. 'Mr Redmayne is the most wonderful architect in the world. His design is exactly what we want.'

'We?' he sneered, rounding on her. 'We, we, we? I was the one who began all this, Letitia. I was the person who explained why a house was needed in London. Given that, I should be the one with the power of decision.'

'Not unless you intend to pay for it,' said his mother coolly.

'What?'

'If the money comes from my purse, Egerton, then I reserve the right to hire the man I want. And that's exactly what I've done.'

'That's so unfair, Mother!' he protested.

'It's the way of the world.'

'But the man is unsuitable.'

'You've never even met Mr Redmayne.'

'I've heard about his brother, Henry. He's the talk of every tavern in the city. It's only a matter of time before he's hanged for his crime. And rightly so,' he added. 'I knew the murder victim briefly. Signor Maldini once gave me fencing lessons.'

'Then he was a poor tutor.'

'Mother!'

'Jack Cardinal made you look like a novice.'

'I'll make him pay for that.'

'Oh, Egerton,' she said, using a softer tone. 'Let's not bicker like this. You've been away for so long. Must the first time we see you again be an occasion for sourness and recrimination? Be ruled by me.'

'It seems that I must be,' he said resentfully.

'And take that grim expression from your face. It ill becomes you. We should be celebrating your return, not falling out with each other.' She embraced him and planted a gentle kiss on his cheek. 'There, the matter is settled.'

'Do not count on it,' he said under his breath.

'You'll soon see that your fears were in vain, Egerton. Wait until you meet him,' she said with a beatific smile. 'He'll win you over in no time. Forget about this brother of his. Christopher Redmayne is a perfect gentleman.'

'Good Lord!' exclaimed Jonathan Bale, staring at him in amazement at the bedraggled figure on his foorstep. 'Is that really *you*, Mr Redmayne?'

'Unhappily, it is.'

'But you are soaked to the skin.'

'I've been in the river,' explained Christopher, trying to stop his teeth chattering. 'Your house was so much nearer than mine that I came to throw myself on your mercy.'

'Of course, sir. Come in, come in.'

Jonathan stood aside so tha this visitor could get into the house. Hearing Christopher's voice, Sarah came bustling out of the kitchen to look at his sodden apparel. Water was still dripping from him. He had lost his hat and his hair was plastered to his head. His cloak was a wet rag over his arm. When he moved, his boots squelched.

'What on earth happened?' asked Sarah.

'I fell in by accident.'

'Fell in?'

'Yes, Mrs Bale. I lost my footing.'

Sarah took control. 'Stand by the fire or you'll catch your death of cold. I'll fetch a blanket for you. Mr Redmayne will need a change of clothes, Jonathan,' she said, pushing her husband away. 'See what you can find.'

Christopher was grateful that the children had been put to bed and were not there to witness his humiliation. Stepping into the parlour, he huddled over the fire. Jonathan soon returned with some clothing and his wife brought a rough blanket on which their visitor could dry himself. They left him alone in the parlour so that he could peel off his coat, shirt and breeches before wrapping the blanket around him. Still shivering, he rubbed himself dry then put on the sober attire that his friend had loaned him. It was much too large and the material was far more coarse than anything he had worn before but Christopher did not complain. He crouched beside the fire and began to thaw slowly out. Jonathan tapped the door and came in. He was carrying a small cup.

'Drink this, Mr Redmayne,' he counselled. 'It might help.'

'What is it?'

'A remedy that Sarah often prepares for me. It's warm and searching.'

Christopher did not even ask what the ingredients were. When he saw the steam rising from the cup, he accepted the drink gratefully and gulped it down. It had a sweet taste and coursed through him with speed. He felt much better. Jonathan took the cup back from him and set it aside.

'Now, Mr Redmayne,' he said, 'perhaps you'll tell me the truth.'

'The truth?'

'I know that you did not wish to alarm my wife but I'm different. This was no accident, sir. A man like you would never lose his footing on the bank.'

'I was pushed in,' admitted Christopher. 'Someone shoved me from behind.'

'Who would do such a thing?'

'I wish I knew, Jonathan. Whoever it was did not expect me to get out of the water again. I was lucky to do so. The river was still icy cold. My clothing was so waterlogged that I could barely move. I flailed around and yelled until someone threw me a rope from the wharf. I was pulled out like a drowned rat.'

'What were you doing by the river in the first place?'

Christopher told him about his visit to the lawyer's office and his subsequent walk to Fenchurch Street. He had gone over ground that Jonathan himself had visited and reached the same conclusion.

'I think that the body of Signor Maldini was thrown in the water not far from the spot where my brother was found by the watchmen. In fact,' said Christopher, 'I may have dived headfirst into the Thames at almost the same point.'

'Why would anyone wish to attack you?' asked the other.

'I may have the answer to that, Jonathan. But, first, tell me your own news. Did you manage to speak to Martin Crenlowe or Sir Humphrey Godden?'

'To both of them.'

Jonathan talked about his visit to the goldsmith and his second encounter with the man at the coffee house that morning. Neither man had struck him as the ideal friends on whom someone like Henry Redmayne could rely. He also had the feeling that both of them were holding back certain details about the evening they spent at the Elephant.

'I was puzzled,' he said. 'They spoke harshly of Captain Harvest yet they had been ready to share a meal with him.'

'One of them actually paid for it, Jonathan.'

'How do you know?'

'Because Henry did not have the money to do so,' said Christopher, 'and I'm certain that the captain did not settle his own bill. He boasted to me about it.'

'You've met him, then?'

Christopher took up the narrative again and explained how difficult it had been to find the elusive soldier. His estimate of the man tallied with Jonathan's own but he had learned things that the constable had not. A more rounded picture of the captain emerged.

'Did you think him capable of murder?' said Jonathan.

'Yes,' replied Christopher. 'More than capable.'

'That was Mr Crenlowe's view as well. Sir Humphrey Godden disagreed.'

'I'd back the goldsmith's judgement.'

'I'd trust neither.'

'Captain Harvest did not have a kind word to say about them.'

'Coming back to this evening,' said Jonathan, pleased that his visitor had now stopped shivering. 'Did you not realise that you were being followed?'

'My mind was on other things.'

'Were there no witnesses to the attack?'

'It was dark, Jonathan. People were hurrying home. Nobody stopped to see a hand helping me into the water. It was a long drop,' he explained. 'Had the river still been frozen, I might have broken my neck on the ice. As it was, I all but drowned.'

'I still do not see why you were set on, Mr Redmayne.'

'I do,' said Christopher, 'and I found it oddly reassuring.'

Jonathan gaped. '*Reassuring*? When someone tries to kill you?'

'It means that I'm on the right track, after all. This was no random assault. Had it been a thief, he'd have snatched my purse before pitching me into the water. I was followed for a reason, Jonathan. Someone knows that I'm on his trail.'

'Who?'

'In all probability, it was the man who *did* kill the fencing master.'

Jonathan was sceptical. 'That's not the conclusion I'd reach.'

'You still think that my brother is guilty,' said Christopher, almost exultant. 'But my dip in the Thames taught me one thing, if nothing else. Someone is trying to prevent me from finding out the truth about the murder. Henry is clearly innocent.'

'I hope, for both your sakes, that he is.'

'But you remain unconvinced.'

'I need more persuasion,' said Jonathan. 'Do you think that your brother would consent to see me in Newgate? It would help if I could talk to him myself.'

'Henry is not in the most receptive mood.'

'Then he'd turn me away?'

'He's hardly in a position to do that,' said Christopher, 'and any visit breaks up the boredom of being locked away. On the other hand, alas, Henry does not share the high opinion that I have of you. He inhabits a different world and knows that you are hostile to it. However,' he decided, 'there's no harm in trying. Leave it to me.'

'You'll ask him?'

'When I visit the prison tomorrow.'

'Did you see him today?' Christopher nodded. 'How did you find him?'

'Close to desperation,' replied the other, recalling Henry's confession about the appeal of suicide. 'But I think that I managed to restore his spirits. When he hears about my swim in the river, he'll be even more heartened. The real killer has shown his hand. We know that he's still in London.'

It was curious. The more the evening progressed, the more drawn she became to him. Determined to dislike the man, Susan Cheever had found him unremarkable on first acquaintance and patently uninterested in her. Jack Cardinal's attention was fixed firmly on his mother and he deferred to her wishes at every point. Susan thought that the old woman was exploiting him but he did not seem to mind, and she doted on him. Mrs Cardinal never stopped telling the others around the table how devoted her son was. His management of the estate was also praised. Brilliana Serle had been responsible for the seating arrangements so she made sure that her sister was next to Cardinal. Her own seat was directly opposite them, so that she could keep them under observation and feed each of them pleasing titbits of information about the other. Susan was relieved to see that Cardinal found it as unsettling as she did.

Brilliana was not the only person who was watching the couple. When she was not listing her various ailments in order to reap communal sympathy, Mrs Cardinal kept a watchful eye on Susan and on her son's response to her proximity. Eventually, she leaned in Susan's direction.

'Do you prefer the town or the country, Miss Cheever?'

'I like both, Mrs Cardinal,' replied Susan.

'You live close to Northampton, I hear.'

'It's the nearest town but it is tiny by comparison with London.'

'Is there much society there?'

'No,' said Brilliana before he sister could answer. 'Neither the county nor the town can provide fitting company for people of quality. That's why I came south in search of a husband,' she added, tossing an affectionate glance at Serle. 'Since I've been here, I've come to see Northamptonshire as nothing short of barbarous.'

Susan was roused. 'That's unjust, Brilliana.'

'I was only too glad to escape.'

'Well, I have fonder memories. It's a beautiful county and we had many good friends there. I still regard it as my home.'

'Quite rightly so, Miss Cheever,' said Cardinal. 'None of us can choose our place of birth but we owe it a loyalty nevertheless. As it happens, I once rode through your county on my way to Leicestershire, and I agree with you. It has great charm.'

'That's what I feel,' decided Serle.

'Nobody asked for your opinion, Lancelot,' scolded his wife.

'But I had the same impression as Jack.'

'That's neither here nor there.'

'I think it is, Brilliana,' said Susan, enjoying the chance to put her sister on the defensive. 'You may pour scorn on the county of your birth but three of us at least can sing its praises.'

'Will you be returning home soon, Miss Cheever?' asked Mrs Cardinal.

'No, not for a while.'

'Did you not wish to be with your father?'

'I preferred to stay here, Mrs Cardinal.'

Serle beamed. 'And we are delighted to have you, sister-in-law.'

'Thank you, Lancelot.'

'I understand that you have a house in London,' said Cardinal.

'Yes,' replied Susan. 'Father and I live there when he has business in the city. If Parliament is not sitting, he retreats to his estate.'

'Do you like London?'

'Very much, Mr Cardinal.'

'What appeals to you most about it?'

'Its size and its sense of activity,' she explained. 'There is so much going on, especially now that rebuilding is so advanced. It's fascinating to watch old streets being renovated and new ones being created alongside them. Then, of course, there was the frost fair. That was a miraculous event.'

'So I understand.'

'Jack offered to take me there,' said Mrs Cardinal, 'but the roads were bad and my poor chest would never have withstood the cold. I have to be so careful, you know. I tire so easily in the winter.'

'You've rallied magnificently this past week, Mother,' he said.

'Only because the weather has improved.'

'I've never seen you looking better,' remarked Brilliana.

'Thank you, Mrs Serle.'

'Mother is well enough to face the travel now,' said Cardinal. 'I've business interests to attend to in London and Mother has agreed to accompany me there for a couple of days. We leave early tomorrow.'

Brilliana was disappointed. 'We hoped that you might linger to dine with us.'

'It will not be possible, I fear.'

'Can we not persuade you, Jack?' asked Serle, responding to a nudge under the table from his wife. 'Stay another day, if you wish.'

'We'd be delighted to have you,' said Brilliana. 'So would Susan. It's rather dull for her to have nobody but us to entertain her.'

'Then why did she not stay in London?' wondered Mrs Cardinal, turning towards Susan. 'I would have thought that you'd built up a circle of friends there by now.'

'Yes, Mrs Cardinal,' said Susan. 'I do have friends in the city.'

'Why desert them for Richmond?'

'Because she wanted to be with her sister,' said Brilliana.

'That's not strictly true,' added Susan. 'I left London with some reluctance.'

'What do you miss most?' asked Cardinal.

'Seeing my friends and visiting the shops.'

'Ah!' said Mrs Cardinal with a laugh, 'that's what is luring me there. The thought of all those wonderful shops, filled to the brim with the latest fashions. If my health will allow it, I intend to visit them all.' An idea made her sit up abruptly. 'But wait, my dear,' she went on, smiling at Susan. 'You prefer to be in London, you say?'

'To some extent, Mrs Cardinal.'

'Then why do you not come with us?'

Susan was immediately tempted. 'That's a very kind invitation.'

'Then let me endorse it,' said Cardinal gallantly. 'We'd love to have you as our companion, Miss Cheever. I'll have to spend a lot of time dealing with my business affairs and it would be a relief to know that someone was looking after Mother.'

'I'd be happy to do that.'

'Splendid news!' He looked at Brilliana. 'Unless you have an objection.'

'None at all,' she said.

'This is better than we dared hope for,' observed Serle, before collecting a kick of reproof from his wife. 'I mean that this will suit everyone.'

'As long as Jack does not abandon my sister completely,' said Brilliana.

'I'll ensure that he does not do that,' promised Mrs Cardinal.

'Then I give the excursion my blessing.'

Susan was thrilled. Having braced herself for a tedious evening in the company of strangers, she had been given an unexpected opportunity to escape from Richmond. Brilliana had condoned the visit because she felt it would throw Jack Cardinal and her sister closer together, but Susan had another objective. Being in London meant a possibility of seeing Christopher Redmayne again and that hope was uppermost in her mind. If she could contrive a meeting with him, she was prepared to endure any number of Mrs Cardinal's long monologues about her ill health.

'Well,' said Cardinal happily, 'this is a pleasant surprise. It will be a delight to have you with us, Miss Cheever.'

'Thank you,' said Susan.

'You'll be able to feed your passion for literature again.'

'Will I?'

'Yes, indeed. I'll take you to the best bookshops in London.'

'I'd like that, Mr Cardinal,' she said warmly. 'I'd like that very much.'

He gave her a shy smile. 'So would I.'

Jonathan Bale insisted on accompanying his friend home. Christopher did not think that he needed a bodyguard but he was grateful for the concern that was shown. Over his arm was the apparel that was still damp from its dip in the river. On the walk back to Fetter Lane, they kept looking over their shoulder but saw nobody following them. Whoever had pushed Christopher into the water had fled from the scene and would have no idea what happened to the architect. For that evening at least, he was safe. At the door of the house, Jonathan tried to take his leave.

'Step in for a moment,' invited Christopher.

'No thank you, Mr Redmayne.'

'But I can let you have your things back when I change.'

'There's no hurry for that, sir. I have work to do. I must go.'

'I'm so sorry to descend on you like that.'

'We are pleased that you felt able to do so.'

'Take a message to your wife,' said Christopher. 'Tell her how grateful I am to her and ask her what was in that remedy. It's revived me completely.'

Jonathan nodded and they exchanged farewells. Christopher let himself into the house, expecting to shed the garments he had borrowed in order to put on some that actually fitted him. He planned to spend a restful hour in front of the fire with a glass or two of brandy. When he entered the parlour, however, he saw something that swiftly rearranged his whole evening for him. The Reverend Algernon Redmayne was waiting for him.

'Father!' he exclaimed. 'How nice to see you!'

'That's more than I can say for you,' returned the old man, looking at his baggy attire. 'What, in the name of God, are you wearing?'

'I had to borrow these clothes from a friend.'

'I did not imagine you had a tailor cruel enough to make them for you.'

'They served their purpose,' said Christopher. 'But how are you, Father? How did you travel? When did you arrive? Has Jacob been looking after you?'

'Yes,' said the servant, emerging from the kitchen with a glass of wine. 'I made your father a light meal then gave him some ointment.'

'Ointment?'

'It was very soothing,' said the Dean. 'I rode most of the way on horseback and the saddle took its toll. Jacob was kind enough to act as my physician.' He took the glass of wine. 'Thank you. I feel that I've deserved this.'

'Shall I fetch a glass for you, Mr Redmayne?' asked Jacob.

'Not yet,' said Christopher, handing him the wet clothes. 'In time, in time.'

His servant backed out and left the two of them alone. Christopher studied his father. The journey had clearly taxed him. Dark circles had formed beneath his eyes and pain was etched into his face. Though he was sitting in a chair, he was doing so at an awkward angle so that one raw buttock did not come into contact with anything. His son bent over him solicitously but the old man waved him away. Only one subject interested him at that moment.

'Has Henry been released yet?' he enquired.

'No, Father.'

'Why not?'

'We have not established his innocence to their satisfaction.'

'The burden of proof lies with the authorities.'

'They feel they have enough evidence to hold him.'

'What evidence?' said the Dean. 'Your letter was short in detail, Christopher.'

'At the time of writing, I was not in full possession of the facts.'

'And now?'

'There's still much to learn, Father.'

Christopher gave him the description of events that he had already rehearsed in his mind, omitting all mention of the fact that his brother was hopelessly drunk at the time when the crime was committed and saying nothing about Henry's impulse to commit suicide. His father was stern and attentive. He was also far too intelligent to be misled about his elder son.

'You say that Henry does not remember what happened?'

'No, Father.'

'Why is that?'

'It was late. He was confused. He believes that he was struck on the head.'

'How much wine had he consumed?' asked the Dean, sipping from his glass. 'I've had occasion to warn him about excessive drinking. It dulls the mind and leads to moral turpitude.' He tapped his glass. 'I only ever touch it myself in times of crisis such as now. Jacob's ointment and your wine have refreshed me after that ordeal.'

'I'm glad to hear it, Father.'

'Was your brother drunk?'

'It had been a convivial evening.'

'He was ever a slave to conviviality,' grumbled the old man. 'I threatened to cut off his allowance if he did not keep to the strait and narrow path of righteousness, and he swore that he would. But righteous men do not end up in prison.'

'What of John Bunyan and many like him?'

The Dean was scornful. 'Do not talk to me of Puritans. They are the bane of my life. Your garb reminds me uncomfortably of the wretches. The point I am making is that Henry should not have put himself in a position where this appalling error could be made.' He closed one eye and stared at Christopher through the other. 'You are certain that it *is* an error?'

'Yes, Father.'

'I would rather know the truth, Christopher. If your brother did commit a murder, tell me honestly. I need to prepare myself before I meet him.'

'Henry is a victim. Of that, I have no doubt. Someone took advantage of him in the most nefarious way. In short, the person who killed the fencing master made sure that suspicion fell on Henry.'

'Then why has his name not been cleared?'

'It takes time to gather evidence. We are working as hard as we can.'

'We?'

'My friend, Jonathan Bale, is helping me,' said Christopher, glancing down at his clothes. 'He loaned me this strange garb.'

'I did not think you had become a Puritan.'

'I'd spare you that disgrace, Father.'

'If only my other son showed me similar consideration,' said the Dean, wincing as he shifted his position. 'But why did you need to borrow those ill-fitting garments?'

'I was pushed into the river.'

Christopher told him what had happened without suppressing any of the facts. His father was alarmed at the news and in no way reassured by his son's claim that he was attacked because he was breathing down the neck of the real killer. All that the old man could think about was Christopher's safety.

'You must not stir abroad alone,' he warned.

'There's no danger if I keep my wits about me.'

'But there is, Christopher,' urged his father. 'This incident has proved it. You should not have walked home on your own this evening.'

'I did not, Father. Jonathan bore me company to my front door. I had the protection of a constable all the way here. And as you see,' he added, tugging at his coat, 'he's a much bigger man than me.'

'And this constable is helping you?'

'Well, yes. He's trying to gather evidence about the crime.'

'I sense a hesitation in your voice, my son. Why is that?'

Christopher licked his lips. 'There's a slight problem here.'

'Problem?'

'Jonathan Bale is not as persuaded of Henry's innocence as I am.'

The Dean was shaken. 'But you said that he was your friend.'

'*My* friend, yes,' said Christopher, 'but not my brother's.'

'This is very worrying. There's obviously room for genuine doubt here. Why does Mr Bale believe that Henry committed this wicked crime? Does he have access to proof that's been denied to you?'

'No, Father. He relies on instinct.'

'Then it's even more disturbing.'

'Not at all.'

'He mixes with criminals every day. He understands their character.'

'He does not understand Henry,' said Christopher, 'or he would

167

know that his arrest is a gross mistake. I know it, his friends know it, and, in your heart, you must know it as well, Father. Surely, you never questioned your son's innocence?'

'Not until I came here.'

'At a time like this, he needs our support and not our suspicion.'

'I'll visit him first thing in the he morning.'

'Let me come with you.'

'No, Christopher,' affirmed the old man. 'I'll go alone. There's only room in a prison cell for the three of us – Henry, myself and God.'

They talked for the best part of an hour but the Dean of Gloucester was patently tired and in discomfort. After saying a prayer with his son, he retired to bed early with a supply of Jacob's ointment. When his father was safely out of the way, Christopher felt able to relax for the first time.

'It has been an eventful evening, Jacob,' he said ruefully. 'I was shoved into the river, dried off at Jonathan Bale's house and put into these clothes, then confronted by my father at a time when I was least ready for him. When I've had a glass of brandy, I do believe that I'm entitled to take to my bed as well.'

'I have to deliver the message first, sir.'

'Message?'

'I did not dare to tell you while your father was here,' said Jacob, 'because you had enough to contend with then. I fear that I've some bad tidings for you.'

'About Henry?'

'No, sir. They concern Lady Whitcombe. The message arrived earlier on.'

'Well?'

'Lady Whitcombe is in London and intends to call on you tomorrow.'

Christopher felt as if he had just been pushed into the River Thames again.

Chapter Twelve

In spite of her protestations of ill health, Mrs Cardinal arose early next morning, got herself downstairs alone, devoured a hearty breakfast and prepared for her departure unaided. She was noticeably less dependent on her son, leaving Jack Cardinal to pay more attention to Susan Cheever. As the two of them waited beside the coach for his mother to join them, he ventured a first compliment.

'May I say how resplendent you look today?'

'Thank you, Mr Cardinal,' she replied, 'but I do not feel it. Winter is the enemy of fashion. When we choose our clothing, we have to think about warmth rather than style.'

'You would be elegant in whatever you wore.'

'Do not tell that to Brilliana. She thinks my wardrobe is dowdy.'

He was tactful. 'Your sister has somewhat different tastes.'

'Are you sure that you do not mind my joining you in London?' she asked. 'I'd hate to feel that I was intruding in any way.'

'Dear lady, you could never intrude on anyone.'

'What about the friends with whom you intend to stay?'

'Lord and Lady Eames will be as delighted to have you there as we are to take you,' said Cardinal. 'My only fear is that Mother will take up all of your time in the city.'

'I enjoy her company.'

'Do not let her lean too heavily on you.'

'Mrs Cardinal is a most interesting lady. I long to know her better.'

'Mother said exactly the same of you.'

He gave a nervous laugh. In spite of the shortness of their acquaintance, Susan had come to admire Jack Cardinal. He was affable, sincere and self-deprecating. He loved his mother enough to tolerate her many eccentricities. Cardinal also had a keen interest in poetry and his knowledge of it was wide. Susan and he had spent the whole breakfast in a discussion of the merits of Ben Jonson's poems. Subdued for the most part, Cardinal had later spoken with such passion about Izaak Walton's *The Compleat Angler* that he made Susan want to read it so that she could judge for herself. Lancelot Serle had been the only person able to contribute to their debate and his involvement was short-lived. His wife had dragged him unceremoniously off so that her sister was left alone with Cardinal.

The two of them were still standing beside the coach when Mrs Cardinal came out of the house on Serle's arm. Her massive bulk was draped in voluminous clothing and her face reduced to a third of its size by a vast, green, feathered, undulating hat that was secured under her three chins by a thick white ribbon.

'Have I kept you waiting?' she asked. 'I do beg your pardons, my dears.'

'There's nothing to pardon, Mother,' said her son, helping her into the coach. It wobbled under her weight. He offered his hand to Susan. 'Miss Cheever?'

'Thank you,' she said, taking it and climbing into the coach.

Mrs Cardinal patted the seat. 'Come here,' she invited. 'Jack will have to travel with his back to the road. He does not mind that but it would give me one of my turns and that would never do. It's such an odd sensation to be driven backwards. I detest it.'

Susan settled in beside her and Cardinal sat opposite. After wishing them well on their journey, Brilliana and her husband closed the coach door after them. Amid a battery of farewells, the vehicle rumbled off. It was a fine day and the bright sunshine was already bringing out the stark lines of the landscape. Susan surveyed the estate through the window. She had been so eager to escape the clutches of her sister that she had not really understood what was expected of her. She sensed that there could be drawbacks to the new arrangement. Mrs Cardinal was very demanding and her own son had warned Susan not to let the old lady monopolise her. As they rattled along, she could feel his gaze upon the side of his face. What sort of man was he and would they be able to spend so much time together without irritating each other? Who were the friends with whom they were going to stay? How would they react to the arrival of a complete stranger? What would the visitors do all day? Susan began to have qualms about the visit.

Mrs Cardinal put a hand on her arm. 'Your sister is a charming lady,' she said. 'She and dear Lancelot make an ideal couple, I always think.'

'They do,' agreed Susan.

'I had the good fortune to enjoy a happy marriage as well. Did I not, Jack?'

'Yes, Mother,' he said obediently.

'Your father was a devoted husband.'

'I know, Mother.'

Her eyes moistened. 'It was so unfair of God to take him away from me like that. It was a tragedy. My dear husband went before his time and it broke my heart.'

'Do not distress yourself about it now, Mother.'

'I just wanted Susan to understand my situation. It was such a surprise,' she said, her cheeks trembling with emotion. 'I was the one with the delicate constitution and my husband was in the rudest of health. Yet he was snatched away first.'

'Father was thrown from a horse,' explained Cardinal, looking at Susan. 'It was a terrible accident. We've still not recovered from the shock.'

'I doubt that I ever shall,' said his mother.

'When was this?' asked Susan.

'Five years ago, Miss Cheever. Five long, lonely, empty years without him.'

'Come now, Mother,' said Cardinal softly. 'We must not dwell on such things, least of all now when we are setting off on a little adventure. It's months since you went to London and there will be so much to do.' He flicked his eyes to Susan again. 'Where would you like to go, Miss Cheever?'

'Wherever you wish.'

'You must have friends of your own whom you'd like to see.'

'I do, Mr Cardinal.'

'Then you must feel free to get in touch with them.'

'Thank you.'

'We shall very much enjoy meeting them,' said Mrs Cardinal, squeezing her arm. 'Our friends are all rather old and a trifle dull. I've told Jack a hundred times that we need the company of younger people or we shall dwindle into dullness ourselves.'

'I cannot imagine that happening, Mrs Cardinal,' said Susan.

'Then help to prevent it.'

'How?'

'By introducing us to friends of your own age.'

'Miss Cheever might prefer to see them alone, Mother,' suggested Cardinal.

'There's no question of that.'

'Why not?' asked Susan, suddenly worried.

'Because I refuse to be left out,' said the old woman with a touch of belligerence. 'We are not simply giving you a lift to London. That would be to make a convenience of us and what we've offered you is true companionship.' She beamed at Susan. 'I'm sure that you appreciate that.'

'Yes, Mrs Cardinal.'

'I'm glad that we agree on that point.'

'We do,' confirmed Susan. 'I'd be hurt if you thought I was taking advantage of your good nature to make use of your coach. That would be ungracious. At the same time, however, I'm determined that I'll not get under your feet. I daresay that there will be moments when my absence will come as a relief.'

'That's too fanciful a suggestion even to consider,' said Cardinal.

His mother nodded. 'I side with Jack on that.'

'There'd be no benefit at all in your absence, Miss Cheever.'

'And so many from your presence,' said Mrs Cardinal as if laying down a law. 'Besides, I made a promise and I've sworn to keep it.'

'A promise?' said Susan.

'To your sister, Brilliana. She told me that you had a habit of going astray and we cannot have that in a city as large and dangerous as London. It would irresponsible of me. I promised her that I'd keep a motherly eye on you at all times, Miss Cheever.' She gave Susan a playful nudge. 'I hope that you've no objection to that?'

'Do you?' asked Cardinal.

'No,' said Susan, forcing a smile. 'I've no objection at all.'

She concealed her dejection well but her heart was pounding. Susan feared that the private meeting with Christopher Redmayne might not even take place. Her escape was illusory. Instead of breaking free from Brilliana, she was taking her sister with her in the bloated shape of Mrs Cardinal. She felt as if she had been betrayed.

Christopher Redmayne could see at a glance that he was not going to like him. Lady Whitcombe and her daughter were as pleasant as ever but Egerton Whitcombe exuded hostility from the moment he stepped into the house. While the ladies sat, he preferred to stand. When they accepted the offer of refreshment, he spurned it with a rudeness that fringed on contempt. Christopher's polite enquiry about his visit to France was met with a rebuff. Whitcombe made no attempt at civility.

'I was so anxious for Egerton to meet you,' said Lady Whitcombe with a benign smile. 'I wanted to still any doubts he has about you as an architect.'

'It's not Mr Redmayne's architecture that's in question, Mother.'

'Then what is?' asked Christopher.

'Your family, sir.'

'Egerton!' scolded his mother. 'You promised not to raise the matter.'

'It cannot be ignored.'

'Your son is correct, Lady Whitcombe,' admitted Christopher, ready to confront the problem honestly. 'You've doubtless heard about the unfortunate circumstances in which my brother finds himself. But the situation is only temporary, I do assure you. Henry is innocent of the crime with which he's been charged and I've every confidence that he'll be released in due course.'

'I admire your loyalty to your brother, Mr Redmayne,' said Whitcombe with a faint sneer, 'but you can hardly expect us to share it. Everyone else in London believes him to be guilty and you'll not persuade me otherwise.'

'I'd never attempt to do so.'

'You'd be rash even to try, sir.'

'Perhaps we can leave the matter there,' decided Lady Whitcombe.

'No, Mother.'

'Are you determined to exasperate me, Egerton?'

'I'm determined to bring everything out into the open,' he said, ignoring her warning glare. 'You may have no reservations about Mr Redmayne but I think it would be foolish and impolitic to link our name with that of his family.'

'A decision has already been made,' she said with steely authority, 'and it will not be changed. Now, let's have no more of your bleating.'

'I must be allowed to speak my mind, Mother.'

'Enough is enough!'

There was a long silence. It was broken by an involuntary giggle from Letitia, who had not taken her eyes off Christopher since she had been in the room and who had blushed deeply at her brother's forthright comments. Conscious that her giggle was out of place, she mouthed an apology then shrank back in her seat. At best, it would have been an unwelcome visit because Christopher did not wish to see his client at such an awkward time. The presence of Egerton Whitcombe made the discussion very painful. Silenced by his mother, he was now glowering. Christopher chose to address his objections in the most reasonable way.

'Lady Whitcombe,' he began, 'it's absurd to pretend that a problem does not exist here. I do not blame your son for adopting the attitude that he takes. It is, alas, one that's shared by the vast majority of people. That's regrettable but understandable. What I propose, therefore, is this.'

'You've no need to propose anything, Mr Redmayne,' said Lady Whitcombe.

'Hear him out, Mother,' advised her son.

'Yes,' added Letitia nervously. 'I'd like to know what Mr Redmayne has to say.'

'It's quite simple,' said Christopher. 'Since my family name is under a cloud, would it not be sensible to set aside the contract that I have with you and leave it in abeyance? As it happens, the weather conspires against us. It may be some time before work could begin on site and, by then, I am certain, my brother's fate will have been decided. His name will be cleared and your son's objections will be removed.'

'Supposing that your brother is hanged for his crime?' asked Whitcombe.

'He did not commit any.'

'Then why is he being held in Newgate prison?'

Christopher took a deep breath. 'In the event that Henry is found guilty – and there have been miscarriages of justice before – then my contract with Lady Whitcombe is null and void. I accept that.'

'Well, I do not,' she asserted.

'It's your son for whom the house is primarily being built.'

'I'm glad that someone else appreciates that,' said Whitcombe.

'Do you consider my offer a fair one?'

'I do, Mr Redmayne.'

'Then that's how we will proceed.'

'No,' insisted Lady Whitcombe. 'I commissioned the house and I'll hold you to the contract that you signed. Whatever the outcome of the trial, I want to see the property built and I wish you to remain as its architect.'

'So do I,' Letitia piped.

'Keep out of this,' snapped her brother.

'I'm entitled to an opinion, Egerton.'

'You simply do as Mother tells you.'

'And you would be wise to follow her example,' said Lady Whitcombe.

'Please,' said Christopher, trying to calm them down. 'I do not wish to sow any family discord here. I'm honoured that you selected me as your architect and would hate to be compelled to withdraw from the project. At the same time, I have to acknowledge that there are peculiar difficulties here so I offer you a compromise. Let us wait. What harm can there be in that?'

'None,' said Whitcombe, partially mollified.

Christopher turned to his client. 'Lady Whitcombe?'

'I need to think it over,' she replied before shifting her gaze to her son. 'Well, Egerton. Did I not tell you what a considerate man Mr Redmayne was? He has taken your objections into account. I think that you owe him an apology.'

'For what?' asked Whitcombe.

'Your bad manners.'

'It's not unmannerly to protect the good name of your family.'

'Indeed not,' said Christopher, quick to agree with him, 'I'm in the process of doing the same thing myself.'

'Even though you may be wasting your time.'

'That remark was uncalled for, Egerton,' said Lady Whitcombe reproachfully.

'We shall see,' he said. 'Well, now that I've met Mr Redmayne, I'll not take up any more of his time. I have friends to call on. You know where to find me, Mother.'

Christopher had hoped they would all leave but it was only Egerton Whitcombe who was shown out. The hostility towards his host was still there but it was not as pronounced as before. Feeling that he had at least achieved a degree of victory, Whitcombe walked off in the direction of Holborn. Christopher braced himself before returning to face the two ladies in the parlour. He conjured up a pleasant smile.

'You must forgive my son,' said Lady Whitcombe when he

reappeared. 'His stay in France has coarsened him somewhat. Egerton is normally so amenable.'

'As long as he gets what he wants,' observed Letitia.

'That's not true at all.'

'Egerton does like his own way, Mother.'

'He takes after me in that respect.'

Christopher sat opposite them and sensed an immediate change of mood. They were not there solely to talk about the new house. Both of them were now looking at him with a mingled respect and admiration. Letitia tried to suppress another giggle but it came out in the form of a squeak instead. Her mother nudged her sharply before looking around the room.

'What a charming house you have here, Mr Redmayne,' she said.

'Yes, Lady Whitcombe,' he replied. 'I'm lucky that it still stands.'

'Was it threatened by the fire, then?'

'Very much so. The lower half of Fetter Lane was burned to the ground. What you saw when you passed them were the new houses that have been built.'

'I prefer this one,' said Letitia. 'It feels so homely.'

'It's also my place of work.'

'That's why I like it so much. Was our house designed in here, Mr Redmayne?'

'On that very table,' he said, pointing to it. 'But it was not so much designed as recreated to your mother's specifications. Lady Whitcombe is rare among clients in that she knows exactly what she wants.'

'Oh, I do,' said the older woman.

Christopher felt uncomfortable at the way that Letitia was staring at him with a fixed grin on her face. Lady Whitcombe seemed to have brought her daughter there for his approval and it unsettled him. He sought a way out.

'I don't wish to be inhospitable,' he said, rising to his feet, 'but I have to visit my brother this morning. Is there anything else we need to discuss?'

'Not for the moment,' said Lady Whitcombe. 'Since we are in London for a few days, there'll be other opportunities for talking to each other.'

'Oh, yes!' agreed Letitia.

'How *is* your brother, Mr Redmayne?'

'Bearing up well, Lady Whitcombe,' said Christopher.

'I must confess that I was shocked to hear of his arrest.'

'I'm grateful that you did not seize on it as an excuse to rescind our contract.'

'Heavens!' she protested. 'I'd never do that. My late husband taught me to be sceptical about the law. Justice is blind, he told me, and it often fails to see the truth. The guilty people are not always the ones who are locked up in prison. From what you say, your brother has been arrested by mistake.'

'Yes, Lady Whitcombe.'

'Innocence is its own protection.'

'It does need some help occasionally,' said Christopher. 'I've vowed to do everything in my power to restore his reputation.'

'That's very noble of you, Mr Redmayne,' said Letitia.

'And just what I would expect of you,' added Lady Whitcombe. 'Your father must have heard the tidings by now. Have you had any response from him?'

'The clearest possible,' replied Christopher. 'Father is not a young man but he endured days in the saddle to get here in order to lend his support to Henry. Had you come earlier, you'd have met him.'

Lady Whitcombe was delighted. 'The Dean of Gloucester is *here*? Then we must have the pleasure of meeting him.'

'Not for a while, perhaps. Circumstances are not entirely propitious.'

'Of course. He has other preoccupations at the moment.'

'When will your brother be set free?' asked Letitia.

'As soon as we can arrange it.'

'I'd be thrilled to meet him as well.'

'Yes,' said her mother, getting up from her seat and motioning Letitia up at the same time. 'We'd like to get to know all of your family, Mr Redmayne. It's not often that your father is in the city, I daresay, so we must not miss the opportunity.'

'I'll make sure that you don't,' said Christopher, anxious to be rid of them.

'Where is the reverend gentleman now?'

'At the prison, Lady Whitcombe. He's trying to comfort my brother.'

During his years as a priest, the Reverend Algernon Redmayne had often been called upon to visit parishioners who had fallen foul of the law and finished up in Gloucester gaol. It was part of his ministry and he discharged that particular aspect of it extremely well. What he did not envisage was that he would one day be obliged to visit one of his own sons in the most infamous prison in London. Its sheer size was forbidding, its history was a black and direful catalogue of the worst crimes ever perpetrated by the human hand. To realise that the name of Redmayne had been entered in the prison records made the old man quiver with indignation. It was a foul blot on the family escutcheon and he wanted it removed. When he was escorted through Newgate, therefore, he was in a mood of quiet determination. His composure was soon shaken.

'Saints above!' he exclaimed as he was let into the cell. 'This is worse than a pigsty! Can they find you no accommodation other than this, Henry?'

'No, Father. This is one of the better rooms.'

'Then I feel sympathy for the poor souls elsewhere. The place *stinks*.'

'Newgate does not have an odour of sanctity.'

'Do not be so blasphemous!'

'I was endeavouring to be droll.'

'Droll?' The Dean was aghast. 'In *here*?'

'I can see that my remark was misplaced.'

Wishing to greet his brother, Henry was startled when his father stepped into the inadequate confines of the prison cell. He backed away instinctively and yet he felt, after the initial shock had worn off, oddly reassured by the arrival of his visitor. He knew the effort it must have taken the old man to reach London and the embarrassment there must have been when the Dean confided to his bishop the reason for his journey. His father plainly shared his suffering. Henry noted how stooped he had become.

'How are you, Father?' he asked.

'Wearied by travel,' replied the other. 'I'm far too old ride a horse across four or five counties.' He rubbed his back. 'It feels as if I've been in the saddle for a month.'

'See it as a form of pilgrimage.'

'If only I could, Henry! But this is a hardly a holy shrine.'

'No, Father.'

'What have you to say for yourself?'

Henry lowered his head. 'I'm deeply sorry about all this.'

'I did not come for an apology,' said the Dean, 'but for an explanation. Your brother assures me that you are completely innocent of the charge but I want to hear it from your own lips. Look at me, Henry.' The prisoner raised his eyes. 'Did you or did you not commit a murder?'

'I do not believe so, Father.'

'Is there the slightest doubt in your mind?'

'No,' said Henry, trying to sound more certain than he felt. 'The taking of a man's life is anathema to me. That was inculcated in me at an early age. I've obeyed all your precepts, Father. I've done my best to live a Christian life.'

'There's no room in Christianity for over-indulgence.'

'I strive to be abstemious.'

'You have patently not striven hard enough. How often have I warned you about the danger of strong drink? It leads to all manner of lewd behaviour.'

'That's why I only touch wine in moderation, Father.'

'You should only ever taste it during communion.' He leaned forward. 'You do attend a service of holy communion every Sunday, I hope?'

'Unfailingly,' lied Henry. 'I've become very devout.'

'I see precious little sign of it.'

He peered at his son and noticed for the first time how pinched and sallow Henry was. There was a day's growth of beard on his face, his hair was unkempt and the clean apparel he had put on the previous day was already creased and soiled. Sympathy welled up in the old man. Putting his hands on Henry's shoulders, he closed his eyes then offered up a prayer for his son's exoneration and release. Henry was moved.

'Thank you, Father.'

'Bishop Nicholson is praying for you daily. He, too, has faith in you.'

'That's good to hear.'

'Christopher tells me that your friends are standing by you as well.'

'Some of them.' Henry became worried. 'What else has Christopher told you?'

'Far too little. I had a distinct feeling that he might be concealing certain facts from me out of consideration for you. I want nothing hidden. In order to make a proper judgement, I need to hear all the relevant information. Do you understand?'

'Yes, Father.'

'Then tell me what happened, in your own words.'

Henry had looked forward to his father's visit with trepidation. Now that the old man had actually arrived, however, it was not as bad as he had feared. Life in prison had stripped him of his sensibilities and habituated him to pain. What helped him was the fact that he felt sorry for his father. He could see the anguish in his eyes and the awkwardness with which he held himself. On this occasion, the Dean of Gloucester was too fatigued to carry his pulpit with him. Henry would be spared a full homily. With that thought in mind, he told his story with more honesty than he had ever used in front of his father before.

In the intimacy of the cell, Algernon Redmayne listened with the watchful attentiveness of a priest receiving confession from a sinful parishioner. Though he said nothing, his eyebrows were eloquent. When the recital came to an end, he let out a long sigh and searched Henry's face.

'Is that all?' he asked.

'It's all that I can remember.'

'I'm surprised that you remember anything after so much drink.'

'I was led astray, Father. It's unusual of me to imbibe so much.'

'At least, you now know what horrors can ensure. A sober man would not have behaved the way that you did, my son. He would not be under threat of death in a prison.'

'I know that,' said Henry. 'I rue the day when I picked up that first glass of wine.'

'You are too weak-willed.'

'It was an unaccustomed lapse, Father. I hope that you believe that.'

'I trust the evidence of my own eyes and they tell me that you are much too fond of the fruit of the vine. You look haggard and dissipated.'

'Even you would look like that after a few days in here.'

'No, Henry. I might pine and grow thin but I would not be so unwholesome.'

'If you saw me in my periwig, you'd think me the healthiest of men.'

'Never,' said the other. 'I've seen too much decadence to mistake the signs. If and when you are delivered from this hellish place, you and I must have a long talk, Henry. The time has come to mend your ways.' His son gave a penitential nod. 'Thank you for what you told me. You spoke with a degree of sincerity that I had not anticipated and it was a consolation. But there is one point on which you were not entirely clear.'

'What was that, Father?'

'Your reason for hating this Italian fencing master so much.'

'I told you,' said Henry. 'I heard that he cheated at cards.'

'*Heard*? Or did you sit opposite him at the card table and witness the act?'

'Drink, I admit to, Father, but gambling has never had much appeal for me.'

'So why were you so outraged that this fellow should cheat?'

'Because it's a dishonourable act.'

'It was not your place to correct him for it.'

'There was more to it than that,' conceded Henry. 'Jeronimo Maldini was not merely a cheat and a villain. He exposed me to ridicule at the fencing school by demonstrating his superiority with a sword.'

'That might anger you,' said his father, 'but it was surely not enough to implant murderous thoughts in your mind. And you did say that, in the middle of an argument, you threatened to kill the man.'

'I did, I did – to my eternal shame!'

'So what *really* made you despise this man?'

Henry blenched beneath his father's gaze. The cell suddenly seemed much smaller. In spite of the cold, sweat broke out on Henry's brow and his collar felt impossibly tight. There was no way that he could tell his father about the woman who had been stolen from him by his rival. The Dean of Gloucester would neither under-stand nor countenance the idea of sexual passion. It was something that he appeared never to have experienced and Henry had come to believe that he and Christopher had been conceived in random moments of religious ecstasy that had long been buried under years of monkish chastity. To explain to his father that he had loved and courted a married woman would be to show contempt for the bonds of holy matrimony. The name of Lady Patience Holcroft had to be kept out of the conversation altogether.

'Well,' pressed his father. 'I'm waiting for an answer.'

'I've already given it,' replied Henry. 'I was goaded by Jeronimo Maldini.'

'But why did he pick on you? There must have been a reason.'

'He took it with him to the grave, Father.'

The old man stepped back and nodded sagely. Henry had been let off the hook.

'I hope that you realise how much you have to thank your brother for,' said the Dean with solemnity. 'Christopher has dedicated himself to your cause.'

'I do not know what I would have done without him.'

'You came perilously close to finding out.'

'What do you mean?'

'An attempt was made on Christopher's life yesterday.'

'Where?'

'On the riverbank. He was pushed into the water.'

'Did he survive?' asked Henry, becoming agitated. 'What happened? Was he hurt? This is terrible news, Father. Who was responsible?'

'Christopher believes the attack was linked to the crime for which you were arrested. He was drenched by the incident but is otherwise unharmed. I'm telling you this so that you'll not give way to feelings of self-pity. You at least are safe in here, Henry,' he pointed out. 'But in trying to help you, your brother has put his life in danger.'

The man watched the house in Fetter Lane from the safety of a doorway farther down the street. He had been reassured when he saw an old man in clerical garb come out of the property with a servant who then hailed a carriage for him. It suggested that a priest had come to offer condolences. Shortly afterwards, three people went into the house. The young man was the first to leave and the two ladies followed some time afterwards. Too far away to see the expressions on their faces, he hoped that the visitors were also there out of sympathy for a bereavement. After an hour in the chill wind, he decided that he would leave but the front door of the

182

house opened again and a sprightly figure stepped out. The man cursed under his breath. Christopher Redmayne was still alive.

Captain Harvest arrived on horseback at the tavern in Whitefriars. Before he could dismount, however, he saw that Jonathan Bale was approaching him. He gave a cheery wave with a gloved hand.

'Good day to you, my friend!'

'Good morning, Captain Harvest.'

'You are getting to know my habits. That worries me.'

'There are a few things that worry me as well, sir,' said Jonathan. 'I wonder if I might take up a little of your time?'

'By all means, my friend.'

The soldier dismounted and held the bridle of his horse. Jonathan noticed the beautiful leather saddle. Harvest looked even more shabby and disreputable than before. There was mud on his boots, a tear in his waistcoat and the vestiges of his breakfast were lodged in his red beard. He gave the constable a mock bow.

'I'm always ready to assist an officer of the law,' he said.

'Your landlord seemed to think you would run from the sight of me.'

'Which landlord?'

'The one you fled because you owed him rent.'

Harvest laughed. 'More than one landlord could make that claim,' he admitted. 'But I do not only pay in money, you see. I reward them with something far more valuable. They have the pleasure of my company and no man could set a price on that.' His eyelids narrowed. 'I hope that you've not come to arrest me for debt. If that's the case, I've money in my purse to pay the fellow.'

'He'd rather have it from your hand than mine,' said Jonathan. 'No, Captain Harvest, I'm not here to arrest you on the landlord's behalf. I came to ask you a few more questions about the murder.'

'You know my view. Henry Redmayne is guilty.'

'I talked to Mr Crenlowe and Sir Humphrey Godden on the subject.'

'Then they doubtless swore that he was innocent.'

'Mr Crenlowe did rather more than that, sir.'

'Oh?'

'He wondered who the real killer might be.'

'You already have him in custody.'

'Not according to Mr Crenlowe and he struck me as an intelligent man. He said that you are a more likely assassin than Mr Redmayne.'

'Me?' He gave a laugh of disbelief. 'Why ever should Martin think that?'

'He was making a judgement of your character.'

'Did Sir Humphrey agree with him?'

'No,' said Jonathan. 'He could not see that you'd have a motive.'

'Nobody had a stronger motive than me to keep Jeronimo Maldini *alive*,' asserted Harvest, tapping his own chest. 'His fencing school was a godsend to me in many ways. I not only earned some money there, I made the acquaintance of the kind of people I like.'

'People who will lend you money?'

'Those who are too wealthy to ask for it back, Mr Bale.' The horse moved sharply sideways and Jonathan leaped out of its way. 'I see you are not a riding man,' said Harvest, patting the flank of the animal to ease it back. 'The two best friends any soldier can have are a good sword and a fine horse.'

'I always fought on foot, sir.'

'That explains a lot about you.'

'Let's return to Mr Crenlowe. How do you answer his accusation?'

'With contempt and outrage,' rejoined the other, eyes ablaze. 'What proof did Martin offer? None, I'll wager, because none exists. When I left the Elephant that night, I went straight to friends. They'll vouch for Captain Harvest.'

'That brings me to another point.'

'What else does that cringing goldsmith allege against me?'

'Nothing at all.'

'I'll crack his head open if he dares to blacken my name.'

'What exactly *is* that name, sir?'

'You know full well. I'm Captain James Harvest.'

'And you've always been a soldier?'

'Yes,' declared the other with pride. 'I fought three times under the Royalist flag then went abroad until the country came to its senses. When King Charles took his rightful place on the throne, I served the army on the Continent. I'm a soldier through and through, Mr Bale.'

'Then it's strange that there's so little record of you.'

'Record?'

'I have a close friend who works as a clerk for the army,' said Jonathan, 'and I asked him a favour. He went back through all the muster rolls that he could find but there was no mention anywhere of a James Harvest, either as a captain or holding any other rank. Which regiment did you serve, sir?'

'Do you doubt my word?' blustered the other.

'Frankly, I do.'

'I don't have to explain myself to you, Mr Bale.'

'It's Henry Redmayne who deserves the explanation, sir. He took you for what you appear to be and was grossly deceived. Do you remember what you first said to me?'

Harvest scowled. 'I regret that I ever saw you.'

'You assured me that Mr Redmayne was guilty of the murder and that you'd stake your reputation on it.' Jonathan grasped him by the arm. 'How can you do that when you *have* no reputation?'

'Take your hand off me!'

'How can you be Captain James Harvest when no such person exists?'

'Leave go!'

'It's my duty to place you under arrest, sir.'

'Damn you!'

'I think that you have some explaining to do.'

'Get off, man!'

Tugging hard on the reins, he brought his horse around in a semicircle so that its flank buffeted Jonathan and sent him reeling. The other man had his foot in the stirrup in an instant. Before the constable could recover, the counterfeit soldier mounted the horse then jabbed his heels into the animal. It cantered off down the street. Annoyed that he had let his man escape, Jonathan was nevertheless philosophical. He felt that he had made definite progress.

Susan Cheever was given an opportunity much sooner than she dared to hope. The coach ride from Richmond had been such a trial for Mrs Cardinal that she took to a day-bed as soon as they reached their destination. Her son stood by to see if his mother required anything, leaving Susan to get acquainted with her hosts. Lord Eames was a distinguished old man with silver hair, kind, cordial and endlessly obliging, but his wife, the frail Lady Eames, though delighted to welcome the guests, was troubled by deafness. Their palatial house was in the Strand and its relative proximity to Fetter Lane was too great a temptation for Susan to resist. Excusing herself to rest after the rigours of the journey, Susan retired to her room then waited a decent interval before slipping down the backstairs and leaving through the rear door of the house. Spurning the danger of being unaccompanied, she walked briskly until she reached Christopher Redmayne's house. Jacob shepherded her into the parlour. He was very surprised to see her.

'I thought you had gone to your sister in Richmond,' he said.

'Chance brought me back to London again.'

'I'm pleased to hear it. Mr Redmayne will be delighted.'

'How long is he likely to be?' asked Susan. 'I cannot tarry.'

'I expect him home very soon, Miss Cheever. He went off to visit his brother in Newgate and then dine with his father. The Dean arrived here yesterday. I believe that the two of them were going to visit the lawyer this afternoon.'

Susan was dismayed. Anxious to see Christopher again to hear his news, she was less enthralled at the prospect of doing so in the presence of his father. She had never met the old man but had heard enough about him to suspect that he would add a sombre note to the occasion. Susan could hardly express her affection for his son in the shadow of the Dean of Gloucester. In the event, her fears were unfounded. Christopher returned alone on horseback and was met by Jacob at the door. When he realised that she was there, the architect positively bounded into the parlour and embraced his visitor.

'What are you doing here?' he asked.

'Take off your hat and cloak, and I might tell you.'

'At once, Susan.'

When he removed his cloak, she saw that he wore a dagger as well as a sword.

'You are well-armed today,' she said.

'Of necessity,' he explained, removing his rapier. 'I also took the precaution of travelling by horse. He'll not catch me unawares again.'

'Who?'

'The man who tried to kill me.'

Susan reached out for him in alarm and he held her hands. Leading her to a chair, he sat her down and told her about the incident on the bank of the river. She was even more upset. Susan could not understand why he was so calm about it.

'The man is still stalking you, Christopher?'

'He will do, when he discovers that I'm still alive.'

'But you must have some protection against him.'

'I have it here,' he said, indicating his weapons. 'Next time, I'll be prepared for him. I'll take care to watch my back.'

'You sound as if you *want* him to attack you again.'

'I do, Susan. It's the only way that I can catch the rogue.'

'And you believe that he's the man who killed that fencing master?'

'Why else would he turn on me?' he replied. 'He knows that I'm on his tail and must be closer than I imagined. I've given him a scare. That's why he struck out.'

'You've given me a scare as well,' she said, touching his hand again. 'Please take the utmost care. I'd be so distressed if anything were to happen to you.'

'It will not, you have my word on that.'

Christopher gave her a warm smile and she relaxed a little. Moved by her obvious concern, he was sorry when Susan gently withdrew her hand. She looked around.

'I was told that your father was with you.'

'He was. We dined together then called on the lawyer to discuss Henry's case. Father is something of a lawyer himself so his support was welcome. Having seen my brother in prison, he knows what a dreadful state Henry is in and wants to secure his release as soon as possible.'

'Where is your father now?'

'Visiting the Bishop of London,' returned Christopher. 'He feels duty bound to defend the family name at the highest level of the Church. I admire him for that.' Still lifted by the joy of seeing her so unexpectedly, he looked at her with an affectionate smile. 'However do you come to be here?'

'Purely by accident.'

She told him about the providential invitation from Mrs Cardinal and her son but did not explain that her sister had deliberately brought Jack Cardinal to Serle Court as a potential suitor for her. It did not seem a relevant detail to her. Unable to believe his good fortune, Christopher grinned throughout.

'So that's why you seized your moment today?' he concluded.

'Yes,' she said. 'I may not have another opportunity.'

'Then I'll have to come to you next time.'

'It may be difficult. Mrs Cardinal and her son know people all over London. This visit is in the nature of a complete tour of their acquaintances. On the ride here, Mrs Cardinal never stopped boasting about the friends she has in high places.'

'Where are you staying?'

'With Lord and Lady Eames. They have a house in the Strand.'

'A mansion, more like. Only the very wealthy can afford to live there.'

'It's a fine place,' she said, 'but I much prefer a certain house in Fetter Lane.'

'You'd have been welcome to stay here.'

'Mrs Cardinal would never countenance that. She watches me like a hawk. I'd better return there now before she wakes up again or it could be very awkward.'

He reached for his cloak. 'I'll make sure you get there safely.'

'Lord and Lady Eames are generous hosts,' she said. 'They could not have been nicer to me. In honour of Mrs Cardinal and her son, they are giving a dinner party tomorrow that sounds like a veritable banquet. Everybody will be there.'

'Except me, alas.'

'Mrs Cardinal was delighted at the fuss they are making of her. The Lord Mayor has been invited, so has the Attorney General, so have many other important people, including Sir Ralph Holcroft and Judge McNeil.'

Christopher was taken aback. 'Sir Ralph Holcroft?'

'Yes. I've heard Father speak disparagingly of him but the man cannot be as bad as that. Apparently, he has a young and beautiful wife. Is that true?'

'Very true,' he said, his mind racing. 'Susan.'

'Yes?'

'I have a big favour to ask of you.'

Chapter Thirteen

Jack Cardinal occupied the bedchamber next to his mother so that he could be summoned instantly, if the need arose. Their hosts had assigned a maidservant to look after Mrs Cardinal but the latter preferred to rely on her son. To that end, she always carried a little bell with her and had the satisfaction of knowing that he was only a tinkle away. While he waited for the sound of the bell, Cardinal mused on the way in which he had made the acquaintance of Susan Cheever. He had liked her at once and found it possible to talk to her about subjects that most of the young ladies he knew would have found irrelevant or boring. Susan had an inquiring mind.

What struck him most about her was a sense of self-possession. She had such poise and assurance. During the visit of her neighbours, Brilliana Serle made certain that she was the centre of attention but it was her sister who had provided the main interest for Cardinal. He was too modest to assume that he had made such a favourable impression on Susan but he was reassured by the fact that she was so willing to travel with them to London. It was a hopeful sign. His mother obviously approved of her. That was an even more hopeful sign. As he recalled the events of the past twenty-four hours, Cardinal's affection for his new friend slowly increased.

He was so lost in fond meditation that he did not at first hear the tinkle of the bell. It was shaken with more urgency. Rising from his chair, he went into the adjoining room.

'How are you now, Mother?' he asked.

'I feel faint,' she said. 'Where is my medicine?'

'I'll get it for you.'

He opened the leather valise that stood on the little table and ran his eye over the selection of bottles. Choosing one of them, he poured the medicine into a tiny silver cup that nestled amid the potions. Mrs Cardinal propped herself up on the day-bed so that she could drink the liquid in some comfort. She closed her eyes tight until it began to have some effect. Her son relieved her of the silver cup.

'That's better,' she announced, opening her eyes. 'How long was I asleep?'

'Well over an hour.'

'The coach would jostle us.'

'The roads are still hard, Mother, and you wanted to make good time. Besides,' he said, 'the journey seemed much quicker than usual – thanks to our companion.'

'Yes, Susan Cheever is a most agreeable young lady.'

'And a most intelligent one.'

'It's not often that I take to anyone as easily as that.'

'Nor me, Mother. She's such pleasant company.'

'I had a feeling that you liked her, Jack,' she said, patting his hand. 'It's wrong for you to be at my beck and call all the time. You need someone like her to bring a little colour into your existence.'

He became defensive. 'I hardly know Miss Cheever yet.'

'But you approve of what you do know, I take it?'

'Yes, Mother.'

'Good. That's a promising start.'

'Do not rush things, Mother. We've only just met.'

'The girl is Lancelot Serle's sister-in-law. That tells you much.'

'I agree,' he said. 'But Miss Cheever is a handsome young lady.'

'So?'

'She'll have many admirers and may already have formed an attachment.'

'Then why was she staying at Serle Court?'

'To be with her sister.'

'And why was Brilliana so eager for us to meet her? Open your eyes, Jack.'

'I do not think she had any mercenary intent.'

'I'd not blame her if she had.'

'Mother!'

'We were invited for a purpose.'

'Yes,' he said. 'To enjoy the hospitality of good friends, that was all.'

'I have a sixth sense in these matters.'

'Miss Cheever would never lend herself to what you suggest.'

'Brilliana would give her no choice in the matter.'

'I'm sorry, Mother. I disagree with you. I see no hidden meanings here.'

'You will, Jack. You will. Where is Miss Cheever now?'

'She went to her room to rest.'

'At her age?' asked Mrs Cardinal in surprise. 'Rest is for ladies of my years and my constitution. It should not be encouraged in young ladies, especially those as robust as she. Fetch her, Jack.'

'What?'

'Fetch her. I want to speak to her.'

'But she may be asleep, Mother.'

'Then wake her up. I did not bring her all the way to London so that she could go to sleep on me. Invite her in here then we'll descend together. Lord and Lady Eames will think us poor guests if we slumber throughout the whole afternoon.'

He was reluctant. 'It would be unfair to disturb her.'

'My needs take precedence over Miss Cheever's,' said his mother. 'Shame on you, Jack! Would you oppose the wishes of a sick woman?'

'I'll fetch her at once,' he promised.

Cardinal went out. He was troubled by his mother's comments. As an eligible bachelor, he was not unused to having available young ladies thrust at him by grinning parents and he had learned to avoid the situations in which that could happen. He did not have the feeling that Susan was being presented for his approval in such an obvious way. If anything, she had been a little distant with him when he first arrived at Serle Court and had made no attempt to engage him in conversation. It was only when she had been invited to join them in London that she showed any enthusiasm for their company. He did not sense that Susan was deliberately trying to ingratiate herself with him. That was what he found so attractive about her. She seemed to be very much her own woman.

He walked along the landing to a room at the far end and tapped politely on the door. When there was no response, he knocked a little harder. Getting no reply again, he rapped on the door with more purpose. There was a long silence. He inched the door open and peeped in, only to find that the room was empty. Cardinal was about to report back to his mother when he heard footsteps behind him. He turned to see Susan Cheever, wearing her cloak and hat, tripping up the backstairs.

'Where have you been?' he asked.

'Oh,' she said, startled to see him. 'There you are, Mr Cardinal.'

'We thought you were in your room.'

'Yes, I was. But I had a headache and felt that a walk in the garden would help to clear it. Have you seen the rear garden? It goes right down to the river.' Having invented an excuse, she began to embellish it. 'I enjoyed my walk so much that I lost all purchase on time. It was fascinating to look at the river now that the ice is melting. I'm rather sad that the frost fair has disappeared but it could not last. What a pity you were not able to see it, Mr Cardinal! It took my breath away.' She removed her hat. 'Have I been gone long? Have you missed me?'

'Very much,' he replied with a smile. 'I'm glad that you came back.'

'I feel so much better for my walk.'

'What about your headache?'

'Oh, that soon vanished, Mr Cardinal,' she said, relieved that he obviously accepted her explanation. 'Going out into the fresh air was the best thing I could have done. My little walk has refreshed me completely.'

Christopher Redmayne had stayed long enough to watch her disappear around the side of the building before he set off again. The sudden change in his fortunes had left him in a state of exhilaration. To see Susan Cheever again so soon was a miracle in itself but there had been another unforeseen blessing. As a result of staying at the mansion in the Strand, she would be able to dine with Sir Ralph Holcroft and his wife. It gave Christopher the perfect opportunity to communicate with the woman whom he believed might hold vital information that could be of direct benefit to his brother. He was tingling all over.

Having accompanied Susan back to the house, he now had to walk home alone and he did not let his feeling of joy distract him from the need to be watchful. His dip in the River Thames was still a painful memory. On the stroll back to Fetter Lane, therefore, he kept his hand on the hilt of his sword and his mind alert. It was still light and traffic was busy. When he reached Fleet Street, he had to wait until a coach and three carts had gone by before he could cross the road. Fearing that someone might lunge out of the crowd at him, he remained vigilant all the way home. No attack came but he did have an uncomfortable feeling that he was being followed. When he reached his door, therefore, he turned suddenly on his heel and stared down the street. His instinct had not betrayed him.

Christopher had been followed but it was by a friend. Jonathan Bale was hurrying towards him.

'Why did you not shout?' he asked when the constable caught up with him.

'You'd not have heard me with all the noise,' said Jonathan, as a carriage thundered past with two horsemen behind it. 'London gets more deafening every day.'

'Then let's step inside where we can hear ourselves.'

They went into the house and made for the parlour. Jacob appeared from the kitchen to take their cloaks and hats. Since the attack on his master, he insisted on wearing a dagger himself even though the likelihood of his having to use it was remote. The two men sat down in order to exchange their intelligence. Christopher felt constrained. Though he had confided everything else to his friend, he had deliberately kept his brother's involvement with Patience Holcroft to himself. It meant that he could not share the exciting news that he had finally found a means of getting in touch with the lady. Instead, he had to enthuse about his father's visit.

'It removed all trace of doubt in my mind,' he explained. 'My brother is innocent. If Henry *had* been guilty of that crime, my father would surely have known it.'

'How, Mr Redmayne?'

'How do you know when your sons have misbehaved?'

'Murder is rather more than misbehaviour.'

'You know what I mean, Jonathan.'

'Yes, I do,' said the other. 'As for my sons, they always look so uneasy that I can see at once if they've been up to mischief. And so can Sarah.'

'It's not quite as simple as that in this case. Henry was so confused.'

'And now?'

'He knows that he could never have killed that man.'

'What did your father think of Newgate?'

'He was horrified,' said Christopher, 'and not merely because one of his sons was being held there by mistake. The whole prison revolted him. Father is like me. He could not believe that a building with such a grand exterior could be so vile and soulless on the inside. That abiding reek turned his stomach. He looked ill when he came out again.'

'Did you visit your brother yourself?'

'Briefly. I took some more food and drink for him.'

'Were you able to mention my request?' asked Jonathan. 'I know that your brother is not fond of me but I would still like to visit him on my own. Would that be possible?'

'Only if you are ready to withstand a torrent of abuse.'

'What did he say?'

'At first, he ordered me to keep you away at all costs.'

'And then?'

'He changed his mind. Henry told me that he so hated being locked up alone in a prison cell that he'd welcome a visit from his worst enemy. Those were his exact words.'

'I see.'

'You'll have to make your own decision, Jonathan. But I'd better warn you that he was very upset when I told him that you were taking a particular interest in his case.'

'That does not surprise me.'

'Henry seems to have forgotten a previous occasion when you helped to get him out of trouble. All that he remembers is the way that you upbraided him afterwards.'

'He deserved it, Mr Redmayne.'

'Oh. I agree. But it did not endear you to him.'

'We'll never be close friends, sir.'

'He's still prickly. Your visit may be in vain.'

Jonathan pondered. 'I'd still like to go,' he said at length.

'Would you like me there with you? It might make it a little easier.'

'No, I'll go on my own. I'm used to talking to prisoners in their cells. They give things away without even realising it sometimes.' He studied the glow on Christopher's face. 'You look happy, sir. Has something else happened?'

'A pleasing encounter with a dear friend, that's all,' said Christopher evasively. 'What's really given me new heart is the discovery that the man who killed Signor Maldini is frightened enough to strike again. I have him on the run, Jonathan. It's only a question of time before I find out who he is.' He rubbed his hands. 'But you would not have called if you did not have news of your own to impart? What have you learned?'

'What we both suspected about him, Mr Redmayne.'

'About whom?'

'Captain Harvest.'

'He's entertaining company, I know, but I'd not trust him for a second.'

'Nor I,' said Jonathan. 'You met him at the Hope and Anchor. I began to wonder why he chose to spend time in a sailors' tavern when, if he'd gone elsewhere, he could have found plenty of old soldiers to talk to about his days in the army.'

'That puzzled me as well.'

'I found out why.'

'Was the gallant Captain Harvest discharged with dishonour?'

'I doubt if he ever bore arms in war. Whenever I was with him, I felt that I was being tricked. So I tried to trick him myself.'

'He'd not have expected that, Jonathan. What did you do?'

'I pretended that I had a friend who worked as a clerk in the army and told him that the man had looked through all the muster rolls without finding any trace of a Captain Harvest. The trick worked,' he said with a smile of self-congratulation. 'He believed me. When I asked him what regiment he served in, he knew that the game was up and fled on his horse. He'll not be so easy to track down again.'

Christopher was intrigued. 'If he is not Captain Harvest, who is he?'

'I do not know, Mr Redmayne, but I intend to find out.'

'Did he not try to talk his way out of it?'

'He tried and failed, sir. His eyes betrayed him.'

'This is news indeed!' said Christopher with a laugh. 'You look so honest that he never suspected that you'd dupe him. Bravo! You tricked a master trickster, Jonathan.'

'Then I let him get away.'

'That was unlike you. Well, this puts a different complexion on the whole thing. I did suggest that he might be involved in the murder but we thought he'd have no motive.'

'Mr Crenlowe believed he might be guilty.'

'Did he say why?'

'No, it was just a feeling that he had about the man.'

'Yet Sir Humphrey Godden disagreed with him.'

'Very strongly. I think that Mr Crenlowe had suspicions of Captain Harvest – or, at least, of the man who was passing himself off under that name. The murder brought those suspicions to the surface.'

'Perhaps I should call on him again.'

'You'd fare better than me, Mr Redmayne. I learned little from the goldsmith.'

'You learned that he was not as pleasant a man as he appeared to be.'

'He showed you more respect, it's true.'

'What about Sir Humphrey? Should I see him again?'

'I think that someone should tell him how completely he was fooled. Let me do it. That fraudulent soldier deceived them all, including your brother.'

'And me, Jonathan. His voice, manner and gestures were so persuasive.'

'I fought in an army, sir. You did not. He troubled me from the start.'

'You've done us all a service by unmasking him,' said Christopher. 'It raises all kinds of new questions. How close was he to Jeronimo Maldini? Did the Italian know his true identity or was he taken in as well? Why was 'the captain' the only one of Henry's friends who did not stand by him? I think we know the answer to that,' he decided. 'It was as I guessed. He accused my brother to divert attention from himself.'

'We need to catch him, Mr Redmayne – and soon.'

'But where *is* the mysterious Captain Harvest?'

Sir Humphrey Godden dined at home with his wife for once then set some hours aside to work on his accounts. It was a tiresome exercise but he stuck to his task, going through his bills in order and making the appropriate entries in his ledger. When a servant entered, his master looked up in the hope that he had brought some refreshment but the man had only come to inform him that he had a visitor. Sir Humphrey was not pleased to hear the name that was whispered in his ear. Setting his quill aside, he marched out of the room and into the hall, expecting to see a familiar face and distinctive apparel. Instead, he was looking at a big, broad-shouldered man in dark clothing that robbed him of all of his flamboyance. Where there had once been a red beard, there was now a clean-shaven face. Coming to a halt, Sir Humphrey stared with incredulity at his friend.

'I was told that Captain Harvest was here,' he said.

'He is,' replied the other with his telltale grin.

'Is that *you*, James? What have you done to yourself?'

'I'll explain that, Sir Humphrey.'

'Why have you come here?'

'I need to borrow some money.'

Sir Humphrey was in two minds, wanting to turn the visitor away yet held back by invisible ties of friendship. Eventually, he glanced over his shoulder.

'Follow me,' he said.

Martin Crenlowe was in high feather at the hope of success. He had spent over an hour displaying his wares to a customer in search of a goldsmith who could fashion some highly expensive jewellery for him. The man had gone away to consider the matter but Crenlowe was almost certain that the lucrative order would in time be placed with him. It was the latest piece of good fortune in what had been a profitable week. Alone in his office, he allowed himself a celebratory glass of brandy. There was a tap on the door then one of his apprentices came in.

'There's a gentleman to see you, sir,' he said.

Crenlowe was pleased. 'Is it the customer who was here earlier?'

'No, sir. His name is Christopher Redmayne.'

'Oh.' He was disappointed. 'Did you tell him that I was here?'

'Yes, sir.'

'Then you had better show him in.'

Crenlowe drained his glass then set it aside. He got to his feet to give Christopher a greeting when the latter was conducted into the room. The goldsmith was apologetic.

'You catch me at a busy time, Mr Redmayne,' he said.

'Then I'll do my best not to hold you up for long,' promised Christopher, 'but there have been certain developments that I felt might interest you.'

'Developments?'

'I believe that you had a visit from Jonathan Bale.'

'Oh, yes, that constable. Not the most prepossessing of individuals.'

'Do not be misled by that dour manner of his, Mr Crenlowe. He's a shrewd man. Jonathan discovered something that neither you, Sir Humphrey Godden, nor my brother had managed to find out.'

'And what was that?'

'Captain Harvest is an impostor.'

Christopher told him how the self-styled soldier had been challenged and exposed by Jonathan and how he had fled from the scene as a result. The goldsmith was very interested in the news but he was not entirely surprised.

'We all knew that James was a rogue of sorts,' he said blandly, 'but he could be such amiable company that it did not seem to mind. And there was no doubting his skill with a sword. We took his word that he'd learned that on the battlefield. Yet now, you tell me, he was not even a soldier.'

'Mr Bale was.'

'I see.'

'He fought at Worcester. He pointed out that there's no place in battle for any refinements of the art of fencing. It's all slash, cut and thrust. You've no time to make use of the eight positions from which to attack or parry that are taught in a fencing school. Strength and speed of action are the qualities needed.'

'I obviously misjudged your friend, the constable.'

'Many people do. You told him that Captain Harvest – to give him the name that he used – might conceivably have been the killer.'

'I begin to think it even more likely now.'

'So do I, Mr Crenlowe. He may have made an attempt on my life as well.'

'Never!'

When he heard about the attack on the riverbank, Crenlowe became alarmed. He needed some time to absorb the implications of what he had been told. Eventually, he pointed a knowing finger at his visitor.

'This is proof positive that Henry is innocent,' he declared.

'That's what I believe.'

'James must be arrested at once.'

'Unfortunately, he's disappeared.'

'Then he must be hunted down, Mr Redmayne.' He shook his head with disgust. 'To think how easily he took us all in! Mark you,' he went on, 'we only ever saw him in convivial surroundings. When drink is taken, one is apt to be far less discriminating. And we did imbibe a great deal. I confess to that fault readily.

James duped us. He knew exactly how to win our confidence.' He moved across to Christopher. 'Have you told your brother about this?'

'Not yet, Mr Crenlowe.'

'It will gladden his heart.'

'Henry is still trying to recover from our father's visit.'

'Yes, he lives in dread of him. He's often spoken to us about the fearsome Dean.'

'Father is only fearsome to those with a guilty conscience,' said Christopher, 'and Henry has had that for years. But there's something else on which I'd like your opinion,' he went on, measuring his words carefully. 'Captain Harvest claimed that the root of the dissension between Henry and Signor Maldini was their mutual interest in a certain lady.'

'Did he say who the lady was?'

'No,' replied Christopher, careful to divulge no further detail. 'Were you aware that my brother had conceived a passion for someone?'

'It's happened too often for us to pay much attention to it.'

'This was patently a more serious involvement.'

'Then Henry was discreet for once,' said Crenlowe, 'for I was unaware of it. And since we know that James was a practised liar, he might well have invented the whole thing in order to give your brother a stronger motive to commit murder. What does Henry himself say?'

'He denies such a lady even existed.'

'There's your answer, then. Disregard the suggestion.'

Christopher was glad that he had not mentioned the name of Patience Holcroft. The goldsmith clearly had no knowledge of her link with the murder victim and the man arrested for the crime. He was confident that Sir Humphrey Godden knew nothing of it either. Evidently, Henry Redmayne had shown uncharacteristic discretion in his dealings with the lady. That only confirmed the strength of his feeling for her.

'Thank you for your help, Mr Crenlowe,' he said. 'I'm glad that I came.'

'So am I, so am I. These tidings about James are very distressing.'

'Have you any idea where we might find him?'

'No, Mr Redmayne,' said the other. 'He had a habit of finding *us*.

I've no idea where the man lodged even. James would just appear when he chose to.'

'He boasted to me that he liked to cover his tracks.'

'He'll have even more need to do that now.'

'Exactly,' said Christopher. 'Since he can no longer swagger as Captain Harvest, he'll have to find another disguise. My fear is that he might flee London altogether but he'd need money to do that. Where would he go to find it?'

Crenlowe was stern. 'Not here,' he said, 'I can promise you that. I made it crystal clear to James that I'd loaned him money for the last time.'

'What about Sir Humphrey Godden?'

'He'd be less likely to expect repayment.'

'Why is that?'

'Sir Humphrey has more money than he needs, Mr Redmayne. He inherited his wealth. I, as you see, have to accumulate mine with the skills I've acquired in my trade. It makes me less willing to advance a loan unless I know that it will be duly repaid. James would never turn to me again.'

'Where would he turn?'

'I could give you half-a-dozen names,' said Crenlowe, 'but the main one has already been mentioned. He'd almost certainly go first to Sir Humphrey Godden.'

Jonathan Bale was even less welcome at the address in Covent Garden than he had been at the coffee house. He was kept standing in the draughty hall for fifteen minutes before Sir Humphrey Godden even deigned to acknowledge his presence. When he finally made an appearance, the man was an unfriendly host.

'Will you stop hounding me, Mr Bale?' he demanded.

'I needed to speak to you again, Sir Humphrey.'

'Well, I've no wish to speak to you. And neither has Martin Crenlowe, for that matter. We are both certain of Henry Redmayne's innocence so we'll have no dealings with someone who is intent on securing his conviction.'

'My only intention is to see that justice is done,' said Jonathan.

'*Your* kind of justice, based on ignorance and prejudice.'

'You are hardly free from prejudice yourself, Sir Humphrey.'

'What do you mean?'

'I was thinking about your opinion of foreigners.'

'It's shared by every right-thinking Englishman. Foreigners are inferior to us.'

'I can see that you have a degree of ignorance as well.'

'Beware, sir!' growled the other, squaring his shoulders aggressively. 'I'll not be insulted in my own home. Nor will I be cross-examined by a parish constable who does not understand the meaning of respect. I bid you farewell.'

'Are you not interested in the news that I bring you?'

'Not in the slightest.'

'Then I'll leave you to the mercy of Captain Harvest,' said Jonathan, heading for the door. 'You obviously have no wish to learn the truth about him.'

Sir Humphrey was jolted. 'Wait!' he said. 'What's this about James?'

'I only came here as a favour to pass on the warning.'

'Warning?'

Jonathan opened the front door. 'Good day, Sir Humphrey.'

'Hold on a moment!' ordered the other, crossing swiftly over to him. 'If there's something that I should know, let's hear it.' He closed the door again. 'Now, Mr Bale. What really brought you to my house today?'

'My sense of duty, sir. I felt impelled to tell you what I discovered.'

Jonathan's description of his encounter with Captain Harvest was slow and rather ponderous. Sir Humphrey Godden listened with growing unease. A chevron of anxiety appeared on his brow and he began to grind his teeth. The strange appearance at his house of his erstwhile friend was now explained. What he could not accept was the suggestion that the man might be responsible for the murder.

'James was something of a scoundrel – we all accepted that – but he was not a malicious person. When you see a man in his cups,' he argued, 'you have a good idea of his true character, and he was the soul of joviality.'

'He was not very jovial when he made his escape from me.'

'I can see why. You tore away his mask.'

'Who was the man behind it, Sir Humphrey? That's what I wish to know.'

'A knave and an imposter, perhaps – but not a killer.'

'Mr Redmayne would dispute that,' said Jonathan. 'He feels that he was the victim of a murderous attack by your friend. When Mr Redmayne was standing on the riverbank, he was pushed into the water by someone who did not wish him to come out again. Fortunately, he survived.'

Sir Humphrey was shocked by the news. 'I'm relieved to hear it.'

'Not as much as me. He could easily have drowned.'

'And he thinks that James was responsible?'

'He considers it a strong possibility, Sir Humphrey.'

'How does Mr Redmayne know that the attack is related to the murder?'

'He was near the scene of the crime when it happened,' explained Jonathan.

'What, in Fenchurch Street?'

'No, some distance away. His brother was found in an alley near Thames Street. It was only a short walk to the river from there.'

'I begin to see his reasoning,' said Sir Humphrey, rubbing his chin. 'It would be too great a coincidence for this to happen so close to the place where the murder must have been committed.'

'Does it alter your opinion of Captain Harvest?'

'No, I still do not take him for a callous murderer.'

'Somebody stabbed the fencing master in the back.'

'I thought that you were ready to hang Henry Redmayne for the crime.'

'I felt that the evidence pointed that way,' admitted Jonathan, 'but I've been forced to think again. What I do know is that the man who called himself Captain Harvest is implicated in some way and that means we have to apprehend him. Have you any idea where he might be, Sir Humphrey?'

'None at all.'

'When did you last see him?'

'On the night when the murder took place.'

'Has he not tried to get in touch with you since?'

'Why should he do that?'

'Because he needs money,' said Jonathan. 'He left his lodging because he could not pay his rent. Mr Redmayne found him playing cards in a tavern in search of funds. I've only met the fellow twice but I'd say that he was an expert at borrowing money from friends. I wondered if he had come to you, Sir Humphrey.'

'No, Mr Bale!' said the other with more force in his denial than was necessary. 'I've not seen hide nor hair of the fellow. He's had nothing from me, I warrant you. I'd not give him a single penny.'

Jonathan sensed that he was lying.

Lady Whitcombe was not pleased with the outcome of their visit to Fetter Lane. Her hopes that Christopher Redmayne would be able to win over her son had foundered. Egerton Whitcombe had been surly and disobedient, aspects of his character that he took care to hide from his mother as a rule. While the architect had behaved like a gentleman, her son had been boorish and she was determined to wrest an apology out of him. Her daughter, Letitia, was thinking along the same lines.

'Egerton was so disagreeable this morning,' she said. 'He was rude and peevish. What made him behave like that, Mother?'

'I think he's still tired after the difficult crossing from France.'

'You always make excuses for him.'

'I make none in this instance, Letitia. I mean to reprimand him sharply.'

Her daughter giggled. 'I long to hear you do that.'

'It will be done in private,' emphasized Lady Whitcombe. 'But Egerton was not the only person who let me down in Mr Redmayne's house. You behaved badly as well. I want him to admire my daughter yet you make strange noises at him then start to argue with your brother. Truly, I was ashamed of both of you.'

'Mother!' said the girl, tears forming in her eyes. 'Do not be angry with me.'

'Then do not give me cause for anger.'

Letitia lapsed into a bruised silence. They were alone in the parlour of the house where they were staying. Lady Whitcombe had been studying the drawings for her new house and reflecting on the quality of its architect. She was not in the mood for idle conversation with her daughter. Letitia waited several minutes before she dared to speak.

'Do you think that Mr Redmayne's brother did commit a murder?' she asked.

'No, Letitia.'

'Yet he has been arrested.'

'Yes,' said her mother, 'and you can see the unfortunate position in which that places Mr Redmayne. People have turned against him in the same unthinking way that Egerton did. It's so narrow-minded of them. Your father taught me the value of tolerance and decency,' she continued, folding up the drawings. 'He lived through turbulent days, Letitia. He saw more than one friend of his sent to the Tower but he never turned his back on them because of that. Nor did he shun their families.'

'Father was a saint,' said Letitia wistfully.

'No, he was a simply human being who understood human weakness.'

'I do wish I'd seen more of him when I was growing up.'

'Your father was a statesman, Letitia. That brings heavy responsibilities. He served his country and we still bask in the reputation that he left behind. It's only when a family is in danger of losing its good name – as in this present case – that you realise how important an asset it is.'

'Yes, Mother.'

'At a time like this, Mr Redmayne needs compassion.'

'It's no use looking to Egerton for that.'

'Letitia!'

'When he went to that house this morning, he was in a foul mood.'

'He'd been listening to too much loose talk in taverns,' said Lady Whitcombe. 'The general feeling is that Henry Redmayne is guilty. Well, I'll not believe it. I'm sure that his brother will soon clear his name.'

'Oh, I hope so. I do want him to design our house.'

Her mother held up the drawings. 'He's already done that. Nothing will stop me having this house built. Whatever happens, Mr Redmayne will be my architect. I'll tell him that when I see him tomorrow.'

'We're going to see him again?' asked Letitia with a grin.

'I am. You will stay here.'

'That's cruel!'

'I choose to go on my own this time.'

'But I like him so. Do let me come with you.'

'No,' said Lady Whitcombe firmly. 'There are a few tiny points I wish to raise with him over the design and I'd prefer to see him in private. Do not look so sad, Letitia. There'll be other occasions. In due course,' she assured her daughter, 'you will be seeing a great deal of Christopher Redmayne.'

Susan Cheever was so grateful that her disappearance from the house had escaped attention that she made an effort to be especially attentive to the people who had taken her there. Friendly towards Jack Cardinal, she was even more courteous towards his mother, asking her about her plans for the stay in London and showing an interest in everything that was suggested. Mrs Cardinal warmed to her and could see that her son was also drawn to their new acquaintance. Lord Eames was an inveterate collector. When he took Cardinal off to see his display of weapons, the three ladies were left alone in the parlour before the roaring fire. Deafness prevented Lady Eames from doing little more than nodding and smiling though any conversation. When the old lady fell quietly asleep in her chair, Mrs Cardinal was able to talk more freely to Susan.

'Have you recovered from the journey yet?' she asked.

'I think so, Mrs Cardinal.'

'I've never known the coach toss us around so much.'

'For the pleasure of coming to London, I'd endure any discomfort. I'm so grateful to you and your son for bringing me. Apart from anything else, it takes away the feeling that I'm imposing on Brilliana.'

'Your sister would never let anyone impose on her.'

Susan laughed. 'I see that you've got to know her.'

'The whole of Richmond knows her. Brilliana has such energy. I am never with your sister but there's a shower of sparks flying from her. Was she always so lively?'

'Yes, Mrs Cardinal.'

'You have a much quieter disposition.'

'Do I?'

'Jack noticed that,' said the other. 'Fond as he is of Brilliana, he could not tolerate her company for this long. He feels that she would wear him out and yet Lancelot seems to thrive on it.'

'He's a very dutiful husband.'

'I suspect that your sister chose with him with great care.'

'She does everything with care, Mrs Cardinal.'

'I gathered that. Your father is a Member of Parliament, I believe.'

'A discontented one,' replied Susan fondly. 'Father thinks that everyone in the chamber but himself is a blockhead. The problem is that he insists on telling them that.'

'Sir Julius is not a man who seeks easy popularity, then.'

'No, Mrs Cardinal.'

'It's perhaps as well that he's not here now.'

'Why?'

'We'll be dining tomorrow with some of the people he would consider blockheads. Three of them sit in the House of Commons so they may know the name of Sir Julius Cheever.'

'It might be more tactful to keep it from them.'

'I hoped at one time that Jack might enter politics but he has no stomach for it.'

'Then he's wise to stay well clear of that world.'

'We'll all be pitched into the middle of it tomorrow,' said Mrs Cardinal. 'They'll be talking politics all around us at dinner. Lady Eames is the only person who'll be spared. Deafness has its compensations. But I'll expect you to talk to Jack,' she said. 'I'll make sure that you sit next to him so that he does not have to listen to all that earnest discussion of the state of the nation. Will you do that for me?'

'With pleasure,' replied Susan, guessing that there was another reason behind the request. 'You told me earlier that one of the guests was Sir Ralph Holcroft,' she went on, keen to know more about him after her visit to Fetter Lane. 'What manner of man is he?'

'Shrewd and sagacious, by all accounts.'

'Did you not say that he had a young wife?'

'Patience is the envy of his friends,' said Mrs Cardinal. 'Sir Ralph is over thirty years older and not the handsomest of men, yet he was her choice of a husband. He claims that she is a greater gift than his knighthood.'

'Have you met his wife before?'

'Only once but that was enough. Her reputation as a beauty is well-earned. She would dazzle in any assembly. Jack was rather overwhelmed by her but every other man in the room gazed at her in adoration. Patience Holcroft is a rare woman.'

'I look forward to meeting her.'

'You may have difficulty getting close enough,' warned Mrs

Cardinal with a chuckle. 'The men will crowd around her and I daresay that Lord Eames will have her sitting at his elbow during dinner.'

'Does her husband not mind the attention that she gets?'

'He revels in it, Miss Cheever.'

'What about his wife?'

'Patience, by name and by nature. She endures it all without protest. But enough of our friends,' she decided, adjusting her skirt. 'You have your own. We long to meet people in your circle as well.'

'It's very small, I fear.'

'No matter. Your sister told us that you had made some good friends in London. Jack and I will insist on being introduced to them.' Her good humour suddenly vanished. 'With one glaring exception, that is.'

'Exception?'

'Brilliana mentioned a young architect named Christopher Redmayne.'

'Yes,' said Susan proudly. 'Mr Redmayne is a friend of mine.'

'Then I'd advise you to sever the relationship at once. His brother, as I hear, has been arrested on a charge of murder.'

'Mistakenly, it seems.'

'Not according to common report. I tell you this for your own sake, Miss Cheever. End your friendship with this architect at once. When his brother is convicted of murder,' she insisted, her eyes rolling, 'the name of Redmayne will be a form of leprosy.'

It was dusk when Christopher left the goldsmith's shop to ride back home. He was glad that he had visited Martin Crenlowe again. There had been a subtle change in the man's manner that he did not understand but he was nevertheless pleased to spend time with someone who had such complete faith in his brother's innocence. As he picked his way along the crowded thoroughfare, he sifted through what the goldsmith had told him, feeling that there was something that he had missed. Christopher did not neglect his personal safety. He was alert, sword and dagger within easy reach.

Inevitably, Susan Cheever soon displaced everyone else in his mind. He remembered the courage she had shown to make contact with him in Richmond and the risk she had taken to visit him that afternoon. Christopher hoped that the time would soon come when their friendship was not so beset with obstacles. When he had asked her for a favour, she had agreed to grant it before she even knew what it was. Everything now turned on the way that she did the favour. All that he had asked her to do was to give a letter, in strictest privacy, to Lady Patience Holcroft. Susan had not even pressed him for details and he had been spared the embarrassment of telling her about Henry's romantic interest or of compromising the lady's reputation.

Reaching the house, he could see candlelight through the gap in the shutters. Since Jacob did not come out to greet him, he surmised that his servant was attending to their guest who must surely have returned from his visit to the bishop. Christopher decided to stable the horse by himself. He dismounted and led the animal down the passageway at the side of the house. Jacob had lit a lantern and it was hanging from a nail outside the stable. Opening the door, Christopher patted the horse and it went through into the stall. Before he could follow it, he heard hurried footsteps behind him.

Christopher swung round to see a figure hurtling towards him out of the shadows.

Chapter Fourteen

He was too slow. His attacker had the advantage of surprise. Before he could even draw a weapon to defend himself, Christopher was hit on the side of the head with a cudgel. Though his hat softened the blow, it still dazed him slightly. He put an arm up to ward off the next few blows and bunched his other fist so that he could throw a punch at the man who was belabouring him. It caught his adversary on the chest and sent him a yard backwards, but he flung himself at Christopher again with renewed energy and knocked his hat from his head. Using both arms to defend himself, Christopher was beaten back against the stable door. Resistance was being bludgeoned out of him. When he felt blood oozing down the side of his face, it prompted his instinct for survival. Christopher tensed himself. As the cudgel descended again, he grabbed the man's wrist and twisted hard but the weapon was not dislodged. It flailed around in his face. With a supreme effort, Christopher swung the man's arm against the wall so that the cudgel was dashed from his hand.

Letting out a cry of pain, his attacker pushed him away and ran back down the passageway. Christopher flung back his cloak and groped for his sword but the man did not want to duel with him. Instead, he pulled a dagger from his belt and threw it hard. Christopher dodged in the nick of time. After missing his face by inches, the dagger embedded itself in the side of the stable with a thud. The man took to his heels. Christopher was too groggy to give pursuit but he staggered out into Fetter Lane in time to see him mounting a horse before riding off at speed.

It had all happened so quickly that Christopher did not get a chance to look properly at the man. All that he knew was that his adversary was young, slim and wiry with a hat pulled down over his face. One thing was evident. It was certainly not the man he had known as Captain Harvest. As he swayed uncertainly on his feet, he did not know whether to be reassured or disappointed by that fact. A moment later, Jacob came hurrying out of the house with a lantern in one hand and a dagger in the other. He saw the blood on his master's face.

'What happened, Mr Redmayne!' he exclaimed.

'Someone was lying in wait for me, Jacob.'

'Are you badly hurt, sir?'

'I'm bruised and bloodied, but it could have been far worse.'

'It's my fault,' wailed Jacob. 'I meant to come out when I heard the horse but your father was busy giving me instructions. Come inside, Mr Redmayne. I'll clean that the wound for you and bind it up.'

'See to the horse first,' said Christopher, steadying himself with a hand on the wall. 'I'm not sure that I can manage that just yet. Oh, there's something I forgot,' he added, going back to the stable to retrieve the dagger. 'This was meant for me.'

Jonathan Bale's visit to the house in Covent Garden had been instructive. Sir Humphrey Godden had denied any knowledge of the whereabouts of the former Captain Harvest with such vehemence that the constable knew that he was lying. That meant either that the impostor had already been to him in the hope of borrowing money, or, more worryingly, that Sir Humphrey was somehow working in league with the man. If the latter were the case, Jonathan decided, it explained why Sir Humphrey had insisted that his friend could not be guilty of the crime. He would have been deliberately shielding an accomplice. There was no doubting the intensity of Sir Humphrey's open hatred of the Italian fencing master. It gave him an obvious motive for murder.

The important thing was to catch the bogus soldier as soon as possible. Jonathan did not think that the man would necessarily leave London. Someone who could evade a succession of creditors with such ease knew how to lose himself in the populous city. As long as he had money to sustain himself, he might go to ground somewhere. Jonathan set out in search of him, having first called at his house to change his clothing. It was an occasion when a common man would be more likely to gather intelligence than a constable. His long black coat was therefore replaced by the garb that he had once worn as a shipwright. It would help Jonathan to blend in more easily.

Since he had twice found his quarry at a tavern in Whitefriars, he knew that the man would not return there. Instead, he went to the Hope and Anchor, the riverside inn where Christopher Redmayne had encountered the quondam Captain Harvest. It was only half-full but the atmosphere was still rowdy. A fierce quarrel was taking place between two watermen who berated each other with mouth-filling oaths. Another man was arguing over the price that an ageing prostitute was putting on her dubious favours. Three drunken sailors were singing out of tune. Jonathan ordered a tankard of beer and bided his time. When the noise finally died down a little, he sidled across to the innkeeper.

'I was hoping to see a friend of mine in here,' he said, looking around.

'And who might that be?' asked the other, a stocky man with bulging forearms.

'Captain Harvest. We agreed to play cards in here this evening.'

The innkeeper smirked. 'Oh, I think that the captain has another game in mind.'

'Does he often come in here?'

'Only when he needs some money and some comfort.'

'Comfort?'

'Captain Harvest has an eye for the ladies, sir,' said the man. 'One in particular brings him to the Hope and Anchor. She's done it time and again.'

'Who is she?'

'That would be telling.'

'If he's not coming in this evening, I need to get a message to him.'

'Leave it with me. I'll pass it on.'

'How will you do that?' The innkeeper ignored him and used a cloth to wipe the counter between them. 'I've good news for the captain,' resumed Jonathan. 'It could bring him some money.' He put his hand on his purse. 'There'd be something in it for you, my friend, if you could tell me where he is.'

The innkeeper was suspicious. 'Who are you?' he asked.

'I told you. I'm a friend of Captain Harvest.'

'What's your trade?'

'I'm a shipwright.'

'Oh?' said the innkeeper, looking him up and down. 'A shipwright, eh? You've the hands for it, I grant you, but that proves nothing. Which ships have you worked on?'

'The last was the *Mercury*,' said Jonathan, naming a vessel that had been launched only months ago. 'We needed the oak from almost six hundred trees to build her. It was nearer seven hundred for the *Silver Spirit*. I was working at Chatham when we built her. I could tell you exactly how we constructed the hull. Would you like me to take you through the mysteries of my trade?'

'No, sir,' said the other. 'I believe you. But I had to make sure.'

'You were right. Never trust a stranger. It's a good rule.' He put some coins on the counter. 'But I'd still like to speak to Captain Harvest.'

The innkeeper eyed the money. 'I'm not sure where he is this evening.'

'But you have some idea, I can see that. Who is this particular lady you speak of?'

'That would be Hannah Liggett.'

'Does she work here?'

'Yes,' said the man, 'that's why the captain always comes back when he needs a bed for the night. Hannah is sweet on him. He'll leave her for months on end but she never turns him away when he shows up here.'

'Where is she now?' asked Jonathan.

'Hannah won't be in for days yet.'

'Does that mean she's with the captain?' The innkeeper was staring at the money. Jonathan added two more coins. 'How would I find this Hannah Liggett?'

The man swept up the money. 'She lives no more than a short walk away.'

When Jacob had cleaned him up, Christopher Redmayne still looked in a sorry state. His father stood over him and clicked his tongue in consternation.

'Attacked on your own doorstep!' he said. 'What a violent city this is!'

'Violence is everywhere, Father,' said Christopher, seated on a chair while Jacob bound his head with a strip of linen. 'You have your share of it in Gloucester, I daresay.'

'Not on this scale. Bishop Henchman was complaining about it earlier. He told me that he feels like a King Canute, vainly trying to hold back the tide of villainy. We have our malefactors in Gloucester but they do not try to murder you outside your own house. That is insupportable.'

'I managed to fight him off.'

'But look at the injury he inflicted on you.'

Christopher winced at the reminder. The scalp wound smarted and his arms and shoulders ached from the bruising blows. He was glad that Susan Cheever could not see him at that moment. He felt battered.

'We'll pray together later,' said the Dean, 'and thank God for your deliverance.'

'Yes, Father.'

'Bishop Henchman will hear of this.'

'You must not trouble the Bishop of London with my misfortunes.'

'But he's taken an interest in Henry's case. The bishop was very sympathetic to our cause. By the time I had finished talking to him, he was prepared to accept that Henry might be innocent of the crime.' Having finished doctoring his patient, Jacob went off into the kitchen. The Dean put a gentle hand on his son's shoulder. 'Who was the rogue who assaulted you?'

'A henchman of a different kind, Father.'

'Henchman?'

'I believe that he may be working for someone else, a swaggering fellow who called himself Captain Harvest to conceal his real name and character. When I talked about the murder with him, he told me that an accomplice was involved. I did not realise that he might have been the person who employed him. Captain Harvest is a genial parasite,' he explained. 'He uses his charm and cunning to live off others.'

'Henry mentioned his name. He thought the captain was a friend of his.'

'Not any more, Father.'

'How did he fall in with such bad company?'

'He's not the only person to be tricked by Captain Harvest. Dozens more were deceived by his plausible manner and smooth tongue. Had it not been for my friend, Jonathan Bale, the captain would have continued his deception unchecked and, I fear, have got away with murder.'

'It's shameful!' said the old man with bitterness. 'All this stems from Henry's reprehensible way of life. That is the *fons et origo* of this succession of horrors. Because your brother is so easily led by false friends, he is now in prison and you have twice escaped attempts on your life. It's unpardonable! I was far too soft on Henry at the prison. When I return tomorrow, I'll make him see the evil consequences of his behaviour.'

'No, Father. Do not mention what happened to me today.'

'But I must. It may bring him to his senses.'

'He's already plagued by his conscience,' said Christopher, 'If he knows there's been another assault on me, he'll suffer even greater pangs. Let's spare him those. It's torment enough simply to be locked up in that prison.'

'Henry needs to show true remorse.'

'I'm sure that he does.'

'I want clearer evidence of it, Christopher,' insisted the other. 'For that reason, I intend to tell him how terribly you've suffered because of him. Thanks to Henry, you were all but murdered by that ruffian.'

'That's the odd thing, Father.'

'What is?'

'The man was no ruffian.'

'He must have been.'

'He hit me hard,' said Christopher, rubbing a shoulder, 'there's no question about that. But he used that cudgel as if he'd never had it in his hand before. A ruffian would have had me senseless with a few blows then finished me off with a dagger. This may seem a strange thing to say,' he continued, 'but I was attacked by a gentleman of sorts.'

Hannah Liggett lodged in a tenement not far from the Hope and Anchor. When he got there, Jonathan first spoke to the landlord and learned that the woman was not inside. She had been seen leaving with a man earlier that evening but he did not fit the description that the constable gave him of Captain Harvest. There was nothing that Jonathan could do except wait. Finding a vantage point from which to watch the building, he turned up his collar against the chill wind and kept his eyes on the street. Several people came and went but none looked anything like the man he sought. Hannah Liggett's room was on the first floor and he watched the shuttered window for signs of light. She did not return to the tenement. It was a long, cold, cheerless wait that yielded no positive result. At midnight, Jonathan went back home.

The first guests arrived by mid-morning and the house in the Strand was suddenly filled with political gossip. Susan Cheever remained on the fringes of the conversation and spent most of her time chatting to Jack Cardinal, who seemed to shy away from the general discussion.

'Do you have no time for politics, Mr Cardinal?' she asked.

'For politics, yes,' he replied. 'It's the politicians that frighten me. Listen to them. They never stop talking about which faction will rise and which fall.'

'You'd not find my father congenial company, then.'

'Oh, but I would, Miss Cheever.'

'He, too, is obsessed with political events.'

'Any member of your family would interest me greatly. Lancelot tells me that Sir Julius is an outspoken man with forceful opinions. We've too few of those in parliament. I'd very much like to meet him some time.' He gave a smile. 'Now that I've made your acquaintance, I hope to see a lot more of you.'

It was the nearest he got to expressing his affection for her. Susan was grateful when his mother detached him with a request to fetch something from her bedchamber. It gave Susan a chance to take a first look at Patience Holcroft, who was just arriving with her husband. They were an incongruous couple. The gaunt and stooping Sir Ralph Holcroft looked years older than his true age while his wife seemed to be years younger than hers. There was a youthful bloom on her that turned the head of every man in the room. She was beautiful yet demure, accepting compliments with a touching modesty. Her husband appeared to bask in the praise that she received. Susan was worried. With everyone forming a circle around the newcomers, she could not see how she could get near Patience Holcroft and, if she was to fulfil her promise to Christopher Redmayne, it was imperative to speak to her alone.

She watched and waited until the novelty of the woman's arrival slowly wore off. Lord Eames voiced an opinion concerning the revenue of the Crown and Sir Ralph Holcroft immediately responded to it. The room was suddenly ringing with heady political discussion again. It was Mrs Cardinal who came unwittingly to Susan's aid. Restored by the smelling salts that her son had brought for her, she swooped on Patience Holcroft and brought her across to introduce her to Susan. When she heard that Sir Julius Cheever was a

Member of Parliament, Lady Holcroft gave Susan a look of sympathy.

'It would be better for you if he'd remained a farmer,' she said.

'Life would certainly be quieter, Lady Holcroft,' replied Susan. 'But your husband is far more elevated than my father. Does it not excite you that he is so close to the centre of events?'

'It does, Miss Cheever. I reap the benefits but I also suffer the disadvantages. Sir Ralph's dedication to his work is remarkable but it does take him away from me. This will be the first time this week that we've dined together.'

'And your husband will spend it talking to other politicians,' noted Mrs Cardinal.

'At least, we are together,' said Lady Holcroft loyally.

'That's so important in a marriage, especially in the early years.' Mrs Cardinal shot a meaningful glance at Susan. 'My husband spoiled me. We saw each other every day at first and were rarely apart after that. Jack, my son, was able to pattern himself on his father because he spent so much time with him.'

'Your circumstances were obviously different, Mrs Cardinal,' said Susan.

'I chose a man who loved the country so much that he rarely stirred from it. Jack follows him a little in that regard, though he does have something in common with you, Miss Cheever,' she said with a fond smile in her son's direction. 'He loves to kick the earth off his boots from time to time and come to London. You are two of a kind in that respect. Oh, look,' she added, noticing that Lady Eames was alone. 'Our dear hostess is being cruelly neglected by all her guests. Do please excuse me.'

She displayed a row of small teeth and moved away. Susan knew that it was time to strike because she might not get a second opportunity. Making sure that nobody was within earshot, she took a step closer to Lady Holcroft.

'I wondered if I might have a word in private with you?' she asked.

'Why?' replied the other.

'I've a letter to give you from a friend.'

Lady Holcroft stiffened. 'A letter? Do I know the person who wrote it?'

'No, Lady Holcroft.'

'Then keep it yourself, Miss Cheever. I do not accept missives from strangers.'

'I was told that it was important to deliver it,' said Susan.

'No matter.'

'It's not what you think it might be, Lady Holcroft.'

'Oh? Why do you say that? Do you know what the letter contains?'

'No, Lady Holcroft but I trust the young man who wrote it.'

'Too many young men have tried to involve me in a correspondence.'

'I can understand that.'

'As a married woman,' said the other, 'I naturally spurn all their attempts.'

'The letter was given to me in confidence by a Mr Redmayne.'

Lady Holcroft recoiled as if from a blow. For a moment, she did not know quite how to react. A stab of pain showed in her eyes. Without warning, she turned abruptly on her heel and walked swiftly away. Susan bit her lip in dismay. She felt that she had let Christopher down badly.

Jonathan Bale studied the dagger with interest. He held it on the palm of his hand to feel its weight. When he called at the house in Fetter Lane that morning, he found Christopher Redmayne alone. His father had visited the prison again and Jacob was at the market to get some provisions for the larder. It enabled them to talk freely about what each had found out since their last meeting. Jonathan was disturbed to hear of the second attack.

'I've never seen a weapon quite like this before,' he said, turning the dagger over. 'And he hurled this at you?'

'Yes, Jonathan.

'Why did he not draw his sword? If you were dazed by the blows from the cudgel, he had you at a clear disadvantage. One quick thrust of a rapier and you were done for.'

'He seemed to lose his nerve and flee.'

'Then he was no practised assassin, Mr Redmayne. If he was the same man who pushed you in the river, you were lucky. He's had two chances to kill you and lacked the skill to take either.'

Christopher smiled. 'I don't propose to offer him a third opportunity.'

217

He no longer wore the bandaging around his head but the bruises had now come out on his arms and shoulders, showing him just how much punishment he had taken. He was grateful to be able to tell his friend about the attack. After handing the dagger back to him, Jonathan described his visit to the home of Sir Humphrey Godden and his night-time vigil outside the tenement where Hannah Liggett lodged. Christopher was interested to hear his opinion.

'You think that Sir Humphrey is hand-in-glove with our Captain Harvest?'

'That was the feeling I began to get, sir.'

'Then why did the captain not seek refuge at the house in Covent Garden? I'll wager that Sir Humphrey could offer him a softer bed than the one he'll find in a tenement near the river.'

'But he could hardly share it with Hannah Liggett there.'

'True,' said Christopher. 'And his friend might not want him under his roof. Captain Harvest – or whatever his name really is – belongs to a part of his life that Sir Humphrey chooses to keep hidden from his wife. Well, Jonathan,' he concluded, 'if the two of them are in league together, they must have an accomplice, for it was neither of them who ambushed me outside my stable.'

'The man who did was not in their employ,' decided Jonathan. 'They'd hire a more seasoned assassin than the one who attacked you. That does not mean you ignore this fellow. I think you need someone to guard you, sir,' he went on, worried for his friend. 'If he's struck twice, he's determined to kill you. Let me act as your protector.'

'My Lord High Protector?' teased the other.

'Your life is in danger, Mr Redmayne.'

'So is my brother's,' said Christopher, 'and he's in no position to defend himself. I am, Jonathan. Thank you for your offer but I can take care of myself. I *want* the fellow to try again. I'll be more than ready for him.'

'As you wish, sir.'

'You keep looking for the man you deprived of his disguise as a soldier. Most likely, he'll have taken on another by now but there are some things even he cannot hide.'

'I'd know him anywhere, Mr Redmayne,' said Jonathan, moving to the door. 'But I also intend to call at Newgate today. Your brother may be ready to speak to me now.'

'Do not count on it,' warned Christopher.

He saw his friend out of the house then returned to the parlour. After examining the dagger again, he slipped it into a drawer. He crossed to the mirror and used a delicate hand to flick hair over the scalp wound that had now dried up. When he heard a tap on the door, he thought that Jonathan had come back but a glance through the window showed that there was a carriage outside the door. Lady Whitcombe had called. Though she was the last person he wished to see at that moment, he conquered the urge to lie low and pretend that he was not at home. Her coachman banged on the door more loudly. As soon as Christopher opened it, Lady Whitcombe alighted from her carriage with the aid of the coachman and surged towards the house. Under her arm were the drawings that Christopher had delivered to her house in Sheen.

'I'm so glad that I caught you at home,' she said, sweeping past him to go into the house. 'Forgive my descending on you like this, Mr Redmayne, but I've had a change of mind with regard to your design.'

'You wish to rescind our contract, after all?' he said anxiously, closing the door and following her into the parlour. 'I understood that I was still your architect.'

'You were, are and ever will be,' she told him before glancing around. 'Is your father not here this morning?'

'No, Lady Whitcombe. Father left earlier. He's visiting my brother. May I offer you some refreshment?' he asked with brisk civility. 'Jacob has gone to market so I have to play the servant today.'

'Oh, we are alone in the house, are we?'

'We are.'

'How convenient!' Removing her hat and cloak, she handed them to Christopher who went into the hallway to hang them on a peg. When he returned, he saw that his visitor was seated in a chair, arranging her dress. 'Come and sit beside me, Mr Redmayne,' she said. 'There's something we need to discuss.'

Christopher took a seat. 'You talked about a change of mind.'

'Only with regard to my bedchamber. I think I'll go back to your original suggestion about the proportions of the room. I was wrong, you were right.'

'Every architect likes to hear that from a client.'

'Before we talk about the house,' she said, 'you must let me apologise for my son's behaviour yesterday. It was very untypical of him. Egerton can be such a delightful young man, as you will in time discover.'

'I bear no grudges, Lady Whitcombe. I admired your son's forthrightness.'

'His father always taught him to speak his mind.'

'He certainly did that,' said Christopher.

'He misses his father greatly,' she sighed. 'Almost as much as I do.' She regarded him through hooded eyes. 'What do you think of Letitia?' she asked.

'Your daughter is a charming young lady.'

'A little wanting in true beauty, perhaps.'

'Not at all,' he said gallantly. 'Good looks are obviously a family attribute. Your son is very handsome. He and his sister are a credit to you, Lady Whitcombe.'

'I hoped you'd think that. Letitia lacks maturity, that's her main fault.'

'It will vanish with the passage of time.'

'That's what I told her,' said Lady Whitcombe. 'Letitia will grow into herself. Believe it or not, I was a trifle gauche at her age.'

'I refuse to accept that.'

She gave a laugh. 'You flatter me, Mr Redmayne. Though, looking back, I have to tell you that I much prefer the blessings of maturity to the blundering of inexperience. Egerton became a man when his father died. Letitia has yet to blossom.' She beamed at him. 'It pleases me so much that you are fond of my daughter. In a sense, it signals your approval of me.'

'That was never in question, Lady Whitcombe.' She laughed again. 'Shall we look at the drawings again?' he suggested. 'I can soon make the necessary adjustments.'

'There are some other adjustments to be made first, Mr Redmayne.'

'Indeed?'

'This is a trying time for you, I know,' she said, reaching out to grasp his arm. 'When one has family anxieties, it's impossible to think of anything else. Patently, you are bearing a heavy burden at the moment.'

'I'd not disagree with that.'

'Well, you do not have to bear it alone, Mr Redmayne. You have friends. Loyal and supportive friends, who are there for you to turn to in moments of extremity. I'd feel privileged to be one of those friends.'

'Yes, Lady Whitcombe,' he said without enthusiasm. 'You are, you are.'

'That means a great deal to me.' She squeezed his arm before releasing it. 'You must have noticed how fond Letitia has become of you. When we came to London to welcome Egerton back, she insisted that we called on you as well. Not, mark you, that any insistence was required. I'd already made the decision to do just that.' She gazed at him for a moment. 'What will happen if your brother is convicted?' she asked.

'That's a possibility I do not even contemplate.'

'Most of London seems to think it a probability, Mr Redmayne. While I hope that he'll be acquitted, I'm compelled to accept that our system of justice is far from perfect. Innocent men sometimes to do go to the gallows. If – God forbid! – that did occur, how would it affect your career?'

'Adversely, Lady Whitcombe.'

'My commission would therefore be a valuable one.'

'It would be the saving of me.'

'Once built, of course, my new house would be a fine advertisement for you.'

'To show your faith in me, in such circumstances, would be an even better advertisement for me. Even if Henry is released, it will take time for me to win back some lost credibility. An architect is only as good as his name and mine is rather sullied at the moment. I'm deeply grateful for the way that you've helped me, Lady Whitcombe.'

'You've helped us as well.'

'Have I?'

'Yes, Mr Redmayne,' she said quietly. 'When you came on the scene, Letitia and I were very lonely. My husband had died and my son was in France for a lengthy period. There was no man in the house until you began to visit.' She touched his arm again. 'I'd like you to visit us more often in future. Will you do that for me?'

Christopher felt distinctly uneasy. Having feared that she was pushing her daughter at him in the hope that a romance might develop between them, he saw that the situation was far more threatening than that. It was Lady Whitcombe herself who had the real interest in him. In trying to involve him in her family, she simply wanted him closer to her. Christopher saw the precariousness of his position. She was his only client at a time when the name of Redmayne was a serious handicap. To lose her commission would be to plunge him into a period of unemployment from which it would not be easy to escape. Lady Whitcombe was trying to exploit his vulnerability.

'Will you do that for me, Mr Redmayne?' she repeated, beaming at him.

'When the house is being built,' he said, 'we are bound to see a lot of each other.'

'Only as architect and client. I wish to see you as a friend – a *close* friend.'

Her fingers tightened on his arm. Christopher decided to play for time.

'Then you shall, Lady Whitcombe.'

'Good!' she said with a laugh of satisfaction. 'Now that we have sorted that out, perhaps we could take a look at the drawings again. I really do need your expert advice with regard to my bedchamber.'

Dinner at the house in the Strand was a sumptuous affair. Served in a room that was almost as large as a baronial hall, it was a veritable banquet. In addition to Lord and Lady Eames, there were sixteen people at a table that was laden with culinary delights. Those with appetites big enough could enjoy soups of various kind, a fricassee of rabbit and chicken, boiled mutton, carp, roast lamb, roasted pigeons, a lamprey pie, a platter of anchovies and a dish of four lobsters. Sweetmeats galore followed, the whole meal washed down with quality wines. Politics remained the chosen subject of debate.

Susan Cheever was at the opposite end of the table from Sir Ralph Holcroft and his wife. Seated next to Jack Cardinal, she engaged in polite conversation while trying to catch the eye of Lady Holcroft. Susan was studiously ignored. It intensified her sense of failure and she did not look forward to reporting it to Christopher. Her neighbour saw how little food she touched.

'Is that all you want, Miss Cheever?' he asked.

'I'm not hungry.'

'A magnificent feast like this makes one feel hungry. It's irresistible.'

'Then you can eat my share as well, Mr Cardinal,' she offered.

'Thank you. How long will you be staying in Richmond?'

'Until my father returns.'

'In the meantime, you must visit us,' he said, coupling the invitation with a cordial smile. 'Your sister tells me that you are a fine horsewoman. Perhaps we could ride out together.'

'When the weather improves,' she said, one eye still on Lady Holcroft. 'I do enjoy riding, Mr Cardinal. I much prefer it to travelling by coach.'

'That's something else on which we agree. Unfortunately, Mother can only get around on four wheels so, naturally, I have to make allowances for her. But there's nothing nicer than a ride to whet one's appetite before breakfast.'

'Your appetite seems to have be whetted today.'

'No,' he said with a guilty chuckle, looking at the food piled on his plate. 'This is not appetite, Miss Cheever. It's sheer greed.'

'I did not take you for a greedy man.'

'Why else do you think I sat next to you?'

The compliment was blurted out so quickly that he felt slightly embarrassed about it and turned away. Susan glanced down the table. Lady Holcroft was listening to an anecdote from her host and laughing obligingly. All that Susan could see was the back of her head. Cardinal looked past her.

'Sir Ralph Holcroft is a fortunate man,' he observed. 'His wife is a perfect example of the trappings of power. Lesser beings would not get near her.'

'You make her sound very calculating, Mr Cardinal.'

'Far from it. I think the calculation was on her husband's part.'

'Does it not encourage you to go into politics?'

'No, Miss Cheever. I'd be bored within a week. I'm very happy with my life as it is. Power and position are such temporary things. They rest on so many imponderables. I'm old enough to remember a time when we had no King on the throne. What happened to those who held sway then?'

'Do not put that question to my father,' she cautioned. 'His answer is apt to be rather trenchant. He'd not approve of his daughter, sitting at such a table as this.'

'I cannot imagine disapproving of you, whatever you did.'

The compliment went unheard. Susan had noticed that Lady

Holcroft had just excused herself from the table. As she walked past, she deliberately looked at Susan before moving on. The signal was unmistakable. After waiting a full minute, Susan made her apologies and rose to leave. She found Lady Holcroft waiting for her at the bottom of the staircase. Susan hurried over to her.

'Where is that letter?' asked the other.

'In my room,' said Susan. 'Shall I fetch it, Lady Holcroft?'

'I'll come with you.'

They went upstairs together and slipped into the bedchamber at the end of the passageway. Susan retrieved the letter from the valise in which she had concealed it then handed it over. She moved towards the door.

'Wait,' said Lady Holcroft. 'There's no need to leave.'

'I don't wish to intrude.'

'Please stay, Miss Cheever.'

Turning away so that Susan could not see her face, she broke the seal and read the letter. Susan watched her shoulders tighten. Evidently, it was a long missive that provoked serious thought. It was some time before Lady Holcroft faced her again. When she did so, her expression gave nothing away.

'What sort of man is Mr Christopher Redmayne?' she asked.

Christopher had never before been so relieved to see his servant. When Jacob returned to the house, bowed down with produce from the market, Lady Whitcombe was poring over the table with her master as they studied the design for her house. Christopher broke away at once, glad to escape from the rub of her shoulder against his and to shake off the uncomfortable feeling that he was, in some sense, a victim of intended blackmail. Lady Whitcombe was quite ruthless. Having commissioned a new home, she decided to acquire the architect as well. Jacob's return made further progress impossible for her and she soon withdrew, confident that she had achieved her objective.

It was not long before the Reverend Algernon Redmayne came back from his second visit to the prison. Over dinner together, he told Christopher how ill and forlorn his elder son had looked. Henry had been perplexed to hear of the latest assault on his brother and sent his deepest apologies. What pleased the Dean was that the prisoner seemed to be showing genuine remorse at last. He was taking responsibility for his actions and vowed to make amends if the chance were granted to him. It had obviously been a harrowing encounter for father and son, but the old man left with a degree of hope. Acknowledgement of sin was the first step towards redemption. His elder son, he felt, had finally taken that step.

Christopher intended to visit his brother as well but he had another call to make first. Wearing sword and dagger, he rode off in the direction of Sir Humphrey Godden's home to see if his own impression of the man matched that of Jonathan Bale. He got within thirty yards of the house when two figures emerged and had what appeared to be a lively argument. Sir Humphrey was gesticulating angrily and Martin Crenlowe was wagging a finger at him. At length, the goldsmith raised his palms to calm his friend then backed away. Christopher waited in the angle of a building so that Crenlowe did not see him as his carriage rolled past.

Sir Humphrey, too, was dressed to go out. Before he could walk off in the opposite direction, Christopher trotted up beside him and leaned over in the saddle.

'Good afternoon, Sir Humphrey!' he said, touching his hat.

'Ah, it's you,' grunted the other, coming to a halt.

'May I have a moment of your time?'

'If it really is a moment, Mr Redmayne.'

'I saw you talking to Mr Crenlowe just now,' remarked Christopher, dismounting from the horse. 'I thought the two of you were good friends.'

'We are, sir.'

'It did not look like it from where I was standing.'

'A slight difference of opinion, that's all,' said Sir Humphrey. 'When we meet again, it will all be forgiven and forgotten.'

'Which one of you has to forgive and forget?' He collected a glare by way of an answer. 'I gather that my friend, Jonathan Bale, called on you again.'

'Yes, Mr Redmayne. Is there any way that you can keep the fellow away from me? I find him the most unpleasant individual. He's so grim and tenacious.'

'He takes his work very seriously.'

'There's nothing more I can tell him.' His manner softened slightly. 'I was sorry to hear that you'd been attacked beside the river,' he said. 'Do you have any idea who the man was?'

'No, Sir Humphrey, but he was not content with giving me a dip in the Thames. If my guess is correct, he came back yesterday and attacked me with a cudgel. I still have the bruises to show for it.'

'Two assaults on you? Why?'

'To stop me finding out the truth about the murder.'

'You think that he was the killer?'

'I did, Sir Humphrey, but I'm not so sure now.' He appraised the other man. 'You look as if you are off on a pleasant afternoon stroll,' he observed. 'Nobody would suspect that one of your friends was rotting in Newgate on a charge of murder.'

'A false charge, Mr Redmayne.'

'It feels authentic enough to Henry. Why not go and ask him?'

'That's what Martin was saying to me. He may have been but I see no virtue in going to a prison. Henry knows that I'll back him. I stand by my friends.'

'Does that go for Captain Harvest as well?' He saw the other man tense. 'Jonathan must have told you how he ripped the mask off him. That's the value of being grim and tenacious, Sir Humphrey. You sniff out fraud. How much money did you give to your friend?'

'Nothing, sir.'

'Mr Crenlowe was certain that he'd come cap-in-hand to you first.'

'I've seen no sign of James – or whatever his name is.'

'Would you have told me, if you had?'

'No,' snapped Sir Humphrey. 'It's no business of yours.'

'It is if your friend was implicated in the murder of Signor Maldini.'

'That's an absurd notion.'

'Mr Crenlowe shares it. Is that what the two of you were arguing about?'

'No!'

'Or was he reproaching you for lending money to a proven impostor?'

'What Martin and I said is a matter between the two of us.' He made an effort to rein in his temper. 'Listen, Mr Redmayne. I admire you for what you are doing and I'll be the first to congratulate Henry when this ridiculous charge is finally exposed for what it is. Beyond that, there's nothing I can do.'

'You might try telling the truth, Sir Humphrey.'

'That's an insult!'

'It was not meant to be,' said Christopher. 'It's a heartfelt plea for information that can lead us to the man who did kill the fencing master. You may choose to absolve the man known as Captain Harvest but I'd not dispense with him so easily. He has much to answer for, Sir Humphrey. Where can we find him?'

'How should I know?'

'Because you are the person to whom he's likely to turn.'

'Well, he did not!' rejoined the other, reddening visibly. 'Do you and Mr Bale not understand the English language? James – Captain Harvest –call him what you will – has not been anywhere near me. Now, you can either believe me or not.'

After looking him full in the eye, Christopher mounted his horse again.

'I think that I prefer to believe Jonathan Bale,' he said.

A return to the Hope and Anchor, and a second visit to the tenement, had both been in vain. Hannah Liggett was not in the former and had not been seen in the latter since the previous day. Jonathan had once again taken the precaution of shedding the attire he wore as a constable. Dressed as a shipwright and walking beside the river, he felt the pull of his old trade. It had been laborious work but it had brought in a regular wage and was fraught with none of the hazards he met as a humble constable. The moments he had savoured most were when the ships he had helped to build were finally launched into service. Even those occasions, however, rewarding as they were, did not give him the intense satisfaction he got from arresting a dangerous criminal.

After eating a frugal dinner in an ordinary, he trudged back along Thames Street. What he expected to glean from a visit to the prison, he did not know but he felt that he should at least try to speak to Henry Redmayne. He also wanted to find out how the man had coped with imprisonment. That could be telling. When he got to Newgate, he reported to the prison sergeant who recognised him at once.

'What's this, Jonathan?' he said, looking at his clothing. 'A constable no more?'

'I'm an officer of the law, whatever I wear.'

'Who have you brought for us today?'

'Nobody, Isaac,' said Jonathan. 'I've come to visit a prisoner. Henry Redmayne.'

'Mr Redmayne, eh?' The sergeant checked his ledger. 'He's a popular man.'

'What do you mean?'

'You're the third visitor today. His father was here this morning, a reverend gentleman with an air of holiness about him. The other man has just gone to him.'

'Was it his brother?'

'No, it was a strange, haunted fellow,' said the sergeant. 'But he was generous to me so I'll not keep him from his friend. Here!' he called, snapping his fingers at a turnkey. 'Show Mr Bale where he can find Henry Redmayne.

'How has he behaved while he's been in here, Isaac?'

'Quiet as a lamb, Jonathan. We'd be happy to have more like him.'

The turnkey unlocked a door so that Jonathan could follow him through it. After locking it behind them, he led the constable down a long, cold, featureless passageway with the footsteps echoing on the cold stone. When they turned a corner, the turnkey pointed to a cell door that was open at the far end. A slim young man was being ushered in by another turnkey who locked him in with the prisoner.

'That's Mr Redmayne's cell,' said Jonathan's companion. 'You'll have to wait. There's no room in there for three of you.'

Jonathan thanked him and strode on down to where the other turnkey was waiting.

'I've permission to see Mr Redmayne.'

'*Everybody* wants to see him today,' replied the man, curling a lip.

'Who's in there now?'

'A friend of his.'

'Did he give a name?' asked Jonathan peering through the grill. A loud gurgling sound came from inside the cell. 'Quick!' he yelled. 'Open the door!'

'Why?'

'Open the door, man!'

Grabbing the key from him, Jonathan unlocked the door and dived into the cell, Henry Redmayne was on his knees, his face purple as his visitor tightened the cord that was around his neck. Jonathan punched the attacker on the nose and sent him sprawling into the straw. Before he could recover, Jonathan pounded him with a fierce relay of blows until he was too weak to fight back. Blood streamed freely from the man's nose. Henry, meanwhile was spluttering in the corner. Watching from the doorway, the turnkey tried to defend himself.

'I searched him for weapons. How was I to know he had that cord with him?'

'Take hold of him,' ordered Jonathan, lifting the other visitor from the floor with one hand and pushing him into the arms of the turnkey. 'He should never have been allowed in here. I'll speak to the prison sergeant about this.'

The turnkey hustled the man out. Jonathan turned to Henry, who was still holding his throat and retching. He put an arm around the prisoner's shoulder.'

'How are you now, sir?' he asked.

'Grateful you came, Mr Bale,' gasped Henry. 'You saved my life.'
'Who was he?'

'A madman. As soon as he came into the cell, he tried to strangle me.'

'Do you know his name, sir?'

'Oh, yes,' said Henry, finding it painful to speak. 'It's Pietro Maldini.'

'Maldini?'

'He thinks I killed his brother.'

Chapter Fifteen

Sir Ralph Holcroft and his wife were the first to leave the house in the Strand and the other guests soon followed. Nobody had eaten more voraciously at the table than Mrs Cardinal, who was so bloated that she had to be helped into the parlour by her son. The chair creaked beneath her weight as she lowered herself into it and she began to wheeze badly. Jack Cardinal was dispatched upstairs to fetch one of her potions. His mother would not accept that she had brought the discomfort on herself. She turned to Susan Cheever, who sat beside her.

'The cook was to blame,' she said, raising a hand to cover a discreet belch. 'The choice was too great and the quantities too large. It would have been discourteous to our hosts to refuse such exquisite food.'

'Yes, Mrs Cardinal,' said Susan.

'Though you seemed to partake of very little.'

'What I ate, I enjoyed immensely. I'm not used to such rich dishes.'

'Nor am I,' complained Mrs Cardinal, shifting her position on the chair to ease the pain in her stomach. 'The lamprey pie was a mistake. At home in Richmond, our fare is rather simpler, as you will discover when you visit us.'

'Thank you.'

'But I'll not forget this dinner for a long time, I know that.'

'Nor will I,' said Susan.

Cardinal arrived with the potion and helped his mother to take a small amount.

'Keep it by me, Jack,' she said, 'in case I need to have some more.'

'Yes, Mother,' he agreed, sitting opposite her.

'You are a proper physician, Mr Cardinal,' observed Susan. 'Whenever your mother sends for some medicine, you know exactly which one to bring.'

'I'd be lost without Jack,' said Mrs Cardinal, beaming at him. 'Now, then,' she went on, nudging Susan gently, 'let me into your little secret. I watched the pair of you talking for hours at the table. What was the subject of your conversation?'

'Anything but politics.'

'It's true, Mother,' said Cardinal. 'Though her father sits in Parliament, Miss Cheever has little interest in what happens there. Neither do I when I hear the kind of ceaseless banter that was filling the house earlier on. It was tedious. We preferred to talk about the merits of living in the country.'

'And what conclusion did you reach?' asked his mother.

'We agreed that rural pleasures had the greater appeal.'

'Not that the city is without its charms,' added Susan. 'Especially when it's as large and exciting as London. I know nothing of politics but I was nevertheless fascinated to meet so many important people from that world. It was a privilege to be at a table where the leading issues of the day were being discussed so earnestly. When my father talks about such things, he tends to rant and rave. A much more civilised debate went on at the table.'

'Lord and Lady Eames always hold a dinner party like that in our honour.'

'I'm very grateful to have been part of it, Mrs Cardinal.'

'You'll meet more of our illustrious friends in time,' said the old woman grandly, 'but we must not forget one of the other reasons for this trip to London.'

Cardinal smiled. 'Mother wishes to visit some of the shops.'

'I intend to visit *all* of the shops, Jack. I begin tomorrow morning.'

'Then you'll have to manage without me, Mother, for I have an appointment with my lawyer. However,' he said, turning to Susan, 'I'm sure that Miss Cheever will be happy to accompany you on your mission.'

'I'd not dream of going without her and I daresay that Miss Cheever would feel hurt if I did.' She clapped her hands. 'Tomorrow morning, it will be, then.'

'I'm afraid not,' said Susan. 'I already have a commitment.'

Mrs Cardinal was peremptory. 'Cancel it. I need you with me.'

'It's not possible to cancel it, Mrs Cardinal. I've already accepted the invitation.'

'From whom?'

'Lady Holcroft. She's picking me up in her coach at ten o'clock.'

Susan had to contain her amusement at their reaction. Jack Cardinal's mouth fell open in surprise and his mother began to quiver all over, astonished that Susan had aroused such interest in

Lady Holcroft and peeved that she had been robbed of a companion on an expedition to the shops. Grabbing the potion from her son, she took another swig from the bottle.

By the time that Christopher Redmayne arrived at the prison, his brother had recovered from the shock of the attack in his cell but his neck still bore an ugly red souvenir. He stroked it ruefully as he explained what had happened. Christopher was stunned.

'He tried to *kill* you, Henry?'

'He would have succeeded, had not your friend, Mr Bale, pulled him off me. I could never bring myself to like that constable but I owe him my sincere gratitude.'

'I hope that you had the grace to tell him that.'

'I did my best,' said Henry, 'though my throat was on fire at the time.'

'Why did they let the man into your cell in the first place?'

'He told them he was a friend and bribed the prison sergeant.'

'Did nobody suspect that he was Jeronimo Maldini's brother?'

'He gave a false name, it seems, and his English is good. He's lived here much longer than his brother. Pietro is a musician,' said Henry, still rubbing his neck. 'Perhaps that's why I felt I was being strangled with a lute string.'

'Where is he now?'

'Being charged with attempted murder. I know one thing, Christopher. If they keep him in Newgate, I've no wish to share a cell with him or with any other member of the Maldini family. They are much too hot-blooded for me.'

'Before too long,' said Christopher, 'you won't even be in here.'

'No, I'll be dangling from the end of a rope.'

Henry looked more harassed than ever. His brother had brought another change of clothing for him but Henry showed no interest in it. The visit from his father had left him thoroughly jangled and the attack had shaken him even more. As long as he was in prison, he felt, he was at the mercy of everyone. The promised release seemed no nearer.

'Father was impressed by the way you conducted yourself today,' said Christopher. 'He felt that you were showing true contrition.'

'I'd have shown anything just to get rid of him.'

'Henry!'

'He kept on and on at me, Christopher. I felt that I was strapped into a pew at the cathedral while he directed a venomous sermon at me. At least, that crazed Italian tried to put me out of my misery quickly. Father raged on until I was reduced to tears.'

'He only does it out of love for you,' said Christopher. 'And you must admit that you do give him good reason to censure you. Your life is so irregular.'

'All that I can think about now is my death.'

'No more of that kind of talk!' warned his brother. 'You promised me.'

Henry sighed. 'I'm sorry, but the whole world seems to have turned against me.'

'Not entirely, Henry. Those who know you best still believe in you.'

'Thank you.' He took the apparel from his brother and put it on the stool. 'What really hurt me about Father's visit was the way that he harped on about you. Because of me, he said, there'd been a second attempt on your life. That upset me more than anything else, Christopher. Were you injured in any way?'

'Cuts and bruises. Nothing serious.'

'It's always serious when someone tries to kill you. I discovered that earlier on. It was a dreadful experience but there's one consolation to be drawn from it.'

'What's that?'

'Pietro Maldini won't be able to attack either of us again.'

Christopher blinked. 'You believe that he was the man who stalked me?'

'I'm certain of it,' said Henry. 'He confessed as much. I'd killed his brother, he told me, so he'd tried to murder mine. When he failed to do that, he decided to throttle me instead, even though he knew that he'd be throwing his own life away as well. They'd never have let him out of here.'

'They should never have let him in.'

'Somehow, they did. It means that you can stop watching your back.'

Christopher was strangely disappointed. When he heard about the assault on his brother, he had never connected Pietro Maldini with himself. He was so convinced that his attacker had been involved in the murder of the fencing master that it took him some time to accept the truth. He had simply been stalked by a vengeful Italian brother. He chided himself for being misled.

'Did you have a chance to talk to Jonathan Bale?' he asked.

'No, he went off to make sure that they locked that lunatic up. And he was going to protest to the prison sergeant on my behalf. They've a duty to keep me safe in here.'

'And to prevent you from harming yourself,' said Christopher, remembering the razor that had been dropped into the cell. 'Well, if you've not spoken to Jonathan, you've not heard about Captain Harvest.'

'What's that reprobate been up to now?'

'Quite a lot, Henry.'

Christopher told him what Jonathan had found out then described how Martin Crenlowe and Sir Humphrey Godden had responded to the news. Henry was sour.

'The villain!' he cried. 'What was his real name?'

'We still haven't found that out.'

'Martin never really trusted him. I, for my sins, did. Sir Humphrey was the one who gave him the most money but, then, he had much more to give than the rest of us.'

'Was he close to Captain Harvest?'

'Not really, Christopher. None of us were. Why do you ask?'

'Because I think that there's some link between them that goes beyond a casual friendship. When the captain wanted to borrow money, the first person he always turned to was Sir Humphrey Godden. What did Sir Humphrey get in return?'

'James could be a very engaging companion.'

'I think that it may go deeper than that. Mr Crenlowe has been fairly helpful but Sir Humphrey has been awkward with both Jonathan and me. Why? He's supposed to be on your side.'

'He is, Christopher. We've been friends for years.'

'There's been precious little evidence of that friendship. He clearly has a short temper. When I called on him earlier, he was having a quarrel with Mr. Crenlowe. I had the feeling that it might be about the so-called Captain Harvest.'

'One way and another, James has caused so much bother.'

'It may be a lot more than bother, Henry.'

'What do you mean?'

'Supposing – for the sake of argument – that your fake soldier had a hold over Sir Humphrey. Supposing, for instance, that Sir Humphrey had employed him on a very important assignment.'

'Assignment?'

'The murder of Jeronimo Maldini.'

'That's impossible!'

'Is it? We know that Sir Humphrey loathed the man as much as you.'

'Yes, but James liked him. He and that scheming Italian were friends.'

'No,' corrected his brother. 'Jeronimo Maldini was befriended by someone called Captain James Harvest. So were you and so were many others like you. The captain had a gift for ingratiating himself with people. But we now know that there's no such person as Captain Harvest. Under his real name,' said Christopher, 'he might not have been quite so fond of the fencing master. He could be our killer.'

Lady Whitcombe was too fond of her son to be angry with him for long. When she and her daughter called on him that afternoon, she embraced him warmly and accepted a kiss on both cheeks. Egerton Whitcombe was in a much more pleasant mood. He even bestowed a peck on his sister.

'I'm sorry for what happened yesterday,' he began.

'Let's put that aside, shall we?' said his mother magnanimously. 'You were in an ill humour, Egerton. I choose to forget it.'

'I was simply trying to protect the family name.'

'Nobody does that more assiduously than me.'

They were in the room that he had hired in the tavern in Holborn and he was dressed to go out. While he preened himself in a mirror, Letitia admired his new coat and his shining leather jackboots.

'You look very splendid,' she commented. 'Where are you going, Egerton?'

'To meet some friends.'

'Do we know them?'

'Not yet, Letitia. Some of them are still new to me at the moment.'

'It's important to widen our circle at all times,' said Lady Whitcombe. 'Your father was most insistent about that. To the end of his life, he was meeting new people and forging new alliances. You must do the same, Egerton. Cultivate those who can help you to advance in life.'

'I do, Mother. When I have a house in London, of course, it will be far easier.'

'Work on the foundations could begin in a matter of weeks.'

'Yes,' said her daughter. 'Mother went to see Mr Redmayne about it earlier on.'

Whitcombe frowned. 'Is this true?'

'We had a few matters to discuss, Egerton,' said the older woman. 'And I needed to apologise for the way that you'd conducted yourself at the house. It was unseemly.'

'It was necessary, Mother. Someone needed to put Mr Redmayne in his place.'

'You were there simply to meet him, not to cause him offence.'

'It's that brother of his who is causing the offence,' said Whitcombe. 'One of my friends is a lawyer and he says that there's no way that Henry Redmayne will escape the noose. Do you not see what I am trying to save you from, Mother? You risk employing an architect whose reputation will soon be in tatters.'

'But Mr Redmayne is a genius at what he does,' said Letitia with passion. 'You only have to look at his drawings to see that.'

'I prefer to look at his name, Letitia. That's what everyone else will do.'

'Not everyone,' said Lady Whitcombe. 'Some people are more discerning.'

'When I met him, I discerned a man whose career is about to come to an end. And I cannot find it in my heart to offer him any sympathy,' said Whitcombe, brushing a speck of dust from his sleeve. 'His brother stabbed Jeronimo Maldini in the back. I once went to the Italian for fencing lessons. He was a brilliant teacher.'

'He could not teach you how to get the better of Jack Cardinal,' said Letitia with a giggle. 'You met your match in him.'

'That was a long time ago,' said Whitcombe, caught on the raw. 'Things would be different now. The point is that Signor Maldini was a fine man who provided an excellent service to his school. I introduced Father to him once. He liked the fellow as well.'

'We like Mr Redmayne.'

'Who cares for you opinion, Letitia?'

'I do,' said Lady Whitcombe, 'because I happen to share it.'

Her son was appalled. 'Would you link our family with the name of Redmayne?'

'Yes, Egerton. I believe that I would.' She smiled to herself as she recalled her earlier meeting with Christopher. Her voice then hardened. 'I suggest that you start to get used to the idea.'

Jonathan Bale had just finished talking to the prison sergeant when Christopher caught up with him. Turnkeys were standing in readiness as a new prisoner was being delivered to Newgate. The two friends stepped aside so that they could have a private conversation.

'I cannot thank you enough,' said Christopher, shaking his hand. 'Henry told me what happened. He's indebted to you, Jonathan.'

'I was only too pleased to help.'

'That man should never have been allowed near my brother.'

'I've just been saying the same thing to the prison sergeant,' explained the other. 'Isaac admits that they made a gross mistake. The man seemed harmless and he offered a tempting bribe. Nobody guessed that he might be Signor Maldini's brother. When he let him into the cell, the turnkey thought he had no weapon on him, but a length of cord was concealed about his person somewhere.'

'Henry was caught off guard or he'd have put up more of a fight.'

'He's still alive, Mr Redmayne, that's the main thing.'

'Yes. Where's his attacker now?'

'Safely locked up.'

'I want to see him,' said Christopher.

'There's no point, sir.'

'Yes, there is. He's the man who pushed me into the Thames then attempted to kill me on my own doorstep. I'd like to take a good look at Pietro Maldini.'

'Then I'd advise you to do it later,' said Jonathan. 'He's in a very excited state at the moment. Only a desperate man would try to commit murder inside a prison. It's a form of suicide.' Christopher winced at the mention of the word. 'Give him time to calm down. We can speak to him then. His testimony could turn out to be very valuable.'

'Why?'

'He can tell us about his brother, Mr Redmayne. Everything we've heard about the murder victim has come from people he taught at his school. They only saw one side of the man. Pietro Maldini will be able to tell us about the other sides.'

'That's very true, Jonathan.'

'Leave him here awhile. He's not going anywhere.'

They were let out of the prison and stood together in the swirling wind. Both men had to hold on to their hats to stop them from blowing away. Christopher told his friend about his second visit to Sir Humphrey Godden. The constable was intrigued.

'Why did he and Mr Crenlowe fall out?' he wondered.

'I wish I knew, Jonathan.'

'Did you ask Sir Humphrey?'

'He told me to mind my own business.'

'He'd have used even stronger language to me,' said Jonathan with a chuckle. 'There's no pleasure in standing in the cold, waiting for Captain Harvest to show up, but I think I'd prefer that to another talk with Sir Humphrey. He looks down on me.'

'He may look up to you when he hears that you saved Henry's life.'

'I doubt that. If he was involved in the murder, he could *want* someone to remove your brother. With the chief suspect dead, the case would be closed. The real killer, or killers, would have got away scot free.'

'Not as long as I've breath in my body.'

'That goes for me as well, sir.'

'But you were so sure at the start that Henry was guilty.'

Jonathan gave a penitential nod. 'I no longer feel that now, Mr Redmayne. We are pulling in the same direction now.'

'That's a relief!' said Christopher. 'What will you do next?'

'Bide my time until I can return to the Hope and Anchor this evening. If a certain person is still not there, I'll keep watch on that lodging again. What about you, sir?'

'I need to go home.'

'Your father will be horrified to hear about the attack on your brother.'

'It may induce more sympathy in him for Henry,' he added, 'Father has been too harsh on him today. Also,' he added, 'I want to put Jacob's mind at rest.'

'Your servant?'

'Ever since I was cudgelled outside the stable, Jacob has patrolled the house with a dagger in his belt. He looks outside the front door every ten minutes. There's no call for that any more. Pietro Maldini is behind bars.'

As soon as he saw his master's horse go past the window, Jacob leapt into action. Pulling the dagger from its sheath, he scurried out in time to watch Christopher dismount. Jacob swivelled his head so that he could scan Fetter Lane in both directions for any signs of danger. Christopher handed him the reins.

'Put your weapon away, Jacob,' he said. 'The man will not strike again.'

'How do you know?'

'He's under lock and key in Newgate.'

'Is he?' said the old man in astonishment. 'How did he get there?'

'He took refuge in the prison out of fear of you,' teased Christopher. 'Stable the horse and I'll explain what happened. Is my father still here?'

'No, sir. He's paying another visit to Bishop Henchman.'

'I'll have news for him when he returns.'

While Jacob led the horse to the stables, Christopher went into the house. After removing his coat and hat, he saw a letter waiting in the middle of the table. Snatching it up, he broke the seal and read the contents. His spirits soared. Written by Susan Cheever in a neat hand, the letter was short but explicit. Christopher was to present himself at a certain place and time on the following morning. No details were given but he required none. She had somehow contrived a meeting for him with Lady Patience Holcroft. He was so pleased that he kissed the letter with delight.

When Jacob eventually joined him, Christopher was still holding the missive.

'When did this come?' he asked.

'About an hour ago, sir.'

'Did Miss Cheever bring it herself?'

'No, sir,' said Jacob. 'It was delivered by a man. He slipped it under the door.'

'Have you any idea who he was?'

'He did not stay long enough for me to find out, Mr Redmayne. Good news?'

'The very best, Jacob,' said Christopher. 'The very best.'

Jonathan Bale waited until the children had been put to bed before he left the house. His wife gave him a parting kiss on the doorstep. She looked at the shipwright's garb that he was still wearing.

'This is just like old times,' she said.

'Not exactly,' he replied. 'I won't come back with the smell of pitch on me tonight, or with the sound of mallets still ringing in my ears.'

'As long as you return safely, that's all I ask.'

'I will, Sarah. Do not fear on my account.'

He set off on the long walk to the Hope and Anchor, wishing that the wind was not quite so blustery nor the sky so black. There was plenty to occupy his mind. Now that he had come round to the view that Henry Redmayne was, after all, innocent of the crime, he had to find another culprit. The former Captain Harvest was a possible suspect but he schooled himself not to rush to judgement. While the man was clearly guilty of a number of offences, there was no direct proof that murder was one of them.

When he reached the tavern, he popped his head inside but the man he was after was still not there. Jonathan adjourned to the tenement and spoke to the landlord, only to be told that Hannah Liggett had not been seen all day. Undeterred, he took up the vantage point that he has used on the previous evening and resigned himself to a long wait. In fact, his stay lasted less than an hour. He was still crouched in his hiding place when he felt a hard object strike him on the shoulder. It was a small stone and it was soon followed by another missile. Jonathan dodged behind the angle of a building for protection.

There was no need for evasive action. His unseen assailant was already riding away on his horse. Jonathan recognised the mocking laugh of the man who had called himself Captain Harvest. He had obviously been warned about the constable. The vigil was decisively over.

Any hopes that Mrs Cardinal had of being invited to join them soon faded. When the coach arrived next morning at the house in the Strand, she insisted on coming out with Susan Cheever so that she could exchange pleasantries with Lady Holcroft. Wearing her cloak and hat, Mrs Cardinal was ready for an outing.

'May I ask where the two of you are going, Lady Holcroft?' she said as Susan clambered into the coach. 'I'm intrigued to find out.'

'I offered to take Miss Cheever for a ride around the city.'

'But you hardly spoke to her yesterday.'

'Precisely,' said Lady Holcroft. 'That's why I wanted to spend time with her today. Goodbye, Mrs Cardinal.'

'You make me feel very envious.'

'I envy you that visit to the shops, Mrs Cardinal,' said Susan sweetly. 'Goodbye.'

To the old woman's disgust, the whip cracked and the horses pulled the coach away from the house. She stamped back into the house to complain to her son. The two younger ladies, meanwhile, were driven along the Strand and into the much narrower confines of King Street. Though she had written the letter to Christopher, Susan had not been in a position to deliver it so Lady Holcroft had sent one of her footmen to Fetter Lane. She had stressed that the meeting should take place elsewhere. Accordingly, Susan had suggested the family house in Westminster.

Lady Holcroft said nothing on the journey and Susan did not try to draw her into conversation. As they pulled up outside the house, however, Lady Holcroft flipped back her hood to look up at it with interest.

'This is your home, Miss Cheever?' she asked.

'When my father is in London.'

'It's a beautiful house.'

Susan swelled with pride. 'Mr Redmayne designed it for us.'

When they went inside, Christopher was already waiting for them in the parlour. Susan could see from his eyes how grateful he was to her. She introduced them then swiftly withdrew to leave the pair alone. Lady Holcroft did not remove her cloak. She perched on the edge of a chair and waited. Christopher took a seat opposite.

'Thank you so much for agreeing to see me, Lady Holcroft,' he said. 'I know how embarrassing this must be for you but it could be such a help to my brother.'

'How is Henry?'

'As well as can be expected.'

Christopher was conscious of being weighed up. He could see that it would be fruitless to tell her about the attempt on his brother's life or about the privations he was suffering. Lady Holcroft was patently uneasy about her connection with Henry and with Jeronimo Maldini. She wanted her stay at the house to be as brief and painless as possible. Though her face was pinched and her eyes filled with suspicion, she was still beautiful and Christopher was bound to wonder what had attracted her to his brother.

'Miss Cheever assures me that you are very discreet,' she said.

'I am, Lady Holcroft.'

'There's no need to explain the delicacy of my position. I could see from your letter that you understood it very well. It's the only reason that brought me here.'

'I see.'

'I did know your brother,' she confessed. 'His work at the Navy Office brought him into contact with Sir Ralph and that was how we became acquainted. I allowed his admiration to me to develop to a degree that was perhaps unwise. But it went no further than that,' she said quietly, 'and I wish to make that clear. Whatever Henry has told you, we did not – and could not – ever go beyond the bounds of simple friendship even though that friendship gave me, at the time, much joy.'

'It was so with my brother, Lady Holcroft.'

'I did not mean to hurt his feelings, Mr Redmayne.'

'He attaches no blame to you,' said Christopher. 'He looked elsewhere to do that.'

'Then he was mistaken in doing so.'

'Oh?'

'Our friendship had run its course,' she said with a faint hint of irritation. 'The pleasure was waning, the risks seemed too great to take any more. When I explained this to Henry, he accepted it like a gentleman. That should have been an end to it. But,' she continued, pursing her lips, 'someone else came along soon afterwards and, for a number of reasons, that person aroused my curiosity.'

'May I ask how you met him, Lady Holcroft?'

'He was at Court one afternoon. His brother was one of the musicians there and he had been invited along to hear him. We met by chance,' she said, looking away, 'and that's all I'm prepared to tell you about it. Henry, I know, took a different view of it all.'

'He felt that he had been dispossessed.'

She flashed her eyes at him. 'He never possessed me, Mr Redmayne,' she said with controlled anger. 'He had no claim whatsoever upon me. I told him that a dozen times. He was nursing an illusion.'

'Henry is rather prone to do that,' admitted Christopher. 'But illusions can exert a tremendous power. In my brother's case, it provoked an extreme hatred. Not of you, Lady Holcroft – that would be unthinkable – but of the other person we are talking about.'

'Go on.'

'It made the two of them sworn enemies. They were rivals for your affection.'

'No!' she said sharply. 'What kind of person do you take me to be? I do not play one man off against another like that. Henry was never more than a friend and he ceased to be that. It was weeks before...' She broke off and took a deep breath. 'This is very painful for me, Mr Redmayne. I hoped that these chapters in my life were closed. I'm afraid there's little I can add that may be of help to you.'

'Answer me this,' he said. 'Do you believe that my brother is guilty of murder?'

'I'd not be here if I believed that.'

'Thank you, Lady Holcroft. That means so much to me.'

'Henry would never hurt me deliberately,' she said, 'and I was deeply upset by that particular death. Even though my friendship with that gentleman had come to an end, I was stricken by the news. And I was even more distressed when your brother was arrested for the crime. He'd not *do* such a thing to me.' She lifted her chin with patrician pride. 'He'd not dare!'

Christopher began rearranging questions in his mind. Lady Holcroft was not at all the helpless victim of an Italian lover that he had been led to expect. Nor did she requite his brother's love in the manner that Henry had implied. There was a hard edge to her. She would divulge nothing that would be of use to him unless she was sure that it did not compromise her. Yet he saw a potential weakness. She had something of a temper. If he could play on that, he might find out what he wanted to know.

'Henry could not bear the way that his rival treated you, Lady Holcroft.'

'They were not rivals,' she retorted. 'Not in the sense that you mean.'

'They were, in Henry's imagination.'

'That was always far too lively, Mr Redmayne. It was one of the things that persuaded me that our friendship had to end. Your brother, alas, began to make certain assumptions.'

'About what?'

She was curt. 'That's a private matter and, in any case, no longer relevant.'

'It is to Henry. He still reveres you.'

'I've not encouraged him to do that.'

'But it explains why he was deeply upset when you were cast aside.'

'I beg your pardon!' she said with indignation.

'Henry claimed that the other gentleman took advantage of you.'

'He did nothing of the kind, sir.' Cheeks blushing, she jumped to her feet. 'I regard that as a cruel insult.'

'It was not intended to be, Lady Holcroft.'

'Neither you nor your brother know anything about that particular friendship.'

'But the gentleman did bring that friendship to a sudden end, did he not?'

'No, Mr Redmayne,' she snapped, wrestling to contain her fury. 'I did that. No man would ever cast me aside. I dispense with *them*.' She moved to the door. 'Good day to you, sir. I can see that I made a grave error in coming here.'

'The error was entirely of my brother's making,' he said, rushing to intercept her. 'Henry is the victim of a misunderstanding. He felt sorry for you because he thought that you were abandoned when the other gentleman tired of you.'

'It was I who tired of him and his infernal questions.'

'Questions?'

'You are standing in my way, Mr Redmayne.'

'What sort of questions did he ask?'

'The wrong ones, sir,' she said coldly. 'And you have done the same.'

Christopher stood aside. 'Thank you for coming, Lady Holcroft. I appreciate it.'

Without a word, she swept past him into the hall and out through the front door. A moment later, he heard the coach pulling away from the house. Susan came into the parlour with a look of consternation.

'Lady Holcroft has just left without me,' she said.

'That was my fault,' admitted Christopher. He gave her a warm smile. 'I suppose that I'll have to take responsibility for getting you back to your friends.'

Susan relaxed visibly. 'There's no hurry,' she said.

A cold night in Newgate had left its imprint on Pietro Maldini. On the advice of Jonathan Bale, the Italian had been locked in a cell with fifteen other prisoners, sharing their stink, deafened by their noise and recoiling from their abuse. They mocked his accent, they reviled his nation and more than one of them felt obliged to punch or jostle him. He was already in pain. The blood had been cleansed from his face but nothing could be done about the broken nose and it throbbed unmercifully. After a sleepless night, Maldini was hollow-eyed and frightened. The fierce rage that had brought him to Newgate in the first place had been drained out of him.

Jonathan had him moved to a small private room so that he could talk to him in relative comfort. Maldini was pathetically grateful even though the constable had been the person who stopped him from achieving his objective. Stripped down to shirt and breeches, he cut a forlorn figure, the once handsome face disfigured by the broken nose, the neat black beard caked with wisps of straw. They sat either side of a bare wooden table. Jonathan explained who he was and why he had come. Maldini was in a daze. His command of English was good, his accent quite pronounced.

'What will happen to me?' he asked.

'You'll have to stand trial on a charge of attempted murder, sir,' said Jonathan. 'You tried to kill Mr Redmayne and we believe that you made two attempts to kill his brother as well.'

'I had to do it. That man, he stabbed Jeronimo in the back. I want revenge.'

'People are not allowed to take the law into their own hands in this country. In any case, you attacked the wrong people. There's growing evidence to suggest that Henry Redmayne is not guilty of the murder and his brother, of course, was not involved in any way. You might have killed two completely innocent men.'

'No,' denied the other. 'Henry Redmayne, he stabbed my brother. Everyone say so. Jeronimo's friend, he told me it was true.'

'His friend?'

'Captain Harvest.'

'Ah,' said Jonathan. 'I had a feeling that he might be involved somehow.'

Speaking slowly, he told the prisoner how the soldier had been exposed as an impostor and how he was liable for arrest on a number of charges. Maldini listened with increasing discomfort. When he heard that the man was under suspicion for the murder as well, he was confused.

'No,' he said, 'this cannot be. The captain, he was Jeronimo's friend.'

'I know that he worked at the fencing school with your brother.'

'It was more than that. Jeronimo, he told me this man was a great help to him.'

'In what way, sir?'

'He did not say. My brother and me, we did not speak often. Our lives, they were very different. But I still loved him,' he asserted. 'When I hear of his death, I have to get revenge. It's – what do you call it – a matter of honour?'

'I see no honour at all in trying to throttle a man to death,' said Jonathan harshly, 'especially as he may well turn out to have nothing to do with this crime.'

'But he did. He was there. He had an argument with Jeronimo.'

'So did one or two other people, by the sound of it.'

'I still think Henry Redmayne, he is the man. That's why I went in search of his brother. He stabbed my brother, I wanted to kill his.'

'How did you know where to find Christopher Redmayne?'

'I was told where he lived.'

'By the same Captain Harvest, I daresay.' Maldini nodded. 'He deliberately set you on. That means he incited murder. We have another charge to hang around his neck.'

'Jeronimo always trusted him.'

'Enough to turn his back on the man. That was his mistake.'

'This captain, he told me, was very useful to him. Jeronimo, he relied on him.'

'At the fencing school?'

'For something else. My brother, he did not tell me what it was. He liked to keep secrets. It was the same when we were boys at home in Italy. Jeronimo was very private.'

'Yet he led a very public life,' said Jonathan, perplexed. 'How much privacy can you have if you spend all day teaching pupils to fence? Your brother was surrounded by people.' He pulled a face. 'Unfortunately, the captain was one of them.'

'All I know is what Jeronimo tell me.'

The Italian shrugged his shoulders. He looked thoroughly miserable. Though he did not condone what the man had done, Jonathan nevertheless felt sorry for him. Impelled by a desire to avenge the death of his brother, he had sacrificed his own life.

'Did you meet any friends of his?' asked Jonathan.

'No, sir.'

'Did he ever mention Sir Humphrey Godden to you?'

'No, sir.'

'What about a Mr Crenlowe? He's a goldsmith.'

'Ah,' said the other, 'that name I know. My brother, he say that this man make some jewellery for him. Mr Crenlowe. That was his name.'

'Did your brother tell you who the jewellery was for?'

Maldini gestured with a hand. 'Who else but for a lady?'

Jonathan had the feeling that the man could provide valuable information about his brother but he was not certain that he was the best person to elicit it from him. Maldini needed more time to understand what was happening to him. He was still too bewildered by the turn of events. Jonathan leaned forward on the table.

'We both want the same thing,' he said. 'We want your brother's killer to hang. You tried to do the hangman's job for him and that was a terrible mistake. You were wrong about Captain Harvest being a friend. He's a criminal. And you are wrong about Henry Redmayne as well.'

'No,' protested Maldini, 'he is the one. Everybody knows it.'

'Most people *think* it, I agree. Those of us who know Mr Redmayne, and who have looked into this case, are certain that he's innocent. I won't try to convince you of that. I can see that it would be a waste of time. However, tell me this. If – and I only ask you to consider it – if someone else stuck that knife in your brother's back, would you help us to catch him?'

'Yes, of course. But the killer has already been arrested.'

'On false evidence in my view,' said Jonathan. 'That's why his brother is moving heaven and earth to prove his innocence. You can understand that, I think. You know how it feels when you think a brother has been cruelly wronged.'

'Oh, yes,' said the other, knuckles tightening. 'I would have done anything for Jeronimo.'

'You've already done too much.'

Maldini's head fell to his chest. Jonathan felt another surge of pity. The Italian was young, strong and lithe with a promising career as a musician ahead of him. All that had been squandered. Jonathan sought to relieve his suffering a little.

'Where did you spend the night?' he said.

'With a pack of wild animals,' replied Maldini, looking up. 'It was torture.'

'I might be able to get you moved to a cell on your own. Would you like that?'

'Yes, please! Those others, they drive me mad,'

'I'll speak to the prison sergeant.'

Maldini grabbed his arm. 'Thank you, Mr Bale. Thank you, sir.'

'But I expect a favour in return, mark you.'

'A favour?'

'I want you to talk to Christopher Redmayne.'

Maldini withdrew his hand in disgust and spat on to the floor.

The meeting with Lady Holcroft had been less enlightening than he had hoped but Christopher had the supreme consolation of spending an hour alone with Susan Cheever. At no point did she press him about his reason for a secret rendezvous with Lady Holcroft and he was grateful for that. She felt able to confide in him her worries that Mrs Cardinal was showing an interest in her as a possible future wife for her son and assuring him that, while she admired Jack Cardinal, she would never choose him as her partner in life. He was tempted to reveal his own dilemma with regard to Lady Whitcombe but he drew back, still hoping that he could resolve that particular problem.

'What will I tell Mrs Cardinal when I get back to the house?' she asked.

'Tell her that you and Lady Holcroft went for a ride in the coach.'

'She's bound to press for details.'

'Invent some,' said Christopher cheerfully. 'Lady Holcroft will not contradict you. I suspect she'll pretend that this morning did not really take place. The main thing is to get you back before Mrs Cardinal and her son return.'

'Yes,' she agreed, sad to leave. 'I suppose so.'

'I'm deeply grateful to the lady. After all, she brought you to London.'

'She did, Christopher. If the situation were different, I could like her very much. But she will watch me all the time, just like Brilliana. It's almost as if they have a secret pact to marry me off, and I hate it when people try to make decisions for me.'

'I'd never presume to do that.'

'Thank you.' She turned round so that he could put her cloak around her shoulders. 'It's been wonderful to see you again,' she said, facing him again, 'but I know that you have to get back to helping your brother. How is he? I heard his name mentioned more than once at the dinner table yesterday. The comments were not flattering.'

'They will be when Henry is exonerated.'

'How close are you to proving his innocence?'

'Jonathan Bale and I get closer every day, Susan,' he said. 'I've managed to win over the most difficult man to persuade.'

'Who is that?'

'Jonathan himself. He thought at first that Henry was guilty.'

'That must have made for some awkwardness between the two of you.'

'Oh, it did,' he agreed, 'but friendship is an odd thing. It sometimes thrives on differences of opinion. At least, I felt that it did in this case.'

'Does he know that you were coming here today?'

'No, Susan. It was something that even he could not be told about. And he never will. I promised Lady Holcroft in my letter that nobody else would ever be aware that our meeting took place. Apart from you, that is.'

'I can be very discreet.'

'That's why I turned to you.' He gave her a smile of gratitude then remembered what he had been told earlier by Lady Holcroft. 'May I please ask you something?'

'Of course.'

'This is purely a suggestion,' he explained, 'and relates to nobody in particular. Suppose that a certain lady, married and of good reputation, permitted a gentleman to pay court to her in strictest privacy.'

'Yes,' said Susan, 'I can readily imagine that.'

'And suppose that she decided to bring their friendship to a sudden end.'

'Why should she do that?'

'Because he pestered her with questions.'

'Questions?'

'Infernal questions,' he said. 'What sort of questions would annoy a lady most in those circumstances? In short, what would she be least willing to talk about?'

'That's easy to answer,' replied Susan. 'Her husband.'

Chapter Sixteen

When he visited the prison that morning, the Reverend Algernon Redmayne was in a more compassionate mood. Instead of condemning his elder son for his past sins, he brought fresh food and a degree of comfort into the cell. Henry had never seen his father in such a benign state. For his part, the Dean was pleased that his son had taken some pains with his appearance. Henry had washed, shaved and donned the change of apparel that his brother had taken to him. He had even combed his thinning hair into a semblance of order. It no longer looked as if he had just come in from a howling gale.

'Christopher told me about the vicious attack on you, Henry,' said his father. 'It's unforgivable that such a thing should happen. I'll speak to the authorities myself.'

'I was rescued just in time, Father.'

'So I hear. I'll give my personal thanks to this doughty constable.'

'As long as you do not try to engage him in theological debate,' warned Henry. 'You'd find him a stubborn parishioner. Mr Bale is a resolute Puritan.'

'The fellow is also a hero and I salute him for that.'

The Dean insisted on hearing a full description of the attempt on his son's life and Henry was only too willing to give it. His father offered him uncritical sympathy so rarely that he intended to exploit it to the full. He embroidered the tale to make the ordeal seem even worse than it was. Enfolding his son in his arms, the Dean offered up a prayer of thanksgiving. There were tears in his eyes.

'You've walked in the valley of the shadow of death,' he said.

'It's difficult to walk anywhere when someone is trying to strangle you.'

'What went through your mind, Henry?'

'Nothing at all.'

'Did you not think that your end was nigh?'

'Of course, Father.'

'And did you not cry out to God for his aid?'

'I could not say a word,' replied Henry, rubbing his neck. 'The cord was so tight that I could do little but gurgle. I was terrified. I believed that I was going to die and I felt desperately unready.'

'That's what I was hoping you'd say. At that awful moment of extremity, you felt unready to meet your Maker. That's a good and proper feeling, Henry,' said his Father, releasing him at last. 'It shows that you recognised your failings as a human being.'

'Oh, I did that the moment they locked me up in here.'

'What will happen when you get out again?'

'I'm beginning to give up all hope of that.'

'You must never do that!' said the other seriously. 'Christopher assures me that he and his friend will soon apprehend the real culprit. You will then have to be released. I trust that you will resolve to lead a more Christian life.'

'Yes, Father.'

'You fell among evil men and were led astray.'

'I'll choose my friends with more care in future,' promised Henry. 'I've never been a contemplative man but this experience has wrought a profound change in me. I've been arrested, imprisoned, vilified by all and sundry, then attacked by a murderous Italian. If and when I'm let out of Newgate, I vow to start a new life.'

'Why not quit London and return to Gloucester with me?'

'Not *that* new, Father,' said Henry, gulping at the prospect. 'I'd return to my post at the Navy Office and apply myself even more conscientiously than before. To leave the city would give the impression that I'm running away, and I'd never do that. I need to stay here to rebuild my lost reputation.'

'That shows courage and I applaud you. What of this other fellow?' he asked with a glance over his shoulder. 'This demented Italian who tried to strangle you.'

'Pietro Maldini is having a taste of what I've been through. He's learning just how unpleasant it is to be deprived of your liberty and flung into gaol among strangers.'

After an hour of sustained misery, Pietro Maldini began to have second thoughts. The other prisoners would not leave him alone. He was ridiculed, cajoled, pushed, prodded and even tripped up for the amusement of the ragged assembly. The food he was given was inedible and the water too brackish to drink. Life as a Court musician had hardly prepared him for the squalor and intimidation of Newgate. When two men tried to steal the clothes from his back, he had to fight them off with all his strength. There was no way that he could keep them at bay indefinitely. A turnkey appeared at the door and Maldini rushed across to him.

'Take a message to Mr Bale!' he yelled.

'Who?' said the other gruffly.

'The constable I spoke to earlier.'

The turnkey sneered. 'I'm not here to carry your messages.'

'Please!' implored Maldini. 'Tell him I will do him that favour!'

When he got back to his house, Christopher was pleased to see Jonathan Bale waiting for him in the parlour. The constable reported what had happened the previous night during his ill-fated vigil and described his long conversation with the Italian prisoner. Fascinated by what he heard, Christopher was disappointed that he was unable to speak to the man himself. He seized on one item of information.

'At least, we know that the so-called Captain Harvest is still in London.'

'He was taunting me,' said Jonathan. 'He knew exactly where I was.'

'His boldness could prove his downfall. If he does not have the sense to remain hidden, he's bound to make a mistake sooner or later.' Christopher stroked his chin. 'What interests me is the suggestion that he and the fencing master were closer friends than we thought. Did the brother give no details?'

'He knew none, Mr Redmayne.'

'Were the two men involved in some other enterprise?'

'We can only guess.'

Christopher perched on the edge of his table. 'What happened when the body of Jeronimo Maldini was identified?' he asked. 'Did you not go to his lodging?'

'We did, sir. His brother had been there first to take away anything of value as well as items that had a personal meaning for him. We searched the room thoroughly for any clues – letters, documents, a diary even – that would give us clear evidence of who the killer might be. There was nothing.'

'Not even a ledger, showing the accounts from the fencing school?'

'No, Mr Redmayne,' said Jonathan. 'It puzzled me at the time. Signor Maldini must have made money or he'd not have been able

253

to rent the rooms where his fencing school was held. It was very popular yet there was no record of any income from it.'

'There must be. How hard did you look?'

'Two of us were there for half an hour.'

'Would it be possible to search it again?'

'Yes,' replied the other, 'the house is in my ward. I know the man who owns it. He spoke of Signor Maldini as a quiet, respectable gentleman who always paid his rent on time.' He smiled. 'Just as well he did not have Captain Harvest as a lodger.'

'Go back,' urged Christopher. 'Take a second look. If the ledger is not there, find out where his brother lived. He may have taken it when he removed the valuables. Pietro Maldini will have no use for any of his belongings now.' Jonathan got up from his chair. 'Is there no chance that the man might talk to me?'

'I fancy that he may come round in time.'

'I'll call at the prison in due course.'

'Please do, Mr Redmayne. I left instructions that he was to be moved to a cell on his own if he agreed to help us. The place where he's held now is like a menagerie.'

Christopher saw him to the door and waved him off. Jonathan strode briskly in the direction of Fleet Street. Before he could get his horse from the stable, however, Christopher saw someone walking towards him from the Holborn end of the lane. It was Martin Crenlowe. The goldsmith was relieved to see him.

'I was hoping to catch you in, Mr Redmayne,' he said, arriving at the door. 'I had business nearby and decided to take a chance on your being at home.'

'Come in, Mr Crenlowe,' invited Christopher, taking him into the parlour and indicating a seat. 'You were the last visitor I expected.'

Crenlowe sat down. 'I wanted to know how your investigations were going.'

'We are making definite progress, I feel.'

'Good, good. I've something to pass on that may be of help.'

'What's that?' asked Christopher.

'Captain Harvest – or whatever the damn fellow's name really is – came to see me yesterday. He has the audacity of the Devil himself. He told me some cock and bull story about needing to go abroad and tried to borrow money.'

'Did you give it to him?'

'I most certainly did not,' asserted the other. 'I warmed his ears with some ripe language and sent him on his way. He betrayed the lot of us yet all he could do was to laugh in my face. Anyway,' he went on, 'I came to tell you that the villain is still in London and that he's in disguise. He's shaved off his beard and dressed himself like a clerk of some sort. I hardly recognised him at first.'

'What did you do after he left?'

'I went straight to Covent Garden so that I could warn Sir Humphrey.'

'I know, sir,' said Christopher. 'I called on him myself, as it happens, and arrived in time to see you and Sir Humphrey having some kind of disagreement.'

Crenlowe was annoyed. 'Have you been watching me, Mr Redmayne?'

'Not at all. I chanced to come along at that particular time. Sir Humphrey seemed very upset,' recalled Christopher. 'He was waving his arms about in the air. Why was that? Was it anything to do with your former friend?'

'Yes,' admitted the other. 'My warning came too late. He'd already been there and Sir Humphrey had foolishly given him what he wanted. When I remonstrated with him, he lost his temper. I calmed him down and went on my way.'

'Why did Sir Humphrey give the man some money when you did not?'

'He's not always as guarded as he should be, Mr Redmayne.'

'Could it be that the captain had some power over him?'

'That scoundrel had a power over the lot of us,' confessed the other. 'He had the most extraordinary charm when he chose to use it and we were all at its mercy for a time. Apparently, it still worked on Sir Humphrey but I'm proof against it now.'

'The charm obviously worked on Signor Maldini as well.'

'Yes, the captain often borrowed money from him.'

'Was the fencing master able to afford it?' asked Christopher. 'His school was never short of pupils but I would not have thought it brought in a vast amount of money. Yet he never seemed to be short of it. If he had independent wealth, he'd not have needed to give fencing lessons. Where did his money come from, Mr Crenlowe?'

'Who can tell? I never looked into the man's finances.'

'I understand that he once commissioned a piece of jewellery from you.'

Crenlowe started. 'Who told you that?'

'Is it true?'

'I never discuss my business affairs with anyone, Mr Redmayne.'

'This one has a special interest for me.'

'I'm not even prepared to confirm that it took place,' said the goldsmith.

'Pietro Maldini has already done that for us and he has no reason to lie. Perhaps I should tell you that he is at present under lock and key at Newgate. After failing to kill me, he tricked his way into Henry's cell and attempted to strangle him.'

'Heavens!' exclaimed the other. 'Did Henry survive?'

'Thanks to the intervention of my friend, Jonathan Bale, he did. I did tell you that he was a remarkable man,' Christopher reminded him. 'Even Henry accepts that now.'

'So he should. Tell me more. How and when did this all happen?'

Christopher gave him a concise account of the events at the prison. The goldsmith was astonished that the attack had been allowed to take place and reassured to hear that Henry had come through it. He was impressed by what he heard of Jonathan.

'You were right,' he conceded. 'I did not appreciate the constable's true worth. He not only tore the mask away from Captain Harvest, he's saved a man's life. Who would have thought Pietro Maldini desperate enough to act like that? We knew that our fencing master had a brother but none of us ever saw him.'

'The captain did,' said Christopher. 'But let's return to this piece of jewellery.'

'I told you, Mr Redmayne. All my transactions are strictly private.'

'They must also be lucrative, Mr Crenlowe. Nothing in your shop would come cheaply. If Jeronimo Maldini commissioned something from you, it must have been expensive. Was he able to pay for it?' The goldsmith remained silent. 'Very well,' resumed Christopher, 'if you'll not tell me, I'll have to ask someone else.'

'Who?'

'Your client's brother – Pietro Maldini.'

Mrs Cardinal was still annoyed that she had been rebuffed by Lady Holcroft and deprived of a companion for her visit to the shops. In the event, she remained at the house in the Strand and sulked. It took Susan Cheever a long time to mollify her, showering her with apologies and promising to go out with her that same afternoon. By the time that her son returned, Mrs Cardinal had recovered some of her good humour. Jack Cardinal joined the two of them in the parlour and sat opposite Susan.

'Did you enjoy your ride with Lady Holcroft?' he asked.

'Yes,' replied Susan. 'I enjoyed it very much.'

'I've just been hearing about it,' said Mrs Cardinal, 'and it sounds rather dreary. Who could wish to be driven along crowded streets when she could have been helping me to choose some new additions to my wardrobe? But let's put that behind us, shall we?' she went on. 'Miss Cheever was hardly in a position to refuse the invitation. Now, then, Jack. What sort of a morning have you had?'

'A rather dull one, Mother,' he said. 'Lawyers are such cautious creatures.'

'Your father always called them a necessary evil.'

'I seemed to be there for hours.'

'What did you do after you left?'

'I went to the coffee house nearby,' he told her. 'I knew that I'd meet some friends there and I was in need of more lively company. It was very pleasant.'

'Whom did you meet?'

'All sorts of people, including one whom I could cheerfully have avoided.'

'Oh?' said his mother. 'Who was that!'

'Egerton Whitcombe.'

'Such an obnoxious young man!'

'His manners have not improved since I last saw him,' said Cardinal. 'He's just returned from France and is staying here for a week or so. Lady Whitcombe and her daughter have come to London to welcome him back. According to Egerton, they've done nothing but argue since they met.'

'That's unusual. Lady Whitcombe usually indulges his every whim. When Egerton is around, that poor daughter of hers is all but ignored.' She turned to Susan. 'Letitia is appallingly plain and totally lacking in any feminine virtues. She'll be around her mother's neck for ever.'

'Not necessarily,' said her son.

'What do you mean, Jack?'

'The argument with Egerton concerned the new house that his mother is having built in London. The designated architect is none other than Christopher Redmayne.'

Mrs Cardinal was contemptuous. 'He should be dismissed immediately.'

'Why?' asked Susan, stung by the sharpness of her remark.

'You know why, Miss Cheever. The man's name is impossibly tainted.'

'Not if his brother is proved to be innocent.'

'That's highly unlikely,' said Cardinal. 'The talk at the coffee house was that Henry Redmayne would be convicted of murder. It's what Egerton believes as well. That's why he demanded that Lady Whitcombe engages a different architect.'

'She intends to *keep* Mr Redmayne?' asked his mother in amazement.

'So it seems. Egerton vows that it will never happen. Unfortunately for him, Lady Whitcombe holds the purse strings. I fancy that she'll call the tune.'

'But it's madness. Lady Whitcombe will be employing the brother of a convicted murderer. How can she possibly even consider someone with the name of Redmayne?'

'Egerton thinks he has the answer to that.'

'What is it?

'His sister seems to be inordinately fond of this fellow.'

'Does she?'

'And he was very attentive to her.'

'Was he?' asked Susan, feeling uneasy.

'He thinks that Christopher Redmayne has gone out of his way to court Letitia so that he can secure this contract. That's what really provoked his ire,' said Cardinal. 'Lady Whitcombe even hinted that this architect could soon be linked to the family by the bonds of holy matrimony.'

Mrs Cardinal was astounded. Susan felt as if her cheeks were on fire.

The landlord was a short, bustling man with a bald pate. Having no objection to a second search of the room once occupied by Jeronimo Maldini, he led the constable upstairs.

'It's exactly as you found it last time, Mr Bale,' he explained. 'All the furniture belongs to me except the desk. That came from Italy with Signor Maldini. His brother is going to arrange to have it moved.'

'I don't think his brother will have any need for it now,' said Jonathan.

The house was only a few hundred yards from where he lived but it was substantially bigger than anything in Addle Hill. He was conducted into a large, low, rectangular room with a capacious bed against one wall. The room also contained three chairs, a small table, a water jug and a bowl, a collection of swords and an oak desk with ornate carvings. On one wall was a crucifix. As soon as he was left alone, Jonathan began his search, working systematically around the room. He lifted the carpet, he crawled under the bed and he poked into every corner. No new discovery came to light.

All that was left was the desk, a bulky object that had taken two of them to move on the first visit so that they could look behind it. The drawers had been emptied for the most part. All that remained in them were some writing materials and a manual on fencing, written in Italian. Jonathan sat down to study the desk, deciding that it must have had exceptional importance for its owner if he had brought it all the way from Italy. He began to explore it more carefully, pulling out the drawers so that he could reach in with his arm then tapping the desk all over with his knuckles as he listened for a sound that indicated hollowness.

He knew that skilled cabinetmakers could make ingenious secret compartments but he could find none in the desk. He was about to give up when his eye fell on the swords propped up against the wall. Selecting a rapier, he pulled it from its sheath and used it to prod in each of the cavities where the drawers had fitted. Nothing happened at first then he inserted the weapon into another part of the desk and jabbed gently. The response was immediate and sudden. As the point of the rapier struck a small panel, there was a twang as a spring was released and a small door flapped open in the side, and at the rear of, the desk. Jonathan went down on his knees to grope inside the compartment that had just been revealed.

The first thing to emerge was a ledger, containing the accounts of the fencing school but a pile of letters soon followed. Some were in Italian but several were in English. Though they were unsigned, most bore a number to aid identification by the recipient. Jonathan skimmed through some of the correspondence, wondering why an Italian fencing master should be interested in the subjects that were discussed. He then found the most important item in the cache. It was a list of names, against each of which was a number. When he saw the name at the top of the list, he was shocked.

Christopher Redmayne did not relish the idea of being locked in a room with a man who had tried to murder both him and his brother. When he saw Pietro Maldini, however, he decided that he was in no danger. The man looked beaten and hunted. Wearing manacles, he sat on a chair in the corner of the room with his shoulders hunched and his knees drawn up. Released from his cell on the instruction left by Jonathan Bale, he was ready to fulfil his side of the bargain, albeit with great reluctance. He did not even look up when Christopher came into the room. The architect stayed on his feet.

'Do you know who I am?' he asked. Maldini nodded. 'Then you need to be aware of something else,' said Christopher earnestly. 'My brother is not guilty of this crime and I'll prove it by catching the man who was. You can help me in my search.' Maldini simply glowered at him. 'I've not forgotten what you did to me, Signor Maldini, but that's not important at this moment. You acted the way you did because you loved your brother. That's exactly what I'm doing.'

'Your brother murdered Jeronimo,' said Maldini, glaring at him.

'The evidence points that way, I admit, but I had doubts about it at the start. Let me tell you why. Did you ever see your brother take part in a fencing bout?'

'Many times.'

'He was a fine swordsman, I hear.'

'There was no better one,' said the other with pride.

'In other words,' said Christopher, 'he was a man well able to look after himself. My brother was not. On the night when the crime took place, my brother was too drunk even to know where he was going. His only weapon was a dagger. Your brother never went anywhere without his rapier. It was the mark of his trade.'

'What you trying to tell me?'

'I want to ask you a simple question. If the two of them met that night, which would have the advantage? A drunken man with a dagger or an unrivalled swordsman?'

Maldini was confused. 'Your brother stabbed him in the back.'

'How?' asked Christopher, spreading his arms. 'He'd never get close enough to try. Do you think your brother would be stupid enough to turn his back on someone with whom he'd fallen out? Had they closed with each other, there would have been only one winner and it would not have been Henry.'

'You make this up to trick me.'

'Why should I do that? Why should I bother to defend my brother's name if I was not absolutely certain that he was innocent? There's no trick involved, Signor Maldini.' He moved forward to stand over the man. 'Do you think I'd trouble to speak to someone who tried to murder me if I did not believe he could help me? I'm the one with the right to be angry,' he said with studied calmness, 'and you know why. But I put my personal grievances aside for the sake of my brother. Do the same for the sake of yours.'

Maldini was still suspicious. 'What do you want from me?'

'A clearer notion of what your brother was like. Everything I've heard about him so far has been coloured by prejudice. Tell me about the real Jeronimo Maldini,' he said. 'I admire anyone who comes to a foreign country and masters its language enough to make a good living here. Both you and your brother did that. Why did you come in the first place? What made you choose England?'

The prisoner gave a wistful smile. 'We thought we'd have a better life here.'

'And did you?'

Pietro Maldini was resentful at first, feeling that he and his brother had been badly let down in their adopted country, talking about some of the slights they had received. But the more he talked, the more relaxed he became. He spoke with great fondness of his brother and revealed many insights into his character. Christopher was struck by the speed with which Jeronimo Maldini had settled into his new home. He pressed for more personal detail.

'Did he never wish to marry?'

Maldini shrugged. 'Why tie yourself to one woman when you can please many?'

'Is that what your brother did?'

'Jeronimo was a very handsome man. He could take his pick.'

261

'I understand that he bought jewellery from a goldsmith called Mr Crenlowe.'

'That is so.'

'Was he able to afford the high price that must have been charged?'

'Of course!' rejoined the other.

'And did you brother always buy expensive gifts for his ladies?'

'No,' said Maldini with a half-smile. 'He did not need to. The gift they had was Jeronimo himself. That was enough.'

'Except in this particular case,' noted Christopher. 'Why was that?'

'One lady, she was very special to him. He love her dearly.'

'But not enough to marry her, obviously.'

'She already had a husband. Most of them did. Jeronimo, he prefer that.'

'Who was the lady he loved more than the others?' asked Christopher. 'She must have been special to him if he was ready to spend so much money on her. Did he ever tell you her name?'

'My brother, he would never do that. He protect the lady's reputation. But I did watch him seal a letter to her once,' said Maldini. 'He wrote something on the front of it.'

'Well?'

'It was her initial. Her name, I think it begin with 'M".'

Sir Humphrey Godden had enjoyed his visit to his favourite coffee house. He was among friends and able to relax. There was far less gossip to be heard about the murder of the Italian fencing master and that, too, contented him. It was something that he was trying to put out of his mind for the time being. When he finally came out of the building, he was feeling more cheerful than he had done for a week. Then someone stepped out of a doorway and took him familiarly by the arm. It was the man he had first known as Captain James Harvest.

'Good day to you, Sir Humphrey!' he said, grinning broadly.

'What are you doing here?'

'Waiting for you, of course. When I saw your coach, I knew that you were inside. And I could hardly join you,' he went on, indicating the dark suit that he was wearing, 'in this humble garb.'

'I've nothing more to say to you,' growled Sir Humphrey. 'I gave you what you wanted so you can now disappear from my life.'

'That's what I'd hoped to do, Sir Humphrey, but a constable has other ideas.'

'Constable? Are you talking of Mr Bale?'

'The very same. He's a good huntsman. He found out where I was hiding and lay in wait for me. That will not do, Sir Humphrey. I'm too fond of my freedom to risk another meeting with that tenacious fellow.'

'Why tell me?'

'Because you are in a position to help me.'

'You'll get no more money from me,' snarled Sir Humphrey.

'It's not money that I'm after,' said the other, 'but somewhere to hide. You have that huge house with all those empty rooms in it. Nobody would ever think of looking for me there. It would be so much more comfortable than a tenement in Wapping.' He grinned again. 'What do you say?'

'No!'

'Why must you be so inhospitable?'

'You are not coming anywhere near my home,' said Sir Humphrey. 'Find somewhere else to hide or get out of London altogether.'

'I don't have enough money for that. You were the only person ready to help me. Martin turned me away with a mouthful of abuse. We used to be such friends, all three of us.' He nudged the other man in the ribs. 'Do you remember?'

'Look,' said Sir Humphrey, trying to sound more reasonable. 'It's not possible.'

'Why not? I stayed there once before – when your wife was away.'

'That was a long time ago.'

'I still remember how soft and inviting the bed was,' said the other. 'It will only be for a week or so. The trail will have gone cold by then. Mr Bale will think that I've quit the city and give up.' He gave a knowing leer. 'I think that you owe me a favour. Remember what happened to your wife.'

'Be quiet, man!'

'I helped you to resolve the problem regarding Lady Godden.'

Sir Humphrey shook him. 'I won't tell you again!'

Their eyes locked and he began to wilt under the other man's gaze. In trusting the former Captain Harvest, he had been unwise and was now suffering the consequences.

'This is blackmail!' he hissed.

'A week is all I ask, Sir Humphrey. Then I'll be gone for good.'

Sir Humphrey began to weaken. 'My wife must not even know that you're there.'

'I'll be as quiet as a mouse. Lock me in the cellar, if need be.'

'Amid my wine and brandy?' said the other. 'I'm not that stupid.'

'My horse is nearby. Shall I follow you back to Covent Garden?'

'Can you not leave it until after dark?'

'No, I need a refuge *now*.'

Sir Humphrey was trapped. An enjoyable visit to the coffee house had been ruined by a face from the past but he was not in a position to ignore it completely. There was an obligation that could be held over him. He opened the door of his coach as he thought through the implications of the request. With one foot on the step, he turned round and spoke in a grudging voice.

'I'll do it,' he said, 'but let me get to the house well before you do.'

Henry Redmayne was outraged by what he saw as a filial betrayal. When Christopher explained what he had done, Henry took his brother by the shoulders and shook him hard.

'That man tried to throttle me!' he yelled.

'I still have the bruises from his cudgel.'

'Then why did you not avenge the pair of us? I'd have torn the rogue apart.'

'What would that have achieved?' asked Christopher.

'It would have given me profound satisfaction.'

'No, Henry, it would have ensured that you'd have an appointment with the hangman, after all. You were imprisoned for a crime you did not commit. Only a fool would then try to kill someone within the confines of the prison. Pietro Maldini did that,' he pointed out, 'and look where he has ended up.'

'Enjoying a pleasant chat with my brother.'

'There was nothing pleasant about it for either of us.'

Christopher calmed him down and explained in detail what had happened. When he realised that his brother had been searching for information that might lead to his release, Henry was apologetic. He was also angered by the news that his rival had bought some expensive jewellery for a married woman.

'It had to be for Patience,' he decided. 'He commissioned it for her.'

'The name begins with 'M' and that rules Lady Holcroft out.'

'But she adored jewels of all kind, Christopher. They were her real joy in life. Patience deserved to be covered in diamonds and rubies. I asked Martin Crenlowe to fashion a brooch for me but, before I could give it to her, Patience was taken away from me by that fiend of an Italian.'

Christopher loved his brother too much to disabuse him of his illusion. Having heard Lady Holcroft's account of their friendship, he resolved never to mention to Henry that he had ever met her. It would be too cruel. Henry was better left to his fantasies.

'I feel that we have an important clue in our hands,' said Christopher. 'All that we have to do is to identify the woman and it was not, I'm certain, Lady Holcroft. Think of the letter 'M''. Find me a wife called Mary, Margaret or Mildred.'

'I know of none, Christopher.'

'Rack your brains.'

'They have already been racked too hard.'

'Which of your friends has a wife called Maria?'

'None of them,' said Henry. He thought hard. 'But I know a Miriam,' he recalled.

'Is she young and beautiful?'

'Very young and exceedingly beautiful.'

'Yet she's a married lady?' Henry nodded. 'Excellent. Who is her husband?'

'Sir Humphrey Godden.'

Jonathan Bale was rarely excited. His was a more phlegmatic temperament. When he made his discovery at the fencing master's lodging, however, he was thrilled. He walked back to the house in Fetter Lane to report his findings. Christopher Redmayne was not there but Jacob introduced him to the Dean of Gloucester instead. Jonathan received warm congratulation and stern reproof at the same time. While the old man thanked him for his courage in tackling Henry's would-be assassin, he also felt obliged to attest the spiritual superiority of the Anglican Church and to condemn those who dared to question the validity of its tenets. The constable weathered the storm with some difficulty and was glad when the Dean retired to his bedchamber with his Bible.

Christopher arrived back soon afterwards. Jonathan could see that he, too, was in a state of excitement. The architect explained why. Though highly uncomfortable, the talk with Pietro Maldini had been very worthwhile. Christopher felt that a significant connection had been made.

'If that jewellery was intended for Sir Humphrey Godden's wife, we have a motive for murder,' he argued. 'Sir Humphrey must have learned of his wife's infidelity and sought revenge. He engaged the false Captain Harvest as his accomplice.'

'What shall we do, Mr Redmayne?'

'Challenge him at once.'

'Wait until you've heard my news,' said Jonathan, taking the ledger and the papers from under his arm. 'We are dealing with far more than a case of murder, sir.' He handed a sheet of paper to Christopher. 'Do you recognise any of those names?'

Christopher was jolted when he saw that the first name on the list was that of Sir Peregrine Whitcombe. Beneath that was the name of Sir Ralph Holcroft. Of the other seven on the list, he recognised most as senior members of the government. He reached the same conclusion as Jonathan.

'Signor Maldini was a spy,' he declared, remembering what Lady Holcroft had told him. 'He deliberately courted ladies who were married to leading politicians. While he was pleasuring them, he was also asking them about their husbands.' An image of Lady Whitcombe came into his mind. 'Yet I cannot think he was involved in that way with Sir Peregrine's wife.'

'He did not need to be,' said Jonathan, giving him some letters. 'His was the one name that I knew because Jacob told me you were designing a house for his widow. As you see, Sir Peregrine is number one. That means he wrote those letters.'

Christopher leafed through them, staggered by what he saw. Information about the country's naval and military defences was set out in neat columns. There were also reports of meetings of the Privy Council. His head reeled. He was being employed by a woman whose late husband had betrayed his country.

'Sir Peregrine was paid for his intelligence,' said Jonathan, holding the ledger up. 'Here's proof of it. Payments to number one are listed at the back. The man was a traitor, Mr Redmayne. He died before he could be caught.'

'We cannot pursue him beyond the grave,' said Christopher.

'And I'm certain that Lady Whitcombe knew nothing of this. She'd not be so proud of her husband's reputation if she had.' He took the ledger from Jonathan. 'Well, you've opened a door to Hell with this discovery. Did someone find out that Signor Maldini was a spy?' he wondered. 'Is that why he was killed?'

'It could be, Mr Redmayne.'

'How was he unmasked? No wife would dare to admit to her husband that she had been seduced by a foreign spy. That's why the arrangement was so clever.'

Jonathan gave a disapproving frown. 'I see nothing clever in seduction, sir.'

'When he had found out what he wanted to know, he abandoned one lady and moved on to the next. He knew that none of them would ever betray him. Although,' he added, as the words of Pietro Maldini came back to him, 'that's what happened to him in the end. A certain lady betrayed the spy by making him fall in love with her.'

'She wrote these letters,' said Jonathan, handing over the last two items he had found in the desk. 'I felt embarrassed at reading them.'

'Why?'

'They are very fulsome, Mr Redmayne.'

'Are they signed?'

'Only with an initial – "M".'

'That stands for Lady Miriam Godden,' said Christopher, glancing through the first letter, 'and there's no doubt that she loved Signor Maldini, or she'd not have been so indiscreet as to write to him. If her husband learned about this secret romance, he'd have been enraged.'

'It would certainly have given him a reason to go after Signor Maldini's blood.'

'Let's go and speak to him, Jonathan,' said Christopher, pocketing the two letters. 'I've a strong feeling that Sir Humphrey Godden is our man.'

Sir Humphrey Godden was grateful that his wife was not at home. It made it much easier to smuggle his unwanted guest into the house. At the top of the building was a small room that was used for storage. When he had stabled his horse, the former Captain Harvest was hustled upstairs to the room by his reluctant host.

'You're to stay here and keep quiet,' ordered Sir Humphrey.

'There's no mattress,' complained the other.

'One of the servants will soon bring one. He'll also bring you food and drink.'

'A manservant, eh?' said the other with a chuckle. 'I'd prefer to be looked after by a buxom chambermaid. It may get lonely up here.'

'You'll get a hiding place and nothing else.' Sir Humphrey looked at him. 'By the way, I still have no idea what your real name is.'

'I'd prefer to keep it that way. See me as an anonymous friend.'

Sir Humphrey was about to make a tart riposte but thought better of it. After issuing further warnings, he left the room. His guest immediately began to rearrange his accommodation, shifting some wooden boxes into a corner and stacking some bolts of material on top of them. The servant arrived with a mattress and placed it against a wall. He stayed long enough to light a fire in the grate then withdrew to fetch some blankets. The erstwhile Captain Harvest took stock of his surroundings. When the fire had warmed the room up, it would be snug. More important, his refuge would be safe. While he was being looked for in the more insalubrious parts of the city, he was enjoying the hospitality of a house in the heart of Covent Garden. He grinned at his good fortune.

Crossing to the window, he looked down into the street and watched the traffic go past. The grin then froze on his face. Two figures were walking purposefully towards the house. He could not believe that Christopher Redmayne and Jonathan Bale had tracked him so soon to his new lair. He had to get away at once.

They stopped well short of the house so that they could appraise it. Christopher was armed with sword and dagger but Jonathan carried no weapon, relying instead on his strength and experience. Both were alert to the potential danger of accosting a man whom they believed had committed a murder.

'When I confront him,' said Christopher, 'he may try to make a run for it. Go round to the back of the house, Jonathan, to cut off his escape.'

'Give me time to get into position, Mr Redmayne.'

'I will.'

Jonathan set off. After marching past the house, he turned swiftly down the side of it towards the stables. Sir Humphrey's coach stood in the yard, its horses unhitched and returned to their stalls. But it was another animal that caught the constable's eye. Its head was poking out over the stable door and there was something about it that was familiar. Jonathan took a closer look at the horse, peering into the stall to take note of its colour and conformation. A saddle was resting on the edge the manger at the rear of the stall. He felt a shock of recognition. It was the horse that had once knocked him flying outside a tavern in Whitefriars.

He heard a door open and shut at the back of the house. Dodging behind the coach, he crouched down and waited. Heavy footsteps came towards the stables. When Jonathan looked around the angle of the coach, he saw a big, solid, clean-shaven man in dark clothing that deceived him at first. But the man could not disguise everything. He still had the jaunty gait that Jonathan had noticed at their first encounter. It was the bogus Captain Harvest. When the man swaggered towards his horse, Jonathan leapt out and grabbed him from behind, trapping his arms against his sides.

'You'll not be needing your horse now, sir,' he said.

'Get off me!' yelled the other, struggling hard. 'Or I'll kill you!'

Jonathan did not hesitate. Pushing him forward, he rammed the man's head against the wall of the stables. There was a loud crack and a cry of pain. Jonathan released him, spun him round then punched him hard in the stomach. When his prisoner doubled up in agony, Jonathan deftly relieved him of his sword and dagger. Blood was gushing from a wound in the man's forehead and he was panting for breath. The arrest was over.

Sir Humphrey Godden was bristling with irritation when he came out into the hall. The news that Christopher Redmayne had called for the third time did not please him. He was anxious to get rid of him immediately.

'I'm sorry, Mr Redmayne,' he said. 'I'm not able to speak to you today.'

'I think you will when you hear why I've come, Sir Humphrey.'

'There's nothing more that I can tell about what happened that night.'

'But there is,' said Christopher. 'You've omitted the most important details. We've reason to believe that you were involved in the murder of Signor Maldini.'

Sir Humphrey gaped. '*Me*?'

'With your accomplice.'

'What accomplice?'

'The man who claimed to be Captain James Harvest.'

'That's preposterous!' exclaimed the other. 'It's a monstrous allegation. I'll sue you for slander, Mr Redmayne.'

'Do you deny that you and the captain were confederates?'

'In the strongest possible terms.'

'You denied that you'd seen the man for some time,' Christopher reminded him, 'yet he came here yesterday to borrow money. Mr Crenlowe confirms it. Do you wish to sue *him* for slander as well?'

'Get out of my house!' roared Sir Humphrey.

'Not until we get the truth. My brother's life is at stake here. Henry could be hanged for a murder that you and your accomplice committed.'

'I had no accomplice.'

'Are you saying that you were solely responsible for the crime?'

Sir Humphrey was defiant. 'I'm telling you that I'm being wrongly accused and, whatever Martin Crenlowe might say, I haven't set eyes on that impostor we all knew as Captain Harvest.' He flung open the front door. 'Now, please leave at once!'

The words died in his throat. Standing in the open doorway was Jonathan Bale with his prisoner whose arms had been pinioned behind him. In spite of the blood on the man's face, Christopher recognised him as the counterfeit soldier.

'I caught him sneaking out of the back of the house,' said Jonathan. 'I'll need to take him before a magistrate. Can you manage here, Mr Redmayne?'

'Yes, Jonathan.' Christopher closed the door and turned to the red-faced Sir Humphrey. 'Perhaps we could discuss this elsewhere?' he suggested. 'Or do you still claim that your accomplice has never been near the house?'

'Come this way,' said Sir Humphrey.

He led Christopher into the parlour and shut the door after them. Exposed as a liar, he was much more subdued now. Christopher took the letters from his pocket.

'We know about your wife,' he said.

'What do you mean?'

'That's what spurred you on, Sir Humphrey. When you

discovered that Lady Godden was involved with Signor Maldini, you were consumed with hatred of the man.'

'I was consumed with hatred,' said the other with indignation, 'but not for that reason. My wife never even met that slimy Italian.'

'We found letters that proved otherwise,' said Christopher, holding them up.

'Then they are forgeries, sir. Miriam loathes foreigners as much as I do. She'd never let that fencing master within a mile of her.' He snatched the two letters and read through them. 'These were not written by my wife,' he asserted.

'Are you certain?'

'Of course, I'm certain,' said Sir Humphrey, thrusting them back at him, 'and I resent the implication that my wife has been unfaithful to me. Miriam would never do such a thing.'

'But the letters bear the initial of her name.'

'Thousands of other women in London have names that begin with 'M''. Any one of them could have written those letters. No, wait,' he said as his memory was jogged. 'I saw Jeronimo Maldini when women were around. He could not resist using that oily charm on them. He always addressed a lady by the same name. Yes, there's the answer, Mr Redmayne,' he decided. 'That 'M' does not stand for Miriam. It stands for Madonna. That was what he always cooed in their ear.'

Christopher was disappointed. As a result of his talk with Pietro Maldini, vital new evidence had come to light and it was buttressed by Jonathan's discovery at the lodging once occupied by the man's brother. The two friends had come to the same conclusion yet now, it seemed, it was woefully wrong. Unwilling to believe anything that Sir Humphrey told him, Christopher pressed him time and again but the man remained adamant. In the end, Christopher was forced to accept the possibility that he was actually telling the truth. If his wife were not implicated, Sir Humphrey would have no compulsion to seek revenge.

'I did not kill Jeronimo Maldini,' affirmed Sir Humphrey, 'nor was I involved in any plot to do so. What I do know is that your brother is innocent and I want the real culprit caught. Apart from anything else, it will stop you from hounding me any more.'

Christopher was abashed. 'Who *did* write these letters, then?'

'Let me look at them again,' said the other, taking them from him.

'All that I saw before was that my wife could not have written them. It's not her hand.' He studied the looping calligraphy. 'But I fancy she might tell you whose hand it was.'

'You recognise it, Sir Humphrey?'

'I've seen something very much like it, though I could not be sure. I've only ever observed this looping style on invitation cards that we've received. Yes,' he said, studying each of the letters in turn. 'It's a distinctive hand, no question of that. My wife could be more certain about it but I could give you a possible name for the writer.'

'Who is the lady?'

'Rose Crenlowe,' said the other. 'She's Martin's wife.'

Rose Crenlowe was a short, slim, dark-haired young woman with a beautiful face that was distorted by suffering. Her brow was wrinkled, her eyes were bloodshot and her pretty mouth drooped at the edges. The last of her tears were still drying on her cheeks. Wearing a plain dress and with her hair unkempt, she sat huddled on the bed in the attic room. When she heard a key being inserted in the lock, she drew instinctively away. Her husband came into the room with a tray of food for her. His manner was curt.

'Eat this,' he said, putting the tray down on the table. She shook her head. 'Do as I tell you, Rose!' he warned. 'I'll stand no more of your games.'

'I'm not hungry, Martin,' she whimpered.

'You must keep body and soul together.'

'Why? What's the point?'

'You know very well. If this food is not eaten by the time that I come back, there'll be trouble, Rose. Do you hear?' She said nothing. 'Do you *hear*?' he repeated.

'Yes, Martin.'

'The man is dead. Forget him.'

'I'll never do that,' she said with a show of spirit.

Crenlowe raised a hand to strike her and she cowered on the bed. The blow never came. There was a loud banging on his front door and the sound echoed up through the house. The goldsmith went out on the landing and listened as a servant opened the door. When he heard who had called to see him, he locked the door of his wife's room and went quickly downstairs. With his hat in his hand, Christopher Redmayne was waiting for him in the hall.

'Good day to you, Mr Crenlowe,' he said. 'I was told at your shop that I'd find you at home today. I crave a word with you, sir.'

'Must it be here? I'd prefer to talk to you this afternoon at the shop.'

'The matter is too serious to be postponed.'

'Oh?' said Crenlowe guardedly. 'You have news for me?'

'Yes,' said Christopher. 'The man who pretended to be Captain Harvest has been arrested. My friend, Mr Bale, apprehended him at Sir Humphrey Godden's house.'

'What was he doing there?'

'Causing profound embarrassment, by the look of it. He'll not be in a position to do that again for a very long time. I need to raise a sensitive matter with you,' he went on, lowering his voice, 'and it may help if your wife is present.'

'My wife is not at home.'

'Your servant just assured me that she was.'

'Rose is not available,' said Crenlowe sharply. 'You have my word on it. If you wish to speak to me, then perhaps you'll step in here,' he added, taking his visitor into the parlour. 'I hope that your stay will be brief. I need to get back to my work.'

'Then let me broach that delicate subject, Mr Crenlowe,' said Christopher, watching him closely. 'Were you aware of any connection between Signor Maldini and your wife?'

Crenlowe paled. 'Of course not! What are you suggesting?'

'That you had the best motive of all to see the fencing master dead.'

'This is nonsense, Mr Redmayne!'

'If you'd been cuckolded by the man —'

'No!' howled the other, bunching a fist. 'That's not true!'

'I have letters from your wife that Signor Maldini kept at his lodging. They leave no room for doubt, Mr Crenlowe.' He took them from his pocket. 'Do you wish to see them?'

'Put them away! Rose could never have written them.'

'I'd need your wife's confirmation of that.'

'I've told you, Mr Redmayne. She's not here.'

'Yes,' said Christopher, 'but I've reached the stage where I do not believe a word that you tell me. You visited Henry in prison to give the impression that you were concerned about him when, in point of fact, you were the man responsible for putting him there. When you heard that I was trying to clear Henry's name, you offered to help so that you could keep an eye on any progress that I made. Then we come to the jewellery that Signor Maldini commissioned from you,' he continued, putting the letters back in his pocket. 'You refused to admit that it ever existed and I think that I know why. The fencing master played a cruel trick on you.'

'Be quiet!' shouted Crenlowe.

'He wanted you to design a piece of jewellery that he'd give to your own wife.'

Crenlowe went berserk. Rushing at Christopher, he pushed him back with both hands before darting across the room to snatch up a rapier that stood in the corner. He came forward again with murder dancing in his eyes.

'He mocked me, Mr Redmayne,' he said, taking up his stance. 'He was not content with stealing my wife's affections from me, he mocked my trade by getting me to fashion some jewellery that he'd give to her in secret. Can you think of anything more despicable than that?'

'Yes,' said Christopher. 'Stabbing a man in the back then letting my brother go to the gallows for the crime. That's what I call despicable, Mr Crenlowe.'

The goldsmith lunged at him. Stepping back out of reach, Christopher threw his hat into his assailant's face. It gave him time to draw his own sword. The two men circled each other in the middle of the room. Christopher gave a grim smile.

'Let's see what Signor Maldini taught you, shall we?'

Crenlowe lunged again but his blade was parried. When he slashed wildly at Christopher's head, the latter ducked out of harm's way. Roused to a pitch of desperation, the goldsmith attacked again and again but every stroke was parried or rendered ineffective by neat footwork. Their blades clashed once more then locked together. Christopher's face was inches from that of the goldsmith. Crenlowe strained his sinews to force him back but he was up against someone who was younger, stronger and impelled by an urge to vindicate his brother. With a concerted effort, Christopher shoved him away so violently that his opponent tripped and fell to the floor. Before he could even move, Crenlowe felt a searing pain in his wrist as Christopher's rapier drew blood and made him drop his sword with a clatter.

Standing over his man, Christopher held the point of his weapon at his throat.

'Now, Mr Crenlowe,' he said. 'Tell me what *really* happened that night.'

Epilogue

Lady Whitcombe was overjoyed to receive the invitation to Fetter Lane. The thought of spending time with Christopher Redmayne was always a pleasant one but it held an even richer promise now that she had made her declaration to him. Feeling that she was in a position to exert influence over him, she had no hesitation in using it. Since his brother had now been released from prison, Lady Whitcombe had a double reason to rejoice with him. She could mark her closer relationship with the architect and celebrate the vindication of his family's name. Nothing could now prevent Christopher from resuming his work for her. Even her son, Egerton, albeit reluctantly, had accepted that. It was her daughter, however, who was now proving troublesome. They were in the house of the friends with whom they were staying. Lady Whitcombe was about to leave.

'Let me come with you, Mother,' said Letitia, grabbing her arm.

'Not this time,' replied the other, waving her away. 'Mr Redmayne and I have private business to discuss.'

'But I wish to congratulate him on solving that crime.'

'I'll pass on congratulations for you, Letitia.'

'Mother!'

'There's no point in arguing,' said the older woman. 'I'm going alone.'

'I want to see Mr Redmayne,' protested the girl, stamping a foot in rebellion. 'I like him and he likes me. It's so unfair to keep me away from him like that.'

'You'll be seeing a great deal of him in due course, I promise you.'

Before her daughter could throw a tantrum, Lady Whitcombe swept out of the house and stepped into her carriage. During the drive to Fetter Lane, she rehearsed what she was going to say to the young man whose talent as an architect, and whose charm as a person, had so captivated her. When she arrived at the house, he opened the door to her himself and gave her a cordial welcome before taking her into the parlour. Lady Whitcombe had the distinct impression that they were the only people there and that added to her sense of excitement. She took a seat and beamed at him.

'Let me say how delighted we all were to hear your good news,' she began. 'Your brother must be immensely proud of you for what you did on his behalf.'

'I had a great deal of help, Lady Whitcombe,' said Christopher modestly. 'My good friend, Jonathan Bale, deserves much of the credit.'

'But you are the chief architect of this triumph.' She chortled. 'Forgive me, Mr Redmayne. I did not mean to offer you such a feeble play on words. The point is that you were brave and resolute.' She became almost coquettish. 'In your letter, you said that you had something of importance to tell me.'

'Yes, Lady Whitcombe.'

'Well?'

'It concerns your commission,' he said, sitting beside her. 'If I'm to continue in your employ, there's something that must be understood at the start.'

'You must continue,' she insisted. 'I'll hold you to the contract.'

'Yet you had doubts about me earlier on.'

'Only for a brief moment. Be advised, Mr Redmayne,' she said with quiet authority, 'that I'd never release you from the contract. It's legally binding.'

'In that case, we must talk about your late husband.'

'Sir Peregrine?' she asked, quite baffled. 'Why?'

'Something rather distressing has come to light,' he said.

Christopher tried to break the news to her as gently as possible. He explained about Jeronimo Maldini's work as a spy and how certain documents had been found in a secret compartment of his desk. Lady Whitcombe angrily refuted the suggestion that her husband would have had anything to do with the man until she was shown letters in a hand that she identified immediately. There could be no doubting the fact that Sir Peregrine Whitcombe had been willing to betray his country in return for payment. She remembered that her son had talked of introducing his father to Maldini. That was how the connection between them had first been made. It threw her into a panic. If the truth about her husband were to become common knowledge, she would lose face completely and the memory of Sir Peregrine Whitcombe would be reviled. It would mean a dramatic loss of all the things she most prized. Realising the consequences of disclosure, she reached out to grasp Christopher's hand.

'Who else knows about this?' she asked.

'Only my friend, Mr Bale.'

'Will he divulge it?'

'No, Lady Whitcombe,' said Christopher. 'And neither will I, if we can come to an agreement. When the reputation of my family was in danger, you were kind enough to offer me your support. That meant a lot to me at a time when most people were looking askance at the name of Redmayne. I'd like to give you my support in return and prevent your family name from being sullied unnecessarily. Nothing will be served by digging up the mistakes of the past,' he decided. 'This unfortunate episode is now over. Signor Maldini is dead and so is Sir Peregrine. I believe that we should let their dark secrets die with them.'

'That's so generous of you, Mr Redmayne,' she said, squeezing his hand.

'My generosity comes at a price.'

'Name it and you shall have it.'

'I'll remain as your architect,' he said, withdrawing his hand, 'on condition that there's no suggestion of any personal relationship between us.' Her jaw dropped, her face went blank and she looked much older all of a sudden. 'I'm here simply to make sure that your house is built the way that it should be. It's the only basis on which I'll agree to proceed. Do I have your word on that, Lady Whitcombe?'

The disappointment showed in her eyes but it was tempered with gratitude for what he had done. Christopher had the power to hurt her in the most comprehensive way yet he stayed his hand. Instead of being able to reap the benefits of being the widow of Sir Peregrine Whitcombe, she might be ostracised as the wife of a man who sold state secrets to a foreign country. Coping with the horror of what she had learned about her husband was devastating for someone who had trusted him implicitly. She did not want humiliation as well. Lady Whitcombe saw her folly. She had been driven by desire to seek a closer acquaintance with her architect and she had tried to manipulate the awkward situation in which he found himself to her advantage. She had now been hoist with her own petard and it left her in despair.

'Well?' he prompted. 'I still await an answer.'

'Yes, Mr Redmayne,' she said with an effort. 'You have my word.'

Henry Redmayne was so grateful to be back in his own home again that he kept touching his possessions for reassurance and admiring himself in every mirror that he passed. Jonathan Bale was a mute guest, standing in a corner of the parlour and feeling distinctly out of place. The Reverend Algernon Redmayne was a much more censorious visitor, describing some of the paintings on the walls as far too lewd for public display and wondering why his elder son had such a well-stocked wine cellar when he claimed to lead a life of sobriety. The house in Bedford Street, he insisted, did not bear the marks of an owner with true Christian purpose. Henry endured the criticism with a patient smile. Back in his finest apparel again and wearing his periwig, he felt that he could withstand any parental assaults with equanimity.

When Christopher finally joined them from his meeting with his client, a bottle of wine was opened in celebration of Henry's release. Jonathan refused to touch it but the Dean was coaxed into taking a small cup of the liquid. After the toast, the old man became very solemn.

'Learn from this experience, my son,' he said, pointing a finger at Henry. 'A man is judged by his friends and yours were found cruelly wanting. On that shameful night, you broke bread with three vile individuals whose company you should have shunned.'

'Sir Humphrey Godden committed no crime,' said Henry defensively.

'He did, in my estimation,' said Jonathan.

'Yes,' agreed Christopher. 'He withheld information from us. Even when he knew that Captain Harvest was an impostor, he still gave him money and offered him a refuge. In short, he was protecting a wanted man. The law will require him to say why.'

'I can tell you why,' said Henry, sipping his wine. 'Sir Humphrey made the mistake of letting the fellow stay at the house while Lady Godden was away. A party was held there one night at which certain indiscretions took place. James – as we all knew him – was able to lean on Sir Humphrey to buy his silence.'

'How do you know all this?' demanded his father with suspicion. 'I hope that you were not present at this night of degradation, Henry.'

'No, no, Father.'

'Would you swear to that?'

'I was there at the start of the evening,' admitted Henry, deciding that a half-truth was better than a downright lie, 'but I left before any impropriety occurred. It was Sir Humphrey who confided to me that he was guilty of a peccadillo.'

'Murder, theft, fraud, drunkenness and sexual licence!' The Dean threw both hands up to heaven in supplication. 'How did a son of mine become embroiled in it?'

'By sheer accident, Father.'

'Henry is right,' said Christopher, jumping in to save his brother from another homily. 'His real fault lay in choosing the wrong friends.'

'And consuming far too much wine and brandy with them,' added his father.

'I confess it,' said Henry. 'Because I'm so unused to strong drink, it blinded me to what was going on. I thought I was in Fenchurch Street when I was accosted by Jeronimo Maldini that night, but I'd staggered almost all the way to the river.'

'Signor Maldini followed you,' explained Christopher, 'waiting for his chance to attack. What the Italian did not know, however, was that he, in turn, was being shadowed by Martin Crenlowe, who had seen him come out of his hiding place in Fenchurch Street. You walked on in search of a carriage to take you home. Although it was a bitterly cold night, there were still people abroad. Signor Maldini had to bide his time until you reached an alley near Thames Street. Then he challenged you.'

'That's what I remember, Christopher. He was suddenly there in front of me.'

'Fortunately for you, Mr Crenlowe was also there,' said Christopher. 'In knocking you down from behind, he probably saved your life. Signor Maldini would else have run you through. Mr Crenlowe, as we now know, had a score of his own to settle with the fencing master.'

'His wife had fallen for the Italian's charms.'

'I think it may have been the other way around, Henry.'

'Whatever the truth,' said the Dean. 'it was deplorable behaviour.'

'But it gave Mr Crenlowe the urge to commit murder, Father,' said Christopher. 'When the opportunity presented itself, he took it. While Henry was lying unconscious on the ground, Mr Crenlowe bent over him out of pretended concern and took hold of Henry's dagger. He then tried to appease Signor Maldini with soft words. When the Italian was off guard, Mr Crenlowe stabbed him in the back.'

'Yes,' said Jonathan, taking up the story, 'then he dragged the dead body to the river and heaved it in, thinking it might never be found. He did not bargain for the Thames freezing over like that. When my son stumbled on the body that day, it still had Mr Redmayne's dagger in its back.'

'I felt that it was in *my* back,' complained Henry.

'To some degree, it was,' said his father sonorously. 'Instead of confessing his crime, this goldsmith friend of yours let you take his punishment. He stabbed you in the back, Henry.'

'So did Captain Harvest,' noted Christopher. 'He deliberately brought Signor Maldini along that evening so that the two of you would strike sparks off each other. The fencing master knew where you were and that you'd not be in the best position to defend your-self by the time you'd been drinking heavily. By setting you up like that, the captain stabbed you in the back as well.'

'Who *is* this Captain Harvest?' asked the Dean. 'What's the vil-lain's real name?'

'James Wragg,' replied Jonathan, 'and he had been a soldier but not in any English army. He was a mercenary who fought on the Continent for anyone willing to pay him. He'd picked up a smatter-ing of languages along the way, Italian among them. It was the rea-son that he and Signor Maldini were so close. Mr Wragg had a talent for making easy friendships – your son was only one of his victims – and he lured to the fencing school gentlemen whom Signor Maldini had a particular interest in meeting.'

'Why?' said the old man.

'Because they had desirable wives, Father,' said Christopher.

The Dean was appalled. 'Then this unprincipled rogue was a *pan-dar*!' he cried.

He would have been even more outraged if he had known that the women whom Jeronimo Maldini had seduced almost invariably had husbands with political influence, but Christopher kept that information from his father, as from everyone else. The death of the fencing master had brought the espionage to an end. Nobody still alive was culpable. Ladies who had unwittingly yielded up intelligence about their husbands' work while they were in the arms of the Italian, were dupes rather than traitors. Christopher and Jonathan had agreed to remain silent about Maldini's main reason for coming to England.

'Henry is well clear of the man,' said Christopher. 'Let's be grateful for that.'

'You've been given a second chance, Henry,' observed his father. 'Do not waste it. Turn aside from the company of rogues and voluptuaries. Take your delight in the law of the Lord.'

'I will, Father,' promised Henry. 'Newgate was my Damascus. Of one thing, you may be certain. Prison has made me a better man.'

'I pray that it may be so.'

'It is, it is.'

'Yet the punishment was not wholly undeserved.'

'Yes, it was,' argued Henry. 'I was innocent.'

'Innocent of murder,' said the Dean, 'but guilty of sin. In thought and word, you wanted that man to die. You fell short only of the deed itself.'

Henry was soulful. 'I suppose that's true.'

'It is, my son. You'll be haunted by your sin. That dead body of the man you threatened will be frozen forever inside your skull like that corpse at the frost fair. You must pray daily for the salvation of Signor Maldini's soul. Only then will I know that you are not confusing Damascus with somewhere else.'

When the day of departure arrived, Susan Cheever found herself in two minds. Anxious to stay in London, she was yet ready to leave with Jack Cardinal and his mother. Part of her wanted to linger in the hope that Christopher would somehow get in touch with her. Another part of her, however, was deeply hurt that no word had come from him even though his brother had been exonerated. His silence gave credence to the worrying suggestion that the architect was showing a romantic interest in the daughter of his client. Susan was upset. It made her more vulnerable to Cardinal's respectful and unhurried attentions. Indeed, she had come to find both him and his mother such amenable companions that she looked forward to developing their friendship.

They gathered in the hall of the house in the Strand to express their gratitude to Lord and Lady Eames for their hospitality. Servants, meanwhile, took their luggage out to the coach. It included several presents that Mrs Cardinal had purchased for herself and some gifts that her son had bought for Susan. When farewells had been completed, the whole party moved out into the porch and it was at that point that Susan felt the real poignancy of leaving the city. Assisted by Cardinal, his mother was the first to manoeuvre her bulging frame into the waiting carriage. Susan was just about to take his proferred hand herself when she heard hoof beats on the drive. She let out an involuntary cry of joy when she saw who the horseman was. Christopher Redmayne was trotting towards her with a grin on his face.

He reined in the animal and dismounted, taking Susan's hand to kiss it in greeting. Christopher removed his hat politely to be introduced to everyone else. Requesting a brief moment alone with Susan, he took her aside. Cardinal had only to see the two of them together to realise that any hopes he might have had with regard to her were entirely misplaced. He took the disappointment well but his mother was less accommodating. Mrs Cardinal, feeling baulked, sat back in the coach so hard that it shook violently.

The conversation was short and constrained by the presence of others.

'Where have you been?' asked Susan with reproach in her eyes.

'Wrangling with lawyers on my brother's behalf,' he replied. 'It was much easier to put the guilty man in prison than to get an innocent one out again. I came as soon as I could, Susan, and I'm so glad that I caught you.'

'How is your brother?'

'Henry is thoroughly chastened and so am I,' he said, glancing at the coach. 'Another five minutes and I'd have missed seeing you. I just came to ask for permission to call on you in Richmond – provided that your sister does not slam the door in my face again, that is.'

'Brilliana owes you an apology,' she said. Recalling the gossip she had heard, her manner became guarded. 'Will you come on to Richmond after you've visited your client in Sheen?'

'No, Susan,' he said, 'I'll not need to go there again.'

'But I understood that you had become friends with the family.'

'I try to be friendly towards all my clients but Lady Whitcombe

283

has been far too demanding. With luck, I'll not see her or that strange daughter of hers until the house is actually built. Forget my client,' he advised. 'I'll be coming to Richmond solely to visit you, Susan. If you agree, that is. Do I have your permission?'

'No, Christopher,' she said with a smile. 'You have my request.'

'Request?'

'Please come at the earliest possible opportunity.'

Christopher burst out laughing then reached an instant decision.

'Step into the coach,' he said, 'and I'll follow you all the way to Richmond.'